# ADVOCATE

ALSO BY DARREN GREER

*Tyler's Cape* (2001)

*Still Life with June* (2003)

*Strange Ghosts* (2006)

*Just Beneath My Skin* (2014)

# DARREN GREER
# ADVOCATE

*Cormorant Books*

The publisher gratefully acknowledges the support of the Canada Council for the
Arts and the Ontario Arts Council for its publishing program. We acknowledge
the financial support of the Government of Canada through the Canada Book Fund
(CBF) for our publishing activities, and the Government of Ontario through the
Ontario Media Development Corporation, an agency of the Ontario Ministry of
Culture, and the Ontario Book Publishing Tax Credit Program.

LIBRARY AND ARCHIVES CANADA CATALOGUING IN PUBLICATION

Greer, Darren, author
Advocate / Darren Greer.

Issued in print and electronic formats.
ISBN 978-1-77086-471-9 (paperback). — ISBN 978-1-77086-472-6 (html)

I. Title.

PS8563.R4315A38 2016          C813'.6          C2015-907535-1
                                               C2015-907536-X

Cover art and design: angeljohnguerra.com
Interior text design: Tannice Goddard, Soul Oasis Networking
Printer: Friesens

Printed and bound in Canada.

The interior of this book is printed on 100% post-consumer waste recycled paper.

CORMORANT BOOKS INC.
10 ST. MARY STREET, SUITE 615, TORONTO, ONTARIO, M4Y 1P9
www.cormorantbooks.com

*For Steve*
*and for all those whose names I do not know*

*This I regard as history's highest function,*
*to let no worthy action be uncommemorated,*
*and to hold out the reprobation of posterity*
*as a terror to evil words and deeds.*

— TACITUS, *ANNALS*

# PART I

# ONE

∎

I WAS NINETEEN when I first stepped off the path that had been laid out for me. It seemed at the time, like most major decisions in life, arbitrary — coincidental even. I had no idea that one decision would colour the rest of my life, and move me away from my chosen field, mathematics, towards something far more difficult and less precise.

That decision came in the form of a course selection at the beginning of my second year of university. I was flipping through the course calendar in my tiny apartment on Brunswick Street in the Annex in Toronto, looking for an elective, something to round out my complement of courses and that was not related to mathematics. Most students took an art history course, something they could breeze through. For some reason, I found myself in the biology section and came across Virology 201.

I knew nothing about virology.

I knew nothing about *biology*.

I knew algebra, calculus, quadratic equations, and trigonometry.

But this course, virology, struck me as something that might be interesting. I did not realize at the time what my motivations were. I had been in the city for a year, and though I had come with the intention to study and explore, I had yet to meet anyone. Among the community I was nominally a part of, an epidemic was raging.

I was afraid. But I was also fascinated.

I registered for the course. It was a second year biology credit and I had not the prerequisites to get in. I had to obtain special permission from the instructor, who asked why a second year math student was interested in virology. His name was van Denker, a sixty-year-old balding Dutch man in a white lab coat. He had dirty fingernails, which I found out later were stained because of a dye used in the isolation of bacteria and other microbes in a Petri dish. He was sitting behind his desk when he asked me this question.

"I'm interested," I said. "I know it's not math, but I can't help thinking that a working knowledge of microbiology couldn't harm anyone."

"No," van Denker said, looking up at me. "But it usually doesn't *interest* anyone either, besides microbiologists and medical students. Is there some aspect of the class that attracts you specifically?"

I didn't answer him, though I'm sure he knew.

He gave me permission to take the course, though he warned me I would need a basic grasp of first year biology in order to excel. "Cellular theory, genetics, homeostasis," he told me. "Are you prepared to learn all this in addition to the course material?"

I told him I was.

And I did.

I studied hard for that course, not so much to pass, but to understand. Van Denker took a personal interest in me. After class he'd sometimes stop by my desk to ask how "the mathematician" was doing. I gave myself away during the two classes we spent learning about HIV by asking more questions than the other students. When he first put a drawing of the virus on the wall with the mini-projector I held my breath. It was shaped like a dodecahedron and coloured green, with small barnacles all over it. It looked like a child's toy, or a badly made Christmas ornament. That something so small could cause such significant trouble seemed almost a miracle in reverse.

"There you are," I whispered, under my breath.

At the end of the year, van Denker asked if I had learned what I needed from the course.

"Very much," I said.

"Your mark is excellent," he said. "You can see it posted outside my office. Perhaps you'll think about switching majors."

"I don't think so," I told him.

Van Denker smiled. He knew, I believe, exactly where I was headed, and why, though he refrained from asking details. We said our goodbyes, and I never saw him again. But I never forgot his course, or his passion. To van Denker, viruses, which he often called the "antithesis of symbiosis," were a puzzle, an intellectual pursuit of the grandest order. He saw nothing personal in them.

To me they were the enemy.

■ ■ ■

"I THINK YOU should come home," my mother says when she calls the first Thursday evening in July. "The doctors think your grandmother is dying."

My mother says this practically every time she calls now. She is not being alarmist. My grandmother is so often sick that the doctors are always predicting this week or that will be her last. She is ninety-one. She has congestive heart failure, a buildup of fluid around her heart. She feels weak and tired all the time. She sometimes finds it difficult to breathe. There are days she does not get out of bed. Her eyes are too weak to read or knit, and she is too tired to go anywhere. She does not have Alzheimer's; she is spared that final indignity of having to be spoon-fed while her mind unravels like an untamed thread from a spool. What she does have is mild old-age dementia. She forgets names and faces, dates, and sometimes her own family. The last time I was home she did not know who I was. When I kissed her cheek, wrinkled and dry as parchment, and stood back, she looked up at me slyly, but without recognition, as if to ask who was this strange man taking liberties with her?

I ask my mother what makes this time different from all the other times the doctors were prognosticating death.

"She has a lung infection," says my mother. "And her heart has slowed down. She's on oxygen. She's rarely awake. Dr. Willis says her body is shutting down."

"Is she in the hospital?"

"She's home," says my mother. "By the time we caught the infection she was too weak to move. And Dr. Willis believes if she is going to die, she would rather be at home than anywhere else. Jeanette's taken some time off work to be with her, and a VON nurse comes every day. I really think you should come home and say your goodbyes."

I have a lot of resentment against my grandmother. We all do. And although old age and her condition make it harder to express, it's still there, like a subcutaneous wound. But this has never stopped me from going home before. I go at Christmas, and sometimes during the summer. I am not like my Uncle David, who left in 1969 before I was born and did not come home until 1984.

I have never discussed my work with my grandmother. Not once has she asked me about it, though she knows from my mother and Aunt Jeanette what I do. She also knows about my personal life, that I have turned out different, that I have become what she sometimes refers to as "a man of questionable demeanour." This euphemism of my grandmother's has made its way around my office, as I once told a colleague about it. He was delighted, and though that was years ago I still hear men in my office refer to themselves and their co-workers this way. At the outreach centre, we are all, for the most part, "men of questionable demeanour." A few of the women have demeanour issues of their own.

My grandmother would no more ask me about this than she

would my bowel movements. She was raised in a culture of denial and ignorance, and she did her best to instill those values in the generations who followed.

She failed.

In the work I do we do our best to smash denial, to root out ignorance.

I make absolutely no promises about going home to see my grandmother on her deathbed. My mother asks me to give one good reason why.

"You keep saying she's going to die," I say. "But she keeps hanging on. I suspect she isn't as sick as you said."

This is a lie, and my mother knows it.

"It's a miracle she's still alive. Stop dithering. You'll have to come home sometime. Even if it's after she dies, for the funeral."

"But my work ..." I start to say, but my mother cuts me off.

"Don't give me that, Jacob. You can get a week or two off work. I bet you have six weeks of vacation, don't you?"

Seven, I could tell her.

Normally my mother and I don't discuss my job. I am bound by codes of confidentiality. My mother finds it difficult to discuss. I am a counsellor at a men's outreach centre in the city.

My mathematics degree is a running joke among my colleagues. I can explain Fermat's Last Theorem and deal with radicals and imaginary numbers. But my education does not make me a better counsellor. The language of the psyche is so much more inexact than the language of the material universe. When our office receives copies of the epidemiological reports on sexually transmitted diseases, they are given to me to decipher and present to the staff in plain language. For this reason alone I am a valuable employee, which is good, for I frequently wonder about my abilities as a counsellor. My words and advice seem so feeble in relation to what these men are going through. Some use drugs. Some live on the streets. They have no idea how to protect themselves from the machinations of the world they live in.

I have never lived in this world. I grew up sheltered. I've always had a home. I went to university. How can I know what it is like for these men, who every day wake up to face another nightmare?

Men have died on my watch.

I watch them, growing thinner and sicker with every visit to my office, until one day they don't come at all and we hunt them down on the streets or in hospitals, eventually to go to their funerals. The courses I took at community college were at what I used to think of as the fuzzy end of the social sciences. Like most science students, I had a well-rounded contempt for anything that didn't resolve. But I set aside this prejudice for the sake of my studies, and by my third year I had decided that, though I would get the math degree, I would likely work in the counselling field. I studied addictions, family abuse, and disease management. I took part in mock sessions, suicide prevention courses, and youth sensitivity training. Our studies were hands-on, our instructors both passionate and practical. We were being trained to make a difference. In the final year of my math degree I already had a part-time job on a suicide hotline. By the time I finished I would work at a youth shelter for two years before finally getting this position at the outreach for men living with HIV.

My mother was proud of me, though confused. She couldn't help but wonder what happened to the serious, solemn boy who was going to be a mathematician.

I could have told her I was still serious and solemn. Only the mathematician had been lost. By day I was trying to help others. At night I came home and tried to make sense of my life.

"That's about par for the course," my mother said. She worked at a diner in Advocate and had since I was a child. "Did you think I wanted to be a waitress for the rest of my days?"

I was often reminded of van Denker and his passionate descriptions of viral replication and DNA incorporation by integrase enzymes. He would explain something to us in the most technical of terms and then turn around and face the class — an auditorium full of students with neutral or bored expressions — and say, "Don't you see how *amazing* this all is?"

I think one of the reasons van Denker liked me is that I reminded him of himself. I wasn't there to fulfill a course requirement, or ace a credit. He sensed passion in me, even if it was perverse, or misguided. Sometimes, when he asked "Don't you see?", he would look at me, and I would nod as if I did.

I didn't.

The miracle of cellular function and pathogens escaped me. I wanted only to know the how and why. I was studying the virus not because it fascinated me but because I was frightened of it. Whenever I picture the virus swimming in the bloodstreams of my clients, I think of millions of those little dodecahedrons as I saw them in van Denker's class, waiting to swarm and overcome the first T cell to cross their path. I can't help but think of his words: "A virus is the opposite of symbiosis." I thought, by learning about it, I would conquer my fear. All learning about it did was clarify my fear. It is knowledge that has undone me.

"So just tell me," my mother says finally. "Why aren't you coming?"

There is silence on the phone while my mother waits. I decide to tell her part of the truth. "If I came home," I say, "I'd be afraid I'd tell Grandnan what I thought. I'm afraid I'd ruin her last days on earth."

"Is that all?" says my mother. "We've been telling her the truth for years, and she doesn't pay any attention. It's unlikely she'd start now, particularly as she's asleep most of the time."

"Well, you wanted a reason," I say. "I gave you one."

"It's a bad one," says my mother. "I want you to talk to your boss tomorrow and book your flight home."

I relent. "Okay. I'll do it."

When I explain to Anne, my supervisor, in her office at the end of the next day that I am leaving, she asks if I am close to my grandmother.

"I grew up in her house," I say. Which is not exactly a direct answer.

"You must be very sad," she says.

I surprise myself, by telling the truth. "Not really," I say. "She was a difficult woman, and I hold a lot of things against her."

Anne shouldn't be surprised. She deals with counsellors all day, and we have a tendency to practise what we preach. We spill our guts at the slightest provocation. But I am not normally one of these.

"Well, I hope this visit resolves some of those issues," Anne says. "Death has a way of healing, whether we want it to or not."

"Thanks," I say, leaving her office and heading home. I make dinner, read a book, think about Advocate. At ten o'clock the phone rings and I can see by the display it is my mother. I answer and give her my flight information.

"Aunt Jeanette will pick you up," she says. "I have to work."

"Fine," I say.

"And don't think," says my mother, as if we were still having the conversation of the evening before, "I don't know what it is you want to tell your grandmother. I've been wanting to say the same thing for years."

"And have you?" I ask.

"No," my mother admits. "It's too painful. And she has never mentioned it."

"You understand why I might have to," I say. "My job. What I do. It's affected my whole life."

"That was a terrible time," my mother says absently. "I don't like to think about it."

"None of us do," I say. "That's the problem. That's how they got away with it for so long. But someone should hold them accountable."

"By 'they,'" asks my mother, "who do you mean?"

"All of them," I say. "The whole town."

"You're going to speak to the whole town? What are you going to do? Hold a public meeting? No one would come."

"I know, but someone should try."

"My son," says my mother wistfully. "My marvellous son. Where did you get the idea you have to save the whole world?"

# 2

IT WAS ALWAYS a source of annoyance to my grandmother that her house was one street back from the river and not on the river itself. By the time my grandfather was ready to build in Advocate all the waterfront property had been claimed. The old settlers' houses, with a few exceptions, had been torn down, and Cape Cods and colonials built in their place. There was plenty of room in the south, where Main Street turns to River Road and runs for five miles into the village of Great Falls, but that was the poorer section of town, and my grandfather, with an eye to his medical practice, wanted to build somewhere more prosperous.

So he had to settle for the street *behind* the river. He made up for it by building the largest house in the area. Bigger and more impressive houses were built later, but when I was a child my grandmother's house was still intimidating — six bedrooms, a spacious living room, dining room, a washing and sewing room, and a glassed-in, insulated sun porch in the back where every once in a while if she was in a genteel mood she would serve us lunch on Sunday after Mass at the white wicker table with the sun pouring in on us like lemon dish soap.

The bedrooms were never all occupied. My grandparents had

three children, and after my grandfather died and Uncle David moved away, my grandmother named the extra bedrooms guest rooms, though we never had any guests. These were off limits.

Once a month she made my mother and Aunt Jeanette change the sheets and dust.

"Why on earth do we have to?" Jeanette complained. "No one ever sleeps there."

"Because someone might decide to stay tomorrow. And I'm not having them see tumbleweeds on the floor and grimy sheets on the bed, little girl." My grandmother always called my Aunt Jeanette "little girl" when she chastised her.

And because my mother and Aunt Jeanette lived under my grandmother's roof they did what they were told, once a month tidying the guest rooms.

"I feel like a chambermaid," Jeanette would say. "Maybe we should leave a mint on the pillow."

My mother was less vocal than her sister. She did not argue with my grandmother, and didn't mind cleaning the rooms and doing any other work my grandmother wanted done. She said housework was good for the soul, and would sometimes give me a duster and let me help, though I was more interested in stirring up a string of dust from the windowsill into a tiny cloud or mini tornado and watching the motes dance in the sun.

My grandmother disapproved of me working with my mother and aunt. "He needs boys' work, not housecleaning," she said. "If you want to give him chores I can find him something more suited to a young man."

I had no chores other than to fetch the paper when the paperboy would inevitably toss it into my grandmother's marigold patch. In her opinion fetching a paper was not enough responsibility for me. I should've been chopping kindling — an irony, as we heated the house with oil — or fixing pipes or changing fuses in the cellar when they blew. It didn't matter I was only six. My grandmother wanted me to be a man. She worried because I had no male figures in my life.

"David's a man," said my mother.

"Very funny," said my grandmother. "And since when have you seen David around here? Jacob needs a *positive* male influence. You should apprentice him to someone in town."

"This is not the nineteenth century, Mother. We're not making him into a chimney sweep."

"Maybe not. But he needs to be hewing, not dusting. Work defines character. You have to start them off young, before they get away from you."

Arguments over the best way to raise me were common in our house. My grandmother, as matriarch, believed she should get as much say as my mother. My mother quietly but firmly disagreed.

I responded to my grandmother's gruff authority, but secretly kept my heart aligned with my mother. I did not like man's work, or man's toys. If my grandmother said I had to be a chimney sweep, I would be a chimney sweep, but one who disturbed the piles of ash to see them pirouette in the sun. I played with dolls and tea sets in the privacy of my own room, though even at a young age I knew enough to hide these from my grandmother. I watched soap operas with my Aunt Jeanette when she was off in the afternoon, and I was fascinated by my grandmother's gardens and the variety of flowers and plants that grew within them.

All my grandmother's attempts to make me a man's man over the course of my childhood would fail. Once she paid a young man from town to take me fishing in the river. I found it boring, and I did not like the squishy feel of the worm between my fingers as it was strung upon the hook. When my mother asked me how I liked it I told her I didn't, and she told my grandmother I didn't have to go anymore.

"Mark my words," my grandmother said. "That boy will end up different, if you don't get him doing normal boy things."

"What's wrong with different?" asked my mother.

"Fine," said my grandmother. "Just don't blame me when he ends up a social misfit."

My grandmother had it wrong. I would not end up being a social misfit — I already was, and had been since the day I was born. I was an eerie, quiet child, and I think this bothered my grandmother as much as my proclivity for girls' toys. She didn't know how to take me. I think she was afraid I would turn out like her only son, though she never said as much. It was my grandmother's habit to say everything on her mind except that which had true bearing and relevance. She continued to hound my mother to get me engaged in what to her mind were suitable boy activities, and to guard against effeminacy and softness of character when she saw it. Fortunately for me I had a mother who did as she pleased and did not heed my grandmother's warnings at all.

■ ■ ■

ONE OF MY clients who sees me every two weeks is Randy. He is unlike many of the men I see, in that he is not homeless or living in a boarding house. Nor does he abuse drugs or drink much alcohol. "No more than a couple of cocktails at a dinner party," he told me when I asked. He has a good job as a graphic designer at an ad agency, and he owns a condo in the Annex. There was a day when agencies like ours were filled with men like him, but no more. The message has spread: use condoms, be selective, think with your head and not your prick. The number of affluent and middle-class gay men living with HIV dropped considerably in the nineties and early two thousands. The number of poor, addicted men and women, both gay and straight, has risen.

We've had to adapt.

We've become a welfare agency as well as a support network. Addiction counsellors as well as safe sex proponents. Men like Randy in our office are now rare, and they feel uncomfortable sitting in the waiting room with street junkies and prostitutes.

But Randy is a special case.

He contracted HIV eight months ago, on an ill-advised outing to a bathhouse. He negotiated a string of partners without using condoms. He came down with a violent flu and went to see his doctor. He told his MD of the outing, and his belief he might have caught something. The doctor got suspicious and tested Randy for the virus.

It came back positive.

Flu-like symptoms directly after HIV seroconversion are common.

Randy was devastated. Only losers and the self-destructive get AIDS anymore. Men like him, bombarded over the years with safer sex campaigns and condom promotion, are supposed to know better.

What makes it worse is Randy's partner does not know about his one-night escapade. Eight months later and Randy has still not told him. He fears his lover will leave him. He also fears he has passed it on. Before he found out he was positive, they had had one bout of unprotected sex, as they always had when they were both negative and monogamous.

The situation terrifies him.

His work has suffered. He is unable to concentrate and he misses deadlines. He is depressed and does not sleep. His lover is growing suspicious, because they've not had sex in months. He thinks Randy is seeing someone else. In desperation, Randy came to us. I have been seeing him for over a month, but so far have been unable to convince him to deal with the growing crisis and tell his lover the truth. Despite the invention of medications that prolong the patient's life, and keep the worse symptoms at bay, AIDS continues to wreck lives. It wreaks its own special brand of havoc.

Randy is at the stage of being angry at the man who gave it to him. He keeps talking about finding him, and suing him. "Having his ass slapped in jail for the rest of his life," he tells me. I see this stage often, one of Kubler-Ross's stages of grief I studied in college. It is always interesting, if a little alarming, to see something we studied so blithely on paper suddenly manifest itself in real life. It's the difference between reading about the resurrection and actually seeing it.

I try to guide Randy through his anger, to validate it, and move him forward into the next stage. I tell him he can try to find the man who gave it to him, though with the multiple partners it would be difficult. I hope, I say, Randy can find him and he can be charged.

I also hope that Randy will focus his attentions on his own issues and prepare himself to tell his lover the truth. "Getting HIV is not your fault," I told him. "Regardless of the unsafe sex or how you feel about yourself. If he loves you, he will work with you to get through this."

"I wouldn't," Randy said flatly. "I'd be so angry I'd leave. And that's just what he will do too."

"Have you started medications yet?" I asked him.

"I can't," he said. "He'd wonder what they were for."

"You need to start them as soon as possible. Which is another reason to tell him. You can't keep putting your own health on hold because of your fear. This really is a matter of life and death. As long as you're medication-free, your life is at serious risk."

One of the reasons I initially liked him so much when he first came to see me was that he, too, was interested in the technical aspects of the virus. Like me, I think he believed that the more he knew about it the more power he had. Our first few sessions were spent talking — in highly technical language that Randy, with his obvious intelligence, clearly understood — about the mechanics and function of the pathogen.

Randy reminded me of me. I knew I was experiencing transference, but I was powerless to stop it. I am overly invested in his life, which diminishes my effectiveness as his counsellor. What I should do is transfer him to another counsellor in the centre. We are often warned about the dangers of over-investment, about how we can harm rather than help our client by becoming too close.

But I cannot do that. I like Randy. I worry about his reaction if I suddenly stop seeing him. The last thing he needs is to feel rejected.

The day after I book my flight to Nova Scotia, he comes into my office. He forgets to shut the door, so I get up and do it for him. He is only a few years younger than me — thirty-four to my thirty-seven — but today he seems like a teenager. He is more anxious than usual; he keeps crossing and uncrossing his legs and can't seem to get comfortable.

"How are you," I say, as I sit back down at my desk.

"Better," says Randy. "I figured a way out."

"Good," I say. "Tell me about it."

"It's like this," Randy says. "He's gonna leave me if I tell him. That I know for sure. I can't take meds if I don't tell him, so that puts my heath at risk. So I figure the best way to deal with it is to leave *him*. I can tell him the relationship isn't working for me anymore and I want out. He can keep the condo. I'll get an apartment. We can still be friends but he never has to know about the HIV and it'll solve all the problems." Randy says all of this in one breath, as if he has been practising for days.

I am taken aback.

Not at the audacity — and, let's face it, stupidity — of the plan, but by how earnestly Randy believes it to be the only solution. He is not a dumb man. Very few of our clients are. I am amazed he cannot see the dozen or so holes in his schematic; it leaks water like a sieve.

But my job is not to point out the problems. It is to get the client to see them for themselves. And the way we do that, somewhat underhandedly, is to start with praise.

"That would seem," I say, "to get you out of the mess you're in."

"Wouldn't it? It came to me only a few days ago, when I was lying in bed. I don't know why I didn't see it before."

"It would also get you immediately on the medications, which is my primary concern."

"I've already mentioned it to my doctor," Randy says. "We're gonna start as soon as everything is arranged."

"Have you said anything to John yet?" John is Randy's partner.

Randy shakes his head, a smidgen of enthusiasm floating away. "Not yet," he says. "I don't know exactly what I'm going to say."

"Why don't we figure it out together?"

Randy tries to come up with an excuse that doesn't mention the real reason why he is leaving him. Dissatisfaction, another man, seven-year itch. All of these seem inadequate, mostly because they aren't true. By the end of the session Randy has realized he can come up with no suitable reason for the simple fact that he loves John. It is his love for John that has made all of this so difficult. He leaves my office more dejected than when he came in.

It should count as a successful session. I have talked him down off the ledge, as I've been taught to do. But I don't feel good about it.

I call my mother and make sure Jeanette is going to meet my plane.

## 3

MY FAVOURITE ROOM in my grandmother's house was the attic. It could be accessed by a door next to the upstairs hallway closet and a climb up a short set of stairs. One could disappear into it, if one wished, for hours on end.

I was not allowed in the attic.

Both my mother and grandmother considered it dangerous, because there was no solid floor, only beams crossing the upper side of the upstairs ceiling. My grandmother claimed if you set foot in between the beams you would plunge right through, and if she didn't have the bother of cleaning your broken body up from the room below, she would be put to the trouble of repairing the damage to the ceiling of whatever room you happened to break though.

I was always careful to stay on the beams.

The attic ran the entire length of the house. The ceiling was sloped, and when I first stepped up from the last stair I had to duck my head. In order to move around, I had to navigate my way across the beams to the centre of the room under the peak.

I liked the attic for two reasons. One, it was a place where I could get away from my family. I liked the musty, dust-laden, old leather-and-mothball smell of it. There was something comforting about that smell, something that reeked of history and forgotten narrative. I couldn't put this into words, of course, but I sensed that in the attic secrets were kept.

The second reason I was fascinated with the place was that it was full of boxes. My grandmother never threw anything away. If something was not in immediate use, but she had judged it being useful someday, up to the attic it went. My grandmother's fear of me plummeting through the floor into the bedrooms below was ill-founded: there were so many boxes, hardly a square inch of space remained for an ill-placed step.

When I first started sneaking into it, I cleared a path to the centre of the room so I could make my way through box after box. All this was done in stolen moments. I couldn't be gone long before someone would start to wonder where I was. My progress was slow. I studied each item I pulled from the boxes carefully. I read old newspapers. I puzzled over receipts and deeds and math scribblers filled with figures written in faded ink from 1962.

In many of the boxes were clothes, thus the camphor stink of mothballs.

My mother and Aunt Jeanette tried to convince my grandmother to give her old clothes to the Salvation Army or St. Vincent de Paul. The Salvation Army was out, because it was Protestant. St. Vincent was also out because my grandmother said she didn't believe in making first-hand things second-hand things.

"It's an invasion of privacy," she said. "I don't want everyone to know what I wore when I give my clothes away."

"They know what you're wearing when you wear them, don't they?" said Aunt Jeanette.

But there was no arguing with my grandmother. Up into the attic each batch of discarded clothes went. It occurs to me now that, sitting amongst those boxes and working my way through to the heart of them, I was engaged in peeling back strata of time — moving from present through past, trying to read the history of my family through cast-off clothing, old shoes, paperwork, and mementos.

My grandmother was not pleased on the rare occasions I was caught. Several times she threatened to put a padlock on the door, though she never did. I suppose it was because she often lost keys, and because if she ever did need to put anything up there her arms would be too full to stop and undo a lock. She did give me fair warning. "If you go up there again, you'll get a hiding you won't forget." I needn't have worried. My grandmother never "hided" me — my mother wouldn't allow it. But when she caught me playing up there, she would give me a severe dressing down until I swore I would not step foot in the attic again.

I always did, though. It was the only place in the house where I could be entirely myself. I didn't have to worry about sitting up straight or washing my hands or brushing my teeth. I didn't have to listen to anyone argue, or hear the news on TV. For such a big house, it was rarely quiet, and the attic offered peace. The dust lay so heavily on everything it muffled the present. Only the past spoke, in whispers.

■ ■ ■

I WAS EIGHT when I discovered the attic. Some of my earliest finds were boxes of Jeanette's and my mother's old toys. These, for some reason, were not deep in the piles of boxes trapped in some far corner of the room. They were close to the front. Later I concluded they'd been stored in another part of the house until recently. Perhaps my mother and Aunt Jeanette had held on to them for sentimental reasons, and only lately found the heart to store them away.

Whatever the reason, I was delighted with the find. I had my own toys, of course. But the toys in the boxes in the attic were old. And they were girls' things. A tin doll's house, a tea set, cardboard cut-outs of dresses and outfits for a paper doll. There was even a turquoise Easy-Bake Oven, without directions or mixes but with all the pans. It actually worked when plugged in.

I was fascinated.

Not just that my mother and Aunt Jeanette played with these things when they were little, but they were a whole new category of toy. I was tired of my own toys. For the first time I took what I'd found in the attic downstairs to my room, and over the next couple of weeks I played with them.

I saw nothing wrong with this.

I had tea parties, filling the pot with water and pouring for imaginary guests. I dressed the paper doll in outfits. I built costume jewellery from pieces lying at the bottom of the box that must have been a do-it-yourself kit.

My grandmother caught me when I tried to make something in the Easy-Bake Oven. I took flour and water and salt from the kitchen — I had no idea what went into baking a cake — when I thought no one was around, and my grandmother discovered the flour all over the kitchen counter. She knew something was amiss, and burst in as I was busy watching the pan boil in the little oven.

At first she said nothing. She only asked what I was doing.

"I'm cooking," I said.

"And where, pray tell," she said, "did you get *that*?"

She was pointing to the oven, and the other toys scattered around it. I was also having a tea party, for when the cake was ready. Three people already sat innocently on the floor waiting, though my grandmother couldn't see them. When I didn't answer, she asked again.

The one thing I was absolutely not allowed to do in her house was lie. My grandmother didn't like it. It reflected a corruption of the soul, she said. My mother didn't like it either. She told me that honesty solved problems and dishonesty created them, and she always wanted me to tell her the truth, no matter how bad I thought it was.

Aunt Jeanette lied sometimes to my grandmother, about little things — where she was, where she was going. She said it was hard to live with a puritan and not tell a few. But I knew in this case lying would not help. They would know eventually where I got the toys, and that I had been where I was not supposed to be.

I actually thought the attic was the issue.

■ ■ ■

AS SOON AS my mother came home from dinner, my grandmother met her with the words and in the tone she usually adopted when there was trouble in the house. "Caroline! I need to talk to you!"

Aunt Jeanette had already gone to her room. She had no interest in these intergenerational squabbles over my behaviour. They happened frequently enough, and my mother usually could handle them herself.

My mother was tired. It was a Friday, and Fridays were a busy day at the diner. "What now?" she said wearily, taking off her scarf and coat and laying them across the deacon's bench in the front hall.

I stood at the kitchen door with my grandmother. She tried to herd me back into the kitchen so she could get my mother alone, but I refused. I knew it was better, when I was under discussion, to keep myself in my mother's sight. It softened her heart, gave her more of a defence against my grandmother's harangue.

I was to be thwarted this time.

"I want you to come upstairs with me," she said to my mother. "And I want Jacob to stay downstairs. I have something to show you."

My mother sighed and kicked off her shoes. "Let me get a drink of water first," she said. "And I'll be right up."

"You better," said my grandmother. "This is important."

She went first, perhaps to make sure no one tampered with evidence.

I didn't see what my grandmother was getting so upset for. Whenever I had done something wrong in the past she dressed me down, waited for my mother to come home, then dressed me down again when she considered my mother's response too mild or permissive. This seemed different.

"What did you do?" my mother said, as she went to the fridge for her water.

I figured I'd forestall my grandmother, rob her of the element of surprise. "I went into the attic when I wasn't supposed to and I took some stuff."

"What stuff?

"Just stuff," I said. "Old toys I found. That's all."

"You know you're not supposed to go into the attic, don't you?"

I lowered my head, partially in shame and partially, I admit, in calculated humility. "I know," I said. "It's dangerous."

"And you know how touchy your Grandnan is about her old things. You really shouldn't touch anything without permission."

"I know," I said again.

"And now I have to deal with the fallout," my mother said. "Remember, Jacob. It's not just you who has to live in this house. It's all of us, including your Grandnan. I know some of her rules are hard, but the attic rule I happen to agree with. It *is* dangerous. So next time you think you want to go up there, or do something else you're not supposed to do, I want you to remember it affects us all."

This was what I'd expected from my mother. The usual talking to — balanced and reasonable, not too harsh, but effective enough to make me swear on the spot I would not disappoint her again, even if I would forget and make the same or a similar mistake a few days later.

"Okay," I said.

Now she would go upstairs to my grandmother and they would have it out, and though it would start out about me, it would end up being a discussion about the best way to raise a child.

■ ■ ■

THE ISSUE MY grandmother had with the toys in my bedroom was not that I had gone without permission into the attic — though that was infraction enough and worthy of severe punishment, in her opinion. It was that I was playing with girls' things. An Easy-Bake Oven. Tea sets. Paper dolls.

This should have been a minor issue, an anomaly, perfectly natural for a young boy with a curious nature. These days, I've heard, some progressive parents no longer make distinctions between boys' toys and girls' toys. They let their children play with whatever they want.

Jeanette, a self-proclaimed hippie, did her best to inject the reality of a changing world into our daily lives. In retrospect, she accomplished little. Jeanette was too quirky to be taken seriously. Even my mother had little time for her pet causes and intellectual discussions. Jeanette read books, and mounted protests, and indulged in windy arguments over dinner that all of us, me included, did our best to ignore.

My mother was not at the forefront of gender equality. She wore dresses and pantyhose and heels, whereas Jeanette, somewhat ahead of her time, dressed as androgynously as possible. My mother liked perfume, and makeup, and frilly things.

My grandmother approved of my mother's femininity, sometimes as a curative to Jeanette's purposeful manliness. She often referred to my mother as "my prettiest daughter." This infuriated Jeanette, not because she had lost out in the contest of who was better looking, but because my grandmother would think of having such a contest in the first place.

Despite all this, my mother emphatically did not agree with my grandmother when it came to what toys I should play with.

Whatever the results of their argument, I never got to hear any of it. I learned only what I could overhear from snatches of conversation my mother had with Jeanette over the next few weeks. Usually when there was an argument about me, my grandmother was more than happy to drag me into it. She would berate my mother over dinner in front of me, and try to sway me to her side after school when my mother wasn't home. But this time she did not discuss it, and my mother did not carry to me any instructions about what I was or was not to do in my grandmother's presence. She never mentioned the attic.

When I went back up to my room the tea set and oven were still there. No one told me to put them back, or not play with them. I stored them in my closet to be safe, and when I played with them again I did so with my bedroom door shut.

My grandmother wouldn't speak to my mother for two days.

My mother told Jeanette my grandmother was being "ridiculous and neurotic." Jeanette told me I could play with whatever toys I liked and I should just ignore the adults around me who thought differently. My mother came into my room once and sat on the edge of my bed while I was reading a comic. She said she loved me and she would always love me no matter what kind of man I grew up to be.

The whole thing was confusing. It was the first time I remember thinking *all* adults, not just my grandmother, were slightly crazy. I had never considered playing with girls' toys would make me act like a girl when I got older. I was a boy. I *knew* I was a boy, and I didn't believe I would end up wearing women's clothing or makeup because of it. But this is what my grandmother thought. She had experience, she said. It was a proven fact. One had to be vigilant and correct that kind of behaviour when it happened.

My mother put her foot down, which she didn't often do. She told my grandmother she didn't believe in the theory that playing with girls' toys made a boy less masculine, and I could play with whatever I wanted.

Once, my grandmother snuck into my room, took the toys and hid them. They weren't in the attic, or at least in any of the places I could reach. I complained about this to my mother, who found them and gave them back. There was no argument this time. My grandmother never mentioned it, though I suspect my mother had to go into grandmother's room to find them.

Then my grandmother changed tacks. That year, for my birthday and report cards and Christmas, she bought me Tonka trucks, GI Joes, and plastic guns. But trucks were just trucks. I didn't have any inclination to push them through piles of dirt and pretend I was in a job half the men in town already had. I was afraid of the guns. I preferred puzzles and electronics and art kits. These stirred my imagination.

I kept the toys my grandmother gave me, but I didn't play with them. I continued to play with the toys from the attic, because I could imagine people having tea and cake with me, and I liked dressing up the dolls in new outfits. Later, to counter my grandmother's overtly masculine toys, Jeanette and my mother bought me whatever I wanted, including a more up-to-date paper doll set and a newer Easy-Bake Oven with all the pans and pots intact and the packaged mixes to make my own cakes.

Weeks after the argument, when my grandmother came in to call me for supper and caught me playing with the paper doll, she only pursed her lips and told me to come along. Halfway down the stairs, I heard her in the kitchen telling my mother it was too late.

"Too late for what?" said my mother.

"That boy," said my grandmother. "You've got him ruined already. Mark my words."

"I don't care how he turns out," I heard my mother say. "I'll love him anyway."

"I can't believe you're saying that. Of all the irresponsible, ridiculous, dangerous ..."

I came into the kitchen. My grandmother never finished what she was about to say.

# TWO

∎

COMING BACK INTO Nova Scotia after being away for any length of time is always a shock. From the moment we turn off the 104 highway at the Advocate/Trenton exit, I begin to brace myself for the sameness of it all. My mother and Aunt Jeanette are always complaining to me on the phone how everything is always changing, but I see no evidence of this. The first building as we pull off the highway onto Trunk #7 is the Farmer's Co-Op with its tall, cylindrical steel silo jutting up a hundred feet. There are pickup trucks parked irregularly in the yard. Beyond that, the Irving truck stop and small industrial mall, and the Veinot's paper shop, before we turn onto the upper end of River Road and begin the slow sojourn past the Indian reserve and along the river into town.

It is a short jaunt, without time for reflection. Aunt Jeanette chatters the whole way. She picked me up at the airport wearing, typically, a pair of sneakers, faded jeans, and a baggy white t-shirt with *NO WAR* printed on it. Her greying hair is pulled into a bun. She drives hunched over the steering wheel like an old woman, which bothers my mother, who says she looks like she is preparing for an accident. My aunt's driving makes me nervous, too. After she fills me in on all the details of Advocate, she tells me there are several gay men living in town now. I should try to meet them when I'm home.

"Don't tell me you're trying to set me up?"

Jeanette laughs. "It's about time you found someone."

"I'm home for my grandmother's funeral and you're going to play matchmaker?"

"Not her funeral," says Jeanette. "She's just very sick. It could be any day. Or it could be a month."

"I can't stay a month," I say. "And how do you know Grandnan won't get better?"

Jeanette shakes her head. "Not at her age, Jake. She's got pneumonia. Her heart is failing."

I hate to think she better hurry up about it, but I do. I don't say this to Jeanette. I won't say this to anyone.

"Anyway," says my aunt. "If you do happen to meet someone, you should get to know them."

"And what if you're wrong and they aren't gay?"

Jeanette shrugs. "No harm, no foul."

By the time we pull up to the house on Tenerife Street I've absorbed the few changes she pointed out to me. A shop or two. A couple of benches down by the river, that the town council had re-christened Veteran's Memorial Park. It had been known as Founder's Park for years.

My grandmother's formidable brick house always looks the same.

The grass is neatly mowed and bright strips of azaleas, pink and white hostas, petunias, and geraniums are planted neatly in horizontal beds on either side of the front steps. My grandmother chose the flowers and my mother and Jeanette planted them.

A strange car sits in the driveway. A blue, older model Volvo. Boxy. Sensible.

"The homecare nurse," Jeanette explains. "She was watching your grandmother while I was gone to the airport."

"Right," I say.

Jeanette shuts off the car engine and sighs. "Don't expect too much."

I am, in fact, expecting nothing at all, but I don't say this. We retrieve my things from the car and go inside. I have the disturbing sense the house is swallowing me, that I am being drawn back into the dysfunction — the years of arguments and complaint, the religion, the battling perspectives and opposing principles.

I am not prepared for it.

The nurse, a forty-ish, overweight woman with a name tag that reads *Judy* and wearing a blue uniform that matches the Volvo, meets us in the hall. "She's had her medication," the nurse says. "She's sleeping soundly now. Everything is fine."

Jeanette thanks her. I unload my suitcase next to the living room door in the hallway. I avoid the staircase. When the nurse is gone, Jeanette asks if I want to go see my grandmother.

"Why don't we wait until Mom gets home?" I say.

Jeanette looks at me and tilts her head to the side, the way she does when something bemuses or annoys her. "Aren't you at least going to take your things to your room? I'm sure you know where it is."

The problem, and I think Jeanette knows it, is this reminds me too much of other times in this house. I suggest to her instead we just leave everything and have a drink.

Jeanette shrugs. "Suit yourself," she says. "I'm going up to check on Mom."

She takes my suitcase with her when she goes.

■ ■ ■

WHEN I WAS a boy, my best friend was Cameron Simms. He lived on the Protestant side of the river, which made my grandmother suspect he was United, but he assured her he was not. His mother taught biology at the high school. His father was a chemical engineer at the heavy water plant in Trenton. They were, he told my grandmother, both atheists.

It is a testament to the perverseness of my grandmother's beliefs that it was better to be an atheist than a Protestant.

My favourite place to go was Cameron's. His parents were always nice to me. We didn't need to worry about bullies. And if he sometimes became pedantic it wasn't his fault. He was taught that way and I learned a lot from him. We would sit in his backyard and talk, or play Lego blocks or video games in his room. We played Risk, though I usually got beat — Cameron had a five-star general's grasp of strategy — and I could usually wrangle myself an invitation to supper. Then we'd have another hour after to mess around before Cameron decided he needed to get his homework done, and it might be seven or eight o'clock before I was forced to go back to Tenerife Street.

But I didn't see a lot of Cameron in March of 1984. It was cold, with "lots of weather" as my grandmother put it, and for the last two weeks it snowed almost every day. She would often want me home after school to shovel. My grandmother hired her man to shovel out the driveway, but expected my mother and Aunt Jeanette to shovel the paths to the front door and from the back door to the shed. My job was the stoops. My grandmother had assigned me this, along with a few other small chores, to earn my allowance, though she in fact did not pay it. My mother did. But work instilled discipline, and everyone in the house had to have something to do. I didn't mind my job. It took thirty minutes to do each stoop and sometimes I would help my mother and Jeanette with the paths if they were out at the same time.

I didn't mind the snow, but the winters seemed long, and when spring came to Advocate and the house on Tenerife Street, it came as a benediction. The year my uncle returned from Toronto it came early. The first week in April the temperature had risen dramatically to fourteen or fifteen degrees and the snows melted. My grandmother said she could not remember an earlier spring in her lifetime, and she began preparing her yard and her gardens. She removed the burlap from the perennials and bushes. She brought out the wheelbarrow for the rocks that had been forced up through the ground by the frost, picking them up and depositing them behind the backyard shed.

I helped her, simply glad to get out of the house in anything less than a heavy winter jacket and gloves. My grandmother asked me to trim the privet hedge that ran between our property and the neighbour's house to the north. Some days, when they were not working, Aunt Jeanette and my mother would help, too, and the four of us would be out there in our light jackets and boots, raking and turning soil.

April also marked the beginning of what my Aunt Jeanette called our annual "midget convention" — the placing of my grand-mother's variety of little garden gnomes and ceramic angels in the yard. She had a passion for these sculptures and she infested her property with them. There were dozens of these — cherubs in tiny fountains or leaning on walls, gnomes with shovels or red pointed caps — which she sprinkled throughout her azaleas and geraniums and petunias and marigolds. She didn't defend her choices. It was her property and she could do with it as she liked.

When I was younger I liked the placing of the statues, but my grandmother was afraid I might drop them so I was only allowed to consult on the best places to set them. She did let me place them myself when I got older, and when I turned ten she handed the whole business over to me. By then I had outgrown them. They were no more to me than ugly little plaster statues, and I viewed placing them as much a chore as hauling rocks. I never said this to my grandmother, though. She had entrusted me with something she cared about, which was rare enough, and she was still interested enough to come out and inspect my placement and give me a statue-by-statue editorial. "That little man is looking too much towards the front step, don't you think?" she'd tell me. "Shouldn't we turn him a little bit to the north?" Or, "I think the fountain angel should be in the very front of the yard this year. He just *feels* like he should be closer to the road."

The times we placed statues are the only ones I remember, in all my childhood, of having some kind of intimacy with my grandmother. It was our project. We consulted on it. We worked together. I don't remember her once unduly criticizing my choices. When it came to garden gnomes, as in no other area of her life, she became a diplomat. It is a testament, perhaps, to how much I craved a relationship with her that I continued to do this and feigned enthusiasm for it long after the work itself ceased to interest.

■ ■ ■

ONE AFTERNOON IN late May, while my mother and Jeanette were at work, my grandmother received a phone call.

I paid no attention at first. I was at the dining room table doing homework for geography class. I had to identify all the continents, and at least three countries and their capitals within each. I had an atlas. It was easy work, and boring. I was eleven, in grade six, and the year was nearly done.

My grandmother didn't like me sitting at the dining room table. It was antique, left to her by her mother-in-law. It had eight chairs with the likeness of Queen Anne carved in the back. Those chairs were some of her most precious possessions. My deceased grandfather used to say, or so I've heard, that those chairs were "A good place for the arse of a Scot. In the face of a queen." My grandmother was afraid they would break if sat on, so we ate our dinners at the kitchen table, even though it was crowded with the four of us.

I couldn't use the kitchen table for homework, because my grandmother never stayed quiet long enough to let me concentrate, and I found my room too small and oppressive. There was more room in the dining room. I could spread my books out on the mahogany surface and get comfortable. But I was only able to use it if my grandmother wasn't paying attention. Eventually she would catch me and chase me back up to my room. "Good heavens," she'd say. "Don't you know those chairs are priceless heirlooms?"

I heard my grandmother answer the phone and talk into it, though I couldn't hear what was said. A few minutes later she came into the dining room. I knew she was distracted because she didn't mention me being there. She said, "What time is your mother getting home from the diner?"

"Five o'clock," I told her.

"That late?" said my grandmother. "I thought it was three."

My grandmother knew perfectly well what time my mother got off work. I knew it must have been the phone call upsetting her but when I asked her who it was she wouldn't say.

"Just never you mind," she said. "And get up off those chairs. How many times do I have tell you, Jacob Owen McNeil, those are valuable antiques and not for sitting on?"

Reluctantly I gathered up my books and carried them to the kitchen, hoping my grandmother would tell me something about who had been on the other end of the line. I had inherited a streak of nosiness directly from her, and a part of me — albeit a small, naïve part — thought it might have something to do with my father. The man who had sired me. The man I had never met and who had decided, I was told by my grandmother, *not* to marry my mother. It was a shame my grandmother had to bear — a pregnant nineteen-year-old daughter and a bastard grandson who had not been christened because my mother wanted me to make up my own mind when I was old enough. How she ever explained this to her fellow Catholics, to whom decency, marriage, and childbirth were sacrosanct, we never knew. She never mentioned my father. She never mentioned her eldest daughter was an unwed mother.

All I know about my father is he was an itinerant worker who worked on a tree-cutting crew in the county for a season in 1971. My mother fell in love with him, and by the time she knew she was pregnant, the season was over and he was gone. She was never able to find him again.

My grandmother didn't speak to me while she cooked supper. She was roasting beef and was busy basting it and getting it ready to put back in the oven. She muttered to herself all the while, but I could make nothing out. My grandmother did not have a poker face. We always knew what she was thinking by her expression or the way she held herself, and whatever news she had received was not good.

I was determined to wait until my mother came home, when the story would come out. I finished geography and went on to algebra. I was a good student, thorough and conscientious about my work. I hated to make mistakes, and I liked to line my figures up perfectly on the paper so large equations could be distilled magically down to one final and irrevocable number equal to a variable of x or y.

By the time my mother got home, my grandmother had finished her cooking and I had finished my homework. I was still to be disappointed. My grandmother wanted to speak to my mother in my grandfather's den. I stayed seated at the kitchen table, not bothering to strain to hear because the door was shut.

Suddenly I heard my mother squeal.

Someone's dead, I thought.

Less than a minute later my mother came running out of the den, through the living room, and into the kitchen. "Your Uncle David is coming home!" she cried.

"Uncle David?"

I'd never met him. I sometimes forgot he even existed, though my mother and Jeanette talked to him on the phone occasionally, and once in a while they passed it to me. They had not told me much about him. Only that he and my grandmother did not get along, and he left home a long time ago. My grandmother never talked about my uncle.

No wonder she was upset. She was also annoyed her daughter should be so excited over news she found so disconcerting. "I don't know what you're getting in such a fuss about," she said. "It's only for a visit."

"Did he say how long?"

"No," said my grandmother. "I presume a week. Any longer and we'll be put out. I shouldn't agree to it at all."

"Why not?" said my mother. "We've got scads of room."

"It's not just the room," said my grandmother. "It's the extra food and the extra washing. This house is bursting at the seams as is."

My mother ignored my grandmother's grumbling. She called Jeanette at the diner and told her the news. She acted like the screaming, giggling girls in my sixth grade.

I did not share my mother's excitement.

I didn't know my uncle.

I also wasn't used to disruptions at the house on Tenerife Street. I couldn't begrudge my uncle a meal or a bed, like my grandmother did, but I had never seen my mother, usually so cool-headed over everything, get so excited. It bothered me. This Uncle David was an interloper, a rival for my mother's affections, and I resented his intrusion already.

One thing my mother forgot to ask in all the commotion was when my uncle was coming.

"In two weeks," my grandmother said. "By train."

"We'll all go to the train station to meet him," said my mother. "Won't it be great?"

"I certainly won't be going. It's a Saturday, and Saturday is my bridge day, and the church auxiliary meets Saturday night."

"Surely you can miss those things for one day," my mother said.

"I most surely cannot," said my grandmother. "The world may stop for you, Caroline, when someone comes to town, but it doesn't stop for the busy and beholden."

"It's not just *someone*," said my mother, her mood dampening. "It's your *son*."

"Makes no never mind," said my grandmother. "I'll see him well enough when you get home from the station. Though why the man would pick now to come see us, when he hasn't been home in a dozen years, I'll never make out. And what happened to the rest of his school year, I want to know? Doesn't high school go into June in Ontario?"

My grandmother went on, but my mother and I tuned her out.

We went for a walk up Tenerife Street instead, then down to the water along River Street. It was sunny and reasonably warm. She told me about my uncle, but not why my grandmother was so dead-set against seeing him. I was surprised. This was the woman who told me the secret of menstruation at the age of seven when I first began to notice thick white strips of padding in the bathroom garbage can upstairs. I found it interesting that women bled from secret parts of themselves while men did not. My grandmother was horrified that my mother explained it to me. "My heavens!" she cried. "You'll ruin the boy by the time he's ten!"

My mother was not as forthcoming about Uncle David as she was on female reproductive biology. As to why he left home so long ago and never came to visit, she said only that shortly after her father died in 1969, David and my grandmother had an argument and she asked him to leave.

"Why?" I asked.

"Just because," said my mother.

"What kind of because?"

"Your grandmother didn't like the things he did," said my mother.

"What things?"

"Just things."

"That doesn't make any sense." I said, with the inherent logic of a child. "You got pregnant out of wedlock and Grandnan didn't kick you out, and Jeanette told me she smoked so much reefer she threw up all over the living room and she didn't get kicked out. Why should Uncle David be any different?"

I could see I had bewildered my mother. It was an effect I could occasionally produce on my teachers and Jeanette or even on my grandmother. "The questions!" the latter would cry. "The poor boy's tongue flaps at both ends!" But I was determined not to let up on her. I was relentless, tenacious, in pursuit of the truth, as any good mathematician — as I already considered myself — should be.

Finally my mother said, "Your uncle is different from most people."

"Different how?"

"Just different," my mother said. "He's a wonderful man, really. It's just that he's never gotten married and your grandmother doesn't like that."

I knew, or sensed, the situation was more complicated than that, and my mother wasn't telling me everything. She told me when uncle David came I could ask him myself.

"Ask him what? Why he's not married?"

"Yes," said my mother, "if you want to."

"But why don't you tell me?" I was eleven now. Not the eight-year-old who found the boxes in the closet.

When she saw she was not going to get away with a euphemism, or a vagute generalization, or even a good old-fashioned bait and switch, my mother told me the truth. "Your Uncle David is a homosexual," she said flatly. "And your grandmother hates the fact. When she found out she told him never darken her door again."

"A homosexual?" I said, pronouncing the word very carefully, as if it were loaded with explosives. Which, in a sense, I suppose it was in our house. "What does that mean?

"Jacob," said my mother softly, but sternly. "That is something you'll have to ask your uncle. This information belongs to him. It is not mine to tell."

"And so that's why Uncle David never visits? Because of Grandnan?"

"That's why," said my mother.

"Grandnan has trouble getting along with people. There's a kid in my school, Scott Findlay, who's like that. Our home room teacher says he's *obstreperous*."

My mother laughed, as we turned on off the river road and up Fartham Avenue back toward Tenerife. "That is a perfectly fine description of your grandmother."

But I was still not satisfied. I had exhausted my mother with questions, so knew asking more would not yield extra information. I swore to look up the word *homosexual* in a dictionary to find out exactly what it meant before my uncle arrived, but I never did.

2

THE YEAR BEFORE Uncle David came home, when I was ten, my grandmother had a shower installed in the upstairs bathroom at the end of what she called the "north hall." Jeanette and my mother had been arguing for a shower in the upstairs bathroom for years, ever since they were teenagers. The bathrooms hadn't been remodelled since the house was built. They had not installed a shower. Practically every house in Advocate had one, according to my aunt and mother, and it was just silly, in their view, not to have this most common of conveniences in the last half of the twentieth century.

I do not know my grandmother's reasons for having only a bath and not a shower. But I do know whenever my aunt or mother would pester her for one, she would only say a shower was useless and a bath was not.

"A woman's got to soak her parts," she said.

I was too young to understand this argument, but my Aunt Jeanette and my mother seemed to.

"That's medieval," Aunt Jeanette said. "A shower is just as good as a bath. Better, because it doesn't take so long. Look at us now when we have to go anywhere! The three of us and Jacob having to scramble to get in the tub, leaving soap scum everywhere."

"There would be no soap scum if you cleaned up after yourself," said my grandmother, who never missed an opportunity to instill a lesson.

"If you don't do it," Jeanette said, "I'll hire a plumber and have one installed myself."

The argument continued for years.

Because we didn't have a shower, and a bath was such a time-consuming ordeal, I was forced to wash, not every day, but only twice a week, on Wednesday and Sunday night. As I watched TV with Aunt Jeanette in the TV room next to my grandfather's den, my mother would come in and tell me it was bath time. She would have drawn the water and pulled out my favourite inflatable toys. I would stay in there an hour, until the bubbles disappeared and a white scum of soap lay on top of the water like an oil slick, and the water was tepid. Usually it was also black from the dirt that had been on my body.

When Jeanette supervised me, she would always look into the tub and cluck. "See how unhygienic that is?" she'd say, as if making another argument to my grandmother. "How can someone get clean in that?"

After years of resistance my grandmother gave in, though Jeanette did pay for it, as promised, on her meagre wages from the diner. What made my grandmother decide a woman no longer had to "soak her parts" I never knew. Only that one day Jeanette told my mother she had convinced "the old woman" and the plumber would arrive on Monday.

My grandmother refused to use the new shower. She complained about the amount of water being wasted now that Aunt Jeanette and my mother and I were taking showers far more than we bathed.

I lost my Wednesday night bath — my mother said I could just take a shower Thursday morning before school instead — but I insisted on the Sunday night one. Even at the age of eleven I secretly liked the toys, and the bubbles, and the quiet of the bath with only the occasional drip from the faucet marking irregular time.

My mother still took baths occasionally too, by candlelight, with the radio sitting on the toilet seat tuned to an FM classical station. She did not particularly like classical music, she said, except when she was in the bath.

I understood.

At eleven, I should have been more interested in skateboards and bicycles and firecrackers than plastic toys. But I always had my rubber ducky and sailboats in the bath with me. I reverted to some supremely ideal age. I was never a particularly secure boy, despite the efforts of the adults around me to make me so, but I felt perfectly safe and secure in the bath. Enveloped by cool air, silence, and warm water, I was more at peace with myself than I was anywhere else.

■ ■ ■

AUNT JEANETTE HAD a habit of spending twenty minutes or more under the showerhead, driving my grandmother to distraction and forcing her to say Jeanette was draining half the Atlantic and driving the power and water bills into the "elemental stratosphere."

The "elemental stratosphere" was a favourite expression of my grandmother's for defining excess. She had a host of others.

The shower was a source of ongoing tension for them. Whenever

Aunt Jeanette emerged from the bathroom and my grandmother berated her for staying in so long, she always said the same thing. "I was spraying my parts."

The Saturday morning my uncle was due to arrive at the train station at eleven o'clock, Jeanette stayed in longer than usual, perhaps because she wanted to be particularly refreshed for her brother's arrival. My mother and I had awakened late.

My grandmother was up at six, as she always was, but neglected to call us. Jeanette accused her of doing it on purpose. "Why on earth would I do that?" exclaimed my grandmother. "I don't care what time you get out of bed. Sleep until noon if you want to!"

This was not entirely true.

It annoyed my grandmother that, on their days off, her daughters sometimes slept in. She considered the hours between six and nine to be her most productive, and anyone who did not get out of bed to take advantage of this was being lazy, wasting half the day. She would never roust us out of bed directly. My grandmother did not enter our rooms, except occasionally to see if they were clean. Instead she would decide to vacuum outside our doors at seven a.m., or turn the radio in the kitchen so loud we heard it upstairs.

But that morning, not a peep, which was why Jeanette thought she was playing tricks, trying to make it difficult for us to get ready in time to meet my uncle's train.

My grandmother's mood was not improved by the fact her bridge game that afternoon was cancelled. Hazel McLeod from down the street had an attack of gout, and called my grandmother to tell her to find another fourth. But there was no other fourth. It was too short notice.

She was sitting at the kitchen table drinking tea when my mother and I came in for breakfast. Aunt Jeanette was still in the shower.

"That's great," said my mother. "Now you can come to the train station with us."

"It's not 'great,'" said my grandmother sourly. "And I'm still not going. I have things to do around here."

My mother poured me a bowl of cereal with milk. Usually on Saturday my grandmother would have breakfast prepared for us — fried eggs and bacon or ham, cooked tomatoes, sometimes even sliced and fried potatoes. But this morning there was nothing.

For once, though, she did not complain about Jeanette being in the shower too long.

My mother did. It was almost ten o'clock and she and I had yet to clean up.

"What's the point?" said my grandmother. "You're only going to the train station. It's not like the Pope is coming."

"It's an occasion," said my mother. "We should all look nice for him. And smell nice too."

"I smell fine," said my grandmother. She sat, drinking her tea, with a bitter look on her face. She resented the fuss. She resented the bother. I'm sure if she could she would have closed up the house and put a "You're Not Welcome" sign on the door.

■ ■ ■

JEANETTE CLIMBED OUT of the shower at ten fifteen, and my mother was cross with her.

"There's hardly time for me to get ready, let alone Jacob," she said.

Jeanette wore a yellow sundress. My grandmother reminded her it was a train station, and not a cotillion, they were going to. "I know," Jeanette said. "I still want to dress up."

My mother went to the bathroom, and I asked for another bowl of Corn Flakes. Jeanette started working on my grandmother to come to the station. They argued. I took my cereal into the TV room. I was not allowed to eat in any part of the house but the kitchen because my grandmother was afraid I'd drop something and spoil the rugs. But she was too busy arguing with Jeanette to notice. I could hear them from the TV room, so I turned on the television.

*Spider-Man* was on.

I loved *Spider-Man*.

I sat on the sofa and watched the show and finished my cereal. I tried to ignore Aunt Jeanette and my grandmother bickering in the kitchen.

In the end my grandmother decided to go to the station. I'm not sure how Aunt Jeanette convinced her. She could be tenacious; my grandmother said she could argue the boots off a stone statue. Or maybe, her bridge game cancelled, my grandmother decided to go for some obscure reason of her own. Whatever the cause, when I came downstairs changed out of my pyjamas, having time only to comb my hair and wash my face, the three of them were waiting for me in the foyer.

My grandmother wore the same floral print housedress she had on earlier, and she was putting on grandfather's threadbare black greatcoat she sported around the yard in the fall. On a normal day, she would not be caught dead downtown in such an outfit. It was as if she was deliberately dressing down for my uncle. I might be meeting you, that ensemble said, but you aren't anything special.

My mother and Jeanette were smart enough not to mention her getup. Later Jeanette said she looked like a cross between Diefenbaker and an old charwoman. They dressed up, Jeanette in the yellow sundress with a ladies' summer coat that met up perfectly with the hem of her dress and left her legs bare, and my mother in a pair of tight jeans and a white cable-knit sweater. Jeanette looked like a debutante, my mother a sorority girl.

"All ready?" my mother asked.

"Let's get this over with," my grandmother said. "I might not have bridge today, but I do have the auxiliary meeting tonight. And I've got a busy day. Did you start the car, at least?"

Jeanette had, and we all went out and fit ourselves into it. It was a fine day; sun and blue sky, hardly a cloud. My grandmother fastened a clear plastic kerchief over her head to keep her hair in place, though there was no wind. She also called shotgun, though not in those words.

My grandmother disliked Jeanette's car, a Pinto that rode close to the ground and always had something wrong with it. This time it had a loose fan belt that screamed like a child being axe-murdered and gave my grandmother the creeps. "Why don't you get that fixed?" she asked Jeanette. "The whole vehicle is likely to fly apart at any minute."

"It's fine," said Jeanette. "The belt just needs to be tightened."

My mother and I got in the back seat. I was fine because I was short for my age, but my mother, who was reasonably tall for a woman, struggled for legroom. My grandmother thoughtlessly shifted her seat all the way back so my mother's knees were pressed up against it, but my mother never complained.

No one had given a thought to how we were going to fit Uncle David in the car. My grandmother realized, at the same time I did, there was not going to be enough room. "Just you should have went, for heaven's sake. The rest of us could have seen him when you got home ten minutes later."

"It's a homecoming," argued Jeanette. "We all have to be there when he steps down from the train."

Despite Aunt Jeanette's long shower, we arrived at the train station early. Everything I knew about homecomings I had learned from TV. In those shows there are always dozens or hundreds of people waiting anxiously on the platform for the train to arrive. There are shouts and kisses and exclamations. I was not prepared for the desolation of the station, the single ticket agent behind the counter who gave my mother the arrival information, the funereal wasteland of the wooden platform outside as we stood, the only ones there, and waited for my uncle. My grandmother wanted to stay inside. Nobody argued with her. But when we all opted to stand on the platform she stayed with us and sat on a bench.

Aunt Jeanette and my mother talked excitedly. "I wonder what he'll look like," said my Aunt Jeanette.

My grandmother, with less vinegar than usual, had an answer for every question. "He'll look just like he did the last time you saw him," she said. "Only older."

"Maybe he lost his hair," said my mother. "Like Dad did."

"You went up to visit him three years ago," said my grandmother. "Had he lost his hair then?"

"No," admitted my mother.

"Then he's unlikely to have lost it now."

I went over and sat beside my grandmother.

"I fail to see," she said to me, "what the big mystery is. They talk to the boy almost every week on the phone. They know as much about his life as they do about mine."

It was true my mother and Jeanette talked to my uncle a lot. When they put him on the phone with me I had nothing to say to him. To his credit, he didn't baby talk me, as some people do when they are talking to children they've never met. He usually asked me in an adult voice if I was doing well in school and looking after my mother and what were the names of my friends.

I had not seen a picture of my uncle.

I had no idea what he looked like.

My grandmother and I were aligned, she because she resented my uncle for whatever reason, and I because I was jealous.

The wait for the train seemed to take hours.

At quarter after eleven Jeanette stamped her foot once on the platform and cried out, "What is taking so long?"

My mother agreed to go in and ask the ticket taker. She came out five minutes later and said she had been told the train was usually a few minutes late.

"Blueberry Special," said Jeanette. That was the Advocate County nickname for the route from Halifax all the way down to Yarmouth. It was a joke. The train rumbled along so slowly, it was said, you could hop off and pick blueberries and then hop back on again when you were done.

At just that moment we heard a sound from the north, and though we couldn't see the train beyond the bend in the tracks, we could hear it. I stood up, more to see the train than in any anticipation of my uncle's arrival. My grandmother stayed seated. Jeanette and my mother began to jump up and down like schoolgirls.

I was disgusted with them.

So was my grandmother. "I've raised a pair of infants," she said.

The train rounded the corner, crawling slowly but evenly along the tracks. It was silver, long, and sleek. I was expecting, I realize now, a steam train, with billowing smoke and pistons and a horn. The train pulled into the station and rolled to a halt. There was no lifting of fog, no immediate disembarkation of passengers. It just sat there. No one wearing six shooters and a gallon hat got off. I was disappointed. I had watched too many westerns, too many old movies with my grandmother.

In the end the doors slid open and three people got off. One was a young girl with a single small suitcase. She didn't look much older than me, though she must have been, for there was no one there to greet her. Another was a middle-aged, portly man with a satchel and a suit bag slung over his shoulder. He looked like a travelling salesman. The third got out of the last car. He was a tall, thin man with a stoop and more suitcases than he could carry. The porter on the train passed them down to him. He just stood there, helpless.

Jeanette and my mother scanned the faces.

The train did not dally. Apparently there were no passengers to board, for it immediately pulled away.

Jeanette was devastated.

The girl — she reminded me of Anne of Green Gables, though she did not have red hair and a wincey dress — and the salesman walked by us into the station. The tall thin man stayed down at the far end of the platform amidst his bags.

"He didn't come," Jeanette said.

"It must be an error," said my mother. "Maybe he'll be on a later train."

"There is no other train today. This was the only one."

My mother asked my grandmother if this was right, but she was staring intently down the platform at the man on the other end of it. Mother asked what she was looking at.

"I'm not sure," she said, "but I think you better go down and help your brother."

Jeanette slowly shook her head. "It's too thin for David. Isn't it?"

Before Jeanette could argue further, the man left his bags and started walking up the platform towards us. He lifted his arm in a wave, and Jeanette screamed. She and my mother began to run down the platform. Jeanette had worn high heels for the occasion, and they fired on the wooden planks of the platform like shots.

My grandmother and I stayed put. She was studying my uncle carefully from her place on the bench. She was the oldest of us, but there was nothing wrong with her eyesight, or her inner sense. She knew, she said later, there was something wrong with my uncle the minute he stepped down from the train.

## 3

THE KISSING AND the hugging that took place between my uncle and my mother and Jeanette seemed to go on for hours. My grandmother stayed on her bench. I stood beside her and watched my mother and aunt fawn over my prodigal uncle. I didn't leave my grand-mother's side in case I got pulled into this love fest.

My grandmother eyed, suspiciously, the four suitcases still sitting at the far end of the platform. "That's an awful lot of baggage for a short visit," she said. "I hope he doesn't plan on staying the month."

Eventually the three of them returned up the platform, my uncle in the middle and Aunt Jeanette and my mother on either side of him with an arm around his waist.

"Oh brother," said my grandmother. "It's like Old Home Week."

My grandmother could be extremely caustic. Jeanette said once that the woman did not have an ounce of sentimentality in her.

I watched my uncle warily, and scanned my mother's face for signs she had completely forgotten who I was. When they reached us, they stopped, separated, and my uncle looked at my grandmother.

"Hello, Mother," he said.

"Hello, David," she said. "That's a lot of luggage you've brought. You planning on a long stay?"

David shrugged, and Aunt Jeanette shot her a look. My grand-mother still had not risen from her bench, and when my mother suggested she get up and greet my uncle properly, she claimed her thrombosis was acting up and she didn't dare stand.

"Does that mean we have to carry you to the car?" asked Jeanette.

"I'll manage," said my grandmother wryly.

I watched my uncle's face for his reaction to my grandmother's coolness. There was none. He only wore a tight little grin. He was a handsome man, if a little anemic. I stared at him until my mother remembered I was there and introduced me.

"So this is Jacob," he said, bending down and reaching out a hand.

I shook it. I was not used to shaking hands and my uncle's was damp. I fought the urge to wipe my own off on my pants. Unlike my grandmother, I was taught by my mother and the town to hide my displeasure.

"You've lost weight," my grandmother said to him. "Are you not eating well up there in Toronto? And you're pale too. Seems like you're not looking after yourself."

Everyone ignored her, and my mother suggested she and Aunt Jeanette go down and retrieve the bags.

"I can help," said David

"No," my mother said. "You stay here and keep Mom company. We can manage."

I went with them, and as we were walking away I heard my grandmother nattering at her only son. No doubt he'd have to go through the third degree with her. She didn't like him. That was clear. But that still wouldn't exempt him from a thorough interrogation of his life.

On the way down the platform my mother asked what I thought of him.

"He's okay," I said. "He's tall."

"You'll like him," Aunt Jeanette said. "Once you get to know him."

"Then why doesn't Grandnan like him?"

Jeanette grunted, almost like a pig, and said "Grandnan doesn't like much of anybody."

My mother told her to be quiet. "You just have to give it time," she said. "They haven't seen each other in a long while."

This was not an answer. It was another way of saying it was none of my business.

I was given the lightest bag to carry. My mother and Jeanette struggled with the other three. I resented that. The least my uncle could have done was relieve us of one of them. We eventually got them all into the hatchback of the Pinto, and I had to crawl in back in between my mother and David. I was angered even further. I did not want to be close to him, our legs touching. He offered to sit me on his lap if it would make me more comfortable.

"Gee, can I?" I said, with as much sarcasm as I could muster. I'd been good at that from an early age, inadvertently instructed by my grandmother. My mother pinched my thigh, and I stayed quiet.

My grandmother was annoyed because Jeanette could no longer see out the rearview mirror. The bags were piled too high in the hatchback, and she had long ago lost her driver's side mirror when she scraped it off on a building backing into a parking space. "This is a recipe for an accident," my grandmother said. "David's visit will be over before it starts."

We got home without incident and climbed out of the car. My uncle stood in the driveway and looked up at the house.

"Not a thing has changed," he said.

"Nonsense," said my grandmother. "The shutters are green, not blue. The roof's been reshingled. We've kept it perfectly since ..."

My grandmother was about to say, "since your father died" but for some reason stopped herself. Instead she marched, tight-lipped, into the house, leaving us to carry the bags. This time my uncle did help. We then went through the ordeal of my grandmother designating him a room. She could have done this before; in fact she probably had. But she wanted to go through the show of it to illustrate what an inconvenience David's visit was.

Eventually she settled on the guest room next to Jeanette's room. This was the first time I became aware that this was David's old room. There were no mementos. There was no trace of occupancy in the last fifteen years. It was as featureless and sterile as a hotel room. I wondered if there ever had *been* mementos. I knew my room screamed me: *Star Wars* posters and model robots and a red ribbon from a science fair in school. Maybe David had taken all this stuff when he left, or maybe he'd never had any.

He told my grandmother it would do fine. After his bags were stored and he had showered and changed, dirty as he was from such a long train trip, he came down to the pancake brunch being prepared for him. My grandmother opted out. She said she was going over to Hazel's to see how she was feeling. Jeanette offered to drive her, but my grandmother said she would walk. No one mentioned that just a half hour ago she was stricken with thrombosis.

After she left my uncle said, "She hasn't changed much."

"No," said my mother. "Still the same as ever."

"It nearly killed her to give up a spare room," Jeanette said. "She might have to do a little extra laundry. Even though Caroline and I do it all."

My uncle smiled over his pancakes. "I'm sure," he said, "there's more to it than that."

I paid attention, but no more was said. Eventually I left them and went upstairs to my room and played video games, shutting the door behind me because I didn't want to hear the voices drifting up from below.

# THREE
■

BERNADETTE MCLEOD, OR "Deanny" as I came to know her, was
from the proverbial wrong side of the tracks. Not just the middle
class neighbourhood called Mechanicsville, down by the second
bridge, but the area *behind* Mechanicsville, near the old gravel pit
called Meadow Pond Lane.

There was more than just a lane at Meadow Pond. There were
several deeply rutted dirt roads that criss-crossed each other and
around which a shantytown had sprung up like a collection of
toadstools after the Second World War. There were no businesses
to speak of, except a rundown bottle depot at one end. The houses
in between were small, unkempt structures with no paint, or paint
that had faded to the colour of old crepe paper. Yards were over-
grown and marred with the rusting hulks of cars and bicycles
and overturned tricycles. Ragged curtains and sheets hung in
windows. No one knew what, if anything, Deanny's father did. It
was assumed they lived on welfare — the worst sin, according to
my grandmother, next to apostasy.

At the end of May, my friend Cameron's mother decided he
had to "buckle down" and focus on his homework, and that I
should stay away from the house while he studied. Cameron and

I were only in grade six. We didn't have final exams. But Mrs. Simms believed that work habits, especially when it came to academics, should be formed early. She was preparing Cameron for his certain future as a student in university. I was a blatant distraction.

Cameron did not complain. He followed his parents' direction with an almost cult-like obedience, and I was forced to wander the neighbourhood by myself each night after supper without him. My own mother did not enforce rules around homework. She barely ever asked if I had finished it. She was permissive and laissez-faire about child-rearing. If I had homework, I would do it, and if I didn't, I would reap the consequences.

There were no kids my age in our neighbourhood, and even if there were I suspected they would not want to play with me. I could have stayed at home, but since my uncle arrived I no longer liked being inside. I would rather be outside alone than listen to the adults in my house reminisce and ignore me entirely. If the evening was nice I would walk up Tenerife Street, then up and back across Primrose Street. Often neighbours were out clipping hedges, preparing gardens, and mowing lawns. They usually waved to me. I did not wave back. I had money in my pocket, but no desire to go to the stores on Main Street to see what I could buy. I was usually full from supper.

On Thursday night, June 16, I decided to go to the old mill. This was the only place in town besides the Indian reserve that was off-limits to me. It was dangerous, I was told. Twenty years before, it was a chipping and lumber mill that had employed about a hundred men from the town. Then, my mother said, a newer, more efficient mill opened near Trenton, with better equipment, higher wages, and faster production. The old mill had trouble keeping men, and lost contracts to the new mill. They shut it down, sold what equipment they could, and left the rest. My grandmother never liked that the old mill was there, derelict and less than a mile and a half behind her neighbourhood. She said the town should buy the property, level it, and turn it into a park.

So far no one had listened to her.

There were two log ponds at the mill: one in front of the old planer mill, and the other where the lumberyard used to be. You'd have to be crazy to swim in them. They were dark and turbid, with the bark of old logs and bits of plastic and unidentifiable jetsam floating in them. You could imagine that if the light struck them just right, new life would arise — that some sickening, amoebic thing might sidle out of the water and try to absorb you.

It was a fair barometer of my mood that this was the place I chose to go. When I came here before it was with Cameron, whose parents never forbid him from going there. They had a child-rearing policy — I had heard them expound it — of never forbidding anything, and letting Cameron find out on his own what was and what was not safe to do. In Cameron's case this worked. He was, if anything, more physically timid than I was. He would no more have ventured into the old buildings or gone near the ponds than he would wear a dress. He was tempted by the planer mill, however, and he kept looking inside to see if he could figure out what the old equipment was for.

Several times I suggested we go inside and look, but he always turned me down. "Those danger signs aren't there for fun," he said. "A kid could get seriously hurt in there." And because I was a follower, and had no temerity of my own, I had not ventured in.

The mill was deserted, or so I thought. I'd already checked out both ponds and the chip silo. I wasn't aware there was anyone in the mill with me that night until I heard a voice — distinctly female, but hoarse and almost ageless. I stood at the mouth of the planer mill, staring into its dark interior and the hunched brooding shoulders of machinery shrouded in shadow and dust, trying to work up the courage to enter. I didn't like darkness. I thought of the possibility of enormous spiders spinning webs, or snakes. I was beginning to think maybe I *wouldn't* go in; that I had proved myself enough just by walking up here.

I was startled when I heard the voice again.

"Hey asshole," she said, shocking me out of my deliberation. "What the fuck ya up to?"

I spun around and was presented with the strangest looking creature I'd ever seen. She wore red and black checkered pants, a bright sky-blue top, and sneakers that may once have been white but were now almost black. Besides the colourful, clownish clothes — I was wearing clean jeans and a white button-down Chaps shirt, another reason not to go into the mill — she had the thickest mop of curly black hair I'd ever seen, and utterly filthy face and hands. Whatever Deanny had been doing before she met me, she had been doing it well. I was very particular about dirt. I didn't like any on me. She just stood there, legs apart, hands at her sides and curled into fists — though not, I thought, threateningly — looking at me with a mix of curiosity and suspicion. I found out later she'd been watching from behind an old log, to gauge whether or not I was safe. Her head was cocked slightly to one side, and her eyes, as black as her hair, were taking me in, sizing me up, evaluating me. Finally, she said, "Well?"

"Well, what?"

"Aren't you going to speak to me? You asshole."

I was not used to swearing. There was no swearing in our household, and none in Cameron's. Neither of us were used to it. Unfortunately, I told Deanny this.

She smiled. It was not a friendly smile. In no way could it be called nice. It was more carnivorous than anything. Then she let off a string that took my breath away. She achieved a certain poetic intensity, and by the time she was done I was in awe. She smiled again, and this time it was graceful and genuine. "You gonna play with me or what?"

"I guess," I stammered.

"Come on then," she said. "I haven't got all goddamned fucking day."

"What are we gonna do?"

"I got ideas," Deanny said. "If you can keep up."

I didn't know if I could. Deanny ran us all over the mill, and objections I had to any activities were quickly brushed aside in favour of her primary motivation: to do things because we could. We tried things to figure out if they were fun. Just because something was dangerous or illegal did not count as a bona fide excuse, not in Deanny's world. She smoked, and derided me when I wouldn't take one from her pack. I had never smoked, nor did my mother. Jeanette did, occasionally, but only outdoors. My grandmother wouldn't allow lit cigarettes inside her home.

We crawled our way up the conveyer belt to the mill silo, me in a half-terror of falling, until we got inside. It was full of chips and smelled of pine, urine, and old rot. Deanny pushed me down into the chips immediately, before I'd even had a chance to recover from the ordeal of the climb.

"What did you do that for?" I asked, still lying on my back.

"Because," Deanny said. "I'm the king of the mountain, and you're the dirty rascal."

Each time I got up, Deanny would push me down again. She was strong, and I was not a fighter. I could hardly believe I crawled all the way up there to be beaten by a girl.

"Quit it," I said. "I want to look around."

"Forget it," said Deanny. "There's nothing in here. Let's go someplace else."

By the time she was done with me I was dirty and exhausted. She'd forced me into the chip silo, and the planer mill, and my clothes and face ended up as smeared with grease as hers.

A rusted, rundown "pettybone," or forklift, sat unclaimed in the old lumberyard. Deanny insisted we try starting it. The key was in the ignition, but the battery was dead. She wanted to smash the glass in the cab with rocks.

"Why?" I said. "That's destruction of property."

Deanny looked at me with ill-concealed contempt. "Are you that pansy-assed?" she said. "No one uses it. It's a hunk of junk. Who cares if we break a few windows? And even if they do, who's to say it was us?"

And so we broke windows — on all four sides of the cab. They were thick and took many attempts to do so. There was a certain satisfaction in destroying something just for fun. I had never done anything like it before. Cameron and I had a thoughtful, logical, constructive relationship. Deanny was wild and unpredictable; there was a certain crazed anima about her I'd never experienced before. I had to admit it was exhilarating.

After two hours, when it was starting to get dark, I told Deanny I had to go home.

"Mama's boy," she said. "Have to be in before the sun goes down."

"Yes," I said, not knowing what else to say.

Deanny — filthy and glistening, her hands still balled into fists — looked at me and said, "Go the fuck home then."

"Okay," I said. "I will."

Neither of us moved.

"So you want to meet up again tomorrow?" Deanny said first. I had forced her to, by nature of my diffident and restrained personality. I don't know how much it cost her, if it came naturally or not. It was the only concession she made to me all evening. If she hadn't, who knows when we would have seen each other again?

"Where?" I said.

"Here. Where else, fuckwad?"

I went home happy.

When my grandmother saw me she had a fit. "My heavens! Look at you! Your clothes are ruined! Where have you been?"

I lied to her. I told her I'd fallen down into a slough hole by the river. She complained to my mother I was going through clothes like a common labourer and I'd ruined the shirt she had bought me for Christmas. My mother forgave me, and said it was an accident. What could she do? She told me if I was going out at night maybe I should wear older clothes so it wouldn't matter if I got dirty. I agreed. I figured if I was going out again with Deanny I'd better wear coveralls and a hardhat. I wanted to tell my mother about the girl I had met, but something stopped me. I didn't know anything about her or her family or where she lived or what her father did. My mother wouldn't have cared about any of this, of course. She would just be happy I'd made a new friend.

■ ■ ■

MY GRANDMOTHER COULD never be accused of being an aesthete; her tastes ran from the banal to the outright clichéd or hideous. But in the kitchen she came closest to operating with some kind of grace. She believed in slicing carrots because it added not only to the function of the food but its presentation. The way a food *lay* in a dish was just as important as how it tasted. The smell of sliced meat determined the quality of its taste. The right seasoning to a soup, and whether it was folded or stirred, could make the difference between a triumph and a disaster. The rules were both subtle and complex, and my mother and Jeanette failed miserably at mastering them. They were content to let my grandmother make most of the food, and simply eat what was allotted to them — and not without effusive praise. To my grandmother compliments could be as delicious as a delicately spiced slice of ham.

In some ways, though, she was a typical old-fashioned cook. She had a horror of exotic spices and any dish that smacked of ethnicity. I don't think my grandmother was as racist in her culinary habits as she was in real life. She just never learned to cook outside a certain framework, and many of the spices and exotic recipes common later on were not available when she learned to cook as a girl. She was simply out of her element when it came to them and so, as many people do when confronted by the strange or unfamiliar, she denigrated. Curry was not allowed in the house. It stank, and excreted through one's pores. Chinese food was all right from a restaurant, but it had no place in a woman's kitchen. And Thai? Whoever heard of cooking with coconut milk?

As for me, I thrive on making these dishes. They have become my specialty. Whether this is natural for a man who lives in a multicultural city, or I am simply rebelling against my grandmother's narrow habits in the kitchen, I do not know. Deanny, for one, appreciates my cooking. When she comes to Toronto I often have her over for Indian or Thai. Unlike Cameron, we have stayed in touch over the years. She is a lawyer. The fact a girl from her background would end up being a lawyer, and a good one too, is either a testament to inherent equality within the system or a paean to Deanny's tenacity. I tend to think the latter. In high school she worked hard and earned scholarships. She attended Dalhousie and earned more. My grandmother even gave her some money for tuition when she was accepted into law school. Deanny McLeod was my grandmother's favourite example of what a poor person can do when they "pull themselves up by the bootstraps."

Deanny likes my grandmother, now that she is an adult. She's never understood my resentment towards her.

"You didn't have to live with her," I say.

"Your grandmother's old," Deanny says. "You should make allowances."

It is always amazing to me how Deanny has completely reinvented herself. Out of that foul-mouthed little waif I met all those years ago at the mill, she has become a smart, educated, sophisticated woman. I sometimes tell Deanny this. She shrugs.

"We're all two people," she said to me once. "The people we are, and the people we want to be. It's a matter of will and perseverance to turn one into the other."

"Very few people can do it," I said. "You should be proud of yourself."

Deanny handles most of the pro bono work for her firm, which frees up the other lawyers for billable hours. She loves it, and would not, she says, have it any other way. The majority of her clients are the working poor. It's no coincidence that Deanny handles cases that suit her own background. She hunted around, she told me, for a firm with a pro bono policy that pleased her.

Occasionally, Deanny will get a case that, in accordance with the policy of her firm, helps someone living with HIV. I told her once it was strange we should both end up doing the same work.

"Not strange," Deanny told me. "Destined."

"I don't believe in destiny," I said.

"You wouldn't," she said. "Mr. Mathematics. Mr. Logical."

"I just mean it's strange how our past affects our future."

"Only if we let it," Deanny said. "My past has affected my work, but it doesn't cripple my life. I don't allow it. When the day is done I go home to my apartment and cook dinner and watch TV."

I have been home less than a week when Deanny drives down from Halifax to see me. The first thing she does is go and pay her respects to my grandmother. She is in there a half hour or more. I consider going and asking what is taking her so long. My grandmother is comatose. It's not like they can have a conversation. I am surprised to see when Deanny comes downstairs that she has been crying. She dabs the corners of her eyes with a Kleenex and takes a seat beside me on the sofa. When we were kids this is the only room we were allowed in besides my bedroom. We can sit anywhere we want in the house now, with my grandmother incapacitated. Old habits die hard.

"So," Deanny says. "Tell me about your life."

I start to tell her all about the outreach centre, and she stops me. "I said your life, not your work."

"My work is my life," I say.

"Sad," said Deanny. "Still no boyfriend?"

"I don't have time."

"When are you gonna get out there and start meeting some people? Your mother is worried. She thinks you're alone too much."

"Mothers worry," I said. "I'm fine."

"Your grandmother is going to die," Deanny said. "Soon, you know. You should be prepared."

"I am," I said. "I'm home for the funeral, aren't I?"

"Not just about that," Deanny said. "About other things."

"What other things?"

But she enjoys being cryptic. It's possible she knows something I don't; she came down to visit my grandmother a lot. And my mother said that unlike me and her and even Aunt Jeanette, my grandmother always recognized Deanny.

"I must be stored in some accessible neuron in an active part of her brain," Deanny said of it. "She still calls me her little urchin, sometimes. Her little waif."

I offer to take her out to dinner, but Mom comes into the room just as I am asking and insists we have dinner at the house. She cooks, and the four of us crowd around the table in the kitchen and have roast chicken and corn on the cob. Deanny, by her very presence, elevates the mood somehow and we are all laughing and talking and entirely forgetting there is an old woman in a coma upstairs. Deanny quit smoking years ago, but my Aunt Jeanette has not. The three of us go outside to the stoop and Aunt Jeanette lights up.

Deanny says she has to go. "I'll be back down in a couple of days," she says. "I want to see as much of Mrs. McNeil as I can before she goes."

I feel this is directed at me — a criticism, a wake-up call.

It doesn't work.

Deanny can afford to be magnanimous towards my grand-mother. She has been here for it all, but she is not related. She has made forgiveness an art, and I suppose if she can forgive her own father — a drunk, a reprobate, and a man who kept their entire family insolvent throughout Deanny's childhood — before he died, she can forgive anyone.

■ ■ ■

EVERY TIME I MEET her, Deanny has a new boyfriend. I have met some of them. Without exception they are quiet, intense, intel-lectual, and often bespectacled. Her latest is a writer. He has won several awards, and the Internet is lousy with his name. Deanny often dates writers and artists. She is attracted, she says, to the artistic temperament, possibly because she has no artistic ambi-tions of her own. She likes inspiring people, but she isn't inspired by them for very long. She never tells me what happens. The next time I see her, the guy I met last time is nowhere to be found. This time she'll be dating a painter, or a musician.

I have no right to criticize. As much as Deanny seems engaged with a lifelong experiment in serial relationships, I barely have any at all. I am not, despite Deanny's grumbling, an out-and-out virgin. When I first moved to Toronto I had a few encounters, most of them fumbling, awkward affairs that ended badly for me, for him, or for both of us. I was always afraid of sex. Not just because of AIDS, but because of the massive intimacy required. I just do not feel comfortable opening myself up to strangers, and my job keeps me too busy to date and get to know anyone before we jump in the sack together. Faced with this dilemma, I content myself with books, drinks with my colleagues, and my job. I cook, watch television, and occasionally go to a movie or play. It is not a bad life, even if it is not an easy one.

Deanny tells me she wants me to meet her latest, Richard, and to cook curry for them. She also tells me she is inviting another "friend" along for me to meet.

"This isn't you playing matchmaker again," I say. "That never turns out good."

"But this guy is different," says Deanny. "He's the perfect match."

"In what way?"

"He's Russian, for one," she says, as if that makes him instantly desirable.

"So?" I say. "There's a whole country full of those."

"He's a schoolteacher."

"I know nothing of teaching. I know nothing of schoolteachers."

"He teaches high school *math*," says Deanny. This is her pièce de résistance. "Surely that will give you something to talk about."

"You expect us to have dinner with you, and talk about non-linear equations?"

"I don't know what that is," says Deanny. "But I bet Pavel does. That's why he's the perfect date for you."

"Pavel?"

"Russian for Paul."

"Okay," I say. "But I'm not sure I want to meet anyone."

Every time I come home Deanny invites me to Halifax to have dinner and tries to set me up. I rank them by profession. There have been doctors, lawyers, an engineer, an actor, a pharmacist, and an occupational therapist. We rarely made it to the next date.

I am not a traditionally good-looking man. I'm on the thin side, and my nose is too big. Calling it aquiline would be stretching it. Ski-slopish would be more accurate. I inherited it from my grand-mother. And I have skin problems. Not acne, or eczema. Just a slight peeling around my nose and above my eyes. I apply a cream each night before bed, not unaware that my grandmother applies a similar mask as part of her nightly ritual.

This wouldn't be so bad if the men Deanny picked for me to live the rest of my life with were not audaciously, universally handsome. I didn't know where she found them. It was as if she had an Abercrombie and Fitch for professionals and intellectuals. I was usually so stricken by the looks of these men that I had no idea what to say. Dinner, whether out or in Deanny's apartment, was awkward, and I was always quite surprised when they expressed interest and wanted to see me again.

Each man gave his number, but I never called. Deanny always complains about this. She says I will die old and alone and my body will be mauled by cats for a week before anyone finds me.
I remind Deanny I don't have any cats. That I hate them, in fact.

"You know what I mean," she says.

In the end, I agree to another dinner, as Deanny can be tenacious and will not give in until I concede. It is this, I imagine, that makes her such a good lawyer.

"Wear something nice."

"I don't have anything nice," I say. "Jeans and short-sleeves all the way. Unless you count the suit I brought for Grandnan's funeral."

"Just don't sabotage it, is all I mean."

"Do I ever?" I say.

"Very funny," says Deanny. "Just try this time. Pavel is a good friend of Richard's. He's the most amazing person, Jake. I really think you'll hit it off. So does Richard."

"Richard has never met me."

"He knows what I told him. So we'll see you Saturday?"

"Yes," I say, sighing.

My mother is in the kitchen with me, drinking a coffee at the table, and has heard the entire conversation.

"So you're going to Deanny's?" she says, when I hang up.

"Yes. Saturday. For a meal."

She smiles. "And she's fixing you up?"

"Again. She just won't quit."

"She's just concerned about you. We all are. We think you spend too much time alone up there in Toronto."

"I'm not alone. I have my co-workers, and clients. Some days it seems like all there is is people."

"Deanny is concerned about your *personal* life. You're not getting any younger, Jacob. You should start think about settling down."

I've had this conversation, or one similar to it, a hundred times in my life. It is the ongoing theme of the continuing saga of the Life of Jake McNeil, as told by his family and friends. I hate it. I tell my mother I am tired, and she gives up, sighing as loudly as I had with Deanny on the phone. But she lets it go, and I go up to my room.

## 2

ONE LITTLE GARDEN sculpture was a source of tension every year in our home. It was of a little black boy sitting on a wall, fishing. My grandmother always placed it dead-centre on the front lawn. She placed it herself, because my mother forbid me to do it. My mother did not want anyone to see me putting it there. Both she and Aunt Jeanette thought the sculpture thoughtlessly racist; they thought my grandmother should smash it and have it done with.

She refused.

"What's racist about it? It's just a little boy."

"A little black boy," said Aunt Jeanette.

"A little black boy then," said my grandmother. "What harm is there in that? Little black boys exist, don't they?"

"Surely they do," said my mother. "And little black boy statues exist only on the lawns of white people. Black people don't have them."

"I fail to see," said my grandmother, "how you two can find this offensive. No one has ever said a word to me about it."

"Perhaps," said my mother, "if there were some black people in town, you'd hear more about it."

"And perhaps you're forgetting," said my grandmother, "about Henry Hennsey? He lives in town, and last time I checked he is as black as the ace of spades."

It was true. Henry Hennsey *was* black, and he did live in town, in a small, butter-yellow house on Carfax Street in Mechanicsville. The Hennseys had moved there in the fifties from Halifax. At the time, according to my grandmother, it had caused quite a stir. There were no blacks — or any other person of colour, for that matter — in Advocate, besides the Natives, who had been neatly deposited on the reserve a hundred years before. Henry's parents had died years ago and left him the house. No one knew how he supported himself because he didn't have a job.

"Welfare," said some.

"Life insurance," said others.

One of the ways Henry made a living, albeit a small one, was to pick up items from the liquor store for those in town who did not want to be seen buying it. Henry would get it for them, deliver it to their house, and be paid a small stipend for the service. He would go walking up and down Main Street and across the bridges in all kinds of seasons and weather, a forty-year-old, slightly plump man with a wicker basket on his arm.

The basket was to carry food and bottles in. He'd been carrying it since he was a boy, before he was old enough to go to the liquor store. It was said young Henry started doing this when his mother would send him to the grocery store and found the cashiers would not pack his groceries for him. They didn't want to waste a bag on a "nigger."

I was fascinated with Henry when I was boy, and not just because he was the only black face in our town. There was something beautiful about him, with his cocoa-coloured skin and opalescent teeth. The first time I saw a statue of Buddha I was reminded forcibly of Henry. He rarely ever spoke, and when it did it was a quick word of greeting or something practical related to his errand. He always wore green work pants with suspenders and a plaid shirt, and in winter an over-stuffed blue jacket and black and yellow rubber boots. Whenever I walked by he simply turned his pale eyes in my direction, nodded once slowly, and strode on. Occasionally he walked up Tenerife Street, and my grandmother always cooed and delighted in this, for this meant he was delivering booze to one of her friends or neighbours. I never saw him once look at our little black boy on the lawn.

Years before my uncle left home, he had struck up a friendship with Henry. My mother or Aunt Jeanette had not known about it. Neither did my grandmother.

To her frustration, she was also unable to get any information out of David about Toronto, or why he had decided to come home after all these years, or what he did when he went to town or why he was missing the last two weeks of school. Surely he had to oversee final exams. Mark papers. Draw up report cards. She knew he was going for coffee at the diner, because mother or Jeanette served him. But she didn't know what else he was up to.

I think my grandmother was afraid he had a lover. She never said as much — I can't imagine the circumstances necessary to force those words from her lips — but she asked him an undue amount of questions about where he was and who he was with, and she said to my mother and Jeanette he was "up to no good."

"What on earth could he get up to in this town," asked my mother, "that he couldn't get up to in Toronto?" Both Jeanette and my mother knew Uncle David had a lover there, though he refused to talk about him. Nor did he talk about Toronto or his job.

"I don't know," said my grandmother. "But I don't like having anyone living under my roof who refuses to give a complete account of himself."

"Welcome to Gulag Tenerife," said Jeanette. "I hope you find your stay comfortable."

"I'm not running a prison, but neither is this a southern resort. I expect you all to carry your weight, and be responsible. And that includes letting me know what you're up to."

Jeanette had no response for this; later she told my mother, within my earshot, she was surprised my grandmother knew what "Gulag" meant.

David, for his part, ignored my grandmother. When Aunt Jeanette and my mother were at work, he'd stay in the TV room or his bedroom, reading and avoiding my grandmother until they came home. Then we'd have dinner and they'd sit and drink tea and talk. Otherwise he'd wander the streets.

It was Jeanette who saw him with Henry Hennsey when she drove down Carfax Street. She was going to get her hair done at Ilene's Salon on Joseph Street — she always cut down Carfax to get there — and spotted him on the steps of Henry's yellow house. Later that night, at dinner, she asked David about it.

"I used to visit him occasionally," my uncle said, a forkful of mashed potatoes hovering near his mouth. "When I was younger. I quite like him."

"What's he like?" asked my mother. "I mean, I've said hello to him on the street, but I've never really talked to him."

"He's an interesting and intelligent man," said my uncle. "Do you know he's memorized, for every year since 1600, a single important event that changed the world?"

"What nonsense," said my grandmother. "No one can know that many things."

"He does," said my uncle. "I quizzed him."

"What did he know?" asked Aunt Jeanette.

"I said '1692,'" said David. "He told me, quick as a flash, 'Salem witch trials began. Fourteen women and five men hanged in that year. It was also a leap year.'"

"That's amazing," said my mother.

"That's nothing. He can do it for any year. You should try it with him next time you see him."

My mother laughed. "I can just see myself. Running into him, saying 'Hi Henry. What happened in 1717?'"

"He reads a lot," said Uncle David. "We have that in common."

"I don't see what else you have in common," said my grandmother, moodily silent for most of this exchange. Everyone looked at her. "Well, don't stare at me," she said. "I'm not referring to his *colour*. Henry Hennsey delivers booze. If people see you at his house they'll think you're buying liquor."

"So what if they do?" said my uncle. "I care not what people think."

"You don't live here," she said. "You just come and muddy the waters."

There was much clicking of cutlery against plates and shifting in seats, but very little other sound. After dinner, David went up to his room. Grandnan went to the sink to rinse dishes, my mother cleared the table, and I took clean dishes out of the dishwasher and put them on the counter for Jeanette to put away.

My mother asked Grandnan why she had to be so difficult.

My grandmother shook her head. "I'm not being difficult. I'm speaking the truth. I don't care if you like it."

"You don't have to be so cruel. He's having a hard enough time as it is."

"What hard time? Seems to me he has it easy! Home on vacation. Free room and board. Not a worry in the world!"

"Something's wrong," my mother said. She stopped moving dishes and stood in the centre of the floor. "Don't you know that by now? He would never have come home otherwise."

"What then?" my grandmother asked. "I don't hear him saying anything."

"He will."

"Well, until then — and after, for that matter — I'll say what I want in my own house. If you don't like it, you can look for alternate arrangements. How many times have I told you girls that?"

"You're impossible," my mother said.

"I know," my grandmother said. "You've told me countless times." And with that she marched out of the room, the last of the dishes rinsed and set in the sink for me to place in the washer.

A few minutes later my uncle came into the kitchen to steep a cup of tea. My mother and I were finishing the dishes. She apologized for my grandmother's comments.

"No need," said my uncle cheerfully. "You didn't make them."

"I'm curious," said my mother. "What else do you and Henry talk about? Does he ever say what it's like for him to live in Advocate?"

My uncle was rummaging around in the cupboard above the dishwasher for the Tetley. My mother edged him out and found it for him. "Not really," said Uncle David. "We just talk about books, mainly. And history. He's really quite a remarkable man. I went to school with him, you know. He was a grade or two ahead of me."

"Did he say what was the most important, world-shaking event of 1984?" my mother said, smiling. "Was it that David McNeil moved back to the town of his birth?"

He didn't look at her. Instead he busied himself with the kettle and cup and saucer in front of him. "I didn't ask," he said.

My mother's smile melted. I knew the look she gave my uncle. She has this talent, inherited from God-knows-where, of always being able to tell when a person is lying. Many times if I had told a fib I would see my mother grow still and serious all of a sudden and just stare at me gently until I told the truth. It works on Aunt

Jeanette too, who has been known to be less than truthful about certain minor things if the need suits her.

I could see my mother knew David was lying about something.

She said only that she was going to watch TV, and told David to meet her there when his tea was made. He said he would.

At seven o'clock my grandmother came down to watch *Dallas*, her favourite show and the only one she watched regularly. Jeanette and my mother hated it, but stayed to watch it with her if only to be near David, who had never seen it.

"What do you mean, never seen *Dallas*?" said my grandmother. "It's the best show on television."

"I don't watch TV as a rule," said my uncle.

"Neither do I," said Aunt Jeanette. "It's an idiot box, as far as I'm concerned."

"You only say that because you've never lived in a time without it," said my grandmother. "If you had, you'd appreciate it more." This had a certain weird logic no one bothered my grandmother over.

It was an unusually peaceful evening, given my grandmother's comments at dinner. No one mentioned Henry Hennsey the rest of the night. At bedtime my uncle put his head through the doorway to wish me goodnight. I had not warmed up to him since he had come home, which he didn't seem bothered by. But I was stricken with curiosity about Henry Hennsey. I wanted to ask my uncle questions, trapped between my dislike for him and my fascination with Henry.

My uncle saw this, and stepped into my room. "What is it Jacob?"

I cleared my throat and asked him, softly, why he didn't ask Henry Hennsey what the most important event of *this* year was going to be.

"He's not a prognosticator, Jacob," David said. "I can't ask him what hasn't happened yet."

"A prognosti-what?"

"A fortune teller. A seer of the future."

"Oh," I said.

"It's likely the most important thing of this year hasn't happened yet. It's only June after all."

And suddenly my resentment towards him was forgotten, at least for the moment. "So of all the things that happen in a year, how do you tell what's most important?" I said.

"That's a good question," said my uncle. "I suppose it depends on your perspective."

I didn't understand this very well, mostly because I didn't understand the concept of perspective. Very few eleven-year-olds do, because when it comes right down to it we don't have any. At that age, everything is filtered through the self.

As usual when I didn't understand something, I reverted to numbers. "Henry has memorized 482 facts about the world," I said. "And if he memorized every leap year too, and you count that as a fact, then he's memorized 602. That's a lot of information."

My uncle smiled. "You like numbers, don't you," he said.

"I guess," I said. "The square root of pi is 1.77245385091 and so on."

My uncle's smile broadened. "You got me there. I can count to a hundred and that's pretty much it."

"Will you take me to meet Henry sometime?"

His smile disappeared. Not rapidly, but quizzically. "What for?" he said.

I shrugged. "I just want to."

I couldn't tell my uncle that I was interested in Henry because he was black, and because he seemed to me to be the most enigmatic, serene person I had ever seen. I couldn't even explain these things to myself. I just wanted to meet him.

"I'll ask him," said my uncle. "And we'll see what he says. How about that?"

"Okay."

As soon as my uncle left my room, I convinced myself I didn't like him again. But I was excited about possibly meeting Henry.

■ ■ ■

MY UNCLE'S FULL name was David Owen Angus William McNeil. It was a mouthful. He was the only member of our family besides my great grandfather to have more than one middle name. This is because, said my mother, he was the first born, and male, and my grandfather wanted to fulfill the Scottish custom of naming his son after every ancestor he could think of. The Owen in my uncle's name was my great grandfather's. The Angus was for a famous great uncle, and the William for William Wallace, the great Scotsman, from whom my grandfather claimed our family was directly descended. I didn't know until later this is a common claim among the Scots, and we were most likely no more related to the great William Wallace than a flower is to a tree.

It was my uncle's first name that was the most unusual choice. My grandmother, after having named half of Scotland in the middle, wanted it to be something from the Bible. John and Paul were "too Anglo" according to my grandfather, and Matthew and Mark "too soft." No one wanted a baby named Ezekiel or Zebedee. So they settled on David.

David was then, and still is, a common name for boys. There is one in my office in Toronto, who is a decade younger than my uncle would have been today, had he lived.

The biblical David was a hero — a giant-killer, the King of Judea. But my grandmother would remind her oldest son, when she was angry with him, that David was also the murderer of Bathsheba, and a census taker. According to her, the name had its baggage.

My mother told me once that Uncle David hated his excess of names, and when he got older had them shortened on his birth certificate to David Owen McNeil. My grandmother was incensed. "You don't go changing your name just because you feel like it," she said to him. "It's not yours to change. We put a lot of thought in that!"

My grandfather calmed her down. "That name is a handful," he said. "The boy is only trying to make his life more manageable. Besides, he still has them. Just not officially."

Where my uncle was concerned, said my mother, my grandfather was always permissive. Always understanding. And he kept my grandmother in line — until, of course, he died, and David was banished from the house.

Years later, when I asked my mother why Grandnan had let him come home in 1984 after all that time she had no answer. "Maybe he caught her in a weak moment. It had been years since they quarreled. Perhaps she figured it was time."

Whatever the reason, my grandmother did not want to keep my uncle for long.

In the latter part of the first week, he came down with a cold. He slept a lot. He went to bed early, got up late, and looked sweaty and flushed when he came downstairs for breakfast. My mother was convinced he had a fever, and she insisted he go see Dr. Willis, our family doctor who we most often called Dr. Fred.

"It's not serious," my uncle said. "I'll be fine."

Everyone except my grandmother worried about him.

"I don't see why the two of you are making such a fuss," she said. "You don't get half as concerned when I come down with a head cold."

"Do you have a head cold?" asked Aunt Jeanette.

"Of course I don't," said my grandmother sharply. "You know as well as I do I'm as fit as a fiddle."

"Well if you do," said Jeanette, "we'll take care to worry after you, too."

My grandmother harrumphed.

I was in school most days. My uncle, because he was a teacher, was interested in my school work. He asked what I was learning and from whom, and I told him enough to get him off my back. He often asked me about math, and what I liked about it. To that I shrugged. I didn't know. The neatness of it. The resolution of equation into answer. The fact it was impossible to equivocate with numbers. I couldn't put any of this into words, nor did I want to. I just liked it.

He was making an attempt to get to know me. Twice he came into my room while I was reading and sat on the edge of my bed and talked to me. I was hostile to his advances. I answered him in monosyllables and wouldn't look him in the eye.

This didn't seem to bother him. He talked anyway, and told me stories about my mother and him when they were children.

One Saturday, after my mother and Jeanette had just gone to work, he caught me playing with my Easy-Bake Oven. I wasn't baking any cakes — I had run out of mixes — but I was cleaning the burnt cake mix off a pan with a toothpick and running the oven to clean it. My bed was unmade, but my uncle — still wearing his housecoat — sat on it anyway and watched me on the floor. I was mildly embarrassed he caught me playing with girls' toys, but he told me not to worry about it, that he himself had a few dolls when he was a kid. "They were paper and you put cut-out clothes on them. I used to play with them all the time."

I knew, though didn't say, this was likely the same doll set that sat in my closet. I said, derisively, "I thought those belonged to my mother."

My uncle looked thoughtful. "They probably did. But I think I played with them when I was around your age."

"Grandnan says that I shouldn't play with girls' toys or I'll turn out like you."

It was bold, but I didn't like my uncle, and I wanted him to know it. I watched him carefully for reaction to my pronouncement.

He only smiled, slightly, and said, "Turn out like me how?"

"Like a girl or something," I said. "A homosexual."

My uncle looked surprised. "You know that word?" he said.

I shrugged. "Mom told me before you came. She never said what it meant though. But Grandnan says if I play with girls' toys I'll turn out like you. And now you're here and Mom and Jeanette hardly talk to me anymore and Grandnan is in a bad mood. We're all wondering when you're going to *leave*." This was the most I'd said to my uncle since he'd arrived.

I had lied to him. Only my grandmother and I were wondering when he was going to leave. My mother and Aunt Jeanette were hoping he would stay forever. But I wanted to be mean to him. I wanted him to know there was substantial resistance to his presence, and it didn't just come from my grandmother. I had never considered myself a mean boy. I didn't pick fights. I never taunted or provoked. But I took a small pleasure in lashing out at my uncle.

He only smiled at me, and didn't seem at all offended. His smile was vaguely sad.

Eventually I gave him my very limited definition of the word *homosexual*, culminating in my belief that he was so offensive to grandmother because he wouldn't get married.

My uncle laughed, though I honestly did not see what was so funny. When he saw I was offended he stopped. But he couldn't remove the smile from his face. "Me not getting married," he said, "is the least of your grandmother's worries."

"Then what *are* her worries?"

"I'll tell you," my uncle said. "I know your mother wouldn't mind, because we've already discussed it, but I wouldn't mention this to your grandmother if I were you. Sparks might fly."

Sparks always flew when it came to my grandmother, but I promised my uncle I wouldn't.

He launched into an explanation. It wasn't harsh, like my grandmother's elucidation of things would often be, and it wasn't vague, like my mother's. My uncle had his own style. Measured, calm, and assured. He was revealing great secrets, but he did so with the confidence of a seasoned teacher. I listened to him in fascination as he spoke the truth.

···

WHEN MY MOTHER came home on a ten o'clock break to get her watch, she found my uncle and me in my bedroom talking.

"You two seem to be getting along," she said from the doorway.

"Uncle David likes boys," I pronounced. "Grandnan thinks it's because he played with dolls when he was my age."

My mother raised her eyebrows and looked at her brother. He nodded, and my mother looked back at me. I was sitting beside Uncle David on my bed by this time, the Easy-Bake Oven forgotten. "What do you think of that?" she said.

I shrugged. "It's no big deal. I don't see what the big secret was." I knew what a fag was. I'd heard the word on school grounds frequently and had often been called one myself. I had no idea anyone could actually *be* one, however. I really believed it was a figure of speech. Just an insult.

"It's a big deal to some people," said my uncle. "To your grandmother it's a big deal."

"Why?"

"Because it's contrary to what she believes is written in the Bible."

"What's written in the Bible?" I asked.

"A bunch of trash," said my mother.

My grandmother would've been horrified. But I was feeling okay. My sexual education was becoming complete. I was being taught eternal truths, forbidden fruit of the grown-up world. I finally knew what was wrong with my Uncle David, and it wasn't so bad. Other kids might have been turned off or been sickened by that truth, but I was not. I didn't care who my uncle had sex with, and just knowing the truth about him made me warm up to him more.

It still did not entirely explain to my satisfaction why my grand-mother had not wanted to see him for fifteen years. As abhorrent as his homosexuality must have been to her, it still seemed, some-how, out of proportion to her response. But I had a young and logical mind.

After my mother left, Uncle David asked if I wanted to join him for lunch and then a game of *Snakes and Ladders*. *Snakes and Ladders*, my mother must have told him, was my favourite game. I liked it for its unpredictability. You never knew who was going to win.

# 3

UNCLE DAVID HAD been home over a week without making any noises about leaving. My grandmother said a day was an imposi-tion, a week was taking advantage, and two weeks were a species of outrage. She suggested to my mother, twice, that she better ask my uncle what he was up to. Was he broke? Was he in some kind of trouble? Did he plan on staying forever? But my mother refused. So my grandmother did it herself. She asked him for a receipt from his bank account, to make sure he wasn't "pounding on the poor-house door."

He showed it to her, over Jeanette's and my mother's protests. That settled her mind on that subject. "Money's not the problem," she confided in me, simply because there was no one *other* than me to talk to. "So it must be something else. But I'll be darned if I can find out. It's my house. You'd think the three of them were my mortal enemies, they're so close-lipped around me."

I ignored my grandmother, though I too was still unhappy my uncle was staying so long. But if there were alignments to be made, I chose with those against my grandmother, out of habit.

On Saturday, July 7, my uncle told us he was staying in Advocate "for good." I remember the day specifically because my grandmother had allowed us to eat brunch in the sunroom overlooking the backyard. She didn't do this often. It was carpeted in white, and if we spilled something she would have "the devil and witch of a time getting it up." But that morning she relented. We set ourselves up at the white wicker table, overlooking the beds of peonies and petunias in the backyard.

For days, because of his cold, my uncle had worn nothing but pyjamas and a robe. This morning, however, he had dressed. Though he still looked pale, he was smiling. He had filled his plate up to heaping with eggs, bacon, bread, and a healthy dollop of my grandmother's crabapple jelly. He made sure everyone had begun eating when, with a clearing of his throat, he announced he had something to say.

Everyone looked at him. You could tell, whatever it was, it was important. At that moment my uncle reminded me of my grandfather, even though I had never met him. Perhaps it was because he was now the only male member of the family. Perhaps it was because, despite appearing weak and tired, he sat there holding the attention of everyone at the table. Whatever the reason, I saw my uncle differently for the first time that day — as he might have been, perhaps, in front of a classroom.

He said, "I have decided I'd like to move from Toronto and live here in Advocate. If it's okay with you."

In all the arguments, discussions, cajoling, tantrums, and speeches that followed, my uncle did not repeat his request. I suppose, in my business, we would call it a very healthy approach to the situation. Perhaps it was because he knew it wasn't necessary. For the next while, his request would be stated and restated over and over for him.

Like with most major announcements, and one so unexpected, the initial reaction seemed mild. My mother and Aunt Jeanette professed to be delighted. My grandmother said she was surprised and wondered about his job.

"I've quit it," said David.

"Quit!" parroted my grandmother.

"Retired, then," he said. "Money is not a problem, as you know, and I just didn't feel like working anymore."

"No one *feels* like it," said my grandmother. "It's a duty, and a responsibility!"

"Mother," said my mother, though I could see she was concerned too. "Are you sure this is what you want, David?"

"Absolutely," he said. "I want to start a new life. Here. With you."

"But where will you stay?" asked my grandmother nervously.

"Why here of course!" said Jeannette. "In his old room."

My grandmother opened her mouth to counter this, when my uncle said, "No. I'd like to get an apartment in town. Like I said, money is not an issue. And I might pick up some substitution work if I get bored."

To this my grandmother could say nothing, though it was obvious she was disturbed. "But why?" she said. "After all this time? There's nothing here in Advocate for you, is there David?"

"My family is here," David said. "Isn't that enough?"

"It wasn't enough for the last fifteen years," said my grandmother. "I don't see why it should be now."

My mother could see what was coming: an argument. They were as obvious, with my grandmother, as a fire truck racing towards a brick wall. She suggested we just all enjoy brunch and talk the whole thing over later. My uncle had lost that magical authoritative stature he had drawn in my mind a few minutes ago. He looked tired. He hadn't touched a thing on his plate.

Once brunch was finished, my mother, Uncle David, and I stayed at the white wicker table. We could hear my grandmother talking to Jeanette in the kitchen. My mother asked him if everything was really all right — if he hadn't, as my grandmother suggested, got himself in some kind of trouble in Ontario.

He told her he was fine.

"I just need to rest," he said. "And I'd rather do it here than anywhere."

"Even with her around?" my mother asked.

"Yes," said my uncle. "Even with her. I'd put up with her as long as I can be around the two of you. And Jacob."

"Okay," said my mother. "Don't worry. We'll work on her. I'm sure you'll be able to stay in the house if you want."

"I don't," David said. "I'm serious about the apartment. I don't think I could live with her."

"We'll find something," soothed my mother. "I'm just glad you're coming home."

"We'll have to make arrangements for my things," said my uncle. "They're all in storage in Toronto."

"In storage?"

"Yes."

"Then you knew you were moving home all the time?" My mother left it at that, and David went back upstairs to his room. She went out to the kitchen to take some of the heat off Jeanette. The two of them argued quietly with my grandmother about my uncle's announcement.

"He's in trouble," my grandmother said. "It's as plain as the nose on your face."

"It's as plain as nothing," said my mother. "David's finally moving home after all these years. I'd think you'd be glad."

"Glad? I'd be glad to get to the bottom of all this. That's what I'd be glad of."

"You're impossible, mother. I hope you know that."

"Me?" said my grandmother. "I'm not the one turning every-thing upside down here. Rump over kettle. A man just doesn't up and quit a perfectly good job, money in the bank or no, and turn around and move back to a town he's seen neither hide nor hair of for fifteen years, expecting us to all take it lying down like we were rugs under his feet. There's something wrong here, I tell you. Seriously amiss, and if you two don't have the gumption to find out what he's up to, I do."

"Don't go starting anything," my mother warned.

"Mom," said Jeanette. "If you go off half-cocked ..."

"Seriously wrong," said my grandmother again. "A world of ever-loving trouble."

■ ■ ■

THE DAY DEANNY and I are to go shopping for the ingredients for our Indian meal, she meets me in her lobby. Richard is writing, she says. He can't be disturbed.

"So he's living with you?" I ask.

"Yes," says Deanny. "For about a month now. The apartment's big. There's plenty of room. I gave him one of the spare bedrooms for a den."

This surprises me. Of all Deanny's amours, she never let one live with her before. Perhaps this is serious then. I want to ask her, but I know I won't get a straight answer. As invasive as she can be while infiltrating my life, she is often very private about her own. I never complain about it. It is just one of those Deannyesque inconsistencies I have to accept about her.

I drive. Jeanette loaned me her car.

We go to an Asian grocery on Quinpool Road. It is small compared to some of the shops in Toronto I frequent, and it is more expensive. It takes a half hour to buy the ingredients and it is only noon.

I figure Deanny and I will spend the afternoon at her apartment while I cook, but she wants to give Richard a few more hours.

"He finds it almost impossible to write when there is anyone in the apartment. It took him a month to get used to me."

So we decide to go to Citadel Hill. It is a beautiful summer day. Hot, but not too hot. It will be cooler by the water. For all the times I come to Nova Scotia I rarely spend time in Halifax. Deanny usually comes to see me. If I come to see her, we stay at her place and cook or go to a nearby café for lunch.

Halifax is small compared to mammoth Toronto. The traffic and pedestrians on Spring Garden Road are quaint; most parts of the city are within walking distance of each other. I'm reminded of the days I thought Halifax was big, when my mother, Jeanette, and Grandnan referred to it as "the city," as if it were some great metropolis. My grandmother still thinks of it that way, and she rarely accompanied Jeanette and my mother on their occasional shopping trips.

"I get enough crush, fuss, and bother in downtown Advocate," she said. "I don't need the stink and noise of it all."

That my grandmother would ever consider tiny, contained, genteel Halifax as busy or crushing seemed very naïve to me. That I could have once thought of it thus seemed almost as naïve. I was a denizen of Toronto now. The big smoke. My own neighbourhood, near the gay village, has more people in it than downtown Halifax. In the crush of Dundas Square a person really is in the midst of my grandmother's "stink and noise." I think I like Toronto so much because no one notices me. I am as faceless and nameless as the concrete in the streets, the blocks of stone in the buildings.

Going to Citadel Hill is Deanny's idea. In college, she says, she'd often come up here at night before a big exam. Gazing down on the lights of the city and the boats in the harbour comforted her.

"I don't know how you stand Toronto," she says. "Whenever I go there for my work I can't wait to get out. It's not solely because it's big, though that's part of it. Everyone is so tired-looking, and cynical. And all those skyscrapers. Toronto is built to make people feel small."

"Toronto gets a bad rap," I say. "If you like plays, and art, and music, it is the best place in the country to be. Energy. All the time. Everywhere you look. Each corner of the city is another story."

"And how many plays and concerts do you go to?"

I don't answer. She knows very well I don't go to any. I go to work. I stay home. The most adventure I do is shop the ethnic groceries on Gerrard Street East.

We reach the top of Citadel Hill. Halifax's downtown lies below us. Its few tall buildings, tiny compared to Toronto, bristle in a bunch to the north against the flat blue of the harbour. Sailboats dot its surface, tacking and heeling in every direction. Toronto has a harbour too, and sailboats in the summer. But the one area where Toronto cannot compete with Halifax is its waterfront. Halifax has a magnificent harbour, and a strong clear line to the sea. Toronto has a dirty lake. I tell Deanny this, but she is no longer listening.

"I want you to try with Pavel today," she says. "Get to know him. Don't cross him off your list before he has a chance to speak."

"I will," I say.

"That's what you always say, and then you turn to stone."

"I'd just rather meet people in my own way," I say.

"Right," Deanny says. "If it wasn't for me, you wouldn't meet anyone at all. Richard is at least expecting you to be nice to Pavel."

"I'll try."

Deanny sighs. "It would be nice to be on the water today." She says we should be getting back. "We can start dinner, and Pavel will arrive in an hour. Remember. Be nice."

It is my turn to sigh. I am always nice to the men Deanny tries to hook me up with. And they are nice to me. It's just that we rarely find anything in common to talk about. My only subjects are poverty, HIV, and homelessness. What they are interested in often seems remote, academic, and pointless.

Once, Deanny told me I had been damaged by the world. "You have seen the absolute worst of life," she said. "You hold everyone and everything up to that. By that measure, nothing can compete with your sorrow."

She was right. I knew she was right, which is why I at least tried to strike up some kind of conversation with the men she introduced me to, if only for an hour. Yet we both know that in the end I will reject them, or they will reject me, or both. I only go along because I don't want to hurt Deanny's feelings. She has far more invested in these meetings than I do.

# FOUR

■

FOR WEEKS MY grandmother complained bitterly about my uncle's decision to stay in Advocate. She pestered him daily over meals, and in between, to give her his real reasons. She did not buy that he had just quit his job.

Unbeknownst to my mother and Jeanette, she had found the number for his former school from directory assistance and called Toronto to see if she could get more information. They would give her none, citing Uncle David's privacy. My mother and Jeanette wouldn't have known she called at all, if they hadn't seen the Toronto exchange number on a pad in the living room phone table in my grandmother's handwriting. Out of curiosity, Jeanette called it and the school answered. She and my mother confronted my grandmother.

"What?" she said. "I told you I would be getting to the bottom of this. And that's what I'm doing."

"It's none of your business," said my mother. "Leave it alone."

"The boy is under my roof again. So it is my business! Besides, I don't think he's telling us the truth about his position. The man I talked to there said David had resigned, but he had underlying tone. I suspect they let him go. Perhaps he acted inappropriately with a student."

"Mother!" cried Jeanette and my mother in unison.

But there was no talking to my grandmother. She was on a tear, and there were many sumptuous arguments about it between her and my mother and Jeanette. Practically every day she mentioned pointedly how crowded the house was getting.

This was untrue, of course.

The house had held five people when my grandparents were raising their family. We were five now. But it was not in my grandmother's nature to let an issue go. She waited and hoped my uncle would get off his duff and do what he had promised by getting an apartment in town. She even checked the *Advocate Gazette* for places to let, though even she had to admit there was precious little available. Advocate was not a transient town. Most people were there, like my grandmother, to stay. My uncle made a number of calls concerning apartments that first week, but nothing suitable had arisen. He had begun talking about looking for a place in Trenton, to which my grandmother wholeheartedly pledged agreement. This would get him out of the house and thirty miles out of Advocate. Both my mother and Jeanette cautioned him against this. "Just be patient," they said. "Something will come up."

Something did.

That Friday, my uncle was not feeling well again. He begged off supper and stayed in his room. We were sitting down to dinner without him when my grandmother announced triumphantly she had found him a place to let.

When the Catholics first came to Advocate in the 1700s, the Protestants, mostly Lutherans, had already begun settling one side of the river. The Catholics settled down on the other. The Irish and Scottish Catholics hated the Lutherans because the British, in an effort to annoy the French by peopling the province with subjects loyal to the crown, had granted them land, even though they were German and spiritually if not genetically related to that spawn of the devil, Luther himself. The town was named back then, when a Lutheran minister preaching against the Catholics peopling the other side of the river told his congregation they must be advocates for the faith. The Catholics tried to name their side of the river Assumption but the Lutherans won out, and the town was incorporated as Advocate in 1811. The division on either side of the river was a ridiculous situation that persisted for more than a hundred years. By the time I was born, there was no longer any name-calling or religious schism, but the old alliances remained. If you came to town and were actively Catholic you bought, built, or rented on the east side of the river. If you were Protestant, the west.

It was telling my grandmother would find my uncle a place in a small house on the Protestant side of the river. It was a place she would never consider living herself. The bottom half of the house, she said, was vacant, as the former tenants had bought their own house in one of the subdivisions. My grandmother had called the landlord just before supper. It was available at the end of July.

"Another three weeks," she said. "But at least there's an end in sight, thank goodness."

My mother and Aunt Jeanette ignored this. "Did you see it?" asked Aunt Jeanette.

"Of course I didn't," said my grandmother. "I'm not going to be living there. David is. And you know I never go over there, except to the grocery store."

"What if he doesn't like it?" asked my mother.

"He will," said my grandmother. "He can look at it in a couple of days, when he's feeling better. I'm told it's perfectly serviceable, with two bedrooms, one of which he can turn into a den. It's supposed to be clean, with good sewage and water systems. I'm certain he'll like it just fine. I've already told him about it."

"Let's not rush things," said my mother. "He may not be in any state to move out for a while yet. He's still sick."

· My grandmother didn't seem to like this, but she remained silent. My mother and Jeanette began wondering aloud once more, as they had been doing lately, if there was something wrong with David's health.

"He's sick all the time," said Jeanette.

"I don't like how he looks," said my mother.

"Why worry?" said Grandnan. "It's just a cold. If there was something wrong, wouldn't he go to the doctor like everyone else?"

"He's already been to see him," said my mother. "Several times."

"He most certainly has not," said my grandmother pointedly. "I would have known about it if he had. Dr. Willis tells me everything, and I just saw him the other day on Main Street."

"He has, though. I found an appointment card on the table with one scheduled two days ago."

"Did you ask him about it?" asked Jeanette.

"I didn't think it was any of my business."

If it wasn't anyone's business, my mother should have thought twice before mentioning it out loud.

My grandmother was instantly stricken with curiosity at why Uncle David would be going to see Dr. Willis — who we usually called Dr. Fred — so often. She told my mother she would ask him at the first opportunity.

"Don't you dare," said my mother. "It's his business. Not yours."

"He lives under my roof. What he does and where he goes is my business. If there's something wrong with him, I want to know."

This was my grandmother's default argument — that by sheltering us, providing us with shingles over our heads, she had the right to know everything about us and dictate every facet of our lives. Usually it brought on an argument, as surely as mentioning separatism in Quebec, or First Nations land claims. This time, however, it did not. I think, for once, my mother and Jeanette wanted to know as much as my grandmother did why our uncle would be going to see Dr. Fred so often.

After dinner my grandmother went up to Uncle David's room to ask questions, but came down ten minutes later disconcerted and irritable. "He acts like I asked him how much money he had in his bank account," she said.

"You *did* ask him how much money he had in his bank account," said my mother.

"You know what I mean," said my grandmother. "How did I raise such secretive children?"

That was no mystery. If we weren't secretive with my grandmother, we were exposed to her endless criticisms for practically every action we took. We would, in a phrase she often used herself, "never hear the end of it."

My mother, watching television, asked her what she had found out. My grandmother scowled and said, "He told me some story about vitamins and immune systems and this health diet he was on in Toronto. I don't buy it for a minute, and I think I'll ask Dr. Willis about it."

"He won't tell you," said my mother. "Patient-doctor confidentiality. You should know."

"He'll tell me," my grandmother said. "Don't you know yet, my poor girl, that in this town there is no such thing as a secret?"

About this, my grandmother, as in many things concerning small-town life, would be proved correct.

■ ■ ■

ONE AFTERNOON, WHEN he started feeling better again, Uncle David took me to the diner for cheesecake and a Pepsi. It was an effort, perhaps, to get me to warm up to him. No matter what I thought of him, I couldn't refuse. Like most eleven-year-olds, I was a slave to my gut.

My mother sat us in her section and served us, then took ten minutes to sit with us. No one interfered with her taking an unscheduled break. The owner, Mr. Byrd, rarely came to the diner. My mother and Jeanette were his senior servers, and managed the place when he wasn't around.

I talked to my mother, but spoke little to my uncle, cheesecake or no cheesecake. But he talked to me when my mother went back to work. I found myself listening with interest as he talked about his childhood growing up in Advocate. He seemed stuck on this one subject, consumed by it, and I wondered why he was so set on recollection when my mother and Aunt Jeanette rarely mentioned their childhoods.

He recalled the passion with which he went fishing in the log pool, in the river just before Kobetook Lake, looking to catch yellow perch and catfish and slink. These fish my grandmother called "junk fish" because she considered them for the most part inedible. But my uncle said the goal was not to catch something to eat, but to see how many could be caught, and who caught the biggest ones. He called them "fishing derbies" and said practically every weekend there was a derby competition among the town kids. He won a few of them. I asked him what he won.

"Bragging rights," he said.

"No money?"

"Not everything is about money, Jacob. That's your grandmother coming out in you."

On another occasion, as we were coming back from the diner, he pointed to the Carlton Theatre on Main Street as we passed.

"When I was a kid," he said, "you could get in there with a piece of brass."

"A what?"

"A piece of brass. You know. The metal? It started during the war, when they were low on metals and instead of charging the nickel to get in the owner would take pieces of brass which they used for bullets. The owner, the father of Milo who runs it now, found he could still make money from brass once the war was over. So if you didn't have the twenty-five cents to get in during the fifties when I was a kid, you would scrounge a piece of brass from somewhere and pay your admission with that."

I pretended I didn't hear, and didn't respond to his story. And yet, I did think it was cool that, in those dark dim days of my uncle's childhood, an old piece of metal could get you in to the Carlton. Years later, as a teenager and trying to be smart, I carried a brass pipe to a movie with one of my friends. I explained the tradition to the bewildered ticket seller and said it was a perfectly valid way to buy a movie ticket. She disagreed. So did the owner. The price of movies had gone up, and the value of brass had gone down.

A few days later, over breakfast, my uncle asked if I wanted to go with him to visit Henry on the following Sunday. My grandmother dropped her fork and said she disapproved. When everyone stared at her, she shook her head and said it was not because he was *black*. Only that it was unseemly to make casual visits on the Sabbath, especially to those like Henry Hennsey who did not attend Mass.

My grandmother was all about Mass. She constantly pestered us to attend with her, with little result. My mother went occasionally, if only to keep the peace. Jeanette attended for Christmas and Easter. David, since he'd been home, refused to go. The only concession he made towards his mother's religion at all was a St. Jude's medallion he always wore on the inside of his shirt around his neck. He joked that since he was, in the eyes of the Catholic Church, a lost cause, he might as well advertise it.

But my grandmother wasn't buying this. "Anyone who lives under my roof," she blustered, "should be forced to atone for themselves. This is not a spiritual kindergarten, where everyone gets off scot free."

My uncle, who seemed to be practising some type of psychic detachment from my grandmother until he could move into his own apartment at the end of the month, made no answer. He remained silent but cheerful, ignoring her pointed looks and asking my mother to pass him the butter for his toast.

The next Sunday, Grandnan left for Mass with my mother, uttering a parting shot regarding "generational spiritual decline." I went to my room and read until my uncle said it was time to go.

Earlier I had called Cameron — he was always home on Sunday — to tell him I was visiting the house of the one and only Henry Hennsey.

"Big deal," Cameron said. "He's just a person like the rest of us."

"I'm gonna ask him what was the big event of 1884," I said.

"The first edition of the Oxford English Dictionary was published," said Cameron. "It was also a leap year."

I knew Cameron had been studying events for each year, ever since I told him Henry did it. He never said so, but I had seen him in the school library a time or two poring over an encyclopedia, and when I asked him what he was doing he wouldn't tell me.

That was okay. I was doing it too, though I had only made it to 1653.

Henry Hennsey had influenced us without being aware he was doing it. To this day I can remember major events for every year from 1600, though picking events from recent years has been difficult. Sometimes, as my uncle said, it can be hard to see what's important when you're so very close to it.

■ ■ ■

THERE WERE NO little black boys fishing on Henry Hennsey's lawn. Or gnomes. Or angels. The only adornment was a miniature red wooden wheelbarrow heaped with dirt. I could imagine him, in the green workpants and the old plaid shirt he always wore, on his knees spading in tulip bulbs or geranium roots. I pictured him carting off rocks in a real wheelbarrow, like my grandmother, only with a lot less distance to go to round his little yellow house.

My uncle and I walked up the flagstone path to the front stoop and knocked on the door. After a minute Henry opened it, and without a smile or even a nod of greeting asked us to come in. "Tea?" he said to my uncle. "Or something stronger?"

"Tea," said my uncle. "With two sugars."

"And for you Jacob?" said Henry. "I've got some soda pop."

I was surprised Henry knew my name. I had never spoken to him, and I thought he had never taken any notice of me. I agreed to the soda, though Henry didn't say what flavour it was. When he brought it, it was cream soda. My favourite. He told us to go into the sitting room to the left, and my uncle and I did, each claiming a chair across from a small tweed sofa with a painting of a sinking schooner above it. The painting interested me. I had seen many paintings of ships and schooners over the years — there was one of the Bluenose in our library at school and my grandmother had paintings of two others in the upstairs hallway of our house. But I had never seen one that was sinking before. The rigging had let go. The sails flapped violently in a savage wind. The men scrambled fruitlessly on deck for control. I studied it until Henry came back with our tea and soda. He set them on the coffee table and then took a seat on the sofa in front of us, below the painting.

At first no one spoke. Henry studied his pants. My uncle blew on his tea to cool it and I took a sip of my drink. Eventually I drew my eyes away from the sinking ship and looked around the little room. It was perfectly neat and somehow, despite the amount of furniture, did not seem crowded. The hallway ran from the front door only a few short yards down to the back of the house, off which must have been a kitchen, and on the other side a set of stairs climbing back up in the opposite direction. Across the hallway from us was another little room, with a table and chairs and a side-board similar to my grandmother's, only smaller.

It was strange to be in such a small house.

I decided I liked it.

I decided when I got old enough I would live in a house like this. And read books and play games and memorize events from every year since 1600.

I noticed there wasn't a single book to be seen, and yet my uncle had said Henry was a reader. Before I had a chance to check my words, I asked Henry where all his books were. "Uncle David says you have some," I said. "Do you keep them in a library? We don't have a library, but grandfather had a den and it's filled with books. I'm not allowed in there though. Do you have a den?"

My uncle looked at me and smiled. Henry did not change his expression, which could best be described as disinterested. He had a flat face and a wide nose. His lips were thin and dark. I learned eventually that the flat, expressionless face Henry presented to the world belied, as my uncle knew, a fierce passion and deep intelligence. He had learned perhaps to keep his feelings to himself.

Henry did answer me, though. "I don't have a den," he said. "Or a library. But I do have a book room upstairs. Used to be my mother's room. But I don't believe in storing your books in a place where everyone can see. Kind of like hanging your underwear in the living room, only instead of getting a peek at your drawers they get to look at your brain and what you put in it. Books should be private, Jacob. You should only show them to people you want to see, and not every Tom, Dick, and Harry that comes waltzing in your front door."

My uncle surprised me with a laugh. "I never actually considered that before, Henry, but you're absolutely right. It's the way I felt about forcing students to read *Lord of the Flies* or *Heart of Darkness*. If they want to, they'll come to those books in time and in their own way. Making them read them is kind of like forcing an infant to eat chocolate cake. You spoil the experience for later."

"Fine books, both of them," said Henry. "'O judgment! thou art fled to brutish beasts. And men have lost their reason.'"

It was hard to square what was coming out of Henry Hennsey's mouth with how I'd always perceived him — quiet and unobtrusive. No wonder my uncle said he was an intelligent, articulate man. I had not read any of the books they talked about. I looked back and forth between the two of them. Even my uncle surprised me, for I had never seen him talk with such passion as when he discussed these subjects. Soon they moved on to history, and art, and politics. Henry did not get as excited as my uncle. He kept still in his seat, and talked low. But the language and learning were sophisticated. Somehow my uncle had mined him, brought forth what must have always existed below the surface. My respect for uncle David multiplied right there. I was too young to understand much of what they were talking about, but I was fascinated, as the ideas sailed back and forth between them.

I excused myself to go to the bathroom upstairs. When I came back down, and turned into the hallway, their tone was different, the voices lower, more intense. The conversation had changed.

"Have you told them yet?" asked Henry, softly.

I stopped at the newel post.

"No," said my uncle, equally soft, but still clear to me from where I stood at the end of the hallway. "I don't know how."

"You have to tell them soon," said Henry. "All hell'll break loose if you don't."

"I know," said my uncle.

Because I could not see into the living room from where I stood, I did not know what expression my uncle wore when he talked of this mysterious thing. I could tell by the low voices and heavy emphasis it was serious. But what came next surprised me. Shocked me even. I heard something I will never, in all my life, forget. A half-sob, half-choke from my uncle.

I have since heard that strangled sound many times since, in the work I do. It is the inarticulate cry of fear, depression, and despair. Now I know, and perhaps I knew then on an emotional level, it was less for the books and knowledge that Uncle David sought out Henry Hennsey, than for someone with whom he could share his terrible secret.

I announced myself carefully with a feigned stamping of shoes on floor and a sniffle, pretending I had a cold, then went back into the room. Whatever had transpired between them during my absence was now gone, and my uncle was smiling, though his eyes looked sad.

"Ready to go?" he said.

"I guess so," I said, and we made our goodbyes.

On the way home, my uncle was silent. I did not ask any questions.

*Have you told them yet?* Henry Hennsey had asked.

*Not yet,* my uncle answered.

What was this horrible thing that made my uncle, usually so calm and happy, actually cry? What secret was he carrying? I was curious, like so many kids my age. But it was beyond me. And as we walked home from Henry's, from the house of the only black family to live in Advocate in all the long years we had been there, I wasn't entirely sure I wanted to know.

## 2

ONLY A FEW days after we went to Henry's, my uncle felt poorly again and refused to go outside, despite the weather being fine. His constant see-sawing between illness and wellness irritated my grand-mother, who said no one could be sick that often. She suspected my uncle was prevaricating, faking illness in order to avoid taking responsibility for himself. She had to recant when he came down with a violent attack of what she referred to as "summer complaint," a mysterious illness of her childhood.

Dr. Fred came to see him at the house. My grandmother's diagnosis did not sit well with either my mother or Aunt Jeanette. But Dr. Fred did not offer an opinion on it, other than to say that when my grandmother said "summer complaint," what she really meant was a bacterial infection caused by food or water contam-ination. This was more common in my grandmother's day, when food regulation was not as strict and many of the wells were dug instead of drilled and subject to floods or drying up or standing stagnant in the hot days of summer. Dr. Fred told my mother he did not think Uncle David was suffering from bad hygiene or food poisoning, but he would not say what he did think he was suffer-ing from.

My grandmother stuck to her guns.

She knew Uncle David was sick in this manner because of his increasing trips to the bathroom and their unusual duration. The stink, too, was tremendous. She claimed the upstairs hallway was unfit for habitation for hours after he went — and though this was an exaggeration, it was true once David had been in the bath-room, I wanted to wait a bit before waltzing in after him. When he was not on the commode, he was lying on his bed in his robe and pyjamas. He was hot — red-faced and sheathed in sweat — some of the time, and stricken with chills at others. He slept for most of the day, in between bathroom visits. My grandmother grew alarmed.

Dr. Fred came to the house several more times to look at my uncle, and was still vague about what might be the problem.

"A bad flu," he said one time.

"Perhaps a case of sepsis," he said another. "A poisoning of the blood."

In the end my uncle went to the hospital, for two nights. They got the diarrhea under control and gave him medications to deal with the fever. He was sent home, still weak and confined to his bed, and my mother and Jeanette made him soup and tried to get him to eat. They read to him from what books he had brought from Toronto. My grandmother, once she realized David was going to be okay — for a while, when he was in hospital, she acted like she might actually be worried about him — started complaining that not only was the poor boy homeless, he was sick too.

"He's always been sickly," she said. "But this is ridiculous."

"He's not *always* been sickly," my mother protested. "David got sick least of all of us!"

"That's not how I remember it," said my grandmother.

The next day, Dr. Fred again came over and diagnosed my uncle with a case, not of summer complaint, but of meningitis. My grandmother had heard of it, but my mother and Jeanette had to have it explained to them in the kitchen after the doctor had seen my uncle in his room.

"Does he need to go to the hospital again?" my mother asked.

"No," said Fred. "He can stay here. We've given him some antibiotics, and you'll have to keep an eye on him. He'll be very sick for a while yet, but eventually it will get better."

"Is it contagious?" asked my grandmother.

Dr. Fred looked at her, as if weighing his answer. "It could be," he said. "We don't know what kind of meningitis it is. If it's bacterial, some of those can be contagious. If it's viral it isn't. I'll have to do more tests. I've drawn blood, so we'll know in a few days. Meanwhile, just be cautious around him. Jacob is in the most danger. Kids are susceptible to it, more so than adults. I don't think you have anything to worry about. You can tend to him as you normally would. But keep Jacob out of his room."

My mother looked instantly worried. "Should we send Jacob away? To Cameron's for a few days?"

"No need to be alarmist," said Dr. Fred. "It's a tactile contagion, so just keeping him out of the room should suffice. I'll come back and check on him tomorrow."

My mother and Jeanette thanked him, and he left.

"Well, this is a fine kettle of fish," my grandmother said.

"You act like it's his fault," said Aunt Jeanette.

"Of course it isn't," said my grandmother. "How could the boy be at fault for getting sick? It's just difficult to deal with, is all I'm saying. He was supposed to move into his new apartment. What happens now?"

"We'll take care of everything," my mother said. "You don't have to lift a finger." Then she and Jeanette went up to see my uncle in his room.

My grandmother stayed with me in the kitchen. "Don't lift a finger my eye," she said. "A contagion in my own house and I'm not supposed to care one whit about it?"

"What's a contagion?" I asked her.

"A *disease*," she said, emphasizing the word as a snake would a hiss. "The boy has probably not been taking care of himself properly. Running around doing this and that as he always did. He got malaria when he was tromping around in those foreign countries. Did I ever tell you that? Almost killed him. He was sick for months. Why anyone would want to go to a hot, filthy foreign place with contaminated water and infectious mosquitoes is quite beyond me. I've never seen anyone quite like your uncle with the knack for getting himself into trouble."

She had lied to my Aunt Jeanette — she *was* blaming my uncle. You could hear it in every word she spoke. Even I saw how deep her resentment ran.

My mother walked back into the kitchen at that moment. She asked my grandmother what face cloths she could use to soothe my uncle's head. "He's burning up," she said.

"Take the ones under the vanity in the upstairs bathroom," my grandmother said. "They're my old ones. You might as well throw them out when you're done. They'll be no good after."

"You heard what Dr. Willis said," said my mother. "It is only contagious to children. And it might not be contagious at all."

"He didn't say it was only contagious to children," said my grandmother. "He said children were more at risk." My grandmother had my mother there. That was exactly what Dr. Fred had said.

My mother shrugged and went up to get the face cloths. My grandmother sent me out of the kitchen. She was going to get supper ready. "I suppose I'll make him some soup. He should be able to get that down at least."

# 3

THE PRIEST AT my grandmother's church was Father Orlis. He was English, and was educated at the Catholic seminary of Allen Hall in London. He had a master of divinity from Oxford. Why such a grandly educated man would end up in such an out-of-the-way place as Advocate was the real question. From what I understood he *chose* to come to Nova Scotia. My grandmother thought it had something to do with Delilah Smith, who was English, and Catholic, and the wife of the owner of the paper mill, and part of the richest family in town. Father Orlis was in his early sixties, tall, irremediably thin, bald, with pale blue eyes and bushy white eyebrows. The eyebrows gave the appearance of constant disapproval, as if he was judging everything said or done. The strip of white clerical collar and the black vest, or rabbat, didn't help. He lived with the two deacons in the rectory attached to the back of St. Andrew's Church. I was told he had, like Henry Hennsey, a great many books, and when he wasn't engaged in parish business he was busy reading. I couldn't imagine the books of a priest would be very interesting. If my doctor grandfather was interested only in medical books — there were a host of them in his den from Wilde's *Epidemics in Ireland* to *Aequanimitas with Other Addresses to Medical Students, Nurses and Practitioners of Medicine* by William Osler — a priest would likely only be interested in *religious* books.

I liked Father Orlis. Despite the eyebrows, he had a soft, reassuring voice. When he spoke it was as if he was giving his opinion and asking for permission at the same time. He was diffident, for a priest, and he sometimes had trouble meeting my eye. But he managed the affairs of the parish with aplomb, and he always declaimed his parts of the liturgy with grand authority and confidence. My grandmother loved him, both because he was a good old-fashioned Catholic priest and yet he was not so self-assured she felt she couldn't manipulate him. He deferred to my grandmother in a great many things, because she was head of the auxiliary, because she was prominent among the laity, because she was the wife of the dead Catholic doctor. There were three hundred nominal Catholics in Advocate, about half of which were active church members. My grandmother, if not chief among them, belonged to the religious oligarchy, its ruling class. Any good priest or pastor knows in order to survive he must keep this class happy, that it is they who own the church.

Father Orlis was a good priest.

On more than one occasion, he had been to our house for a meal. He visited when anyone got sick — though he was noticeably absent during the period I write about — and he even talked to Aunt Jeanette, asking after her affairs though she refused to attend

Mass. Uncle David met him, and despite his being in "the opposite camp," as my uncle put it, he had not disliked him. "He seems smart," said my uncle. "One of those men devoted to God as an intellectual experience, rather than an emotional one."

"He's devoted to God, period," said my grandmother. "I don't think emotional or intellectual, as you say, has anything to do with it." This was before my uncle got meningitis, and my grandmother was still peeved about him being there.

Uncle David was right about Orlis. He was an intellectual, if a timid one at that. I could easily see him sitting at a desk in the rectory piled high with books and pondering the meaning of God. He was lost in his world of the mind, the importance of the sacraments, the translations of the vulgate, grand cathedrals of theology. He often didn't notice others in the street when he walked down it. He muttered to himself, and his fingernails were chewed to the nub.

My grandmother forgave him these eccentricities. He was a brilliant man, she said. A perfect parish priest. "An Oxford graduate!" she would say, in an almost sexual ecstasy. In the Mass of the Roman Rite, Father Orlis would recite the Agnes Dei during the breaking of the host. My grandmother would always say afterwards that he delivered the best Agnus Dei liturgy of any priest she had ever heard.

My Aunt Jeanette agreed with my grandmother that Orlis was perfect for a priest, not because of his mellifluous speech in Mass but because he was not the type of man she could imagine being married. He had a stoop to his shoulders and he walked slightly tipped forward, as if bowing under the weight of all that brainpower. Even if he wasn't a priest, she surmised, he would be a bachelor, perhaps a schoolteacher, like Ichabod Crane.

Orlis's deacon was Harry, newly appointed to St. Andrew's Church. He had come from Ontario to serve his last years in the diaconate before being ordained. My mother and Jeanette had seen him in the streets of Advocate, and Aunt Jeanette said he was "cute as a button."

"Such a waste," she lamented.

My grandmother was of the opposite opinion, that a life of celibacy and service to the lord was the best use of a life possible. "There's a few young people around here could learn a lesson from that."

Harry was younger than my aunt, at twenty-seven, but she fell in love with him anyway. My mother said it was because he was unattainable. Jeanette always fell in love with men who couldn't love her back. It was defeatist, my mother said, and childish.

Jeanette did not care. "What's wrong with a little looky-feely?" she said. "I don't expect the man to drop out of seminary and marry me."

My aunt, as usual about matters particular to the church, had it wrong. Deacon Harry had already completed his four years of seminary. He was taking his master of divinity from Dalhousie University, to which he travelled one day a week, doing the rest by correspondence.

Living in the rectory with Orlis and Harry was another deacon, Deacon Wilson. Wilson was only a few years younger than Father Orlis. Also a thin, lugubrious, sallow-faced man, he was a "permanent" deacon, which meant he had not gone to seminary and was not eligible to be ordained. He was from Advocate, and technically should not have been living at the rectory at all. He was not paid for his work, and was more like a volunteer to the church. But he had illusions of grandeur and thought he was a priest. Though he didn't go as far as wearing the clerical collar, he did wear a rabbat and a priest's frock, and walked and spoke with an air of ecclesiastical authority that rivalled, if not exceeded, Father Orlis's.

My grandmother did not like Deacon Wilson. She said he had

tone with her. On more than one occasion she asked Father Orlis why they just didn't kick him out of the rectory and be done with it.

"He does no harm," Father Orlis said. "And he even does some good. He's a very effective deacon. He knows this community well."

My grandmother was equally distrustful of the new deacon. Not because he pretended to be a priest — after all, he would be one someday — but because he was so young and handsome. She considered it an unnecessary temptation to her daughter, an invitation to trouble. Jeanette started going to Mass with my grandmother just to lay eyes on him and speak to him when they said goodbye at the door. My grandmother should have been happy something finally brought Jeanette to St. Andrew's, but she was not. She thought it shameful that her youngest daughter was turning Mass into a "peep show."

Jeanette only shrugged when confronted with this accusation. "I like him. What can I say?"

"You're not supposed to like him," said my grandmother. "You're supposed to like God."

"God's not half as cute," quipped Jeanette. "And he's not around to talk to."

■ ■ ■

THE ONLY PART of the church I was interested in was the cemetery. It is one of the oldest landmarks in Advocate. The early Catholic settlers, trying to outdo the Protestants on the other side of the river, planted it with poplars and weeping willows, which gave it a stately, fairy-kingdom atmosphere in spring and summer. I loved the willows, the way their tendrils hung in bunches almost down to the ground. I would wander through them like a green, airy waterfall. The trees seemed to have a personality and a presence of their own that predated the town. They had been there forever, had seen everything, and from my puny perspective — eleven years and four and a half feet — they knew so much more than I did. On days with a breeze their vines rustled and seemed to confer.

But if I was tempted to go into the graveyard to look at old headstones and relax under the trees, I did not do so when my grandmother was there. She visited the cemetery out of respect for her dead husband once a week to lay a flower on his grave, and the few times she caught me she chased me out. "This is not a play yard," she said. "It's hallowed ground, and you can't be running around in here willy-nilly."

Father Orlis had no such compunctions. Once in a while, I'd seen him going around the church from the rectory side, and when he noticed me he'd give me a wave. He never came over and told me how hallowed and sacred everything was. He never told me to stop sitting under the willows, or playing among their low-hanging branches.

Shortly before my uncle went back to the hospital, Father Orlis asked me if I would come in and help him move the Eucharist table back to its proper place. Some workers had misplaced it when they were sanding the floorboards of the sanctuary and neither of the deacons were available. I was a small kid and was not often asked to do anything physical. We went into the church and moved the table. It was strange being inside that dark, cavernous, richly ornamented space alone. It was open all day, for confession and access to the holy water in the fonts, but I never went in. After I was done Father Orlis asked if I would like to come back to the rectory for a glass of juice and a cookie, a reward for helping with the table.

I agreed.

He gave me the juice and cookie in his office, and chatted to me while I ate and drank. As I suspected, the room was lousy with books and papers. Either he had no housekeeper, or he prevented her from doing any work in there.

If this was a novel, he might have tried to assault me then.

Catholics priests have earned such a bad reputation, and their celibacy in community life is supposed to lead to all kinds of transgressions in private, such as sexually assaulting twelve-year-old boys.

Father Orlis did no such thing. He was a decent man, and he knew how to keep his dick in his pants. Deacon Harry, who would eventually become Father Harry, was also decent. No sexual scandals ever rocked our town, thank God. We were spared that at least.

Deacon Wilson was another case entirely. As a lay deacon, he was not required to be celibate. He could have a family or even a girlfriend if he wanted one. But he didn't want one. No one could even imagine Deacon Wilson in a relationship. You'd have to roam pretty far over the Holy Roman Empire to find one willing to sleep with such a brooding, deliberate personality as Deacon Wilson. And even if you could find one, he would not agree to it. If the priests were celibate, *he* would be celibate. If they wore rabbats, *he* would wear rabbats. If they were boiled in oil and hung upside down on crosses, he would be clamouring to be next.

I liked Father Orlis and Deacon Harry; Deacon Wilson terrified me. Whenever he walked by he would flick his eyes in my direction in the barest kind of acknowledgement. I got the sense he didn't like children. During christenings Deacon Wilson was always there, standing beside Deacon Harry and Father Orlis. I imagined if you turned your back on him he would snatch the baby and sink his teeth into its neck. With his pale long face and widow's peak and glittering black eyes, he reminded me of a vampire.

I was glad, when I ate my cookie and drank my juice, he wasn't around. Father Orlis, sitting behind his desk and staring out over a pile of books, asked how my uncle was faring.

"Fine," I said. "He's getting better."

"He's had quite a run of bad luck, I hear."

"He's okay," I said. "Just meningitis."

Father Orlis did not have a widow's peak, or black eyes, and if he did have a pale face it was a reasonably kind one. And he liked babies. But there was something avaricious in his gaze and the way he spoke to me, something that made me uncomfortable. Like he was mining me for information. Priests do this, I know now. They are not just vassals of God, but counsellors to the community. They look for things that might be wrong so they can deal with them when the time comes. I did not know my grandmother had not told Father Orlis about what was going on at home, and that he was trying to get information. He did not come to see my Uncle David, not because he didn't know my uncle was sick, but because my grandmother had not asked. He respected her need for privacy.

But priests are nothing if not gossipmongers with a divine dispensation to be so. He'd likely hear rumours. I was eleven, so it was okay to pump me for information.

I finished my juice and cookie and told Father Orlis I had to go. He asked me a few more questions which I evaded, and when I finally got away I was relieved.

Unfortunately, I went outside into the backyard of the rectory just as Deacon Wilson was rounding the corner.

"What are you doing here?" he said, surprising me, for he rarely ever spoke. "You're not supposed to be here."

"Father Orlis wanted me," I explained, wanting nothing more than to run away as fast as my legs could carry me from him.

"What did he want?" Wilson said.

I wanted to say "None of your business" or "Go suck a lemon" but instead I told him about the Eucharist table and the orange juice.

"Fine," Deacon Wilson said. "Run along now. The rectory is no place for children."

It was no place for vampires either, I wanted to say. But I ran along.

Deacon Wilson had no authority to speak of. He had no say in church or town matters. So he took it where he could get it. I'm certain he was glad to find me in a place I wasn't supposed to be, so he could exercise some personal discretion.

I did not go back to the graveyard. Instead I went home. I'd had enough of the ecclesiastic for one day.

■ ■ ■

WHEN DEANNY AND I return to her apartment, Richard is still in his pyjamas. It's because he can't write in anything else, she says when he goes back to change. No matter the time of day, if Richard is going to write, he changes into them, and then back out when he is done.

I raise my eyebrows, but make no further comment. Writers are weird. *Richard* is weird. He barely speaks the entire dinner, and when I ask him questions about his books he barely answers.

"Richard is an introvert," Deanny explains, in front of him. "I'm an extrovert. That's why we get along so well."

As usual with the men Deanny picks for me, Pavel is achingly handsome, with a certain casualness of demeanour that makes him even more attractive. It is cliché to say the first thing you notice about a person is his eyes, but this is true of Pavel. They are brilliantly black, swimming with empathy and curiosity. It is impossible not to like him a little. It is true he is a schoolteacher. It also is true he is Russian. He seems to have no problem talking about either, and for much of the dinner it is he and Deanny who keep us entertained. He is voluble, expressive, jovial, and expansive. He laughs at Deanny's stories, like the time she soaked all the girls' panty liners in high school in nail polish remover because they made fun of Alison Smith during gym class.

Eventually he turns to me. He has the slightest trace of a Russian accent. Occasionally he will drop articles from his speech, but other than that, his English is perfect and his accent minimal. It is utterly charming. "I hear you are a mathematician?" he says.

"Was," I say. "I am a social worker now."

"I heard that too," says Pavel.

"I took math in college, and got my degree. But it never amounted to much."

I leave unspoken my thought that Deanny and Richard seem to have prepared Pavel well, for he knows a lot about me. I know nothing about him. I ask him about his work. He complains teaching high school math dulls his abilities. Even the most promising students are at little more than remedial level, and the only class he enjoys is calculus, for the small portion of his grade twelve students going on to higher education in math and sciences. Calculus, he says, is something he can sink his teeth into. He enjoys the discussions of limits and integrals and functions and derivatives. "If I can get my students to understand that calculus is the study of change," he tells me, "the way that geometry is the study of shape and algebra the study of operations, they will be successful. The key is to get them to be excited about it. Don't you agree?"

"I've never taught," I tell Pavel. "But yes, I think that would be half the battle."

"Richard and I are abysmal at math," says Deanny. "Aren't we Richard?"

Richard looks at her as if she is an oncoming train. I can see she's trying to push Pavel and me closer together. I am interested in Pavel's background, though, and I ask him about that. He explains to me he lived in Russia until the collapse of the Soviet Union in 1991. He came to Canada in 1992.

"Why Canada?" I ask.

"The weather," he says, and laughs. "It was like Russia. Cold and almost as big. But free. When my country changed all was chaos in Moscow. I wanted stability, and work. It's strange," he says. "Before the fall, everyone hated Russians. Then suddenly you loved us. Everyone was hiring us. I had no problem getting work here, as

I already spoke English. I heard Nova Scotia was paradise. I came here and found job almost right away."

He has lived an interesting life. When he was a student, he studied mathematics and international journalism. Anybody who wanted to make something of themselves, he tells me, had to study something to do with foreign relations or the Communist Party.

"They taught us to despise you," Pavel says, "as capitalist swine. But we were also to study you as much as we could. To find your weaknesses. We all wanted to be part of the *nomenklatura*."

"The *nomenklatura*?"

"The elite," says Pavel. "Members of the party."

I am fascinated. I have never met anyone who lived in Soviet Russia before, and Pavel has no issues it seems with talking about his past. I ask Pavel if he has ever thought of us as "capitalist swine."

"Never," says Pavel. "That's why I studied journalism instead of foreign relations or party politics. I knew from early age the assumptions were flawed. That Americans, and Canadians, were likely no different from us. You looked the same. The truth is probably you were the same. When the Curtain fell, I was relieved. I dropped journalism and studied only math. And decided I would come here when I could. I miss my family. My father is an old Komsomol member and wanted entrance into the party, but was denied because of indiscretions of his own great-grandfather during the revolution. He hates the fact I live in the West, and barely speaks to me. Also," Pavel says, "he is troubled by my sexuality, which I make no secret of."

He smiles at me, and takes a sip of the latte that Deanny has provided with dessert. I don't know what to say. Never has anyone been so open with me in an initial salvo. Pavel has spent the last hour telling me his life story, including his sexual orientation and his relationship with his father. I have told him nothing about me. Despite my apparent openness at my work, and my advocacy for people to say who they are without fear of reprisal, I have never been very good at taking my own advice. I am conditioned by my childhood; I rarely tell anyone anything about myself unless they ask directly. I ask Pavel if his sexuality was okay in Communist Russia.

Pavel smiles again. "It was not," he says. "Marx and Engels did not forbid it, but they didn't like it. The gay laws were abolished after the revolution as being tsarist, but Stalin put them in place again. They were not repealed until 1993. I left before that happened."

"But why would you come to such a small city?" I ask. "Why not Toronto or Montreal where you have half a chance of meeting someone?"

"Have you met anyone in Toronto?" Pavel asks, still smiling.

I have to admit I have not.

"It's not where you are, but how you think. When you are ready, the right person will come along. It doesn't matter if you live in Halifax or Toronto. That thing will happen if it's supposed to."

And then Pavel does a remarkable thing. He winks at me. The lascivious effect of such a handsome man winking at me leaves me completely undone. I drink my coffee and eventually Pavel continues talking.

Shortly after we finish dessert I announce I have to go and Deanny sits up in her chair like she'd been shot. I see her move her leg nearest Richard and imagine that she is kicking him. He looks up slowly from his coffee like a man emerging from a dream. Pavel looks bemused and bewildered. Before I can say any more, Deanny says, "You can't go yet. We're going into the living room."

"Mom will be expecting me," I say. "They don't like me to drive after dark."

"Nonsense. They'd want you to stay out as long as you wanted."

"Really, Deanny. I have to go."

"Fine then," she says. "Pavel, you walk him to his car. I want to talk to Richard alone."

Richard has gone back to his coffee. He is, really, very childlike at times. Almost idiotic. Most writers are, I've found.

It is too late to get out the trap Deanny laid for me. Pavel is already getting up from his seat. She gives me, as we go, a triumphant look. I know it well. It is the same one she used to give me when we were kids and she got something over on me, except back then she also used to stick out her tongue at me at the same time. I can almost see her doing this now. I sigh, and leave the apartment with the handsome Russian schoolteacher in tow.

# 4

FATHER ORLIS DIED eight years ago. My grandmother still mourns his loss, but she did come to accept Father Harry as his replacement. She still thinks of him as a terrible temptation to the parish's younger women, not noticing in her dotage Father Harry has lost his looks. He was always a short, slight man. When he was young and fresh-faced this was charming, but as he got older, it has given him a gnomish appearance, not helped by the fact he wears spectacles. Because he is given to laughter, the skin around his eyes is heavily crinkled, and lines are drawn at either corner of his mouth. He is no more temptation to young girls — what few of them there are, the church is having trouble attracting younger members of late — than would be my grandmother. She never has conceded Father Harry is as good a parish priest as Father Orlis, though she admits his liturgies are "passable." And she did once say Father Harry gave the host better than Orlis. The old man had a palsy hand, and sometimes missed her mouth. My grandmother has relegated herself to the fact that when she dies it will be Father Harry who presides over her funeral. And though she has never said so, one gets the impression she considers this a great honour bestowed upon him.

One morning, after I've been home for a week, Father Harry calls me and asks me to meet him in the cemetery. He remembers that I liked to walk through it when I was a boy. As it is summer now, the branches on the willows are full of tendrils and leaves. We take several turns around the graveyard, and Father Harry asks me if I know my grandmother will be the last person to be buried here.

"Really?" I say.

"Yes," says Father Harry. "The last reserved spot became occupied last year. The only one left is your grandmother's. She sold the other plots when your mother and Jeanette opted to be buried beside your uncle. Once she goes, there will be no more burials at St. Andrew's."

"She will like that," I say. "The last of her kind."

"Agreed," says Father Harry. He tells me he has already administered Unction — the Anointing of the Sick — to my grandmother, as well as the Sacrament of Penance and the Viaticum. I am familiar with the combination of rituals, better known as the Last Rites; I've had history with them. Father Harry knows this history and doesn't mention it. He is only telling me, he says, because he thinks I might like to know, since it is important to my grandmother. My grandmother had not had confession for a long time, and she wasn't able to confess then. My mother and Jeanette were present. Jeanette cried. Father Harry anointed my grandmother with blessed olive oil and said, "May the Lord who has saved you free you from sin and raise you up." He also anointed her hands and said, "Through this holy anointing, may the Lord pardon you of whatever sins you have committed by sight, hearing, smell, touch, taste, walking, carnal delectation."

"What possible sins could a person commit by walking?" I ask him.

Father Henry shrugs. "It's part of the liturgy. It refers to John's exhortation that Christians walk in the light."

"And what on earth is carnal delectation? It's a wonder Grand-nan didn't wake up and give you a slap for that one, for even suggesting it."

"Delectation means delight," Father Harry says solemnly.

"Oh, so you're not supposed to enjoy yourself? Sounds fittingly Catholic."

"It was your grandmother's wish, Jacob," says Father Harry. "It's what she wanted."

"Will you be there when she passes?"

"If at all possible. I told your mother and Jeanette to call me if they even think it's getting close. I know your grandmother did not like me, at least not as much as Father Orlis. But she has served the church well her long life. I'm certain she will go to heaven."

Father Harry suggests we go into the rectory for coffee. Whether he inherited Father Orlis's books is unknown to me, only that the office is as lousy with them as it was when Orlis was alive. He clears off a chair and bids me to sit, then disappears into a back room and comes out with two cups of coffee. "There's no cream, I'm afraid. I forgot to get it from the store. Is black okay?"

"Fine," I say.

"I want you to know I did not invite you down here today just to take a walk or tell you about the Last Rites."

"You didn't?"

"No," says Harry. He sits down behind his desk, pushes aside a tall, irregularly stacked pile of books and looks at me. "I want to tell you something. Just before your grandmother became ill, she had a meeting with me to discuss her funeral arrangements. I think she knew she was not well, but her mind was remarkably clear."

"I suppose she's planning a real humdinger."

Father Henry smiles. "She expects fireworks, yes. But she was also very clear on what she wanted done and *who* she wanted to do it. Your grandmother liked to be in control ..."

"You're not telling me anything I don't know."

"Well, yes, and I think she was afraid her wishes might not be carried out after her death the way she wanted. So she came to me."

"That's ridiculous," I say. "Mother would do whatever it is she wanted. She should know that."

"I don't think she was referring to your mother."

"Then who? Aunt Jeannette? The church auxiliary?"

Father Harry looks at me. I do not understand why he is telling me this. Grandnan is not dead yet. Surely decency demands such a conversation take place after. I tell him so.

"I'm telling you now because your grandmother asked me to. She was very specific about when. If she got sick, and after I had performed the Extreme Unction, I was to let you know."

"Let me know what?"

Father Harry sighs. "She was afraid you wouldn't take it well. That you might refuse to do it. I think her conscience bothered her the last few years, Jacob. I think she has had some regrets."

I am utterly bewildered. Father Harry is talking in riddles. "Just get to your point," I say.

"She wants you to give her eulogy," Father Harry says. "And she wanted you to be told while she is alive, to give you time to absorb it. She thought if they told you a few days before the funeral you wouldn't do it."

I am stunned. Me? The eulogy? Why on earth would she want that? Here I am afraid of confronting her on her deathbed, and here she is giving me the opportunity to do it in front of the entire town. My reaction is swift, and unequivocal.

"I won't do it," I say. "I absolutely refuse."

"She said you'd say that. She wants you to think about it."

"What for? Just to tell you in a week or two, when she finally does die, that I won't and you need to get someone else? Listen, Father. I don't hate my grandmother, okay? She practically brought me up. And I know, that in her way, she cared for me. But I cannot stand up in front of the entire town and sing her praises ..."

I catch myself. I was going to say, *when she denied my uncle just as Peter denied Christ,* but somehow the stricture about speaking about it in our town is still in place, even for me. And now my grandmother wants me to get up and pretend it never happened.

Or so I think.

Father Harry shakes his head and says, "You misunderstand. She doesn't want you to sing her praises. She wants you to explain. She wants you to talk about the year your uncle died. She wants the town to know. She was never able to do it in her lifetime. She never had the courage, and the world she lived in didn't allow it. But she knew the world you lived in did. She chose you, Jacob. She wants you to justify her to the town."

"Justify her? You've got to be kidding me! I can't justify her. I don't know what she was thinking. I never did. That's one of the reasons I've been so damn angry at her!"

"She thinks you can. She was quite certain of it. So just take some time and think about what she's asking. Perhaps if she wakes up again you can ask her about it, though I wouldn't put much hope in that. Even if she does wake up, she'll be very confused. I'm afraid she won't last much longer."

"I —"

"Don't say anything else," says Father Harry. "Do your grandmother a favour by considering what she has requested."

■ ■ ■

EVERY SPRING AND fall, and then again before Christmas, my grandmother cleaned the house from top to bottom. This consisted of waxing all the hardwood floors and shampooing the rugs, dampening down the drapes with a wet cloth, dusting every stick of furniture and every knick-knack and piece of china in the dining room break-front, and taking all the area rugs to the backyard to be beat on the red fence. She employed my mother and Jeanette and me for these tasks, overseeing most of them, and only saved the more delicate procedures, the china and glassware, for herself.

It was not cleaning season when my uncle was diagnosed with meningitis. My grandmother began to clean anyway. My mother thought she was doing it to distract herself from David's illness and the fact he couldn't yet be moved to his own place. She and Jeanette were glad my grandmother was keeping herself busy and tried to stay out of her way.

That Friday my grandmother was in a mood. She said little over dinner. After my mother and Jeanette went upstairs to take a tray up to David, my grandmother decided to take out some of her frustration by cleaning more. Once the dishes were done she asked me to take the duster and dust the picture frames in the hall and the living room. She wiped down the glass bowls and vases on coffee tables and stands. She also switched on the six o'clock news and turned up the volume so she could hear it, wherever in the house she was.

My grandmother was interested in what was going on in the world, but only so she could complain about the godlessness of it later to Jeanette and my mother. Her understanding of world events was limited. She knew the facts, but she didn't know how to interpret them. Violence in the Middle East was due to an "inherent savagery" in the Arab nature. Starving people in Africa was due to an "inclination" to be lazy and indolent. Economic crisis in the US was due to rich men trying to fit themselves through the eyes of needles. Current events according to my grandmother were a muddle of biblical prophecy and racial stereotype, which never failed to infuriate my more liberal aunt.

As we cleaned, my grandmother occasionally commented on a snippet to me. I knew nothing of world events and cared even less. I was too busy dusting portraits of the pope and wilderness scenes and my grandfather's medical degrees, which my grandmother had removed from his den when he died and proudly hung in the front hallway so everyone would see. I was not very tall for my age, so I had to stand on a chair to reach the highest picture. This was of a horse — Pegasus flying through the clouds — which had been given as a gift to my grandmother from a member of her church. No one ever mentioned to my grandmother this was a strange gift for one Christian to give another. Pegasus was a Greek myth, a pagan symbol, and was as far removed from Christ as apples are from oranges. My grandmother didn't seem to notice; if she did, she didn't care. She hung the painting in a place of prominence, and every year since I had turned nine I was obligated to dust it. It was the only time I noticed it. I thought winged horses were stupid. It meant no more to me than my grandfather's Latin inscribed medical degrees.

On the other side of the door from Pegasus was a narrow, waist-high table. Upon it rested a large green Depression glass punch bowl. My grandmother loved Depression glass. She had a china cabinet full of it in the dining room. This bowl sat out because her own grandmother acquired it as a promotional gift in 1932, when her grandfather filled up his De Soto at a gas station and got an oil change. It was one of the only family heirlooms she had, and she wanted to display it prominently. Anyone given a tour of the house was first shown the punch bowl, and given a brief rundown of its history — where it had come from, including the name and proprietor of the gas station; the names of her mother and grandmother, who had owned it before my grandmother; and the day my grandmother received it, which happened to be her wedding day.

Children brought into the house were given the same rundown, though not half as friendly. "You see this?" my grandmother would

say. "That is very old. Worth both a fortune in terms of its sentimental *and* dollar value. It is irreplaceable. You hear me? Irreplaceable!
You are not to touch it. Do not run, jump, or slide around it. You
are to avoid this area at all times. If I catch you doing any of those
things around my bowl, I will banish you from this house."

My grandmother meant what she said. I believed she would
have banished *me* had I broken any of these rules. I was careful to
walk around the table and punch bowl, always conscious not to trip
and fall into it.

Breaking the punch bowl, according to my grandmother, would
be akin to murder.

My mother and Jeanette told her many times she should store
the bowl somewhere safer, where it would be in no danger. But she
wouldn't listen. "It needs to be displayed," she said. "I'm very proud
of it. People should just be careful of it. I'm not going to uproot
and hide away my heritage just because some people don't care to
watch their step." And so the bowl stayed.

As I was dusting Pegasus, my grandmother was dusting the
bowl. It was a delicate procedure. She dared not move it to the kitchen
to wash it, and instead ran a wet cloth around the inside of the bowl.
To get to the underside, she had to lift it off its stand, cradling it in
one arm like a baby while wiping it. .

We were both startled by my mother shouting at the top of
the stairs.

"Mom!" she cried. "Come here. Hurry!"

"What?" called my grandmother. "I'm busy!"

"It's David! Something's wrong!"

"What is it this time?" my grandmother shouted. She was
cradling the bowl in both arms now, and was about to set it back on
the stand.

My mother yelled, "He can't breathe! He's burning up! Call an
ambulance! For God's sake."

"Those two," said my grandmother. "An hour ago he was fine. Now he's sick again. God-knows-what …"

She stopped speaking. The TV in the rumpus room could be heard distinctly from where we stood. So far the news had been of the usual suspects — conflict, economy, politics. But just at that moment, as if orchestrated, we heard the announcer talking about this new disease. AIDS. Acquired Immune Deficiency Syndrome.

My mother and Jeanette tried explaining it to my grandmother before, when the news first started carrying stories about it. But no one made a connection until then.

My grandmother gave a harsh intake of breath. She shoved the bowl back on its stand. The bowl was not all the way on. I watched in horror as it toppled and fell, detonating like a bomb on the hardwood floor. My grandmother didn't notice. She turned halfway around and screamed, "Don't touch him!" with an old lady's dry and piercing squeal. "For God's sake! Don't touch him!" She ran up the stairs as fast as she could. "Don't touch him!" she screamed. "Don't touch him, Caroline!"

I stood on the chair, my duster in hand, looking down. Pieces of my grandmother's precious bowl glittering like jagged emeralds on the dark wood of the floor.

# PART II

■

:

.

# FIVE

∎

THE WORD *AIDS* was never spoken in our house. Not during that period in July, 1984, when it was suspected my uncle had it; nor after, in the late summer, when we knew for sure. There was a barely restrained hysteria then, a sustained but muted mania over something we all knew was there but had a name we could not speak.

The reason it could not be spoken was because of me. This I knew for certain. Whatever secrets were being kept were to deny me knowledge of what was really going on. Conversations stopped when I walked into a room. Forced cheerfulness and idle questions would follow.

"How was your day, Jacob?"

"What did you do outside, Jacob?"

"What do you want for your birthday, Jacob?"

Jeanette and my mother joined my grandmother in this behaviour, and I marvelled at the three of them in collusion over something. Together for the first time in agreeing that whatever this was, it must be kept from me.

And so, of course, I was dying to know.

The night my grandmother smashed her bowl, my uncle was taken to the hospital by ambulance. He did not come out until the middle of August. Those weeks he was away would be the last full days of my childhood, before a long and complicated adolescence began. My mother and aunt and grandmother succeeded in keeping the truth from me, but they knew they couldn't keep it forever. My uncle's situation consumed them to the point that it was as if I didn't exist. I became, for those short weeks, something of a neglected child. I didn't mind. I preferred to be neglected than weighed down by whatever was troubling them. I wanted to know, but I wasn't sure I wanted to be involved.

After a week of hanging about the house and attempting to find out what was going on, I decided to weather the storm by spending as much time away as possible. Unfortunately, in addition to the weirdness at my own house, Cameron began exhibiting a weirdness of his own.

It started simply. One day I called him up to go to his house. He told me I couldn't because his parents were busy waxing the floors. A few days later I ran into him on the sidewalk outside of the library and again suggested we go back to his place. Again he said we couldn't. His father was cutting the grass and didn't want anyone around.

"Isn't your father at work?" I asked him.

"Not today," Cameron said. "He took the afternoon off." He wouldn't look at me while he said it, just kept his eyes cast down. I knew he was lying. I couldn't imagine why. I thought, in my innocence, there were troubles at his house, too.

A few days later, I asked him if he would come to my house. I also told him all about what was going on, so it wouldn't come as a surprise if my grandmother looked at him like he had two heads, or if conversation dried up when he walked into a room. He begged off, saying he was going to visit his aunt in Halifax.

At dinner that night, I complained to my mother that Cameron was being strange.

"In what way?" my mother asked.

"He never wants me to come over anymore. He says his parents are always doing something. Like tonight he said they were going to see his aunt. They never go see his aunt on a week night!"

My mother and Jeanette exchanged glances. My grandmother didn't catch any of it. She was busy feeding her cat, Princess, in the dining room. Jeanette sometimes complained that Princess, who was older than me and weighed almost as much, was the only member of the family who got to eat there. My mother put her arm around me and said she was sure there was a perfectly good explanation.

But that is what parents say when there isn't.

"You want me to call Mrs. Simms and find out what's going on?"

"Why would you do that?" I asked, genuinely surprised. My mother generally didn't get involved in my affairs unless it was serious, like the year before when one of the Shannon brothers gave me a black eye at recess. She called Mr. Shannon and threatened to have the boy arrested. My grandmother was aghast because the Shannons were good Irish Catholics. From her point of view, it was only Protestants who got rough and tumble. But that incident was not to be compared to this. This was a kid thing. Maybe Cameron was mad at me for something that I'd done and I didn't know it. He had done nothing wrong, except to come up with what I was sure were excuses to not have me over or come to my house.

I was tempted to ask my grandmother if she had provoked an argument with Mr. or Mrs. Simms in the supermarket over their atheism, something that had happened once before. My mother beat me to it. When my grandmother came back to the kitchen and resumed her seat, my mother said to her, "Have you been talking lately to Mr. or Mrs. Simms? Cameron's parents?"

"Not recently," she said. "Why?"

"No reason," said my mother.

My grandmother harrumphed and dropped her fork beside her plate without taking a bite. "Now come on, Caroline. There must be a reason. No one asks a question like that out of the blue without some purpose."

My mother shrugged, casually, without guile. "Jacob says that they've been away a lot lately. I was just wondering if you knew where they might be going?"

"Me? For heaven's sake, do you think I take account of every coming and going in Advocate? I don't work for the *Gazette*. Really! Sometimes I think you girls ..."

As my grandmother went on, I realized my mother had not told her the truth. Why would my mother withhold this? Especially now since she had my grandmother riled up about being accused a gossip?

Depressed at the situation in my house, and equally as unhappy with things outside of it, I excused myself and went outside. I picked up a smooth stone and walked around with it, massaging it like a Chinese stress ball. I wanted to throw it through someone's window, but didn't have the nerve. I hadn't met up at the mill with Deanny for a while, because sometimes she'd be there waiting for me and sometimes she would not. I regretted the lack of playmates. After a time, I went back into the house, had a shower, changed into my pyjamas, and went to my room to get ready for bed. For the summer I was allowed to stay up until ten o'clock and watch television with the adults downstairs, but I often chose to stay in my room and read. My mother came in to wish me goodnight and said my uncle would be coming home from the hospital a week from Saturday.

"Good," I said.

My mother smiled, and kissed me on the cheek as I lay in my bed. "I know things have been a little strange around here lately," she said. "They'll straighten out soon."

"Okay," I said.

"My little boy is turning out to be not so little anymore. Have you thought about what you'd like to do for your birthday?"

"I'd like to have a party," I said.

"Really?" said my mother. "You never wanted a party before."

It was true. I never considered I'd had enough friends for one, and inviting bullies and students from school did not seem an appealing option. But I was suddenly thinking I could invite Deanny and Cameron to the bowling alley below the IGA on the Protestant side. I didn't tell my mother about Deanny, but I did tell her about Cameron and bowling.

"Done," she said. "Your birthday falls on a Saturday this year. I'll get the time off and we'll do it that day."

"I'll tell Cameron."

My motivations were twofold: to bring Deanny into the clan, and to force Cameron back into my acquaintance. He liked to bowl, and he couldn't refuse to see me on my birthday. After all, I had gone to Halifax with him on *his* birthday to see the Nova Scotia Museum. With this simple logic in place, I went to sleep.

■ ■ ■

ABOUT MY BIRTHDAY party at the bowling alley, Cameron was evasive. For a week after I told him, he wouldn't give me a straight answer. So the Friday before my birthday, I cornered him in the town library. I'd watched him slip in there when he saw me coming down Main Street. I sat down beside him at a table and asked again about bowling on my birthday. He closed his book and looked at me.

"I can't," he said. "I'm busy."

"What do you mean, you can't?" I said. "It's my birthday!"

"You didn't let me finish. We're going to see my aunt that day."

"You're always going to see your aunt," I said. "Is she sick or something?"

"No," said Cameron, going back to his book. "She just wants to see us a lot."

"So, we'll change it," I said. "What day are you available?"

The town library was deserted. We sat at the centre table, whispering. The librarian, Mrs. Frail, was at her desk. She glanced up occasionally from her papers to make sure we were being quiet as a nun. While nice in all other respects, she was a demon about preserving the acoustic integrity of the room. No loud talking. Nothing above a whisper. It was like being a prisoner of war in there, which is why a lot of kids didn't go.

Cameron didn't glance up from his book. "The thing is, I'm not really available any day," he said. "I'm pretty busy with stuff at home. So I guess I'll have to miss your party."

"What's going on?" I cried.

Mrs. Frail looked up sharply. "Jacob McNeil," she said. "This is not a basketball court, or a hootenanny. It's a library. Accordant tone, please."

"Sorry, Mrs. Frail." Then, more softly, to Cameron, "Are you mad at me or something?"

Cameron, by this time pretending to be fully back into his book, shook his head without looking at me. "Busy is all."

"You lie," I whispered. "You're a liar."

It was the one thing I knew would get to him. He prided himself on always telling the truth, no matter what the cost. When I got a higher mark on a test, he would tell me, seemingly without guile, it was because I got lucky, there was no way I was smarter than he was. It was a principle of his mother's he'd inherited. Liars, she said, both degraded themselves and the people they lied to. It was the worst kind of semantic treachery, and on par with murder or stealing. One of the reasons Cameron often got beat up at school was because he refused to lie to the bullies and tell them what they wanted to hear. Instead of saying he didn't have time to do their homework when they asked, he'd say he would rather be shot and pissed on than help them achieve something they didn't deserve. This commitment to honesty would get Cameron in a lot of trouble in his life. But he would rather be hurt than accused of lying. I really did think he was lying then, and I couldn't understand why. He had always been my friend. Now here he was avoiding me. Without Cameron I had no one. I'd forgotten about Deanny. All I could think of was a birthday party of one. I needed to understand what was going on. Had his mother finally decided I was not worthy to play with Cameron? That I was not good enough for her son? Was it something I had done? Something I didn't do?

Cameron closed his book and set it on the table. He looked over at Mrs. Frail to make sure she was not listening and then leaned in towards me, whispering even lower than before.

"It's your uncle," he said.

"What?"

Cameron nodded. "My mother says I'm not supposed to hang out with you anymore. Because of your uncle. I'm not supposed to tell you this. I was supposed to let you down easy. But you were my friend, so I can tell you. But you can't tell anyone else okay?"

"My uncle?" I said, confused. "Is it because he's a homosexual?"

He shook his head adamantly. "My mother says it's not that. She doesn't care about that at all. It's the other thing."

"What other thing?"

Cameron just looked at me. Studying me. He looked much older than eleven then. Even I could see he was struggling with whatever he was trying to tell me. For a minute, it looked as if he might cry.

"Mom says when it all blows over we can be friends again. It's only now we can't. She says we don't even know how it's transmitted. It could be airborne, or through touch. We just don't know."

"Cameron? What are you talking about?"

"Jacob," Mrs. Frail warned. "If you don't keep your voice down I'm going to have to ask you to leave the library."

"Sorry Mrs. Frail."

"The disease," Cameron said. "The thing your uncle has."

"Meningitis?" I said.

"No," said Cameron. "That's not what he has. He has AIDS."

Mrs. Simms, being a biologist, was familiar with it. Of course she would know. Of course she would be one of the first to figure it out. From this perspective of time and place, her concerns that Cameron might catch it seem incredibly naïve for such an educated woman. But it was a different time, and she was right about one thing. We knew nothing about it.

Cameron explained to me that he couldn't be around me anymore. I would just have to find someone else to invite to my birthday party. Then he went back to his book.

It was my turn to cry. My vision blurred as I left the library and my best friend. I was in a kind of shock. Is this what all the whispering had been about? Is this what I had to look forward to the rest of the summer?

I didn't want to stay downtown.

When my grandmother saw me she asked what I was doing home. Shouldn't I be out playing with Cameron on such a beautiful day? I told her I didn't feel well, and went to my room. My uncle was scheduled to come home the next day. I was depressed. I stayed in my room all afternoon, and when my mother came home at five, she immediately came up to check on me and ask me what was wrong.

I wanted to tell her what happened, but something kept me. It was not loyalty to Cameron and my promise that I would not tell. He had deserted me, so I had no allegiance to him any longer. Perhaps I just didn't want to know the truth.

I lied to her. For once I had no qualms about stretching the truth.

I told her I had a stomach ache.

My mother made me some tomato soup, and sat with me in the kitchen while I ate it. As I said, she had an uncanny knack of knowing when someone was lying. She asked me if something happened that day.

I told her nothing had.

"Are you sure?" she said.

"I'm sure."

"Okay," said my mother. "I know I've said this a thousand times, but if you ever need to talk to me seriously about something, you can. You'll never get in trouble if you bring up the subject first."

"Okay," I said.

The phone rang. My grandmother was upstairs and answered it in her bedroom. She came to the head of the stairs and shouted for my mother. "It's Cameron's mother," my grandmother said. "She said she needs to speak to you immediately."

My mother looked at me. "Did you and Cameron have a fight today?"

"No," I said, and this time it didn't feel like a lie. We had witnessed the end of our friendship, but it wasn't because we had fought. My mother told me she'd be right back and took the call in the living room. My grandmother came downstairs. She asked if I was sure there had been no disagreement.

I told her what I had told my mother.

"Odd," said my grandmother. "I don't think Mrs. Simms has ever called here before."

It was the first of many calls, of many odd things.

My falling out with Cameron was just the beginning.

■ ■ ■

AS FAR AS I could make sense of it later, Cameron went home and told his mother he had told me why he could not be around me any longer. His mother berated him. She called and told my mother Cameron had been insensitive and needlessly cruel, and I did not need to hear what he told me.

"But was it true?" my mother asked. "Did you ask that Cameron not be around Jacob anymore because of David?"

My mother was a waitress. Though she had finished high school, and could read, write, and do basic arithmetic, she hadn't done very well in school. She was not interested in academics, either as a career or pastime. She was no match intellectually for Sharon Simms. But when it came to defending my interests, she was a powerhouse. I do not know what was said, but as I understand it, she swept aside all of Mrs. Simms' well-reasoned, articulate, and intelligent arguments for why Cameron and I should be kept apart.

When Jeanette got home from work, my mother told her about it. "They make assumptions," she said, "and act on them like they're gospel truth. She has actually convinced herself she's doing Jacob a favour!"

"What did you say to her?"

"I said she was as superstitious and as ignorant as everyone else in this town, and if those are the values she teaches her son, I don't want Jacob hanging out with Cameron anyway."

"Why did she call?" said Jeanette.

"To apologize," said my mother. "Can you believe that? For the insensitive way Cameron told Jacob the truth. Which is that they're afraid of David. And these are some of the most educated people in town. What happens when the rest of them find out?"

"Maybe they won't," said Jeanette.

"They will," my mother said. "Some of them already suspect."

If these events weren't enough, something else happened. After my mother's call to Mrs. Simms ended, she realized I wasn't really sick. She made me eat supper with the rest of them. Everyone was quiet. There was much clinking of forks against plates and the silence was oppressive. The grandfather clock in the dining room chimed six. It had a solemn, lugubrious effect on an already depressing meal.

My grandmother stayed particularly silent. Then, seemingly apropos of nothing, she dropped her fork and said, in surprising distress, "I can't take it! He's coming home tomorrow, and this is just the beginning!"

"The beginning of what?" asked Jeanette.

"Don't you see?" said my grandmother. "The Simms are right. Who knows what this means? Jacob is here. We don't know if it's even safe! We don't know what to do. I can't take it, I tell you! It's not tolerable!"

And then my grandmother did a remarkable thing. Something I had never seen her do before. She began to cry. For the second time that day, I was in a state a shock. My mother and Jeanette did their best to calm her down, but in the end she left the table and went to her room. My mother checked on her and then came back down to finish her dinner with us. But no one was hungry.

"What's going on?" said Jeanette. "Is the whole world going crazy?"

"Not the whole world," said my mother. "Just Advocate." She looked sympathetically at me. "You don't know what's going on, do you?"

I shook my head.

"Maybe we should tell him," Aunt Jeanette said. "What Cameron hasn't already said, that is."

"Soon," my mother said. "Let's let things settle down first."

We didn't finish our meals. We scraped them into the garbage and did the dishes. My grandmother wasn't there to rinse so I did it for her. I was grateful for something extra to do. While we worked in the kitchen, the grandfather clock in the dining room ticked with more authority than I had ever noticed before.

## 2

HOW THE NEWS broke in town about the nature of my uncle's illness was never revealed to me, not even later when we began to talk about it openly. Perhaps my grandmother, once she figured it out the night she smashed her Depression glass bowl, mentioned it to a bridge partner. Perhaps his string of illnesses, coupled with his known proclivities, was enough. David himself had told my mother and Jeanette. Dr. Fred admitted afterwards to my mother that he had surmised David's condition on his first visit, shortly after he arrived home. Still, there was no clear explanation how the town knew.

Only that it was increasingly obvious they did.

Uncle David was kept in isolation in the hospital. He told my mother that every nurse who came into his room was gowned and gloved. They seemed terrified, and never stayed long. He was not allowed to use the bathroom, but was given a plastic bedpan that was removed by a man in a Hazmat suit. He slept on worn sheets and was given threadbare towels; he suspected these were burned after his use. The only person not dressed as if he were in a radiation zone was Dr. Fred. But he was not my uncle's doctor in hospital. He could only visit, and express his displeasure at the way my uncle was being treated.

The first sign something was amiss in the town at large came the day my uncle returned from the hospital. That Friday afternoon, my grandmother's bridge tournament was cancelled. One after another her bridge partners called and begged off with some ill-prepared excuse. By the time Hazel — who lived down the street and was one of her closest friends — called, my grandmother was resigned.

"Perhaps you could find a fourth from your list, Millicent?" Hazel suggested.

"I think," said my grandmother dryly, "the list wouldn't do me much good today, Hazel."

■ ■ ■

MY GRANDMOTHER MADE certain to be out of the house when my uncle arrived. She still held the faint hope he would get an apartment in town, and kept calling around for places to let on his behalf. She was always told nothing was available. The man who had offered my uncle the apartment on the Protestant side rescinded shortly after David went into the hospital. No one questioned why.

The bout with meningitis, and whatever else my uncle had, took a lot out of him. When he returned from the hospital, he was not able to walk on his own. Jeanette had borrowed a wheelchair from the hospital to bring him from the car up the walk, but he insisted on standing up and making his way up the front stairs and through the door. I stood in the front hall and watched, fascinated. He was hardly the same man. He was pale, gaunt, and exhausted, weaker and thinner than before he had gone. He held on to the doorjamb to ease himself in to the house, then rested for a while in a kitchen chair.

When he said he would make his own way up the stairs to his room, I was surprised that neither my aunt nor my mother offered to help. As much as they loved him, they were refusing to touch him. After he was up, and his door was closed, they sat over coffee at the kitchen table. They said nothing, and occasionally looked at each other in some wordless communication designed, I was sure, to exclude me. I was baffled. My uncle was home. They should have been happy.

Dr. Fred came by later that afternoon to see how my uncle was doing. He was remarkably free from the hysteria of the nurses and support staff at the hospital. After a little research, he was confident the disease my uncle had, the *underlying illness*, was sexually transmitted.

My grandmother refused to believe it. She still wanted David away where it was safe; she warned me to stay away from him and not to go into his room. My mother didn't challenge my grandmother's proclamation. Though she claimed to believe what Fred said, she must have had some lingering doubt.

While he was in hospital, my uncle had developed two purple spots, one on his cheek and one on his neck, each about the size of a dime. My mother and Jeanette asked Dr. Fred what they were. He said they were a rare form of cancer called Kaposi sarcoma, not uncommon in patients with AIDS. There were no treatments. Uncle David also had a bacteria in his cerebrospinal fluid normally found only in the feces of birds.

Dr. Fred showed himself to be a consummate physician. By his own admission, he knew little about AIDS. There was precious little written about it. There was no one local he could consult, and there were no reported cases in Nova Scotia besides my uncle. He contacted my uncle's physician in Toronto to ask him about it, but the man knew little more than Dr. Fred, and as of yet there were no treatments. So Dr. Fred treated each opportunistic infection separately, with antibiotics and antivirals.

"I don't understand how he could be so sick," my mother said in the living room, while I eavesdropped from the stair. "In June he was just fine. A little thin, maybe, but ..."

"He wasn't fine," Dr. Fred said. "Tom has been symptomatic for over a year. The weight loss is simply part of it. All the other illnesses I have mentioned to you, with the exception of the meningitis, were diagnosed before he came home."

"And so you're telling us ..."

"Yes. I'm telling you."

"Hold on," my mother said. Before she said more, she got up and looked into the hall, where she found me sitting there. "Jacob," she said. "Would you excuse us a minute? Go up to your room while Dr. Willis and I talk."

I did so, resentful that I was being excluded. I passed the closed door to my uncle's bedroom. Over the next few months, I would get very used to that closed door, and tiptoeing past it so as not to disturb him.

■ ■ ■

IF DEANNY MCLEOD ever understood exactly what my uncle had, or if her parents had heard the rumours now virulently sweeping the town, she never mentioned it.

I still hadn't told my mother about Deanny or where I was going. Not because she was from the wrong side of the tracks — I knew my mother and Aunt Jeanette would not care about that, though my grandmother would — but because everything was too weird at my house to invite friends over. So I kept her a secret.

We met at the mill when she could get away. We broke every window in every abandoned vehicle, investigated the old buildings and machinery so much they were stripped of their intrigue and mystery. Deanny got bored. We had done pretty much everything we could there, and looked for somewhere else to play.

She invited me to her house on Meadow Pond Lane.

I had been to Meadow Pond Lane on several occasions. When I collected bottles and cans for Christmas money, my aunt drove me to the depot to cash them in. But I had never walked through it. Poor neighbourhoods, like rich ones, seemed exclusive. Deanny's house, with a weedy, scrofulous lawn, was small, pink, and unadorned, except for one plant dangling under an eve, undeniably dead, its brown stalks and leaves collapsed around the rim of its white plastic hanging pot, an exhausted spider. Everything about Deanny's place was impoverished, even the two twisted spruce trees growing behind the outhouse.

The first time I was there, Deanny did not invite me in. She was as foul-mouthed as she'd been at the mill, and spoke in a loud voice. I kept waiting for someone to come out and see who I was, but no one did. I suspected either her parents weren't home — belied by

the presence of a rust-eaten blue Dodge Charger in the driveway —
or they didn't care. I assumed, correctly as it turned out, that she
was an only child.

I liked Meadow Pond Lane.

I shouldn't have. It was so disordered, so small, so derelict
compared to what I knew. But that was the reason I liked it. I never
had to worry about sitting on an antique chair or breaking a
Depression glass punch bowl. On Tenerife Street I could get
away with nothing, for if I did something untoward either my
grandmother would see me or one of her friends would call her up
and rat me out.

Deanny didn't once ask to go to my house to play. She was
content to stay at Meadow Pond, and to educate me in its ways.
Freed from the suffocating rationalism of Cameron and math class,
and the domestic rules of my grandmother, I went to town. We lit
matches and set off caps and firecrackers. No one blinked an eye.
We walked on the hoods of abandoned cars and tried to smash
windshields with rocks and slashed up the vinyl on seats with
jackknives. I was not a physical boy. This was the closest I'd ever
come to delinquency and it was exhilarating. Deanny showed me
the ropes. She told me what to do and how to do it. She took satisfaction in corrupting me.

From the time my uncle returned from the hospital, until my
birthday, Deanny completely transformed my life. It's no wonder
I paid little attention to the dramas playing themselves out in my
house. There would come a time when I could no longer ignore
them. Until then I was content to play and unshackle myself from
academic expectations and social pretensions. Deanny taught me
how to be a child, at a time when I was being asked to grow up
too quickly.

# 3

MY MOTHER WAS confused about why my uncle was not bouncing back from his illness. In her experience, people got sick and then they got better. David was thin and pale when he went into the hospital, it was true, but there was no reason, she felt, he shouldn't get his strength back. He seemed to be feeling better, making his way around without assistance. But he was feeble. Dr. Fred explained that the meningitis had beaten down my uncle's immune system, and the *underlying condition* would not let it bounce back. Other illnesses, like the bird virus and the purple spots, had taken more serious hold, and, as usual with patients with AIDS, my uncle David seemed to get seriously ill seriously fast.

My mother and Aunt Jeanette suspected David stayed in his room to spare my grandmother. She claimed she couldn't stand the thought, let alone the sight, of him. When they begged him to get out of his room, he would only say that he would rather stay in. He made no requests to go out. He'd made no requests for anything. So they spent time with Uncle David in his room, and continued to bring him meals on trays. My grandmother began to live on the phone in her room, talking to her old bridge partners even though they would no longer come to her house. I spent most of my time at Deanny's.

This state of affairs continued until Dr. Fred told my mother that David had to get out more. "He's rotting away up there," he said. "This disease is as hard on the mind as it is the body. He needs some relief from it."

My mother didn't say anything. In his room, David was barricaded from the prejudice of my grandmother. My mother also wanted to shield him from the ugly truths playing themselves out beyond his door.

Uncle David didn't know, for example, that I had been asked to stay out of the town library. One afternoon, when I had walked in to get a book, Mrs. Frail told me I would have to stay away for a time, until this thing with my uncle straightened itself out. My mother was incensed. She called Mrs. Frail, who prevaricated. I was being prevented, she said, from entering the library due to a town ordinance.

"What ordinance?" asked my mother.

"I don't remember. Perhaps you should contact the mayor." Mrs. Frail would say no more.

At dinner my mother said if she wasn't so angry she would be forced to laugh. "Don't these people hear themselves? Don't they know how ridiculous they sound?"

Jeanette nodded.

My grandmother stayed silent. She had overheard when Dr. Fred said David needed to get out more. After he left, she asked what the mechanics of such a venture might be. "Surely you know you can't just waltz out the front door with him," she said. "The neighbourhood would never allow it."

"I'm tired of what the neighbourhood will and won't allow," said my mother. "I'm sick to death of having to dance around their ignorance."

"Mark my words," said my grandmother. "Trouble will come of it."

"I don't care," my mother said. "If Dr. Fred says it will be good for him, then we'll do it. Who would you rather keep happy? David? Or a bunch of gossipmongering cowards with not a drop of sense or understanding?"

These were unusually harsh and vicious words for my mother, who normally didn't speak poorly of anyone. But she was angry, and I think Dr. Fred's gentle remonstrance had made her feel slightly ashamed. She had allowed the reaction of the town to dictate her own behaviour, and denied my uncle some comfort and relief because of it.

∎∎∎

ON THE DAY of my twelfth birthday, I got up at eight and went downstairs, forgetting for the first half hour I was actually twelve. I only remembered when I glanced into the living room and saw the gifts wrapped in brightly coloured paper and stacked high on the living room sofa. I always got a lot of gifts on my birthday; in a way, it was better than Christmas, because there were no socks or pants or running shoes among the lot. They were always toys, and things I had specifically asked for. Even my grandmother usually went all out and bought me three or four things. This year I asked for a Commodore 64 to replace my old Vic-20, and was anxious as to whether or not I had received it. The Commodore was an expensive gift, and though usually there was no limit on what I could ask for, I was not sure the Commodore fit my grandmother's dictum of "within reason."

I was tempted to check the size and heft of the presents for the most likely candidate, when I heard scuffling of slippers in the kitchen behind me. I expected my mother, but when I stepped inside I saw it was my uncle standing in front of the fridge with the door open. He was looking for something. This was the first time since he had come home from the hospital I had seen him outside of his room, except to go to the bathroom.

As my uncle reached one bony hand into the fridge he became aware of me.

"Hello Jacob," he said.

He looked worse than usual. I almost didn't recognize him. But his voice sounded exactly the same. Calm and measured. It was strange hearing my uncle's voice coming out of this very sick man.

"Hello, Uncle David."

"Can you find the margarine for me? I can't seem to locate it."

Nobody else was around. My mother and Jeanette had taken my grandmother to town at exactly eight so she could beat the rush at the grocery store. He stole these few moments to emerge from his prison on the second floor and get some toast and tea. I'm certain, in retrospect, he hadn't known I was there.

I found the margarine for him. He poured the tea. I poured cereal for myself.

My uncle asked me to sit with him. I was suddenly as fearful as the rest of the town of catching whatever it was my uncle had. This was only natural. I was only twelve, and for weeks I had been hearing concerns about his infectiousness, mostly in regards to me. I had not given it much thought before because I barely saw him. His disease remained mysterious and remote. Yet here he was this morning. I imagined those purple flowers blooming on my own face. My own hands so elongated and thin. My own eyes so sunken in their sockets. I shrank away from my uncle's every movement, even when he reached forward to dip his knife in the margarine, which he did several times.

He must have noticed this. After he had finished only one piece of toast he said he guessed he would take his tea and go back upstairs. He had difficulty carrying it. The hand with the cup shook. As he passed the doorjamb he held on to it for support. The cup was shaking so badly I thought it would spill.

I should have offered to help him. But I didn't. God help me, I didn't.

At that moment I was as guilty as everyone else in the town in thinking my uncle was a doomed pariah.

It was a terrible tone to set for my birthday.

■ ■ ■

BY TEN O'CLOCK, everyone had come back from the grocery store. I asked my mother if we could go pick up Deanny. I had only told her the night before that Deanny was coming, and my mother was delighted, though she was worried about Cameron not being present. Deanny was to be my only guest. My mother knew better than to invite anyone else. Besides the fact I didn't have any friends from town, none of their parents would let them come.

My grandmother used this as another opportunity to state what an effect this whole affair was having on me. "The boy can't celebrate properly," she said. "I hope you realize what a toll this must be taking on him, Caroline."

My mother had the decency not to answer.

She agreed readily it was time to pick up Deanny. By then I had spoken of her a few times, but not much. My mother knew she lived on Meadow Pond Lane. My grandmother did not. I was afraid to tell her about Deanny, in case she viewed the arrival with all the enthusiasm of having a leper, or another case like my uncle, over for the afternoon. I knew what she thought of Meadow Pond Lane and those who lived there.

I was a little worried, I admit, about Deanny spending any amount of time with my grandmother. She swore more than any kid I'd ever met. Since I hadn't seen her in the presence of adults, I didn't know if she toned it down for them. My grandmother did not like swearing. She did not allow it. She was currently not talking to Jeanette, who had called her a bitch the day before over an argument about my uncle. *Bitch* was barely in Deanny's vocabulary as a mild curse word. She preferred *cunt* and *fuck* to practically any others. I couldn't imagine what would happen to my grandmother if she heard those coming out of Deanny's mouth. A heart attack, or an aneurism. She might banish her from the house never to return, and forbid me from ever stepping foot on Meadow Pond Lane again.

Because my mother didn't drive, my Aunt Jeanette picked up Deanny. I went with her. My mother stayed home to ice my birthday cake and get ready for the party. Although I didn't realize it, both my aunt and my mother were prepared to love Deanny, if for nothing else than because she was allowed to come to our house when everyone else was being warned to stay away.

Even past the point where her parents must have known what was going on, Deanny was never asked to stay away from Tenerife Street. If she was, she never listened. Her parents were either completely indifferent, or more educated than the rest of the town. I tend to think the former. Deanny's father was always drunk, and Deanny's mother was so busy trying to hold the impoverished household together she didn't have time to inquire after her.

Deanny herself was never afraid of my uncle's "cooties." She told me before the party she was kind of excited to see him. "Is he all gross?" she said. "Like sores and stuff?"

"Some sores," I told her, thinking of the little purple spots. "And he's kinda thin." I told her about the bird infection in his brain.

"A bird brain," Deanny said. "Cool."

Deanny had made an attempt, I realized as soon as she came out of the house, to dress up. She didn't have much fashion sense, nor money to adhere to one if she did. Most of her clothes were hand-me-downs or bought from Frenchies in town. She rarely wore jeans, mostly pull-on polyester slacks and largish tops that hung too far down. Today the slacks were canary yellow, the top lime green. The same old filthy sneakers. Her hair was still wet from her bath. She came to the car, not smiling, and climbed in the back seat.

I turned around and introduced her to my aunt. Then I held my breath. Anything at all could have come out of her mouth at this moment.

But all she said was "Hi." She scowled and looked out the window.

My aunt said hello, it was nice to meet her, and backed out of the driveway. She tried to engage Deanny in conversation the entire way back into town, but my friend wouldn't respond. She only looked out the window with that fierce, angry expression on her face. I would learn, over the years, this was Deanny's default look, one she assumed in times of uncertainty or shyness. It was a self-defence measure. It was easier to look mad and have people leave her alone than look vulnerable and have them attack her, or worse, pity her. She would come around, eventually, as the day wore on. But for the first few hours it was uncomfortable. Even to my grandmother she would give barely more than a word.

My grandmother, for her part, acted with shocked surprise when she saw her. "Good heavens," she said, as soon as Deanny was out of earshot. "Who dresses that child?"

"Mom!" hissed my mother. "Cut it out."

"She looks as if she just stepped from Barnum and Bailey's."

Deanny was suitably impressed with my grandmother's house, which would have, on any other day, perhaps made her more favourable in my grandmother's eyes. My grandmother loved it when guests complimented her decorating skills, or the carefully designed interior of her home. As soon as Deanny stepped in the front door, behind me but ahead of my Aunt Jeanette, she said, "Holy shit! Look at this place. It's a mansion!"

Unfortunately, my grandmother was in the kitchen and heard every word. She came into the hallway wiping her hands on a dishtowel and said, "We don't talk that way here, little girl. This is a house of God."

"No kidding," Deanny said, completely unperturbed. "It's like a church in here."

I suppose, to Deanny, who lived in a rundown shack on Meadow Pond Lane, the house on Tenerife Street did seem grand. There were bigger houses in town, but Deanny had not been in any of them.

This was her first introduction to Advocate society, though I did not think of it that way. One of the benefits of growing up with two waitresses as influences was that I was not a snob. This despite my grandmother's best efforts to make me one. I didn't look down on people for where they lived or what they did for a living or how much money they had. I never thought of the house I lived in as particularly impressive or grand. It was a house.

If Deanny had any thought about tearing through it the way we ran through her yard my grandmother soon set her straight. She laid down the law. "You can't go into the living room," she said. "I've spent too many years collecting what's there to have it all broken in an afternoon. And the study is out, and the same for all the bedrooms except Jacob's. You can play in the TV room, but not the dining room. It's filled with my china. And if you go outdoors stay away from my flowers and my gnomes."

Deanny stared up at my grandmother, who had, perhaps unconsciously, hunched over my little friend like a witch from a fairytale. I stood there, embarrassed for both of them. Jeanette came to the rescue. "Geez Mom," she said. "Give her a break. She just got in the door."

"Just going over the dos and don'ts," said my grandmother. "Now run along and play until we're ready for you. And remember what I said."

I took Deanny up to my room.

"Goddamned," she said. "It's like living with Hitler."

"Worse," I said. "Hitler didn't have fine china."

Deanny laughed. That was the first time I remember Deanny laughing at one of my jokes, and it felt good. Cameron didn't laugh at anything I said. He rarely laughed at all. Deanny and I played in my room for an hour, until my grandmother called us down for lunch — hotdogs and french fries — after which my official birthday party was to begin.

It would just be my family, and Deanny. I wasn't excited.

Deanny was, though. She was hoping she would see my uncle.

"He won't be there," I told her. "He hardly ever comes out of his room."

"Can we go in and see him?"

"Not allowed," I told her. "I haven't been there in ages."

"Dammit Jacob! This place is like a fucking prison!"

"Don't let my grandmother here you talk like that. She'll kick you out."

"That's the thing," said Deanny. "You can't kick people out of a prison. You can only keep them in."

Deanny was smart. Smarter even than I had given her credit for.

■ ■ ■

THE THING I hate most about birthdays is the singing of the dreaded song. It's not that one person is always off-key — I am not that much of a puritan — or that it is copyrighted and a royalty should be paid to the patent holder every time it is sung, and that a documentary about Martin Luther King Jr. was unavailable for many years because the song was sung in it and the film couldn't clear copyright. No. I hate the song because its singing is tinged with moments of supreme embarrassment, where every eye is upon you, you don't know what to do with your hands or what expression you should wear on your face — outright mortification generally considered to be unacceptable — and you just want to find the nearest set of floorboards and slither down the crack between them.

I knew nothing about copyright laws when I was twelve. I only knew I was dreading the moment when the cake would come, the embarrassment, and the blowing out of candles that would follow.

Deanny seemed to enjoy my discomfort. She sang directly into my face, and her breath smelled like spearmint gum, which she had been chewing all morning to mask the smell of smoke on her breath. My mother and Aunt Jeanette and my grandmother kissed me, and then we set to opening presents. The cake presentation and attendant musical humiliation took place in the kitchen, but my grandmother thought it safe, now that refreshments were taken and there was nothing to spill on the carpet, to retire to the living room. I was seated on the floor with gifts piled up around me like a fortress, and I opened them one by one.

I got the Commodore 64.

It was one of the first presents I opened. Being from my grandmother, it was the most expensive gift. Deanny was impressed by the sheer number of presents. She didn't know what the computer was and I had to explain it to her. I opened the rest of my gifts — toys and books and games — and everyone oohed and awed over them. At the end of it, after my grandmother had cleared up the wrapping paper, my mother surveyed me on the floor surrounded by a mountain of gifts and asked if I was happy.

"Yup," I told her. "Can I go set up my computer?"

"I don't see why not," said my mother. "We'll go to the bowling alley at three."

Deanny and I went into my room to hook up the computer. I had received several games compatible for the system. I loaded one, *Adventure Quest,* for Deanny. It was a game I had played many times at Cameron's. She was puzzled by it, and admitted to me she had never played a video game before. In this respect, I considered her hopelessly uneducated, and did my best to show her the fundamentals. She thought it was boring — moving a bunch of stick figures around on a screen — and wanted to go outside instead. But I was already a child of the virtual. I had moved into this electronic world, and I insisted we stay inside and play.

Deanny chewed gum, snapped it, and looked around my room for something to do. Unfortunately, she found the Easy-Bake Oven and other assorted girls' toys in my closet. "Are these yours?" she asked.

"No," I answered quickly. "They're just there."

"Liar," Deanny said, grinning maliciously. "I think you play with them. What, are you a fag or something?"

I ignored Deanny's question, and asked if she wanted to go outside.

"I hope you don't play with girls' clothes too," Deanny taunted. "Jacob in a little dress. Jacob with high heel shoes."

"Quit it," I said. I wanted to be mad at her, but I couldn't. That she was taking an interest in my life, even if it was a negative interest, pleased me. I suggested we go for a walk downtown and spend some of my birthday money. I had raked it in that afternoon, almost thirty dollars in cold hard cash.

She had opened her mouth to answer, when my door opened — slowly, as if a ghost was entering.

In a way, it *was* a ghost.

It was my uncle.

He was no longer in the blue bathrobe. He was wearing jeans and a white sweater, even though it was warm outside. Despite his attempts to dress himself up, the effect was ghastly. The clothes he had brought with him were now too big, and dangled off his frame. He had combed and wetted his hair, but hastily, so that licks of it stood up here and there. His face was marred with purple spots as it always was and his breathing was shallow. He was deathly pale.

"Jacob?" he said.

Deanny was still in my closet, so he did not see her as he came into the room. In one hand he held a small wrapped gift. He cleared the door and looked at me, where I stood in front of the computer, and smiled.

"I brought you a present," he said. "Happy Birthday."

Deanny stepped out from the closet. She had to, otherwise she wouldn't have been able to see my uncle. She was drawn, despite herself. The general wheeziness of his breath, she said later, frightened her. Deanny admitted to being frightened by very little. But the image in her mind's eye of my wasting, physically dissolute uncle needed to be matched with the reality.

As soon as he saw her, my uncle asked, "Who's this?"

When I introduced him, Deanny said a timid hello. I had never heard her be timid before, and I was as fascinated with that as I was with my uncle's arrival. He had not been in my room since he had grown really sick, and I had not expected to see him. I made no move to retrieve the gift, and my uncle was forced to make his way over — he looked as if he was walking on glass — to hand it to me. I realized then my uncle was probably, at that point, even sicker than he looked, and he was dressing up and pretending he was all right for my sake.

The present was wrapped in plain purple paper with no bow. Almost the colour of my old Easy-Bake Oven.

"You don't have to open it now," said my uncle. "I just wanted you to know I was thinking about you. Did you have a good birthday, Jake?"

I nodded. Suddenly I felt like crying. Part of it was seeing my uncle with Deanny in the room, for the first time seeing him through someone else's eyes, so tired and thin and sad. Another was the gift he gave me, so small and inconsequential compared to the sheer volume and size of the other gifts I had received, but one he must have wrapped himself and made such an effort to come down the hall and give to me. I was so overcome that, not wanting to cry in front of my friend, I tore the paper off the gift and let it fall to the floor.

As I suspected, it was a book.

"It's used, I'm afraid," said my uncle. "I could have given your mother money to pick me up something, but I wanted to give you something of my own. I hope you'll read it. It's my favourite novel."

My uncle's favourite novel was *To Kill a Mockingbird* by Harper Lee.

I had never read it.

That is no longer the case.

That book is now *my* favourite novel, and though I didn't know it then, my uncle had given me his most prized possession. It was a first edition, signed by the author herself: "With Best Wishes, Harper Lee."

It was worth about two thousand dollars in 1984 and much more than that now.

My mother had no idea what he gave me, and he did not tell me what made the book so special or that it was worth so much money. He only told me that I was to look after it. "It means a lot to me," he said. "And I hope someday it will mean a lot to you."

I should have hugged my uncle. But he seemed to understand I couldn't and he turned to go. He told Deanny it was nice to meet her. She, speechless for a change, only nodded. She was being confronted by the Great Presence. Years later, when we were both adults, she would tell me meeting my uncle that day was one of the most significant moments in her young life. "Death has a way of cutting through the thin veneer of daily living," she said, "and forcing you to consider how things really are, and not how you want them to be. Seeing your uncle like that made me kind of scared and excited at the same time. I think it was the first real thing I had ever witnessed, like the first time you have sex and realize the power of the everyday. I'll never forget it."

Deanny and I went downstairs. We played in the yard, and after that my mother took us bowling.

# 4

MY MOTHER AND Jeanette had decided that the afternoon of my birthday would be a good day to take my uncle outside. The weather was fine and we could all go together. But I did not want to go on a walk with my uncle. I did not wish to show him off for Deanny and the neighbourhood. He was a human being, not a sideshow exhibit or circus freak. At twelve I had not much developed in the way of moral philosophy or ethics, but I still did not think it right to accompany my uncle just so Deanny could see the spots on his face. Upon receipt of his gift, I had discovered a new and strange kind of sympathy for him. I did not want to feel sorry for him in front of my friend or mother.

Deanny beat us all at bowling. She threw the ball at the pins as if they had done her personal injury. Whenever she knocked any down, she shouted, "Samurai!" My mother and Aunt Jeanette got a kick out of this. When I bowled, Deanny would try and psyche me out during the set-up. "Sucker!" she'd call out. "Watch out for the gutters. They've got your name on it!"

When I complained Deanny was being a bad sport and breaking my concentration, my mother told me to hush. "She's your friend, and your guest," she said. "Let her have her fun."

I was glad when bowling with Deanny the Samurai was over

When we got home, my mother went upstairs to get my uncle. Aunt Jeanette took the wheelchair from the garage and wrestled it open and into place on the front walk. I told Deanny I was not going on the walk. I wanted to stay home and play video games instead, and I thought she should do the same. She whined about it.

"But I want to go," she said. "Maybe your uncle needs the company."

Deanny no more wanted to provide company than I wanted to provide moral support. Our friendship was still new, but I "laid down the law," as my grandmother would have it. "You can go if you want," I said. "But I'm staying here."

She nodded, and went outside. A few minutes later my aunt came to my room and told me I was coming along, that I was not to leave my friend alone for the sake of a video game. I was mad at Deanny for going over my head, but I couldn't refuse. My aunt so rarely gave me orders.

■ ■ ■

MY GRANDMOTHER SAID she did not want my uncle walking in the neighbourhood because he might catch cold, get pneumonia, get sicker than he was. This was a lie, designed to make her opposition more palatable to her daughters. It was not that she wasn't concerned with the health of her only son; she was, or she would never have relented and let him stay with us. My grandmother believed beyond the point of reason the disease was contagious, and she knew for certain the town believed it.

Walking past her bedroom, I noticed my grandmother's door was still shut. I thought I heard her talking in there, and assumed she was on the phone. Later we would find out she was — to Hazel, her bridge playing partner and the town gossip.

That afternoon, however, we were all unaware my grandmother was setting us up. We busied ourselves getting my uncle in the chair and down the walk, which proved to be no easy task. He could walk around the inside of the house, but he did not have the stamina to take a walk down the street any distance by himself. No matter what he thought of the wheelchair, he had to use it if he wanted to go outside. There would soon come a time when he couldn't get to the bathroom without help from a walker or his sisters, but at this stage my mother left the wheelchair outside and let my uncle come down the stairs and out the front door on his own. He did so slowly, still wearing the jeans and the sweater. My mother asked him if it wouldn't be too hot for him.

"I don't think so," he said. "I'm feeling a chill today."

Despite my mother's contempt for my grandmother and her irrational fears, she had a few of her own. No one was allowed to touch David. As difficult as it was to watch him make his way slowly down the stairs, holding on to the banister with both hands, we were not to help him. Her directions for me were clear. Don't go into his room. Don't touch him at any cost. Deanny and my aunt waited outside and my mother and I stayed inside to watch, making sure he didn't fall. If he had, I don't know what we would have done. Perhaps my mother would have got rubber gloves — something she actually did later on, when he got so ill he needed to be helped out of bed — or called the ambulance, leaving him shattered and broken on the floor, the way my grandmother's bowl had been.

But my uncle made it, and when he reached the bottom, panting for breath, he smiled. "This walk will kill me, I think," he said.

"Nonsense," said my mother. "It will be good for you."

Another few minutes and he was out the door. Once outside, and down the front steps, he sat in the wheelchair and Aunt Jeanette pushed him down the walk. We all took up our places. Jeanette pushing. Deanny beside the chair, remarkably close to my uncle. My mother on the other side of the chair. Me, trailing behind.

"What a wonderful day!" said my uncle. "I'd forgotten what the outdoors was like."

"Let's experience it then," said my aunt. "Ready, David?"

"I'm ready," said my uncle.

My aunt pushed him slowly forward and our little caravan began to proceed north on Tenerife Street and away from the embedded silence of my grandmother's house. I felt glad for my uncle suddenly, glad that he could get out, that he could feel the warmth of the sun on his face for the first time in over a month. It was a fine day, as all the days that summer were. The upcoming school year held promise, I felt. Despite losing my best friend and being banned from the library I would get through this. Perhaps my uncle would even get better, and life would go back to the way it had always been.

This optimism would be short-lived. The town, and my grandmother's phone call, would make sure of it. Later, when my mother asked her why she had done it, she said it was because "people had a right to know. To be safe in their own yards."

"Safe!" my mother had cried. "What on earth is going to put them in danger?"

My grandmother didn't answer. We all knew what she thought, and my mother knew how ridiculous it was. We were trying to give

David some sunshine and hope, and my grandmother was acting like we were bringing Typhoid Mary to town.

"I hope you know what you've done," my mother said finally. "You've ruined a perfectly good day for him."

"I can't help it," my grandmother said. "I'm only doing what I think is right, Caroline."

My grandmother was so often doing what she thought was right, only to discover days and years down the road it was wrong. But she never admitted this. One of the chief characteristics of my grandmother's personality is she could never admit to a mistake. She could act it, by being contrite in certain situations or mellowing for a time. But she'd never admit to one directly.

■ ■ ■

THE STRANGEST THING about Tenerife Street was its name. It was, for a hundred years, called Maple Street, until the nineteen sixties, when the town went on a spate of renaming streets and parks to make itself seem more exotic. The experiment was doomed. Advocate has never been alluring. It is practical. Prosaic, and utilitarian to the extreme. Set fifteen miles inland, it is a mill town with nothing to offer tourists except a small museum and a picnic park by the river. But the municipal council thought that by simply changing a few names, they could make it a destination.

When it came to my grandmother's street, it was because a man on the council had just returned from a trip to the Canary Islands and thought "Tenerife" sounded suitably romantic. He proposed the name change at one of their meetings, and residents of the street were given a chance to speak on the subject.

Both my grandmother and grandfather spoke against. Yes, Maple Street was a misnomer. There were no maples — it was lined with oak and chestnut trees. But my grandmother did not think this justified naming her street after some city on some island she had ever heard of. "You might as well name it German Street. Or Egypt Avenue," she said. "All of them make about as much sense."

Despite the impassioned pleas, the name was changed, though for years my grandmother refused to acknowledge it. Eventually, though, because of mailing addresses and giving directions, she was forced to capitulate. She still complained. "Naming a street after a foreign town makes about as much sense as naming a pig after a barn." She called it Maple Street in her conversations with old friends, and she never forgave the family of the man who first proposed changing it. Several times Grandnan's friends suggested she run for council, but she always turned them down. She was content with criticizing rather than affecting any change. It was safer that way.

The rest of us never thought of Tenerife Street as anything else, even though my mother, Jeanette, and David were old enough to mark the change. Jeanette liked it. She said though it didn't add any spice, at least it wasn't xenophobic. "Nigeria Street would have been better, I think."

Uncle David had been to the actual Tenerife. He told my mother and Jeanette this as we walked on the afternoon of my birthday.

Deanny was silent, but kept stealing looks at my uncle, as if surprised such a rational, semi-normal voice could come out of so sick of a man. Because we were wrapped up in my uncle's story it took us a few minutes to notice something was not quite right. My mother saw it first.

"It's quiet as a ghost town," she said. Indeed, whereas on any other fine Saturday men and women would be on their lawns and in their gardens, there was nothing. The lawns were immaculate and empty — as devoid of life as the tundra. No children. No husbands puttering and waving. Nobody in windows. No dogs. No cats.

We all noticed it.

"Seems like there's something good on TV," said my uncle.

"Or something bad outside," said my aunt.

My uncle reacted — his head moved slightly back and to the side, as if trying to see Jeanette — but then he stopped and focused forward. He must have known what my aunt was thinking. He must have been thinking it himself. His shoulders didn't slump, though. There was no sign of capitulation or defeat.

"Who cares?" my mother said. "Let's just enjoy our walk."

But Jeanette wasn't listening. "What do they think? They're gonna get it just by being outside?"

"That's exactly what they think," said my uncle. "As hard as it is to believe."

"Damn ignorance," said my mother. "I wish they'd all go to hell!"

My mother rarely said things like this, and it took us all by surprise. She was to the left of my uncle, and didn't see what I saw. He reached out to take her hand, then thought better of it, and pulled it quickly back into his lap.

"Don't worry about it, Caroline," he said. "It's not their fault. They just don't know."

"But getting it from the air? Can they be that stupid?"

Deanny and I were both confused by this sudden turn in the conversation. I kept silent, but Deanny spoke up. "Get what?" she said. "Your cooties?"

Our trip that day could have been ruined — would have, I think — if it wasn't for Deanny. My uncle broke into great peals of convulsive laughter. He laughed so hard he had to lean forward to recover. He began coughing. Jeanette stopped pushing the wheelchair and she and mother grew concerned. He waved them away. "Cooties?" he said to Deanny. "That's what you call this?"

Deanny just shrugged. "That's what it is, isn't it?"

"Yes, Deanny," he said, and though I was behind him I could sense the smile on his face. "It's cooties. A bad set, I'm afraid. But I like that word the best of all I've heard. Thank you for telling me."

"No prob," she said. "And if anyone says anything to you about them, I'll take care of them, Dave. Leave it to me."

"I'm sure you will, Deanny," my Uncle David said. "I don't doubt that for a second."

■ ■ ■

TENERIFE STREET RUNS straight for six blocks and then curves off before it ends on Fartham Avenue. Our plan was to go to Fartham and then see how my uncle felt. We no longer discussed the absence of neighbours, or Tenerife.

Aunt Jeanette and my mother and David started the remember game, which they often did, about various incidents from their childhood. They recalled the time when they were little more than toddlers, and David had got hold of a pair of scissors and cut all their hair. Unfortunately this happened the day before my grandmother had scheduled a family portrait to be taken, and she had to take them all to the hairdressers to have it fixed.

"They did the best they could," Aunt Jeanette said, "but we still looked awful. In those photographs we look like Larry, Curly, and Moe." My mother and uncle laughed. Deanny didn't laugh, but she did start to skip alongside my uncle in the wheelchair. This was the only feminine trait she had, and one I did not dare make fun of.

When we came around the corner, Deanny's skip died, as did the laughter. There, in front of John Collins' house, not twenty yards from us, was gathered a small knot of people. Most of them men, and all of them from the neighbourhood. The two women with them stood behind, and when we turned the corner one of them pointed. The men, who had been talking together, turned to face us. So surprised were we by this impromptu gathering of people on the sidewalk that we stopped.

"What's going on?" said Jeanette. "A fire?"

Her supposition was understandable. Usually gatherings like this only took place on the street when there was something wrong in one of the houses. We assumed there was something amiss in John Collins' house, but before we could ask, Collins himself stepped forward. He was a short, bald, stocky man of about fifty who had lived in the neighbourhood fifteen years — still a new neighbour, in my grandmother's eyes. "Hello!" he called out, even though we were close enough to hear if he talked normally.

"Hello," called my Aunt Jeanette back. "What's wrong? Is there a fire?"

Collins smiled, but it seemed forced. My Aunt Jeanette must have thought so too, for she just stood there, her head cocked to one side, puzzled.

"No fire," said John. "I was wondering if I could talk to one of you for a minute?"

My aunt shrugged, and began to push my uncle forward. He, for his part, said nothing. I think he knew what this was about long before Jeanette and my mother figured it out.

Collins raised his hand. "Not all of you," he said. "Just you Jeanette, if you don't mind. Please leave David behind."

The first clue. My aunt looked at my mother.

"Go on," my mother said. "Go see what they want."

"You come with me," Aunt Jeanette said.

It was the strangest thing. We had known these people for years. They had been to my grandmother's house and we to theirs. They had eaten our food, sat beside us at church, driven past us a thousand times and waved. And now suddenly they felt, if not dangerous, then at least worthy of caution. I knew nothing of lynch mobs then. If I had, I would have realized this is what they felt like. Not that they were going to hang my uncle from a tree. Not exactly. But when my mother and Jeanette said they would be right back and went over to talk, and the crowd gathered close around them, I felt a sudden, seemingly irrational fear in the pit of my stomach. Surely I had nothing to fear from people I knew as well as this, but the sensation persisted.

I started to step forward, but my uncle reached out and grabbed my arm to stop me. I forgot at that moment I was not supposed to touch him, and I guess he forgot he was not supposed to touch me.

"Easy Jacob," he said. "Let's just see what all of this is about."

It started calmly enough. At first my mother and Jeanette were just talking. No one touched them. There were no reassuring hands laid on unreasoning shoulders. Then Jeanette, who was fully obscured by those surrounding her, could be heard over the low voices of the others. "You've got to be kidding!" she said. I could not hear my mother, but I could see her. Her expression was one of supreme annoyance melding to anger. I had seen her wear it only when in the throes on an unwinnable argument with my grandmother. Someone was standing beside her, and I could tell, far from being angry with her, they were only trying to reason with her. But my mother wouldn't listen.

The scene being played out was obvious, even to me. Jeanette and my mother were getting a talking to for bringing my uncle out into the street. They told my mother and Jeanette all kinds of nonsense. That AIDS was transmitted through the air, and through mosquitoes, and even that it crawled over grass. That bringing my uncle out in daylight and in fresh air put the entire neighbourhood at risk. That no one knew anything about this disease, and that our family had no right, no right at all, to play with the lives of others.

"It's a judgment from God," said one.

My aunt screamed, "If it was a judgment from God, you'd all have it!"

"Oh Christ," my uncle moaned from his chair.

Eventually my mother stormed back over to us. She was enraged. "You'll never guess …" she began, but my uncle interrupted her.

"I know," he said. "Let's just go home."

"Go home!" cried my mother. "How long do you think it'll be before they ask us to move! How can we let them get away with this?"

"I'm tired," said Uncle David. "I don't have the energy or the will to fight them, Caroline. Let's just leave."

Jeanette gave another screech and started walking towards us. The knot of people had drawn even closer together now, more unified. She turned halfway and shouted back at them. "I don't know how you live with yourselves! You're superstitious, uneducated, mindless fools! Every single one of you."

She too tried to tell my uncle what had happened, and once more he asked to be taken home instead.

"But if we do that," Jeanette said, and I could see she was nearly in tears, "they win."

"It's not about winning or losing," Uncle David said. He was not near tears. He was too sick, and too used to such displays, to be much moved by them. "It's just about maintaining a little dignity. And the only way I can do that now is to get back to bed. I'm very tired."

There was nothing more anyone could say. They agreed to go back.

No one had noticed Deanny. She had been standing beside my uncle's chair, clenching and unclenching her fists, watching the scene play out before her. Of all of us, I think now, she was the most affected by it. I'm not sure why. Perhaps because of her family, of having to deal with little knots of opposition all her life. Or perhaps she had some empathy for my uncle. She knew what it was like to have cooties, and to have no one want to play with you because of them.

The men and women on the other side of invisible line were talking together and looking furtively over at us. Deanny stood still, staring violently back at them. Then she took two steps forward and let out a stream of invective so powerful that it took my breath away.

Deanny was always a master at swearing, but nothing I had seen in her to date matched this. She called them everything she could think of, including some words and phrases I'm sure had never been heard on Tenerife Street. Before she was halfway done, she had the mesmerized attention of every man and woman in the opposing camp. My mother, Jeanette, and my uncle tried to stop her, but they couldn't. She kept shouting until the band of people, under such an onslaught, began to disperse.

Under any other circumstances she would never have gotten away with it. They would have spoken back. Taken her in hand. Tried to teach her a lesson. A dozen other clichés on how to discipline a child. But they didn't.

When Deanny was done, there wasn't a single person left. They had all gone back to their homes. She cursed the last one in the door. After she finished, she turned to us. Her expression was vague. No one knew what to say to her. She had done what we could not. She had chased them away, and because they had gone without so much as a word of protest, she had proven to us, and to them, that they knew they were wrong.

My aunt only told her to come along. My mother put a hand on her shoulder. My uncle asked her mildly where she had learned the word *cooties*.

# SIX

∎

WHEN I WAS a boy, my favourite festival in Advocate was the Orange Day parade. It was held each year to celebrate the victory of William of Orange over James II in the Battle of Boyne in 1690.

As a boy I did not know the etiology.

I only knew in our town the day was considered special, as much of a holiday as Easter or Thanksgiving. On the Catholic side of the river, booths were set up on Main Street to serve food and host games of chance and a band was hired to play. The same happened on the Protestant side, on Orange Street — also named after the indefatigable Protestant pretender to the crown — parallel to the river. Visitors to the town for the festival would go back and forth across the Main Street Bridge to partake of the festivities on both sides.

Aunt Jeanette and practically everyone else on the Catholic side went to the Protestant celebration as well, but my grandmother kept her feet planted firmly on our side of the river. Catholics did not celebrate Orange Day. Orange was Protestant. What the Catholics *did* celebrate was Lemon Day.

Lemon Day and Orange Day drew visitors to our town. No one had ever heard of a town so neatly divided along religious lines that one mocked the rituals and festivals of the other, hundreds of years after such antipathy was considered unusual. No one had ever heard of a Lemon Day parade.

When it was first held, a hundred years ago, in sardonic answer to those marching across the river, it was in deadly earnest. The Catholics were both taunting and professing; they wanted to let the Protestants know they weren't the only ones proud of their faith. The lemons were an afterthought, to show how silly it was to march down a street on a hot summer day in honour of a man named after a tropical fruit. There was never any violence on parade day in Advocate, though. Perhaps this was owing to the geographical separation by the river.

In the 1980s, when I was old enough to witness, the divide was more a joke than anything. A large painted papier-mâché lemon, the size of a kitchen table, was drawn on a wooden cart down Main Street with lines of people walking behind bearing fresh lemons in their hands. On the Protestant side they bore oranges, signs of their faith, and pictures of William III. Occasionally someone on the Catholic side would carry a picture of Pope John Paul II.

Now, I'm told, the parades are dying out. Religious schism is no longer the curiosity it once was. Either it is taken very seriously, as it is in the Middle East, or no one pays any attention at all. The latter is the case in Advocate. Fewer and fewer people march in the parades each year, and fewer tourists come to see them.

But when I was boy, it was still an event. Both parades were an accepted part of Advocate culture — and an important one too. They drew hundreds, from around the province and even the Boston States, who wanted to see such a display of religious antagonism, even if it was now only for show. Thus the booths and the food and the games. Local shopkeepers made a lot of money on that day, and it brought much needed revenue for the town.

I was four before I was allowed to march in the parade, with my mother and Aunt Jeanette and my grandmother. The lemon my grandmother gave me was too big for my hand and I kept dropping it. I was fascinated by the papier-mâché lemon drawn on the wagon by old Colin Meizner. I thought it was real — the great grandmother to the itty-bitty baby lemons we held in our hands. I thought when the parade was over, we would cut it and each get a piece. I didn't realize that lemons are sour; my only experience with them was lemonade, which was sweet.

My grandmother wanted to give me a small photo of the pope, but my mother wouldn't let her. She said she didn't want this to be political.

"Political?" said my grandmother. "What's political about a little boy showing his devotion to his faith?"

She had forgotten that technically I was not a Catholic. I had still not been baptized. My mother insisted I could make that decision for myself when I was old enough. "And what if something happens in the meantime?" my grandmother often said. "Are you going to be responsible for the direction of his soul?"

Ironically, the Lemon/Orange Day parade — the most religious celebration in Advocate — held the least religious tension, both in our family and in the town, of any holiday. We all had a good time. I remember the marching bands, always dropping my lemons, the hotdogs from the Ladies Church Auxiliary booth, Aunt Jeanette trying to win stuffed animals for me at the dart-and-balloon game and failing until the man took pity on her and gave her a small one. Because of my grandmother's conditioning, I was at first nervous about crossing the bridge to the Protestant side, which my mother and Aunt Jeanette always did to spread their money evenly around the town. But there was no difference, other than they wore orange shirts instead of yellow ones. The Protestants seemed to be having as much fun as we were, and there were just as many people.

■ ■ ■

I REMEMBER VERY little rain that summer. It was one of the hottest on record. My grandmother predicted, based on her trusty Farmers' Almanac, we would have a drought. Each day the farmers and the gardeners hoped for rain, but none came. Skies dawned blue and remained unblemished by cloud morning, afternoon, and evening. Water holes and mud sloughs dried up, and the level of water in the river fell dramatically, exposing banks and fluvial beds.

My mother and Jeanette looked forward to work because the diner was air-conditioned and my grandmother's house was not. They knew better than to ask her to buy one. She said they ate kilowatts the way elephants ate peanuts, and an oscillating fan and a drawn blind were as much a defence against the heat as anything else.

My grandmother didn't seem bothered by the heat. In a blue sun hat, white cotton blouse, and long slacks, she'd spend hours in the garden on the hottest days, barely breaking a sweat. She mowed the lawn at high noon. When my mother complained she was pushing herself too hard, Grandnan only waved her eldest daughter away. "These temperatures are nothing," she said. "When I was a child we got them every day in summer for a month, and we were still forced outside to do chores. Hot and cold, Caroline, are no deterrent to hard work and discipline. Things must be done, and they don't get done themselves just because of a little weather."

Deanny and I had taken to rock hopping — making our way across the river from rocks to hard deposits, exposed by low water level. Our goal was to see if we could make it the entire way across without touching water.

My grandmother heard of what we were doing, and warned us to stay away. Not just because we could fall in and drown — which was unlikely, since we stayed upstream where the low water meant little current — but because the standing water was filled with mosquitos and germs. "Beware the dog days," said my grandmother.

This was the name given by old wives to that time of year when the water was at its lowest and potent with disease.

Deanny and I didn't care about germs. We only wanted to see who could make it to the Protestant side without falling and stepping in mud up to our knees. Deanny usually won. She could leap from rock to rock with impressive balance and grace. Once, because of the way she landed on one foot on a rock and managed to hold herself there, teetering back and forth, never falling, until she steadied and brought her leg down, I said she should have been a ballerina.

She didn't like this.

She scowled at me.

Deanny didn't like to be told she could do anything feminine, even in a contest such as this. I was an ape, she said. I had the balance and grace of a box of nails. I could fall in and drown in duck shit for all she cared.

I never called Deanny a ballerina again.

I should have said she looked like a samurai. That would have suited her better.

## 2

MY UNCLE WAS in hospital several times that summer. Once, when infections surged in his body and his temperature rose to 104 and he became delirious; another, when he caught pneumonia. Each time, the ambulance came. Each time he stayed a few days before he was sent home. My mother and Jeanette questioned Dr. Fred as to why he was not being kept longer. He was getting worse, they said — shouldn't he be at the hospital where better care was available?

Dr. Fred admitted he should, but there was opposition at the hospital over my uncle's presence. The nurses refused to touch him and even the doctors were nervous. They continued to burn every-thing he touched, and wore Hazmat suits when they went into his room. Dr. Fred began to administer medications himself, setting up his IV. Once, he carried in Uncle David's tray when the orderly refused. Fred believed my uncle was better off at home, where at least my mother and aunt were willing to look after him. Even the ambulance attendants were afraid to touch him. They too wore gloves and gowns and facemasks and handled him as little as possible. Dr. Fred said it made him angry, that these people who had sworn an oath to heal couldn't get past their own prejudice to attend to a patient. It made him, he said, want to give up medicine and become a water polo instructor. Dr. Fred was resigned to the prob-lem, however, and he taught my mother and Jeanette how to care for my uncle.

He admitted he had called a friend from medical school who worked in Toronto to ask how they were dealing with similar patients. The problem, he was told, existed there as well — this unreasoning fear by the medical professional that in caring for an AIDS patient they themselves would get it. Fred figured it was worse in Advocate, because this was their first case. "Though," he told my mother, "if I know anything, David won't be our last."

After the incident on Tenerife Street, my uncle seemed to with-draw into himself. Though the door to his room was always open, so he could call out in case he needed anything, he came out less often. From my glimpses as I walked by, it was like a hospital in there, with trays and piles of extra blankets and the smell of camphor Aunt Jeanette rubbed on my uncle's chest when he had trouble breathing. Most times he lay on his bed, reading a book or resting. Sometimes he saw me and waved. Other times he didn't notice me at all. When my mother and aunt asked specifically what was wrong with him, Dr. Fred listed off a half dozen illnesses. These seemed to change from day to day.

By the middle of the summer my grandmother had given up hope of finding him his own place. No one wanted to rent to him. His condition had become common knowledge, and our neighbours and the townspeople wished to contain the problem to our house alone. My grandmother complained of this at every meal, after the ritual of preparing a tray that my mother or Jeanette would carry up to my uncle.

My mother would go in to see my uncle again before she came in to say goodnight to me. When I asked how he was, she would sigh and shake her head. She should have lied and said he was fine, but she was unable to keep up the charade. "Not well," she would say, or "Bad tonight."

The mood of the house became more somber with each passing day. The deeper my uncle sank into the swamp of his illness, the further we descended into the bog of our own despair. There was little laughter, and less relief. The canned gaiety of the television sounded tinny and false, and normal conversation was dampened by what was taking place upstairs.

My mother and Jeanette and even my grandmother became focused on petty details during this period. They set before themselves small tasks that could be accomplished in the face of the insurmountable.

My grandmother became obsessed with cleaning and rearranging things. She started wiping down walls, and moving furniture, and clearing out the garage and the basement. She corralled Deanny and I to assist her. We spent one afternoon polishing every piece of silver in her dining room cabinet, another mopping already spotless floors. With the promise of payment, and under her supervision, we went through every box and bag in the garage as she told us what to throw out and what to keep. She trusted us with red paint to redo the fence in the backyard as long as we didn't get any on the grass or her row of hostas.

My mother and Jeanette were more direct in their efforts. They fussed constantly over my uncle so that even he, as sick as he was, must have been driven to distraction by their constant presence.

I was able to escape these assignments by playing with Deanny for hours on end at the old mill or in the river, or riding beside her on my bike. Until I met her, Deanny hadn't owned a bike. My mother bought her one. She was wise enough not to get a girls' bike, without the crossbar and painted some hideous colour like purple or pink. This bike was black, with no speeds, and it looked rather mean. Deanny loved it. We ranged all over the town, usually with Deanny in the lead, shouting at me to catch up. She was impetuous, maniacal. We raced across bridges, dirt roads, and sidewalks. We flew through parks, narrowly missing mothers and babies on blankets. Deanny once wanted us to ride on the rails of the train tracks to see how far we could go before falling off. I took a spill after twenty feet. Deanny went nearly a hundred yards before she toppled off, laughing. We raced around and around the silos and ponds at the old mill, and the more muck she could find for us to slog through the happier she was. I came home coated in filth, and my grandmother screamed at me not to step foot in the house until I had washed myself off with the garden hose.

Their lives were shrinking while mine was expanding. Though I did not always feel as exhilarated as Deanny did sailing thirty kilometres an hour down a hill — there was always a little fear in me — at least I was spared the soul-killing routine maintained in my grandmother's house, this insistence on doing something small because nothing larger could be done. I stayed out of the house from waking until dusk, and only came home for meals and when it was time for bed.

Once Deanny was gone, I dreaded stepping back into the silence of the house. I usually went straight to my room and played video games until it was time to sleep. I had strange dreams. One was about sailing on a ship. Somewhere in the hold was a casket with a body. I could not get this out of my mind. In another, I was on a snow-covered plain, surrounded by wild dogs that wanted to tear me apart and eat me. I would wake up in the dead silence of the house, the pitch dark of my room, sweating, terrified. Some nights I barely slept at all.

■ ■ ■

WHEN CAMERON AND I were friends, we used to go to the Saturday Matinee at the Carlton Theatre all through the summer. Admission was a dollar. All the town kids went. The ticket-taker was a fat, grey-haired lady named Hilda. She smoked incessantly and she hated kids. She was constantly telling us to hold our horses and not to make a mess inside for someone else to clean up. We filed by her kiosk respectfully, in case she took it in her head to ban us for the day, which she would do with little provocation. Once inside, there was no such compunction. The kids laughed and talked and joked and flattened cardboard popcorn boxes and sent them sailing through the air. We booed and hissed in the event the projector broke down, which invariably it did, and we talked right along with the movie and made the dialogue coming from the small, tinny speakers in the theatre difficult to hear.

It was a zoo in there. Though I never threw popcorn boxes and didn't talk to anyone besides Cameron, I enjoyed the chaos of it, the one chance in the week for the inmates to run the asylum. The movies always started with a *Hinterland Who's Who*, a short documentary about a Canadian wild animal. Cameron liked these, but rarely got to hear them. The kids booed and catcalled throughout these as well. They did not, above all things, want to be educated about sandpipers, snowy owls, or wolves on a Saturday afternoon. They howled and pretended to be monkeys. Cameron said once it was like being locked in a room with a troop of troglodytes. I had to look the word up to find out it meant chimpanzees.

Deanny, however, did not like movies, and since our friendship began we hadn't gone. But when she discovered that *Cujo,* starring Dee Wallace and Danny Pintauro, was playing, she decided she wanted to go. Later I would joke about how the last movie we watched at the Saturday cinema had to be about a contagious St. Bernard.

My mother didn't want me to go. Jeanette had already seen it, and she had read the book upon which the film was based. She said it was disturbing. "The little boy dies," she told my mother. "I can't see how anyone can make a film where a little boy dies. It's hard to watch."

"Did he die in the book?" asked my mother.

"Yes," said Jeanette. "But it's harder to take on film, for some reason."

"I think it's all twisted nonsense," said my grandmother. "There's plenty enough going on in real life without going to see some string of horrors concocted by some man down south with too vivid an imagination and no sense of moral decency."

For once my mother agreed with my grandmother, and tried to talk me and Deanny out of seeing the film. "Aunt Jeanette can take you both to the beach, or even into the city for the afternoon, right Jeanette?"

"Right," Jeanette said. "It's not a very good movie, anyway."

But Deanny didn't want to go to the beach or the city. She wanted to see *Cujo.* Deanny didn't read, except what was required in school. She was not much for the suspension of disbelief either. She didn't want so much to see the movie to see the little boy die at the end, as to see *how* the sick filmmakers could make the little boy die at the end. In this sense she was not so far off from the perspective of my grandmother, except Deanny approved of it. She wanted the guts. She wanted the gore.

She would be disappointed. Though we never actually saw *Cujo* at the cinema, we eventually watched it on video. Deanny pronounced it a dud and not worth the effort we had put ourselves through to see it. Tad Trenton did not die horribly mangled in the jaws of a rabid St. Bernard. He died of heat exposure in a car or an asthma attack, she could never figure out which.

Years later, Deanny said she could never watch Pintauro as a sweet little kid on TV's *Who's the Boss* without expecting a large dog to spring out of the closet to tear him to pieces. She said this long after *Cujo* and Pintauro had faded into obscurity, and reruns of *Who's the Boss* were off the air. I had to remind Deanny it was us, and not little Tad, who'd been torn to pieces that day. Though she never liked to admit it, she knew I was right.

■ ■ ■

MY MOTHER TAKES Saturday off so she can look after my grandmother. She encourages me to get out of town, and elicits the help of Deanny, who calls me up and invites me for brunch. I borrow the car from Aunt Jeanette, who says I'm to take as long as I want. She can walk home from the diner.

I should have smelled a rat.

I drive into the city to meet Deanny at a café on Spring Garden Road, and am surprised when I find Pavel sitting beside her. The last time I saw him was at Deanny's dinner party, when he walked me to my car and gave me his number.

I hadn't called.

If anything, Pavel is more exuberant than Deanny, though it's tempered by his masculinity and his Russian accent. When he sees me he stands up and smiles broadly. He shakes my hand vigorously, then sits back down. I shoot a glance at Deanny, who refuses to meet my eye.

"I ran into Pavel on the street and asked him to join us. I hope you don't mind."

"Of course not," I say, knowing this is a lie. "Where's Richard?"

"Writing."

A waiter comes to take our order before I can say anything else. We all order a generous breakfast. Before it arrives, Pavel talks mathematics. He does so naturally, without guile, not trying to impress me. It is what he knows and loves, and he knows I love it too. Deanny takes a backseat, acts demure, listening and smiling, saying nothing. Before long, we are knee-deep in it. I relish the discussion because it is impassioned and lively, and I enjoy coaxing from my memory formulas and concepts I haven't given a thought to since university. Before long, we have forgotten about Deanny entirely.

At the end of the meal she excuses herself to go check on Richard. "Why don't you two go for a walk together," she suggests. "I'll catch up with you later."

Despite knowing the entire day has been engineered by Deanny to throw Pavel and me together, I agree. Once she is gone, we take a stroll down Spring Garden Street towards the waterfront. For a while we have nothing to say. To break the silence, I ask Pavel if he misses Russia.

"Of course I do," he says. "It is my mother country. The source of me, in some way. And Moscow is a great city. Dirty, vile, fast, and rude. I love her very much."

"Do you ever think you'll live there again?"

"Perhaps," says Pavel thoughtfully. "Maybe at the end of my life I will move back again. But for now, Canada is my home. Little baby Halifax my new city. And what of you? Do you miss Advocate?"

I laugh. "Hardly," I say. "It's not the same, is it? Advocate is one tiny little town, not a country. And there's really nothing to miss, besides my mother and aunt."

"But it is a part of you, is it not? The way Moscow is a part of me?"

"Perhaps," I say. "But if it is, it is not a good part."

Pavel shrugs. "I would like to go there someday. Perhaps you will invite me."

"Perhaps," I say, surprised at his boldness. We spend the rest of the day together, and Deanny, the sneak, does not meet up with us. I realize halfway through the afternoon that I like Pavel, in ways I hadn't liked the other men Deanny introduced me to. Perhaps it is because of his nationality, his bizarre energy. Perhaps it is because of his stunning looks. Or maybe it's just because we both like math, and I find him easy to talk to. I tell him about my grandmother's request for a eulogy just to hear what he has to say. I haven't even told my mother this much.

Pavel walks me back to my car and stands with me at the driver's side door. We speak for a time, while I fiddle with my keys. And then suddenly he does it. He leans over and kisses me. I am not expecting it, and it is not a slow graceful advance as you see on TV. It is fast, and precise. As swift and as calculated as a cheetah taking down a gazelle. My heart thumps with fear and desire. Pavel pulls away and smiles at me. I can't remember the last time I was kissed.

"You'll call me?" says Pavel.

"Yes," I say, still disconcerted. "I will."

"If you don't, I will call you. Deanny gave me your number."

We say our final goodbyes and then I drive out of the city to Advocate. I don't know what to expect, or to think. Pavel has kissed me. He clearly likes me. I clearly like him. I curse the complication. It would be easier for everyone if my grandmother died peacefully, I went to the funeral, and returned to Toronto. But I can tell Deanny and Pavel will not give up.

When I get home, my mother asks me about the visit.

I shrug. "We didn't do much."

"Was it just you and Deanny?"

"It was," I lie. "Why do you ask?"

"No reason," my mother says. "I'm glad you had a good time."

When Jeanette comes home she asks me the same questions. I begin to wonder if she and my mother and Deanny are not in on this Pavel thing together. I decide I won't give them the satisfaction.

I am a lone ranger. I pride myself on this. I learned early you cannot rely on others. The only exceptions are Deanny, my mother, and Jeanette.

Pavel is a blip, an indicator that I could perhaps have something more if I want it.

I'm not sure I want it.

# 3

WHEN DEANNY AND I went to the theatre to see *Cujo*, we went an hour early. We bought our tickets from Hilda and went to the concession stand for popcorn and soda. Then we navigated the short hallway to the theatre proper, drew aside the worn but heavy maroon velvet curtains, and stepped into the fray. There was never a way to sneak in unnoticed. This was a hushed moment for me, because it was always so full, stuffed with potential danger. The hallway deposited us at the front of the theatre, where we had to turn and face the kids sitting in their seats staring up at the screen.

Whether it was the lighting, or the reflection of the white screen on their faces, everyone looked anemic, their pale faces floating over popcorn boxes. They were staring at us as we entered.

There were always catcalls and, for some, hellos. Not the latter for Deanny and me. They called us names and blocked the aisle and made it as uncomfortable for us as they could, until we found seats somewhere near the middle with too few kids to keep us from taking them. We settled down and waited for the hubbub to subside. The teasing and the name calling was no worse than for Cameron and me, but I felt a queasiness in my gut, as I knew the seats around me would fill up and it was anyone's guess who would sit there. Someone mild-mannered, or at least indifferent. We had many minutes left to go before the movie started. I ate my popcorn nervously while Deanny scanned the room for potential enemies. She wore her most aggressive expression — eyes narrowed, lips pursed, cheeks puffed. No one cared to take her dare, or they forgot about us. We talked infrequently.

Deanny said she hoped the movie would be good, though if it was it would be lost on these losers. She said this loudly, trying to provoke, but no one took the bait. Groups in the front hollered questions and comments to groups in the back. Waves of laughter broke against the screen. Words like "fuck" and "shit" rose up from the jumble of conversation and stood out in stark verbal contrast. There was not a single adult. No wonder I was always terrified, and it is amazing to me now that I stayed.

But this was the world I lived in.

If I wanted to venture out of my house I had to tolerate such things. And besides, I had Deanny. Up until then she'd kept the monsters off me. They were scared of her. She looked mean, and they didn't know her. They might have justified themselves by saying she was just a girl, and they didn't beat up girls. They were taught better. But it was their fear of her that kept them away. Right up until that day, Deanny made certain no one touched me. They continued to call me names, and her too. But they never laid a finger on me. That was more than I could say for when Cameron and I were together. Several times they had driven us from the theatre altogether and we had to walk home without seeing the film. I was grateful for Deanny, and if I still didn't feel entirely safe, I could at least be certain we would make it through the movie together.

We sat through most of the hour before the film without anyone sitting in the seats around us. I was hopeful no one would, and the lights would go down and we would be safe, but a group of seven came in at the last minute. Three boys and four girls. I knew all of them from my school. Two of the girls were in my grade and the others were older. Immensely popular, from good families and with nice clothes and fashionably cut hair, they stood at the bottom of the theatre waving and shouting at people they knew, with two of the girls scanning for seats.

I scanned too. I was hoping there would be others, but I could see there weren't. The only place these kids could sit together was with us.

I counted their number.

Then I counted two seats on the other side of Deanny and three on the other side of me to the aisle.

I knew what was going to happen before Deanny did. She was busy glaring at some boy in the row below who had whispered "Deanny Dirt-Digger."

The seven kids from below started to make their way up the aisle. They stopped in a little group and looked at us.

I knew all their names.

I knew all their families.

One of them, George, lived on the street behind my grand-mother. He had never touched me. In fact, he had never spoken to me. He was two years older, and played basketball. He wore the red and white of the Junior School basketball team. He always wore it. Deanny called guys like George "Varsity Dicks." She said it should be the name of the team.

"Hey McNeil," George said. "Give us your seats."

I would have done so in a heartbeat, if I had been alone. Cameron and I would have got up and sat separately and we would have counted ourselves lucky not to be pounded into the ground. I actually started to move, when Deanny laid her hand on my arm.

"Where do you think you're going?" she asked.

For a moment, it was as if Deanny was the bully. It was such a stark, threatening question. I froze.

George looked at her and repeated his request. I actually thought he was being quite reasonable for the Saturday Matinee. He could

have just as easily plucked us out of the seats and tossed us down
the aisle and kids would have cheered. There were no grown-ups in
the room, and Milo the projectionist couldn't see. Even if he could,
he had a rule not to interfere in the matinee drama, unless property
was being damaged.

"There's seven of us," George said, "and two of you. "You've got
seven seats between you. Find someplace else to sit."

Deanny held me in place. "Not likely, dickhead," she said. "You
find someplace else."

"What a mouth," said one of the girls.

"You wanna make something of it, Barbie Doll?"

The girls made faces, like they couldn't be bothered with the
likes of Bernadette McLeod. But I noticed no one took her up on
her offer.

"I know you," George said. "You're that kid from Meadow
Pond Lane. Not a pot to piss in and already you think you own the
town. Well, you don't own this town, bitch. I don't care if you are
a girl. If you don't give us those seats, we'll take them. Simple
as that."

I could hear, and feel, how quiet everything had become. Every
eye in the theatre was turned towards us. It was not just a matter
of two kids being ousted from their seats. That happened all the
time. It was something else. The tension that had been building
around my uncle over the stories these kids had been hearing at
home was about to break. It had gone unspoken, and now it was
coming out.

Deanny sensed it too. She stood up and tried to take a step across
my legs, to get closer to George. The girls stepped back. George did
not. I grabbed Deanny's leg. "It's okay," I said. "Let's just move."

"Like fuck," said Deanny. She sounded so grown-up, so adult.
She made her way over me and stood in the aisle in front of George.
He was a step below her, but still taller. She would get clobbered.

A chant started in the room, soft but quickly gaining in strength. "Fight, Fight, Fight, Fight."

"I'm not gonna hit you," George said. "You'd probably run to your momma, and have me thrown in jail."

"I fight my own battles," said Deanny.

The chant was louder now, almost overwhelming. And then, with seemingly great power, George held up his hand and the chanting stopped. Deanny stood fuming. The other kids stood watching. George put his hand down and turned away from Deanny. He looked at me.

"AIDS fucker," he said.

He repeated it, louder this time. Then began to chant it. He beckoned for the crowd to follow. They did. Soon everyone in the theatre was shouting it. "AIDS fucker! AIDS fucker! AIDS fucker!"

Deanny took a swing. George casually blocked her. The crowd did not stop chanting. Another kid grabbed me and wrestled me out of my seat. By this time the entire theatre was in a lather, calling for George to "beat the living shit out of us."

It was really no contest. George easily overpowered Deanny. He called her a "fucking bitch" and slapped her once curtly on the side of her head, then wrapped his arms around her and lifted her. Deanny screamed, shouting every epithet she could think of, until George eventually put a hand over her mouth. The kids continued to shout as Deanny and I were escorted outside. She tried to scream through George's clasped hand and I went placidly. Even in the lobby we could hear the chants from inside. They had not abated. Hilda stepped out of the ticket booth and asked what the hell was going on.

George, still covering Deanny's mouth and fighting her to keep still, told Hilda we tried to fight someone and Milo told them to throw us out of the theatre. Hilda looked at Deanny, who pleaded with her eyes, and at me, my mouth not covered but saying nothing, and nodded uncertainly. "If Milo told you," she said. "Though I don't like the methods."

The boys opened the doors, deposited us unceremoniously on the sidewalk, and shut the glass doors behind us.

The chanting stopped — that or we could no longer hear it. Tears of rage and hatred streamed down Deanny's face. She pounded against the doors to be let back in, but Hilda had locked them, and was shaking her head.

Couldn't Hilda hear what the kids were shouting? Didn't she know Milo would never have asked kids to eject other kids from the theatre?

"You dumb bitch!" screamed Deanny. "You fucking whore cow!"

Those words alone ensured we were barred from the theatre for life, though we never tried to go back after that day.

When Deanny calmed down — though she was still crying — we looked for our bikes.

We couldn't find them.

All the other bikes were leaning against the theatre wall — no one locked their bikes in Advocate in those days — but ours were not. We walked home in silence. We never did find our bikes. Whoever stole them must not have ridden them, and instead destroyed them or kept them locked away in a garage or basement. My mother offered to buy us new ones, but Deanny refused. She would walk, she said. She would find the bastard who did it and beat him to a bloody pulp.

Deanny and I were more defeated that day than Cameron and I had ever been. Neither of us ever told my mother what happened at the theatre. I wanted to, but Deanny was adamant. "Not a word," she said. "Not a goddamned fucking word."

■ ■ ■

EVERYTHING CHANGED AFTER that day in the theatre. Deanny became interested in what exactly my uncle had, and why everyone, even the assholes in the theatre, knew more about it than we did. Their families, it seemed, weren't afraid of saying the word. Why was mine?

She said we should study it.

"You mean go to the library?" I said.

"Where else do you study crap, idgit?" she asked me. "Besides the john."

Deanny suggesting we go to the library was unusual, to say the least. I had only known her since the beginning of the summer. Then she was all daredevil, mud and adventure. I had yet to see her in school where, despite her reputation, she was studious and diligent.

She knew asking my mother or her parents would be useless. They would tell us nothing. "If we want to know about it, we have to learn ourselves."

There were two problems.

First, I had been banned from the library, so Deanny had to go alone.

The second was that the library had nothing about AIDS.

It was 1984.

A library in a big city would have had little about it. Our little broom closet, with just under two thousand volumes, over half of them encyclopedias and *National Geographics*, had nothing. Most of the written work published on AIDS was in medical journals, to which the library did not subscribe. Even if it had, they would have been over Deanny's head.

We tried the encyclopedia. The most contemporary was the 1983 *Britannica*.

Not a mention. In between *aid* — a medieval tax — and *Aidan, the King of Dalriada*, there was no entry.

Although we didn't realize it then, that was likely the last encyclopedia or dictionary in the world that would not have that word. That's how big a deal it would become. We were living in a seminal era, one that would be defined by a single crisis. But we couldn't know that.

After a half-hour fruitless search — with the young, pretty but incredibly nosy second librarian Mrs. Goddard constantly asking what she was looking for — Deanny gave up. Outside on Main Street, she met up with me and said we would just have to go to the horse's mouth.

"My uncle?" I said.

"Hardly," said Deanny. "No one in your house tells us anything. We'll go see Dr. Fred."

I suspected Deanny was right: it was no use asking my mother and Jeanette. Forthright in all other matters, they'd been frustratingly close-mouthed when it came to my uncle and his illness. If we wanted to know anything we would have to go elsewhere. But it seemed a hare-brained scheme to me, this attempt to extract information from my uncle's physician. "He won't tell us," I said. "He has to protect Uncle David's confidentiality."

"We won't ask him about your uncle, dummy," said Deanny. "We'll just ask about the disease."

"Why do you want to know, Deanny?"

She shrugged. "Everyone else seems to know something about it. I don't have a goddamned clue."

"What if he won't tell us?"

"He'll tell us," Deanny said. "He has to. He's a doctor, isn't he? Aren't doctors supposed to educate people?"

This argument seemed specious to me. Doctors were supposed to *heal* people. Teachers were supposed to educate. I thought we might have a better chance with Mrs. Simms, the biology teacher at the high school.

"You mean the same Mrs. Simms who won't let her son play with you?"

She had me there, I had to admit.

The thing was, I wasn't sure I wanted to know exactly what AIDS was. My uncle had it. Of that I was certain. And there were fears it was contagious. That I also knew. Beyond that, my understanding was nebulous — deliberately so, it occurs to me now. If I knew too much, perhaps I wouldn't want to live in my own house. Perhaps I would be the one chanting "AIDS fucker" along with my peers. I went along with Deanny, because I went along with her in everything, and I trusted her. But I did so with trepidation.

When she went ahead and made the appointment with Dr. Fred, she told his secretary she had chronic tendonitis.

"An eleven-year-old?" the secretary had said. "Shouldn't your mother be making this appointment?"

"My mother has chronic assholinitis," Deanny shot back. "In the form of my father. Please make the appointment."

And so the appointment was made, for August 4 — the Tuesday before the week, my mother said later, everything really went to hell.

■ ■ ■

ON THE DAY we were to go visit Dr. Fred, my mother got me out of bed early and said she had a favour to ask me.

"What is it?" I asked.

"Your aunt and I have to go into town for a little while and your grandmother's visiting Father Orlis. I was wondering if you could stay home for a few hours in case your Uncle David needs anything."

"Okay."

What my mother didn't tell me was that she and Jeanette were going to the unemployment office in town to put in a claim. A few days before she and Jeanette had suddenly and mysteriously been laid off from the diner. Mr. Byrd, who was a timid man and had always liked my mother and Jeanette — and gave them the run of the place when they were on shift — didn't tell them the truth at first. He said the diner wasn't busy enough this summer for all the help he hired.

"Doesn't it make sense then," Jeanette asked him, "to lay off the summer people rather than full-time staff?"

"I didn't think ... I mean I don't know ...," said Mr. Byrd.

It didn't take long, with my mother and Jeanette working on him in tandem, for Mr. Byrd to admit the truth. A number of people in town had approached him about my mother and aunt handling food in the diner.

"They thought they might get sick," said Byrd. "I told them I didn't think so, but they threatened to have the diner shut down if I didn't let you go. It's only for a time, a few weeks at most, until this all blows over. In the fall you can come back again."

Jeanette was incensed, my mother resigned. She said it was only for a few weeks and they could use the break to take care of David. Jeanette wanted Mr. Byrd to give her the names of those who complained, so she could confront them. My mother said it was best they didn't know. She told Jeanette and my grandmother not to tell me about their lost jobs. But my grandmother couldn't help it. She spilled her guts to Hazel McLeod on the phone and I overheard every word.

I asked my mother at bedtime why Mr. Byrd thought she could make people sick.

"Because they're ignorant," she said, "No one is getting sick around here except your Uncle David. You do understand that, don't you Jacob?"

"I do," I said.

And so, that Tuesday morning when she and Jeanette went into town, I agreed to stay home. "Don't go in David's room," my mother said. "And don't bother him unless he asks you for something. If he does, ask him if it can wait until we get home. I don't want you in his room unless it's an emergency. Okay, Jacob?"

"Okay," I said.

This routine had not changed since my uncle had first been confined.

I was not allowed in, period.

Whatever my uncle had even my mother was still fearful I would get, despite her bluster about ignorant people.

It shames me now I was so uneducated.

I could have listened more closely to the taunts and jibes of my peers. Perhaps even they, with all their venom, could have taught me something.

Once, when Deanny's father was drunk, she asked him about it. He told her it was a disease that kills queers. "Good riddance too," he said. "As far as I'm concerned."

This was unhelpful, and when Deanny asked how they got it, he mumbled something under his breath and told her to go away.

My mother later told me people get it from being intimate with each other, but she did not explain why she thought I could get it from being in my uncle's room. He was unlikely to get intimate with me.

"That's the thing, Jacob. We know very little about it."

And that was about as much information as we got. No wonder Deanny wanted more. It wasn't just because she was intellectually curious — she was, more than she ever let on — but here we were living amidst a situation we knew nothing about. That day at the theatre had shown her this was on everyone's mind. And if this was the case, Deanny thought it better to be armed with knowledge than with stones. "We find out the truth of this thing," she said, "and we throw it back in their faces." Forewarned is forearmed. A little knowledge is a dangerous thing. A lot of knowledge is a nuclear weapon. Whatever her reasons, she was determined to go to Dr. Fred to get some answers.

I still wasn't sure I wanted to know more than I did at present. I would rather look forward than backward — to our plans, for instance, of walking in the Lemon Day parade. Deanny was planning on making a sign that said "Suck a lemon." My grandmother would have a fit.

The Lemon and Orange Day parades should have already taken place on a weekend in July, but the weekend it was scheduled, a water main broke on Orange Street across the river. It took the town maintenance crew almost the whole weekend to stop it. Meanwhile the street was flooded, along with many basements. Deanny and I went over, took off our shoes and rolled up our pants, and played in it, till my grandmother found out and sent my mother over after us.

The Protestants, of course, could have no parade that weekend, and it was suggested that it be rescheduled to a weekend in August to give time for merchants to lure visitors back to the town. Some of the Catholics hadn't wanted to. They, my grandmother chief among them, were delighted that the Lemon parade could carry on while the Orange was sidelined in the streets. There was an emergency town hall meeting because of it, where those old divisions on either side of the river materialized again. My grandmother was there, arguing on the side of tradition. The Lemon parade should go on, she said. It was unfortunate that the Protestant side was flooded, but God sometimes works in mysterious ways.

Everyone was relieved when the Catholics finally relented and both parades rescheduled.

Deanny showed up at my door at ten-thirty. "We're gonna miss the goddamned appointment," she said.

"What can I do?" I asked her. "I had to say yes."

I agreed to stay home with my uncle in part because if my grandmother was not back in time, it might mean I'd have to cancel on Deanny. She certainly couldn't fault me for staying at home to take care of the man we were going to see the doctor about.

"Well," said Deanny. "She better show up, is all I can say."

Or what? I wanted to ask, but didn't. Deanny asked if my uncle wanted anything.

"He's in his room," I said. "The door's shut and he hasn't used the walkie-talkie."

My aunt had bought a set of walkie-talkies so my uncle could call downstairs if he needed anything. My mother and Aunt Jeanette also brought down my grandmother's walker — several years prior, she had broken her pelvis during a fall while cleaning the kitchen cupboards — and gave it to my uncle. He was now so weak and tired, he had difficulty getting about on his own. He rarely bothered to change out of his pyjamas and housecoat and only used the walker to go to the bathroom and sometimes into my mother's or Jeanette's room.

One of the walkie-talkies sat bluntly silent on the kitchen counter. Deanny sat at the kitchen table, twiddling her thumbs, literally, and stared at the mute walkie-talkie with resentment. It seemed she forgot we were going to the doctor out of concern for my uncle, if that was ever the case. Right now he was a hindrance. If we missed our appointment, she would be in a foul mood all day. I told her she could go without me and fill me in later.

"No," Deanny said. "You're his nephew. Dr. Fred won't say anything to me alone."

When my grandmother showed up at ten to eleven, Deanny immediately jumped out of her chair.

"Goodness," my grandmother said. "What are you two doing here?"

I told my grandmother I was charged by my mother to look after my uncle.

"You didn't go into his room, did you?"

"No," I said. "He didn't ask for anything."

"Run along now," my grandmother said, "and don't forget to come back for lunch."

We wouldn't be home for it. Our appointment didn't end until quarter to twelve. In those days, doctors scheduled their appointment for more than ten minutes at a time.

Since we didn't have our bikes anymore, Deanny said we had to run. It was a ten-minute walk to Fred's office but we ran the entire way and got there in five. His receptionist said he was running late and told us to take a seat.

"Great," Deanny said.

We sat alone in the waiting room. I asked Deanny what we were doing there.

"Aren't you curious?" she said. "Don't you hate when people keep things from you?"

I didn't. I was used to it happening, and I wondered in this case if they, rather than keeping things from us, just didn't know. But I didn't say this. Instead I sat there and waited for our appointment. I hadn't been to the doctor's office in two years. I'd had the chickenpox and Fred had given me some liquid medicine that tasted like molasses and brine. The memory of the taste of it was still strong.

We waited twenty minutes, and two other people came into the waiting room after us. I didn't know them. They were older, perhaps summer people from the lake. They stared curiously at us, two kids just barely in our teens and waiting without an adult. This annoyed Deanny.

"Child leukemia," she said. "With both barrels."

Nonplussed, the couple settled their eyes on magazines rather than risk Deanny's sarcasm again.

Finally Dr. Fred came out of the white-painted door next to the reception desk and said, I'm certain facetiously, "Master McNeil. Miss McLeod."

I could see Deanny was surprised he knew her name. She forgot, perhaps, that she had given it to the receptionist to make the appointment. She hopped up and brushed past Dr. Fred, who held the door open. She was able to slip underneath his arm without him lifting it. I did the same.

"Nice to see you, Jacob," said Dr. Fred, after he closed to the door behind him. "The room to your right please."

There were only two rooms. The other contained a photocopier and medical supplies. Fred's office contained a pine desk, a black leather swivel chair in front of it, another wooden chair with a cushion beside the desk. A steel examining table was jammed firmly against one wall.

"Not enough chairs for both of you," said Dr. Fred. "One of you will have to stand or hop up on the table."

"Not me," said Deanny. "I'll stand."

"Don't worry," said Dr. Fred. "I'm not going to examine you Deanny. Unless of course that tendonitis is acting up."

Deanny looked nervous. She stood cradling her arms and chewing her lower lip, which she always did when she was unsure of herself. Dr. Fred took his seat and motioned for me to take the other. I liked Fred and, unlike Deanny, I was not suspicious of him. He was a handsome man, with the solid build of a football player. My grandmother first visited him shortly after he bought the practice from Dr. Bell — who had bought it from my grandmother when my grandfather died — and said she could not possibly go see a doctor who was so young and good-looking.

"He can't know anything about medicine," she said. "He's barely thirty and he looks like he belongs on some varsity team. I'll have to get another doctor."

My grandmother did not get another doctor. Though she was convinced, based on appearances, Dr. Fred would miss some vital diagnosis and let her die of cholera or bone cancer, he now owned the practice that had once belonged to her husband. To go anywhere else would feel like betrayal.

She fully changed her mind about him when he started dating Jeanette, who was wild about him from the first and actually manufactured symptoms in order to have an excuse to go see him. My grandmother got excited at the thought of one her daughters marrying a doctor, and she thought it prudent from then on to see Dr. Fred in his office whenever necessary and let him know, subtly, he had her full permission and support.

Jeanette did not marry Dr. Fred. She got tired of him, as she got tired of everyone. He remained a bachelor for many years, only marrying a woman from Halifax when he was almost forty.

I took the seat across from Fred. He eased back, crossed his legs at the ankles and said, "So what brings you two here today? I'm sure it's not tendonitis, is it Deanny?"

Deanny didn't answer. I was surprised. I couldn't figure out what was bothering her. Was it that Fred was a doctor, and the surroundings unfamiliar? Had she chickened out, now it had come down to asking Dr. Fred questions? I could tell she was waiting for me to start.

Dr. Fred looked between the two of us with mild bemusement. I don't think he had any idea what we were doing there. But it didn't seem right to just ask him questions outright about my uncle's illness — what it was, why it was troubling everyone so, why I wasn't allowed in his room. I realized just then it was my mother I should have been asking these questions of, and demanding answers. Deanny complained they'd not told us anything, and this was true, but neither had we asked much. I suddenly felt foolish.

Dr. Fred uncrossed his legs and sat up straight in his chair. "Come on now," he said. "Something must have brought you two here today. What is it?"

Deanny couldn't wait any longer. "We want to know what AIDS is," she blurted out. "We went to the library and there's nothing about it. Those assholes in the theatre called Jacob and me 'AIDS fuckers' and we want to know why. We want to know why Jacob is not allowed in his uncle's room, and if we can get it from just being near him, like everyone says. And if we can, how come we're not sick yet? And ..."

"Whoa!" said Dr. Fred. "That's a lot of stuff. Does your mother know you're here?" he said to me.

I shook my head.

"His mother doesn't tell him anything. No one talks about it," said Deanny.

"I see," said Dr. Fred. "You said the kids in the theatre called you 'AIDS fuckers'?"

It was strange, hearing a doctor say the word *fuckers*. Under other circumstances we might have laughed.

"Yes," said Deanny. "Just before they grabbed us and threw us outside and Hilda locked the door on us. I've never been so mad in my life."

"And Milo let them get away with this?"

Deanny nodded.

"I think," said Dr. Fred, as if reading my mind, "you should be asking your mother these questions, Jacob. They seem more suited to her than me."

"I told you," Deanny said. "They don't answer. They don't tell us nothing."

Dr. Fred twirled a pencil on his desk. Then he looked up and said, "What do you want to know?"

"What is it?" said Deanny.

Dr. Fred directed most of his answers at me, though Deanny was asking the questions. His voice was soft, and considerate. He had remarkable bedside manner, which is why he was such a popular physician. Soothing but not unctuous, precise, not conde-scending, his tone remained even and reassuring. He gave us all the information we needed, and more. AIDS, he told us, stood for Acquired Immune Deficiency Syndrome. It was a new disease. The first case in Canada had been discovered only a few years before, and my uncle was one of the first in the country to come down with it. We knew very little about it. It attacked and destroyed the immune system and opened up the person to a host of diseases that eventually killed him.

I asked Dr. Fred about the spots on my uncle's face and neck and hands.

"A type of cancer," he said. "Caused by the illness."

"And the thinness?" asked Deanny. "He looks like a skeleton."

"Body mass wasting," he said. "Also caused by AIDS."

"Is he going to live?" I asked.

"No," said Dr. Fred, looking at me with great sympathy but a steady gaze. "I'm afraid he's not. His days are numbered."

"So why is everyone acting so retarded?" asked Deanny. "How do you get this thing anyway?"

"Through sex, for one," he said. "Some people are afraid you can get it through touch, or the air, or mosquitoes. We've tried to explain to them we don't think that's how it is transmitted, but they won't listen."

I told him about not being allowed in my uncle's room.

"They're just being cautious," he said. "They're pretty sure you can't get it that way, but they don't want to take any chances. You understand, don't you Jacob?"

"And what about the library? And Mom's job at the diner?"

"Stupid," spat Fred. "Silliest thing I've heard in all my years as a doctor. People are just being ignorant and mean."

Deanny asked him about her father saying it killed queers.

Dr. Fred sighed. "The issue is complicated," he said. "So far, it does just seem to affect gay men and drug addicts."

"That doesn't make sense," said Deanny. "Why would a disease just affect one type of person?"

"We don't know," he said. "That's why people are being so heart-less and senseless about this. On one hand, they say it only affects gay men and so 'good riddance,' as your father says. On the other they're worried about getting it themselves. I've never seen such confusion and hysteria surrounding a disease, and I hope never to again. Eventually people will settle down and see how stupid they've been, but until then we have to weather the storm."

Although I didn't know it, Dr. Fred was dealing with the fallout of my uncle as much as we were. Because he treated him, he had lost patients, and was also being ostracized. One man refused to get up on his examining table because my uncle had been on it. When Fred insisted AIDS could not be caught from tables or toilet seats or bug bites, he was pushed away even more.

Dr. Fred told us that if we were his kids, he'd be going to Milo and giving him hell about what had happened in the theatre, and insisting the perpetrators be brought to justice. However, he also cautioned that we were unlikely to change any minds in town about the situation. It would have to run its course.

Deanny asked him if he thought we could get it from touch-ing my uncle, or being in the same room. She asked him for an honest answer, and not one he would expect my mother to give. He seemed to think about this a while, and then said, "No. I don't think you or Jacob is in any danger at all. It seems nearly impossible to convince people of that, but it is what I think. You are both fully safe from this disease."

"Great," Deanny said. "Then we'll start helping him more."

Deanny, it seemed to me, had not come to the office to become a champion for my uncle. She had come to see if there was any basis for the fear of the town, and to get back at those in the theatre who had thrown us out that day. She was to become a crusader, and she'd found my uncle as a cause. It was the first time I'd seen this in her, though the tendency must have been there all along.

Fred answered the rest of our questions, but when we left, I felt no more satisfied than I had before. I didn't understand what we were supposed to do with our knowledge. We still faced the same taunts and prejudice. We were still barred from the theatre. But Deanny looked replete.

"We're experts now," she said.

"Experts on what?"

"On what your uncle has, dummy."

"But how does that help us?" I said.

"You'll see," said Deanny. "Knowing things always helps, Jake."

It was, I realize now, the first time Deanny had ever called me by my name.

# SEVEN

■

THE NOMINAL LEADER of the Lemon Day parade, the one who walked in front of the lemon cart with the papier-mâché fruit, was named Byron McNeil. No relation. He was my grandmother's age, worked at the post office, and had been involved in the town in various capacities all his life. A committed bachelor, it had been more than once suggested his bread was buttered on the wrong side, as my uncle's was. But there was no evidence for this, other than he lived alone with three cats and had never looked at a woman in all his life. He appointed himself Marshal of the Parade years before, when he dressed up us a town crier and with shouts of "Hear Ye! Hear Ye!" assumed the traditionally unoccupied space in front of the lemon cart. Now, some fifteen years later, it had become a new tradition.

My grandmother didn't like Byron. She called him a busybody and a gossip — a sterling case of the pot and the kettle — and she said he was from the "Other McNeils," Scottish Protestants of the United Church who had been living in town almost as long as the Catholics. It bothered my grandmother that Byron would lead the Lemon Day parade and not the Orange, as he was not Catholic. It diluted, she said, the spiritual message, and turned the whole event into a fiasco.

No one listened to her.

Whatever spiritual significance my grandmother drew from the parades had long been bled out of the rest of us. You could be any religion you wanted, short of a devil worshipper, and take part. My grandmother bewailed this, but couldn't change it. The best she could do was carry a placard with a religious message, and hope someone noticed. Neither could she do anything about Byron and his silly costumes and heretical beliefs at the head of the parade. She could make sure we all took part and marched in a group and spent the majority of our money on the Catholic side.

My mother always gave me ten dollars to spend on games of chance and hotdogs and potato chips, and she let me run freely about the streets once the parade was over. Early in August Deanny and I did extra work in the yard so my mother would have a reason to top up her pockets, too. Deanny didn't like to take anything she did not earn. My mother had learned to create projects for Deanny to balance the disparity of cash in our pockets.

On Thursday my grandmother began planning where we would march — front, middle, or end — and she managed to inveigle her way into an auxiliary meeting and take over the running of one of the booths. She wasn't being informed of proper times and locations of meetings, and she had to keep her ear pretty close to the ground to find out, but once she was there, no one had the guts to say anything to her. My mother thought perhaps things were starting to settle down. No one besides my uncle had gotten sick. Whatever fears they had that AIDS was floating magically around in the air had perhaps started to abate. Jeanette noticed the lines in front of her at the grocery store were getting longer again, and people were saying hello to her on the street. Mr. Byrd had even discussed giving my mother and Jeanette their jobs back.

"They've finally come to their senses," my mother said. "Thank goodness."

"For now," said Aunt Jeanette. "I still don't understand what came over them in the first place."

My grandmother, who had never acknowledged the crisis to begin with, didn't say anything about it. She was only happy the auxiliary had allowed her to run the quilting booth on parade day.

■ ■ ■

IF IT SEEMED the rest of the town settled down about the issue of my uncle, Cameron and his family did not. I did not receive a call from him, nor an invitation to visit. When I encountered him on the street, he would cross to the other side and ignore me. He didn't do it haughtily, or with arrogance. He seemed almost ashamed of himself, and refused at all times to meet my eye. He acted as if I didn't exist, probably because it would be easier for him if I didn't.

My mother said she didn't know what garbage Mr. and Mrs. Simms were feeding their son, but for smart people they were being unbelievably stupid. Although she didn't know it, it pained me to hear her run Cameron and his family down. Before I met Deanny, they were like a second family to me. I spent nights and ate meals at their house. Went on family days to the museums in Halifax with them. Twice had gone camping in Digby and had even met Cameron's aunt and his grandmother. Mr. Simms helped me with homework, and talked to me seriously about my future as if I was his son. He was, though often distant and remote, as close to a father as I had ever had. I missed him as much as Cameron.

Mrs. Simms I didn't miss as much. She was harsh, and too stringent for my taste. I was certain it was she and not Mr. Simms who had forbid Cameron from playing with me. "Just for a time," she might have said. "Until all this AIDS business is over with."

But the "AIDS business" would never be over with. Not with people like Mrs. Simms in the world, who were both smart and ignorant at the same time. It is no crime to be either, but an unpardonable sin to be both.

2

AUNT JEANETTE WANTED to take my uncle in the wheelchair out into the Lemon Day parade. "It would likely be his last," she said. "He should be able to enjoy the day as much as anyone else."

My mother was set against it. "Look at what had happened when we took him for a walk," she said. "The street shut up tighter than a drum! If we took him into the parade there would be sheer panic."

This was years before the AIDS marches began, when we pinned on our red ribbons and took to the streets in defiance and protest. It occurs to me now that Jeanette, ever the rebel, had, by wanting my uncle to be wheeled into the fray, suggested the first AIDS march years before anyone else thought of it.

She had a history with marches, having organized many.

I remember her march of one on the Protestant side of the river, against the Americans. It was during the Gulf of Sidra incident in Libya in July of 1981, when everyone thought it would end up in a war. Her sign read *Sidra Is a Sin: No Violence!* A few people honked their horns. A few more told her to get out of the way.

"Have you asked David about this?" said my mother. "Perhaps he doesn't want to be treated as a signpost or a cause? Maybe he just wants to rest."

I rarely heard my mother get angry at Jeanette, but over this she did. And it turned out Jeanette had not asked my uncle what he wanted. She only assumed David was as incensed over the situation as she was.

He wasn't.

"I've always hated those parades," he said. "Even as a boy, I never understood them. What's the point of going out there to march for two different Gods? I'd rather stay home and read."

When Jeanette asked who would stay home with him, as we all planned on marching in the parade, he seemed to get angry. "I'm not a child," he said from his bed. "Or an invalid. Yet. I can take care of myself for a few hours."

Neither my mother nor Jeanette said anything, but they looked worried. When he was in bed it was possible to fool yourself into thinking — aside from the purple splotches and the body mass wasting — he was okay. But when he got out of bed and used the walker, he looked so fragile and moved so slowly he made us worry for him. It looked as if he wouldn't be able to get up on his own if he fell. My mother and Jeanette made him promise, if they brought to him everything he needed before they left, that he would not get up.

David agreed, sighing. But when one of them volunteered to stay at home with him — after all, they said, it was only a parade — he wouldn't hear of it. "If I disrupt this family any more than I have," he said, "I wouldn't be able to live with it. Go. Have a good time. I'll be fine."

By then, my uncle had admitted to my mother and aunt he had lied about his job in Toronto, proving my grandmother's instinct correct. He had not quit. He had been fired in early 1984. It was done subtly, on some pretext or another. Somehow, they had discovered the nature of his illness.

It did not occur to me then that practically every plan my uncle laid had collapsed. Forced to leave his job. Coming home to find his own place and die in peace, only to be stuck in his mother's house with his sisters looking after him, which was the last thing he wanted. Yet I never once during this period saw my uncle cry, or fall into an unshakeable despair. He just accepted. He negotiated each day as it came and if he thought about the future and what it might hold he didn't talk about it.

My respect for him growing, I began to slip into his room when my mother wasn't around. I was still not allowed in there, but I remembered Dr. Fred's words that I was in no danger, and Uncle David didn't seem to think I was either. I sat near his bed, but not too close, on a chair, while Uncle David told me of his travels. He talked about riding an elephant in India and swimming with a school of tiger sharks in Thailand. He inspired in me a desire to travel to these places, though I never would because of my work. I talked to him about the town. He seemed interested in a child's secret places. The mill. The river. The museum. Once I brought my TV to his room and hooked up my Atari and taught him to play video games. He was amazed.

"This is the way the world is going, Jacob," he said. "Into this incredibly detailed, stunningly visual electronic world. One day we will live here, and the real world, the world of flesh and blood, will be left behind."

That my uncle could think of the crude graphics of an Atari console as "stunningly visual" strikes me as quaint and antiquated now. But it didn't then. If he had lived long enough to see the Internet, and the changes it has brought upon us, he might have realized, as early as that, he had been right.

My uncle also had something besides intelligence. I saw in my uncle, despite his fragile condition and the deteriorating circumstances of his life, something I saw in none of the adults around me and in my town, not even my Aunt Jeanette and my mother. It was genuine integrity. I've since learned how rare a quality that is. When I encounter it now it is not at the board meetings of our agency or the round tables of politicians and government bureaucrats. I see it mostly among the clients, who have earned it through hardship and suffering. It is no wonder I ended up doing what I do.

I was attracted to this quality in men at the impossibly young age of twelve, even if I could not articulate it.

I began to spend more and more time with my uncle when the others weren't around. He seemed always glad to see me, no matter how tired he was. A couple of times, when my mother walked by and saw me in there, she looked like she might step in and object. But when she saw my uncle chatting, perhaps she decided whatever comfort and fleeting happiness he could wrest by having me beside his bed was worth whatever risk there may have been to me.

My grandmother never caught me, though. If she had, she would have had no compunction about chasing me out. My grandmother's ignorance persisted long beyond the point where it should have dissipated in the face of fact. The same would be true for Advocate. In the larger world, however, this fear and ignorance would melt away after a few years, once more was learned about AIDS — its means of transmission, its causes, its treatments.

A few short years seems nothing in the span of a lifetime, but for us, who lived in the middle of it — in the blitz, so to speak — it seemed an eternity. My uncle would be long dead before attitudes began to change. He lived in the most suspicious, superstitious and reactionary years of the disease.

My grandmother was the personification of these attitudes. She led the trials, even though they were against her only son.

It is for this, more than anything else, that I cannot forgive her.

■ ■

OUR MILKMAN'S NAME was Charlie. I never knew his last name. I only knew he was one of the last people to keep a job antiquated by modern grocery and convenience stores. He bought his milk from wholesalers in Trenton and delivered to people like my grandmother, who preferred her milk in glass bottles.

There are no milkmen now.

It is a dead trade, and even when it was available some people would rather pick up their milk at the store than pay the few cents extra it cost for delivery. My grandmother was not one of these. Milk from a bottle, she said, tasted better. The wax-lined interior of a carton spoiled the taste. She ordered three bottles a week, some of which she used for baking, and the rest I drank.

I was a lover of milk.

I loved the taste, the luscious, silky feel of it in my throat. I often drank it straight from the bottle though I never let my grandmother catch me. If she did, she'd make me drink the entire thing and then take the cost out of my allowance. She had methods for boys like me, she said. If I continued to drink so much I would turn into a cow. My mother thought it was healthy. Vitamin A and Vitamin D. She offered to buy extra bottles so I could drink freely, but my grandmother, perversely, refused. "What on earth would Charlie think if I bought five bottles a week? That we were taking baths in it?"

I had to be content with what milk I could steal from the fridge when my grandmother wasn't looking. I offered Deanny some, but she hated the stuff.

"You'll get rickets," I said. "Everyone has to drink milk."

But Deanny refused. She preferred water. She knew nothing about the milkman, because he didn't deliver to her house. No one on Meadow Pond Lane had milk delivered. Deanny said her mother liked milk in her coffee, but couldn't afford it, so used whitener instead. Then she asked why, if Charlie delivered milk, they didn't deliver pop, too?

"They do," I told her. "From the Poppe Shop."

Deanny had never heard of the Poppe Shop. So my mother ordered a case each of root beer and cream soda for Deanny to try. She loved it. "Now that's what I'm talking about," she said. "This stuff *will* give you rickets!"

I don't think Deanny actually knew what rickets was. My grandmother knew, and agreed with Deanny. "All that sugar and carbonate isn't good for anyone," she said, "let alone a growing girl. You'll stunt your growth."

Deanny didn't care. She drank it all in two days.

My grandmother was horrified. "You'll be peeing red all week."

"I'll be *seeing* red all week," Deanny told me later, "if your grandmother doesn't leave me alone."

That my grandmother was starting to take an interest in Deanny was encouraging, and a sign her mood had begun to improve. She stopped cleaning the house, and began shopping for sweaters for us to wear to the parade that were exactly the right shade of yellow. The colours we had been wearing before were mismatched, she said, and not truly lemon at all, but amber and maize. "We should all coordinate and wear the proper lemon. There are more shades of yellow than any other colour, and it wouldn't hurt us to do things right for a change."

"Sweaters?" said my mother. "It's August, for God's sakes!"

"Makes no never mind. A little discomfort is worth the spectacle."

My grandmother had this habit of occasionally getting stuck on some incidental in our lives. One year she decided, irrationally and without notice, the ornaments on the Christmas tree should not be factory-made glass balls, like everyone else had, but home-made, so we spent most of December stringing popcorn on thread and building angels and snowmen out of pipe cleaners. Another time, she decided the house should be photographed more, and in every season, and in every light, and from every angle, for a special album to be kept for future generations. It was a useless enthusiasm, and Jeanette complained it was like living with Leni Riefenstahl. "I'm sure the house will be here for future generations to see if they want to," she said.

"Unless it burns down," said my grandmother. "Or one of you, after I'm dead, decides to paint the eves and shutters some godawful hippy colour like that dreadful purple you always wear, Jeanette. I want it preserved as it is now, as your grandfather left it."

This time, my mother and Jeanette didn't mind the lemon obsession. It meant my grandmother was no longer moping about the house. Uncle David was still sick and, as Dr. Fred pointed out, dying. But now at least he could do it in peace.

# 3

YEARS LATER, MY grandmother would say that what happened next was the devil playing tricks. I do not believe in the devil, unless it is the small mean part that exists inside every one of us. My grandmother was right, however. The next thing did appear, from the outside at least, to be a nasty intervention — some kind of dark cosmic joke. Charlie the milkman delivered early in the morning, before dawn. I never met him, though I sometimes woke and heard him pull up to the curb, heard the clink and rattle of bottles as he removed them from his truck. It never occurred to me that during all that was going on with the town, and their fear of us, Charlie didn't stop delivering. Either he didn't know what was going on at our house, or he didn't care

When his eleven-year-old daughter first got sick, the day before the Lemon parade, it was uncertain if Charlie made the phantom connection.

The rest of the town did.

That Friday morning, when we got up, there was no milk. My grandmother was annoyed. I had drunk the last of it the night before and she wanted some for her tea. She wondered aloud what had had happened to Charlie, who had not missed a delivery for a decade. She sent Jeanette down to the grocery store for some, and called Charlie's wife, who told her Rebecca, their daughter, was sick.

"What kind of sick?" my grandmother asked.

"We don't know," said Mrs. Charlie. "She woke up with fever, and she threw up. She acts like she got the flu, but it was so bad Charlie took her to the hospital. We're scared half to death."

My grandmother hung up the phone thoughtfully. She told my mother about the conversation, and looked nervous about it. There was no milk for my cereal, so I was forced to have butter and toast. My grandmother always burned her toast, and it was dry and hard to eat without milk to wash it down.

My mother said she was sure it was nothing, and that Rebecca would be fine.

My grandmother didn't look so certain. "You don't think …" she said.

"Think what?" said my mother.

"Your brother," said my grandmother. "Perhaps what he has …" She stared ahead, hoping my mother would take up the line of her reasoning.

My mother refused. "Don't tell me you believe that load of nonsense everyone else is taking on about. You know what Dr. Fred told us."

"But he doesn't know," said my grandmother. "No one does, Caroline. It's possible. Isn't it?"

"If anyone was going to get sick," said my mother, "wouldn't it be us first? We're always around him."

"I suppose so," said my grandmother. "I just hope Rebecca's all right."

I didn't know Rebecca. She was a grade behind me. What I had seen of her, she was a small and diffident girl. No trouble to anyone. Deanny wouldn't look at her twice.

When Jeanette came back, she said, "The grocery store is shut down."

"What?" said my grandmother. "It's Friday morning for Lord's sake! It opens at eight."

"Closed up tight. I saw people in there but they wouldn't open the doors. Convenience store too. I saw Henry Hennsey walking downtown and he told me a bunch of people got sick and are at the hospital."

At this my grandmother became truly alarmed. "I've got to get on the phone."

She went into the living room. Jeanette sat down at the kitchen table.

"What do you think is happening?" my mother asked.

"I don't know," said Jeanette. "But I don't think it's good news."

"You don't think ..." said my mother, exactly the same way my grandmother had.

"I told you," Jeanette said, "I don't know. Dr. Fred said it wasn't possible."

"But so many people getting sick at once? What on earth can it be?"

"Brace yourself," Jeanette said. "The shit is about to hit the fan."

■ ■ ■

BY NOON THERE were thirteen people in the hospital with fevers, puking and crapping themselves. Now, in the cold light of day and years after the event, we know it was the water. It had been, as I said, a dry year, and in dry years water stands and becomes fetid. Wells evaporate. Town reservoirs grow hot and stale. Bacteria breeds. The water main break in July, it was also surmised, might have allowed dirty water to run across the surface and encounter something spoiled before being reabsorbed into the giant aquifer beneath the town. Those bacteria then sat for weeks in the above ground reservoir on the outskirts of Advocate, before finally being drawn into people's homes.

In any other year and in any other time it would have simply been a case of water poisoning. A boil water advisory would have been put in place, and for a few weeks or a month people would have been put to the inconvenience of travelling seven miles out of town to the Carlsbad Springs to fill up containers and lug them home.

But it was not another time. It was not another place.

It was 1984, in Advocate.

It seems silly now to mistake water poisoning for an outbreak of AIDS. But the dialogue was not rational, the understanding weak. People had been waiting for months for someone to get sick, and when the person finally did, it didn't matter if they had a deep cough and cancer or vomiting and diarrhea. They immediately jumped to conclusions.

By three o'clock twenty people were sick, and the local radio station from Trenton carried the news about the second cancellation of the Lemon parade. There was no mention of the Orange. So far all the people who got ill were from the Catholic side of the river. This was simply by chance, but no one knew that then, and there were all sorts of wild speculations that the virus incubated on our side of the river alone. That God was striking us down, one by one, because my uncle, even though he was miscreant, was nominally Catholic.

My grandmother spent all afternoon on the phone. By five o'clock it was established fact my uncle was responsible for the illness, and many were in hysterics. She received a phone call just before supper from the mayor, who "expressed his concern."

Even though my grandmother likely believed what everyone else did, that the "chickens had come home to roost," she still gave the mayor a piece of her mind. "Sloppy government," she told him. "You should be looking to contain this, Thompson, and start pointing fingers afterwards."

I don't know what exactly Thompson replied. My grandmother

never said, other than that he suggested, politely, my grandmother "relocate" my uncle until it all sorted through.

"Why on earth would we do that?" my grandmother asked. "The boy can barely walk let alone be relocated."

Thompson mumbled some reply and my grandmother hung up on him in annoyance. When my mother asked her what was said, Grandnan only harrumphed, and said things would have been done differently in her day.

Jeanette wondered how they were going to cancel the Lemon Day parade one day before it was supposed to happen. The Trenton radio station would reach those from town and surrounding areas who planned to come, but anyone from farther away wouldn't get the notice. She would be surprised when she heard.

Roadblocks were to be set up on the river road to the south and the roads off the highway to the north. The RCMP would man them, along with local volunteers. The town was effectively under quarantine. A team of specialists were being sent in from Halifax to determine the origins of the sickness, though few people had any doubt where it came from.

Dr. Fred came over after supper to talk my mother and Jeanette. "It's ridiculous of course," he said. "Everyone who is sick has the symptoms of bacterial infection. Nothing else. But none of them will listen. They are convinced they're all dying of AIDS."

"And what about the other doctors?" asked my mother.

"They're on my side, for once," sighed Dr. Fred. "They realize something gastrointestinal is going on, though some of the nurses are frightened. Some have left their posts and gone home. The head nurse is threatening to have them fired. She's doing her best to maintain order. We've had sixty people without any symptoms asking if there's a test for AIDS. Nurse Jones tells them to go home and only give her a call when they start shitting their pants. She's a tough old bird. I wish we had a hundred like her."

Twice while Dr. Fred was at our home the phone rang. The first time was a hang up. The second time a nameless woman screamed at my mother to get my uncle out of town and to stop trying to kill them all. After the call ended, my mother stood bewildered with the phone in her hand and asked what was happening.

"Paranoia," said Dr. Fred. "Hysteria. This is what happens when the dam breaks."

"But don't these people listen?" said Jeanette. "They've been told they can't get it. What do they want us to do, for God's sake? Burn him at the stake?"

"People are foolish animals," Dr. Fred said, "when they're faced with something they don't understand. They're scared. They're confused. They're looking to take it out on someone."

"Well," said Aunt Jeanette, "they won't take it out on him. He only has God knows how many days left, and he deserves to live them in as much peace and dignity as possible."

"I agree," said Fred. "This will blow over. We'll find the cause of this illness. I suspect the water supply myself, so I wouldn't drink any if I were you, unless you boil it. Until then you'll just have to batten down the hatches. Maybe don't answer the phone. I suspect they'll stop short of a posse at the door."

■ ■ ■

DR. FRED WAS wrong. Five people arrived at our door at six o'clock that Friday evening, shortly after supper had concluded and my grandmother had started the dishwasher with its slow, soporific drone and occasional squeak. When the knock came, my grandmother wondered aloud who it was. I stood in the hallway and looked when she opened it.

Standing there were Marjorie Moore, the head librarian; Joe Gall, the owner of the convenience store; and Thompson, the mayor. We had no doubt these three were representatives of the town. They had been chosen, rather than coming of their own volition. There were two others, but when I later asked my mother who they were, she said it didn't matter.

"I'm surprised," said my Aunt Jeanette, "they weren't all wearing masks and surgical gowns. Or rubber gloves, when they knocked at the door."

Neither my mother nor Jeanette spoke to these people again, long after all the fuss had died down and things went back to normal. My grandmother said they were being "unchristian." She was, she said, perfectly willing to forgive and forget and let bygones be bygones.

"That would be a first," said Jeanette.

But my grandmother was, in some ways, more practical than Jeanette or my mother. Thompson would remain mayor until 1990, a year after I went off to university in Toronto. My grandmother couldn't very well not speak to him and keep her nose in town business. She had to compromise. Besides, as my mother and Jeanette had to know, she felt differently from the start about things. She may have even instinctively understood what was going on when she opened the door to the five townspeople standing on her front stoop that night. Aunt Jeanette and my mother were upstairs attending to my uncle. They had not heard the doorbell, or they ignored it if they had. My grandmother politely greeted all, and asked what she could do for them.

"We have something to discuss with you," said the mayor, who, at that moment, didn't seem very mayor-like. Thompson wouldn't look my grandmother in the eye, and he stood at the front of the phalanx like he had been pushed. He was stocky and balding, and wore rimless glasses, as well as a blue sweater and jeans and white sneakers, his summer uniform. He blinked like a bemused owl.

"What do you want to discuss?" my grandmother said lightly.

Just then, my mother came down the stairs and saw the crowd at the door. She asked my grandmother what was going on.

"Thompson was just saying he'd like to talk to us," my grandmother said. "Won't you come in?"

Whenever anyone came to the door in an official capacity, my grandmother always turned into a model of good manners and civility — provided she agreed with the purpose of the visit. In this case, assuming she knew what the visit was about before anyone stated it, she must have also known her invitation would be refused. Ours was the house of plague. Those people were no more likely to step into it than they would a World War II battlefield. But she invited them in anyway.

There was some slight shuffling of feet as Thompson politely declined, and a few wavering gazes. It was as if they were a gang of naughty school children waiting to be scolded.

My mother stood beside my grandmother at the door, blocking my view. "What's all this about?"

"Well," said Thompson. "You must know that ..."

His tone dropped to a restrained mumble.

Aunt Jeanette came down the stairs and stood behind my mother and grandmother. My grandmother stepped back and my aunt assumed her place.

Thompson's voice rose again. "We know how difficult this is for you, but the town is sick. We all know that whatever this is is spreading, and lives are in danger. We have to ask you to move your brother before something worse happens."

"You silly old fool," said Jeanette.

"Jeanette!" reprimanded my grandmother. "Be civil!"

"I will not!" cried Jeanette. "He should know better. You all should. Shame on you. Each and every one!"

"Fine for you to say," a woman's voice came from the back. "You don't have any kids. What about us parents who are only concerned for the safety of our children?"

"I have kids," said my mother. "And do you see anything wrong with him?"

I'm not sure when my grandmother slipped away from all this. I didn't even notice she was gone until it was all over. Later my aunt said she had chickened out. My mother disagreed.

"She's ashamed," she said. "For once, Mom is on the wrong side of the tracks. And she doesn't much like it."

I stood behind my aunt and mother and listened to them argue. It got heated. Voices rose. Another woman threatened legal action. "You're putting us all at risk and there ought to be a law. If there isn't, we'll get Thompson here to introduce an ordinance. How many people have to get sick before you do something about him?"

"They're sick because of the water," Jeanette said. "That's a fact. And when you all find out it's true you'll be shamefaced and begging forgiveness."

"From the likes of you?" the woman said. "Not likely."

If my mother wasn't there to restrain her, I'm not sure Jeanette wouldn't have stepped outside and challenged this woman, whoever she was, to a duel.

In the end, nothing was resolved, and Thompson suggested they go. The woman who picked a fight with Jeanette gave one parting shot. "You've ruined this town," she said. "The parade cancelled. The hospital full. When someone dies of it you'll be sorry."

Jeanette looked like she was about to say something else, but my mother shut the door. She and Jeanette just looked at each other.

"I just want to scream," my mother said.

"Scream then," said Aunt Jeanette. "Let's make them hear us."

And my mother did. A short, high-pitched bark of frustration.

My grandmother shouted down from upstairs, "What's the matter?"

"You are!" Jeanette called back. Then she burst into tears.

My mother hugged her and told her not to worry, and Jeanette
sobbed on her shoulder. I had seen Jeanette cry before. But not
like this — great gusts of emotion that seemed, in a sense, out of
proportion to me.

"They're idiots," my mother said. "They'll see the truth eventually." After a few minutes Jeanette pulled away and asked my mother
what they were going to do.

"What can we do?" said my mother. "It's not like they can kick
us out of town. When they find out what's wrong with all those
people they'll pull in their horns. Meanwhile we just take care of
David."

Jeanette wiped her eyes with her hands, and marshalled herself.
She said she'd be damned if she was just going to sit around and
let them get the better of her.

"Don't do anything rash," my mother said.

"I just wish …" said Jeanette, and let the thought fade.

My mother watched her carefully. She knew her sister well.
"What?"

"I've got an idea," said Jeanette. "Do we have any markers? Any
bristol board?"

"Somewhere in the house," said my mother. "For Jacob's school
projects, I think."

"Good," said Jeanette. "I think we should march in the parade
tomorrow."

"Jeanette," said my mother gently. "There isn't going to *be* any
parade tomorrow."

"Oh yes there is. It only takes two for a parade, and I bet we
can get more than that."

"What are you thinking?"

"Someone has got to make a stand," Jeanette said. "Someone
has got to get it into the open. And I think I know how to do it."

My mother would have asked her more questions, but my

grandmother came to the top of the stairs and asked if the guests
had gone.

"I wouldn't call them guests," said my mother.

"They're gone," said Aunt Jeanette. "No thanks to you."

"All this fuss," said my grandmother. "All this unnecessary
commotion."

"The woman lives in a river in Egypt," said my aunt.

"De Nile," said my mother.

Suddenly, and shockingly, they burst into laughter.

■ ■ ■

THAT NIGHT, MY mother decided to officially let me visit with my
uncle. She sat a chair near the door, not too close to his bed, and
asked me to sit in it and help keep him company. He had a terrible cold and kept clearing his throat and coughing. The sheets were
pulled up to his waist and he sat up in bed with the pillows behind
him. He kept shifting his weight, as if he was uncomfortable, and
his hands lay on top of the sheets twisting nervously, like emaciated
birds of prey. He smiled at me and the effect was ghastly. Even his
voice seemed to have changed — thinner, more a croak or a whisper. He kept taking sips out of a glass of water with a straw beside
his bed. No one mentioned the little committee at the door. They
didn't bother to inform him of the cancellation of the Lemon Day
parade, either. Whatever inklings my uncle had of the resistance to
his presence in the town he picked up by osmosis — by the attitude
and gestures of his sisters, and by their refusal to talk about certain
things. When he asked about the parade, they changed the subject.
When he asked about my grandmother, they said she was great, which
he must have known was a lie. My grandmother was never "great."

She still did not come in to visit him.

She might bring him his tray if my mother and Jeanette were
out, but she wouldn't linger. Uncle David told my mother he now

saw and heard less of his mother than he did when he was in Toronto.

"Don't worry about it," my mother said. "She's busy with the spring cleaning."

"Caroline," David said. "It's August. Spring has been over for months."

"Summer cleaning then," said my mother. "What are you reading David?"

My uncle's illness did not prevent him from reading books. He read everything. Because the library refused to lend them any books, in case my uncle contaminated the volumes, my mother and Jeanette bought him what he needed. The book that lay open-faced on his bedside table was a tome, the thickest book I had ever seen.

"*War and Peace*," my uncle said. "I've been putting it off for twenty years. I figured I'd better get it in."

"Is it good?" asked Aunt Jeanette. I could see they were relieved to have the subject turn to the tangible and uncontroversial. My uncle briefly explained what he liked and what he didn't about the book. "It's strange," he said finally, "to spend your life reading stories other people have made up. Lately I've begun to wonder if there is any value in it."

"Of course there is!" cried Aunt Jeanette. "*War and Peace* is one of the great works of literature."

My uncle shrugged, and through his pyjamas I could see how thin his shoulders were. They tented the shoulders of his pyjamas tops, rather than lifted them. It gave the impression of his clothes being more substantial than he was. "I don't know," said my uncle. "I mean, I love literature. I always have. In some ways, I guess, I've dedicated my life to it. But it seems the occupation of the living rather than the dying."

"Don't talk that way," my mother said. "No one here is dying."

The silence was awkward, and prolonged. My mother and Jeanette seemed determined to keep up this pretense of hope. They fussed over him, and talked to him, and tried to keep up a facade of normality. They thought they were helping him, but even I, at twelve and not skilled in the ways of the world, could see they were not. My uncle was defeated, and he wanted to talk about that defeat. Perhaps needed to. He knew the reality, even if his sisters didn't, and he wanted to stop pretending and just give in to it. But he was unable to, in the face of his sisters' denial. It made for an atmosphere even more depressing than the situation would normally be.

I asked if I could be excused. I had said nothing except hello to my uncle since I came into the room. When I got up to leave he smiled and thanked me for visiting.

My grandmother accosted me at the entrance to my room. "What are they doing in there?" she said.

"Just talking," I said.

She looked me up and down anxiously. "You didn't touch him, did you?"

"No Grandnan," I said. "I didn't."

"Good," said my grandmother. "I'm making some cocoa. Would you like some?"

I declined. It was the dead of summer, and though it was nine o'clock at night, it was still warm enough in the house that I suspected I would have trouble sleeping even with the fan in my room.

My grandmother only made cocoa when she was upset about something. She was waiting, I suspected, for my aunt and my mother to come out of David's room so she could talk about the events of the day. The posse at the door. The sickness in town. The cancellation of the parade. My grandmother had an iron constitution. Nothing ever phased her. She met adversity with strength, conflict with resolve, contradiction with bullheadedness. But tonight I noticed how pale and strained she looked, her face lined with care and wrinkles, her hair grey and wispy. She looked old to me then, of immeasurable years. I felt, for the first time since my uncle had

come home, and maybe for the first time in my life, slightly sorry
for her. It must have seemed everyone was against her, in the house
and in the town. If grandfather had been alive he would have taken
her side. Together the two of them would have dealt with this. But
she was only one old woman, with two full-grown and headstrong
daughters and a son who was dying.

I said nothing to her.

There was nothing to say.

My grandmother went downstairs to make her cocoa and I
went into my room to get ready for bed.

■ ■ ■

THE ONE VISITOR my uncle had, and who came regularly to the
house despite the warnings of the town, was Henry Hennsey. I
don't remember him entering my grandmother's house before then.
I would have recalled that, for even after he started visiting a lot,
and my grandmother no longer stood on ceremony with him, his
presence still seemed strange to me. I wondered if Henry had been
the only black man to ever see the inside of my grandmother's
house. Likely he was, for as I've said there were very few black
people in Advocate over the years.

My grandmother did not complain. She was glad of any visitor
in those days when no one came to see her. She fussed over him.
She offered him tea and cakes and told him there was no need to
remove his shoes. The rest of us were still shouted at if we happened
to take two steps across the marble tiles without taking off our shoes
and placing them on the mat.

Henry was more than civil with my grandmother, and he usually
accepted the tea and sweets, and sat down at the table in the kitchen
to talk with her before going to see my uncle. But it was my uncle
Henry came to see, and his visits with my grandmother were kept
short. I don't know what Uncle David and Henry talked about.

My mother never said, if she ever knew. Knowing Henry and my uncle, it would not be inanities. Maybe they talked about literature. Maybe they talked about *War and Peace*.

More likely, they talked about the town. I could almost hear my uncle complaining about his sisters' well-meaning, but frustrating, efforts to shield him from what the townspeople were up to. I could almost hear Henry cautioning my uncle against judgment, defending my mother and Aunt Jeanette for their good intentions, while at the same time giving my uncle a blow-by-blow of what was really going on in Advocate. It was Henry Hennsey who told my uncle, when he came to visit early Saturday morning, what my Aunt Jeanette had planned. She had called him the night before and asked if he would march in the new parade with her and anyone else she could convince to come along.

From the beginning, mother disagreed with Jeanette's approach. She did not doubt her dedication to my uncle. She did not question her intentions. But marches, of which Jeanette was very fond, were not an effective way, in her opinion, to deal with the problem at hand. "What good will it accomplish?" she argued. "A couple of people with signs and placards annoying them. I just don't see the point."

"There's plenty of point," said my aunt. "Someone has to start telling the truth. To speak up. We have to make ourselves heard."

My mother was suspicious this was just another cause for my aunt. "David probably won't like it," she said. "You know how he feels about a fuss."

David did not like it. When Henry told him what Aunt Jeanette had planned, he called her into his room with them. I stood outside the door in the hallway, out of sight, able to hear clearly.

"What's all this nonsense," said my uncle, "about you having a march?"

"It's a protest parade," said Aunt Jeanette. "In your honour."

"I don't want anything in my honour, Jeanette," said Uncle David. "I didn't come home to make this kind of trouble."

"I know you didn't," said Jeanette. "But we've got to stand up to these people, David. We can't let them walk all over us."

"Yes we can," David said. "Who cares what they think? Let them fly to the moon and back if it makes them happy."

"I'm marching," said Jeanette. "I'll keep your name out of it."

"It's silly," said David. "What do you think Henry?"

Henry didn't answer right away. Then, finally, he said, "I agree they could use a good swift kick in the pants. Though I'm not sure this is the way to go about it."

"It's one way," said my aunt. "You should come, David. We'll wheel you. Don't you want to be a part of this?"

"Not really," he said. "I'm a part of it enough already."

"But don't you want to show them who it is they're doing this to? Don't you want to stand up for yourself?"

"Jeanette," said my uncle, not unkindly, "I *can't* stand up for myself. I can't go anywhere without that damn walker or that damn wheelchair. I can barely breathe, for Christ's sake. And you want me to take part in some kind of an AIDS march, or whatever you want to call it?"

It was the first time, to my knowledge, the word had been spoken in our house. It had been thought and deliberated over no end, but no one had had the guts to say it. Even our detractors in town and on the school board, in the little ad hoc committees of denial and prejudice, had not said it to us directly, though it must have been bandied around endlessly behind closed doors.

The use of the forbidden word did not deter my aunt. Instead she embraced it. "That's what we'll call it. The AIDS march! Perhaps we'll hold it annually."

My uncle did something unexpected then. He laughed. It was a dry, weak laugh, more of a quick bark than anything, but I was certain it was a sign of merriment. He was making fun of my aunt. "Go ahead," he said. "Have your little march, if it makes you feel better. It won't change anything."

"It might," said Jeanette. "Henry? Are you still coming?"

"I suppose," said Henry. "Though I'm inclined to agree with your brother it won't change any minds. People think what they want to think, and neither dynamite nor thunderstorms can change that."

"We'll see," said Jeanette. "David? You'll think about coming with us? You could use the air."

"No. What time are you going?"

"We start at two. From here on Tenerife Street, then down Main Street. I'll get Jacob to help me make up the signs."

At the mention of my name I scooted off into my room. Jeanette had already laid out pieces of white Bristol board and markers on my bed. I was bewildered by what we were supposed to do with them. After a few minutes, I went downstairs and called Deanny. She knew about the Lemon Day parade being cancelled. She was disappointed because she wanted to carry her sign that read *suck a lemon*.

I told her she could still get to carry a sign.

"Really?" she said.

"Really. Jeanette's having a protest march. For my uncle."

"I'll be right over," Deanny said.

She hadn't asked what the march was about, specifically, or what were the events that spawned it. Like Jeanette, she was spoiling for a good fight.

■ ■ ■

IN ALL THE excitement, neither my aunt nor grandmother had thought to ask what had become of the parade on the Protestant side of the river. We'd heard only of the Lemon parade being cancelled. We all assumed the Orange one was too.

Around noon we heard of the roadblocks being set up at either entrance to the town diplomatically informing tourists of the sickness, the fact that its cause was thus far unknown, and that travel into Advocate was ill-advised. This did not stop the organizers of the Orange Day parade from holding theirs. It was not a joke parade organized in satirical response. It was a legitimate socio-religious event. They did not inform my grandmother of this, though she thought they should have, and the radio station in Trenton carried no news of it. While Jeanette was busy with Deanny downstairs in the living room making up protest signs on bristol board, the participants in the parade on the other side of the river were marshalling.

Dr. Fred told us no one had died overnight at the hospital. A few people had been released, including Rebecca, the milkman's daughter. To test the theory of the contaminated water main, the experts from Halifax were analyzing samples from the water tower that stands on giant iron stilts overlooking the town just beyond Mechanicsville and from the aquifer on the protestant side.

In a few hours, they would prove Dr. Fred right. The cause of the outbreak of illness was *E. coli*, not AIDS. But my mother and Jeanette would refrain from saying "I told you so." The mood of the town did not change at all. It may have been *E. coli* this time, they said, but next time it could be AIDS. It was still a crime that my uncle be allowed to die in the town, among them. It was still possible his disease would spread.

As months and years passed, following my uncle's death, the town did grow ashamed of its behaviour. Some justified it by claiming that they just didn't know. "We were all a little crazy then," Mayor Thompson said. "A little fearful. You can't blame us for that, can you?"

My mother and Jeanette could, and would. A long time would pass before they resumed their pre-Uncle David social positions in town. Jeanette at one point talked of moving, but my mother did not want to uproot me from school and Jeanette wouldn't leave without my mother. I blame the fact that neither my mother or Jeanette ever married on those days, a mute form of protest that went on for their rest of their lives, though they both might have been unaware of it.

As soon as it was all over, my grandmother blended back into the town as if nothing had happened. They welcomed her gratefully. It was understood that Jeanette and my mother did not matter. As long as my grandmother was able to put the summer of 1984 behind her, all was well. At home, we never spoke about that year.

I went back to school, and though I was still teased mercilessly up to grade eleven, I was never teased about Uncle David. It was as if the entire town had swum through the river of Lethe, the waters of forgetfulness. By the time I had left Advocate to study in Toronto, and had been in that city for a number of years, enough time had passed. Even my mother and Jeanette had seemed to soften somewhat, if not entirely. They had become involved in the life of the town again.

I was the only one who couldn't let it go. It is no wonder I became a counsellor, an advocate for those who couldn't speak for themselves. My mother was touched, she said, that I would choose a career in memory of my uncle. I don't think she realized how damaged by those times I really am.

■ ■ ■

MY MOTHER HAD no intention of going on any AIDS march with Jeanette. She told her so at breakfast and again, after lunch, when Jeanette had made all the signs and was waiting for two o'clock, when they could begin. Jeanette would not say who, if anyone, she had convinced to come with us.

"A few select people," she said. "Who aren't blind and stupid and have their heads up their asses."

"Language!" my grandmother said. "This isn't a saloon!"

"No one uses the word *saloon* anymore, Mother," Jeanette said. "It's tavern or bar."

"Whatever," said my grandmother. "No swearing in this house. And I should forbid this marching business too. Caroline is right. It's ridiculous."

"I never said it was ridiculous," said my mother. "Just ineffectual."

"We have to stand together," Jeanette said. "If I go and you don't the town will think we're divided. It won't look good."

"I don't care how it looks," said my mother. "I plan on going to the next town council meeting and giving them a piece of my mind. I think that will work better."

"Why don't you do that?" said my grandmother. She could understand going to town council meetings and giving them a piece of her mind. She'd done it often enough. And though it was also a public display, it was a lot less public than a parade down the middle of town.

But Jeanette was determined. She would go it alone if she had to, she said. But she never thought her own sister would shy away from a little controversy.

"I'm not shying away from anything," said my mother. "You do it your way, and I'll do it mine. You can get Deanny and Jacob to march with you."

"I plan on it," said Jeanette. "Let me know if you change your mind."

That might have been the end of it, if my mother hadn't received a phone call a half hour later from Mr. Byrd, the man who owned the diner.

"I'm sorry," Mr. Byrd said. He told my mother he'd had the same posse at his door. They said they suspected the sickness came from the diner, and they were willing to pass a town ordinance to shut him down unless he removed my mother and Jeanette permanently from the payroll.

"They can't do that," my mother said. "Only the health department can shut you down."

"They can," said Mr. Byrd. "Under an emergency town ordinance. And they say they'll do it unless I let you go. I can fight them, but that will take time. Until then, if I want to keep the place open, I'll have to do as they ask."

"But you don't believe them?" said my mother. "You don't believe Jeanette and I could actually make anyone sick?"

Mr. Byrd answered, but too slowly for my mother. She could tell by the delay he did believe it, or was at least entertaining the possibility. She hung up. She had been stunned into silence.

She went upstairs and told my aunt, who was in Uncle David's bedroom, what had happened. Deanny and I were in the room with them. Jeanette had made us bring the bristol board signs up to show him.

"I'm sorry," David said.

My mother told my uncle not to apologize. It wasn't his fault.

"It is," he said. "I should never have come home."

"Thank God you did," said Jeanette.

In the end, my mother agreed to march in the parade. She said we would accomplish little. We'd be a ragtag band of dissenters lost amidst the cries and howls of the mob. But any stand is better than no stand. Any action is better than no action.

I sometimes wish my mother could see the AIDS marches that take place in Toronto. Tens of thousands strong with banners and pride and inexhaustible determination. She would be proud, I think, that we may have had the first one in the country. Everything large begins as something small; the most mighty rivers start off as a trickling stream.

■ ■ ■

I DON'T THINK Jeanette, more than my mother, could ever entirely forgive my grandmother for not marching in the parade with us that day. It was entirely Jeanette's enterprise, her brainchild, and she thought my grandmother should at least make an effort. My grandmother thought Jeanette was being "silly as a goose" and in some ways I agreed with her. I'm not sure what Jeanette expected to accomplish. She knew the minds of those in town and how they felt about things. Surely she didn't expect to change them. To my mother she said she just wanted to "rub their noses in it," which was originally the source of my mother's complaint. When you rub someone's nose in it, she said, your hands tend to get dirty, too.

Jeanette had waited a long time for a real cause which she could get behind, and she felt she had found it in my Uncle David. I don't know how many people she called that day, people she felt would be sympathetic to our cause and willing to stand up for it. She must have known she would be largely unsuccessful. Even those who agreed with her were unlikely to want to march with placards through the streets and stir up trouble. Most begged off, and in the end only three other people showed up: Henry Hennsey, a young man Jeanette knew from the Indian reserve, and to our utter and complete surprise, Deacon Harry. By the time he arrived at the door, my grandmother had already retreated to her room. She was not a retreater by nature, but she was overwhelmed by the small, seething cauldron of civil disobedience in her living room.

Jeanette had piled the bristol boards with their sayings on the living room sofa and I had gone through them with Deanny while my mother and Jeanette had lunch. *It's a disease! Not a curse!* read one. *Judge not, lest you be judged!* read another. Deanny was particularly proud of the one she had made. *Cooties won't kill you. Stupidity will!*

It was so Deanny-esque it made me laugh.

Before my grandmother went upstairs, she pleaded with my

mother and Jeanette. "You'll ruin us in this town," she said, bursting into tears. "I hope you know that."

"We've already been ruined," answered Jeanette. "Look what they've done to us!"

To this my grandmother had no answer.

Afterwards my mother said she felt sorry for her. "This is the worst thing that has happened to her since Dad died."

When Deacon Harry showed up my mother asked him what Father Orlis thought about the whole thing.

"He doesn't say much," said the deacon. "I think he believes the town is being hysterical, but he can see the point. In the twelfth century, priests and monks were afraid to give the last rights to victims of the plague. This is a very old scenario."

"What did he think about you coming out with us today?" asked my Aunt Jeanette.

Deacon Harry looked at her sheepishly. "He doesn't know. I thought it best to reserve the debate until after the fact."

"Right," said Jeanette. "Do you want to carry the *Judge not lest you be judged* sign?"

Deacon Harry, who had worn plain clothes — jeans and a white button-down shirt and high-top sneakers — shook his head and said he should carry something a little less "job related."

He eventually ended up with *Compassion is the cure to all ills.*

My mother carried *Hatred hurts more than sickness.*

Henry chose *Judge not.*

Deanny took hers and Aunt Jeanette took *It's a disease.*

The young man from the reserve, whom I had never met and whose name was Darcy, had something written in Mi'kmaq on his card. Jeanette had always had friends on the reserve. The land we lived on, she often told us, did not belong to us but to the Indians. We had stolen it, and we would either have to give it back or pay mightily for what we had so blithely taken. Jeanette's talk of Native justice made my grandmother furious. She considered Natives to be ne'er-do-wells and alcoholics who lived off the generosity of the state and contributed nothing to the town. There were many heated arguments about this at the dinner table when I was young. But so far, Darcy was the first Native to come to our house, and he seemed to come in peace. When Jeanette asked him what his sign said, he shook his head and said it was simply about joy.

"Amen," said Aunt Jeanette.

Mine, created for me by my mother because I couldn't think of anything to say, read *God is Love*.

■ ■ ■

ALL IN ALL, there were seven of us that day. A Native man, a black man, a deacon, two waitresses, a twelve-year-old boy on the cusp of puberty, and an eleven-year-old girl from the wrong side of the tracks. We were hardly intimidating. All of us were used, somehow, to being on the outside, and so perhaps it was fitting we were to represent the conscience of our town.

I felt self-conscious, I remember, stepping out the front door, sign in hand, walking down Tenerife Street. Perhaps we all did, for there was very little conversation. Somewhere from the street behind a lawn mower brayed. There were no cars, nobody on the lawns. A breathless hush seemed to have gripped the neighbourhood. We imagined we were being watched through windows, though the truth is that no one had the slightest clue what we were up to. The sickness at the hospital and the cancellation of the parade had dampened the mood of the town. If anyone saw us walking the remaining few blocks of Tenerife Street towards Cornwallis, they did not rush out of their houses and scream at us.

Jeanette, who was bristling for confrontation, was disappointed in the lack of reaction. She asked we hold our signs to the sides so people could read them from their windows. But there seemed to be no one in the windows. As we swung towards Main, the faint tattoo of a marching band could be heard. Jeanette cried, "The Orange parade!"

"Yes," said Deacon Harry. "It's not cancelled. Didn't you know?"

"No," said my mother. "We didn't."

Jeanette looked as if she didn't know what to say. The reality of the parade in motion across the river took some of the wind out of her sails. Prejudice in pockets is harder to fight than blanket intolerance. Obviously the Protestants were not giving in to the hysteria. Obviously they had thought the town safe enough to hold their annual march. Jeanette looked helplessly at my mother.

"What!" my mother said. "This is good news, Jeanette! At least some people have their heads screwed on straight."

Jeanette nodded. "We'll march down this side of the river," she said. "This is the side we should be worried about anyway. God-damned Catholics."

She looked at Deacon Harry. "Sorry, Deacon," she said.

"No worries," said the deacon. "I say it myself."

Henry Hennsey laughed.

We held up our signs and continued down Cornwallis to Main. The usual traffic was there for a Saturday. Some stared at us for brief moments, then carried on their business. We marched through downtown in silence. There were no taunts or catcalls. My aunt was again disappointed. She expected active resistance. She expected Kent State. We couldn't march in the middle of the street because of the traffic, so we stayed on the sidewalk. Anyone who met us politely stepped aside and let us pass. They scanned the signs and placards, but refused to meet our eye.

Only one woman spoke as we passed. "You should be ashamed of yourselves," she said.

"For what?" shouted Jeanette. "For caring about a sick man? For having compassion, and love? It's you that should be ashamed, lady."

The woman refused to give in. She stood on the sidewalk, a safe distance away, and told my aunt this was all her fault, she had brought my uncle here, and the entire town was sick, and it was a plague upon our house. Jeanette wanted to stay and argue, but my mother and Deacon Harry talked her out of it.

"Let's just march," my mother said.

"Show them solidarity, Jeanette," said Deacon Harry. "Let God deal out the punishments."

It was an unsatisfying affair. Once we had marched the length of Main Street, with just that single comment and no protest, we turned back. Jeanette was disheartened. "Apathy," she said.

"What did you expect?" my mother asked. "Cheers?"

"I want them to notice us!" cried Jeanette. "I want them to acknowledge!"

"That's not how it works," said Henry, speaking from experience. "You become invisible. That's the Brutus cut."

Darcy, the Indian, nodded. We could have marched up and down Main Street all day and not elicited more responses. We saw a number of *Closed* signs in the window of shops that would have normally been open on a Saturday. Jeanette wanted to go over to the Protestant side and try our luck there in the midst of the celebration, but my mother wouldn't let her. "They're keeping up the tradition and doing the right thing," she said. "Why would we protest them?"

"We should protest all of them," said Jeanette. "They all need to hear the truth."

In the end we went home, more defeated by the lack of response than anything. Deacon Harry said we should take comfort from the fact that we had tried. "The point was made," he said. "That's the best we can do."

Jeanette wanted to put the signs up against the house for the neighbours to see. She actually did it, but my grandmother went out and removed them as soon as she got the chance. Jeanette couldn't find them again. She suspected my grandmother had burned them in the fire pit out back. The next year, after my uncle had died, she made up new signs. We marched in the Lemon Day parade with them. No one commented on them then, either. Even my grandmother ignored them. It was a meagre attempt at change, but at least it *was* an attempt.

The Monday after the parade, while the infection was still ravaging the town, Jeanette went to the grocery store. No cashier would wait on her. Whenever she stepped up to a wicket a *Cash Closed — Use Next Cashier* sign was set down. When she went to another, the same thing happened, until all the cashes were closed and she was left with a cartful of unpaid groceries. When she complained to the manager, he said it was a coincidence that all the cashiers were taking a break.

"And no one is checking through customers?" asked Jeanette. "Surely you don't expect me to believe that."

"Believe what you want," said the manager. "I'm only telling you what I know."

When Jeanette asked him what she was supposed to do with all her food, he told her to take it and go. "You can send us a cheque," he said. "Or pay us later."

"I have to handle a cheque," said Jeanette. "You might get it that way too."

The manager scurried away from her, with more speed than she would have expected if the building had been on fire. Jeanette did not send him a cheque. She kept the food. After a few tries over the next while, with similar results, she had to send Henry to the store for us. The situation was ridiculous, as bad as the divisions between the Protestants and Catholics when the town was founded hundreds of years ago.

All that week, we continued to receive updates of people in

town who believed they had contracted AIDS from the air — even
after they had been sent home from the hospital, cured from their
poisoning. The weekly *Advocate Gazette* carried a story about the
epidemic, full of factual errors and supposition. I still have the article
cut out with the headline *Strange Contagion Strikes Town*. It was
published after they had been informed it was bacterial infection.

My grandmother felt the effects of the shunning, too. When she
went to the meetings of her auxiliary or sewing circle, the doors
were locked against her and no matter how much she pounded on
them, she was not let in. "I know you're in there!" she cried. "I know
what it is you are doing."

The only place people did not prevent her from was Mass. A
lot of people stopped going while the sickness gripped the town.
Those who went gave my grandmother a wide berth. No one
wanted to stand in line for Communion with her, and for a while,
Father Orlis, likely because he was afraid to touch my grandmother's mouth, even stopped giving it. She was horrified that her
hallowed traditions were being uprooted and upended, and was
incensed she was no longer receiving the Body and Blood of Christ.
She complained about it to Orlis, who told her when things settled
down again in Advocate everything would go back to normal. "For
now," he told her, "we have to take precautions."

Even I felt the sting, because when I went to the corner store
on Main Street the proprietor would see me through the window,
flip the *Open* sign to *Closed* and lock the door.

Other shopkeepers did the same.

Our alienation was complete. The hysteria and calumny had
reached an apex, and our popularity and once assured respect
had reached its nadir. We could have fought it, but we didn't. We
were too exhausted and disheartened, too shocked at the blatant
prejudice and blind ignorance to do any more than shake our heads
and try to get on with our lives.

The weekend following the parades, Aunt Jeanette wanted to have another march, but she could get no one except Deanny to go with her. They marched down Main Street alone, eliciting no more response than they had before. Jeanette said she would march every Saturday if need be, until people finally got the message.

She stopped eventually. My uncle got sicker, and she was needed at home. Deanny wanted me to go, but I refused. And even if I wanted to, my mother wouldn't have let me. "That part of it is over," she told Deanny. "We have to get ready for this next part."

"What next part?" Deanny said. My mother wouldn't say, but Deanny knew. I knew, and I was much slower picking up on verbal cues than Deanny. Act III would be the deathbed scene, and we all had our particular roles to play. The time for worrying about the town was over.

# PART III

■
:
.

# EIGHT

∎

THAT FALL I began, unbidden, to think about men.

It is surprising to me now I didn't think about them earlier, that some glimmer of my own sexuality had not shone through, either in dreams or waking fantasies, before that year. I have a theory my psychological sexual development was delayed by the arrival of my uncle into our lives. I had refused to give it mental room. Given his own sexuality and what had resulted from it, I did not allow myself the possibility I too might be like him. I even had dreams sometimes in which I caught what he had, in which I was thin and had to be helped to the bathroom by my mother and Jeanette.

I had begun the process of puberty before my uncle arrived. My mother and Jeanette schooled me in what to expect. Sudden growth spurts. Occasional breaking of my voice into a higher register, the eventual lowering of it. Growth of the testicles. Pubic and armpit hair. Frequent erections. Wet dreams. Masturbation. They held nothing back and informed me fully, to the horror of my grandmother.

Initially, I found the whole thing distasteful, and then when it began to happen I fell into a sort of existential wonder. How could my body undergo such a radical set of changes in such a short period of time and still retain my own personality?

Sex would be of an interest to me, my mother said.

Girls would become an issue.

Despite having gone through this odious process for months —
checking the volume of hair under my arms and on my groin every
time I showered — girls had *not* become an issue. The size of my
penis grew, but my desire for women was not commensurate with it.
The only woman I knew well besides my grandmother, my mother,
and Aunt Jeanette was Deanny. I certainly felt no desire for her.
She had already gone through puberty and, when she was in a mood,
she said she was "on the rag." She had the beginning of breasts.
And though I'd not seen her naked I suspected she also had hair on
her groin.

The thought revolted me.

This alone should have been enough to tell me where my
tendencies lay, but I missed all the clues. I often had erections, but
I didn't masturbate. I had no sexual fantasies. I convinced myself
what I felt was not desire, but simple physical stimulus. My cock
rubbing against the fabric of my jeans if I had neglected to wear
underwear. Mistakenly brushing my hand against it while rolling
over in bed and causing it to sit up, a dog at attention. It is unfortunate, perhaps, all that desire came roaring to the surface at precisely
the time my uncle was dying in our house, with a disease somehow
related to his sexuality. If I could have stopped it I would have. If
I could have delayed it until some other time, I would have done
that also. But biology is insistent. It does not consider niceties and it
has its own immutable sense of timing. If it wants a thing it takes
it. It took me.

It started with a dream.

I was standing before an older boy in my school. I was in my
underwear. He was in his also. He pushed his down, took my hand
and put it on his engorged penis. I came in my sleep. The sensation was so glorious and powerful I woke up gasping for breath,
my whole lower body convulsing with the ejaculation as my erect

penis emptied itself of sperm. My heart beat madly. I was confused, frightened, wildly exhilarated. My sheets were a mess. There was spunk everywhere. Guilty, but still feeling that golden aching release in my cock and balls, I got up and gathered the sheets in a ball. I replaced them with fresh ones from the hall closet and started the washer in the basement in the middle of the night. My grandmother asked the next day what on earth my sheets were doing in the wash.

I had already prepared a lie.

"I peed myself," I said. "Too much milk I guess."

"Jacob!" cried my grandmother. "You're twelve years old!"

I shrugged. I would rather my grandmother think me a bedwetter than a pervert. I was afraid, I think, she would be able to tell the content of my dream simply by looking at the issue of it. The dream troubled me all day. I wasn't supposed to dream of men. My mother said it would be girls I would be interested in. I couldn't tell Deanny, and I told Deanny everything. I was miserable. But that night in bed, I found myself masturbating over the memory of the dream. Again I came, not as powerfully as the night before but still gasping, and convulsing. And once again I felt depressed and hopeless. I had done it again, this time consciously and so twice as guilty. I did not think of my uncle then. I swore to myself if I did it again I would think of girls. But whenever I did there was no lustre to the hand-motion. I threatened to wilt. Substitute with an image of a naked man and I was off to the races, coming sometimes in less than a minute. Night after night, I performed this desperate experiment on myself, always with the same results.

During the day I wallowed in self-pity.

At night I jerked off to beat the band.

I was your typical teenager, until it occurred to me if I did this with any men in reality I could end up with what my uncle had.

This sobered me.

For weeks I didn't masturbate.

My body tempted me cruelly. My cock stood up every night in eager anticipation but I would not give in. I wasn't going to be like that. I wasn't going to incur the wrath of God and the contempt of the world only to die a miserable death. I would deny it. If my body wanted to be that way, then let it. I wouldn't.

The body won, as it always does.

I did it again.

After that I stopped fighting. I took a box of Kleenex to my room to spare the sheets and masturbated as often as I could. Sometimes three times a day. But I swore I would never touch a real man. Never fondle him, or kiss him, or take the chance of catching something in our passion.

Many gay men make this promise to themselves when they are young — this I've learned from counselling. As far as I know, I'm the only one who's ever kept it.

■■■

ALTHOUGH NONE OF us were prepared for it, I was prevented from attending classes in Catholic school in the fall. I should have been in grade seven, after graduating from the elementary on the Protestant side in June. There had been no indication by the principal or my teachers that I would not be allowed back in school in September.

My mother tried to register me in the public school on the Protestant side, but was stymied there also. When she went to see the principal, he did not give her a flimsy excuse as others might have done. He told her directly I was not permitted back for the year due to the possibility of contagion.

She asked how they could know I was exposed to anything contagious.

"We don't," he said. "And that's just the problem. Until all that is sorted out, Jacob will have to stay home from school. If he wants to do an equivalent study program at home we can supply you with outlines and study guides. But I'm afraid, for the beginning of the year at least, he'll have to stay away."

My mother argued. She threatened to call the school board. She threatened to print a letter in the *Advocate Gazette*. She called the superintendent of schools in Trenton, though he already knew something of the case and said the principal was only being cautious and keeping me home from school for a few weeks would not hurt anybody. The decision, she was told, was precautionary, and made without prejudice. The same would be done with any family in any similar situation, no matter what the cause, and the school was entirely within its rights to ask me to stay home for the protection of the other students.

"What other families?" my mother asked on the phone. "What other similar situation?"

"Lice," he told her, with no apparent irony. "We can ask a student to stay at home because of lice."

"Lice?" said my mother. "You're actually asking me to believe this is the same situation as if Jacob had lice?"

"I realize it may seem different on the surface," the superintendent explained, "but I believe the principle is the same."

For several days after, my mother would shake her head and wonder out loud how a collection of people could be so damned stupid. She expected, I think, for someone — the school board, some advocacy group, a concerned citizen — to swoop in and save the day, to rescue her from the insanity that seemed to be gripping the town.

She would wait a long time.

What she didn't understand was all the concerned citizens were concerned in the wrong way — they all agreed with the school's decision. None of them said as much to her directly, and if she asked them why a young boy should be kept from his education due to fear and what she regarded as overreaction, they avoided making comment or meeting her eye, as if to say "Why make a fuss? It's only for a few weeks."

My mother was outraged I was being denied my education, but she knew further action was pointless. She did not write the letters to the *Gazette*. She had given up trying to fight the town. Instead, she and Jeanette began home-schooling me. Since neither one of them had jobs anymore, there was plenty of time.

They had both left high school more than a dozen years before. The curriculum had changed drastically in that time, and the public school was sensitive enough to the situation to supply me with brand new textbooks for all my classes. We worked through them together. In math, I was beyond both the textbooks and my mother and Aunt Jeanette. For English and history, they asked my uncle David if he would instruct me, and gave him the textbooks to choose the lessons.

I could see playing teacher again took a lot out of my uncle.

His breathing wasn't good.

That August he had picked up a respiratory infection. Dr. Fred was treating it with antibiotic without much success. My uncle rarely got out of bed anymore except to be helped to the bathroom. Sometimes his breathing was so laboured it could be heard all the way down the hall. At night I had trouble falling to sleep for the sound of it. I found my own breathing would sync to his, and I would roll over and place my head under the pillow, trying to stop it. My grandmother complained the sound of it kept her from sleeping.

"Jeez, Mom," said Jeanette. "Why doesn't he just die and get it over with, right?" The subject of death came up more and more, as if we were all girding ourselves for it, that by mentioning it a lot it would make it more palatable when it finally came.

Despite my uncle's weakened condition, he made one hell of

a teacher. One of the books on the syllabus for that year in grade seven was *Lord of the Flies*. He made me read it and then we discussed it "in class."

I loved that book.

The idea that beneath the thin veneer of civilization lay a much older savage reality appealed to me. I'd seen it, when kids my age acted one way in front of adults and entirely another when they weren't around. The theatre, for example, was one descent into madness. School another. The streets of Advocate, in alleys and parks and anywhere one could be cornered and torn apart, a third. My uncle said the book was "chock full" of symbolism, and the key to understanding the meaning of Golding's book was to recognize them for what they were.

A symbol, he told me, is the visual representation of an idea.

"A key can be a symbol for freedom, or imprisonment. A rose for love, or sex. An apple is often symbolic of death or poison. Water for creation. The sky for God."

What I liked about my uncle's style of teaching is that he did not talk down to me, as so many of the teachers had in my school. He expected me to understand the books we read on their own merits, rather than dissecting them and making them accessible to me by fitting them into my world. I was in Golding's world when I read, and I had to pay attention. The author was trusting me with a very important truth and wasn't watering it down. He was letting me have it with both barrels.

I read *Lord of the Flies* in two days.

I credit my love of literature now to my uncle, who showed me what a privilege it is to be invited into an author's world and shown his secrets. Every day, when he was feeling up to it, he would ask me into his room and we would discuss the book. He would drill me about what I read. Despite being on the lookout I missed most of the symbolism and my uncle had to explain it.

"What does it mean when the boys build huts and are unable to complete them?" my uncle asked.

I shrugged. I hadn't noticed this part.

"It's one of the most obvious symbols in the book, Jacob," he said. "It's beginning to break down. Civilization, which has barely taken hold in these young men, is represented here by structure. Construction. The huts symbolize man's separation from nature, and the fact the boys start to build them and then let them collapse is Golding's way of showing the lines that separate civilized man from bare savage are already beginning to blur, and they have been there no more than a week."

"Tell me about Piggy," I said.

"*You* tell me about Piggy."

And so I told my uncle. Piggy was just like me. And Cameron. Different from the rest and always getting picked on.

"True," said my uncle. "But he also represents reason. There is no place for reason within the heart of primitive man. And so they stone him to death. They obliterate their own higher faculties for the sake of their own savage heart."

My mother, who once or twice had sat in on these sessions, wondered aloud over dinner one night if *Lord of the Flies* was not too morbid for a twelve-year-old. My grandmother opined most of the books they taught in schools nowadays were trash. Sex and murder, and she wouldn't give ten cents for any of them.

"Oh, I don't know about that," said my mother. "But this book does seem a little harsh. What's the name of the boy they kill?"

"Piggy," I told her.

"Cute," said Jeanette.

"They drop a big rock, and push him off a cliff," I said.

"Oh," said Aunt Jeanette.

My uncle assured my mother *Lord of the Flies* was standard reading for Junior High students everywhere. "Better they learn it from a book than on the streets," he said. "It's not a hopeful story, but it connects with kids. It teaches something valuable."

I think my mother let me go on with the lesson because it seemed to be doing Uncle David as much good as it was me. As weak as he was, he seemed to energize slightly when he was teaching again. He could barely talk above a whisper, but his voice became impassioned. That my uncle had loved being a teacher was obvious, even to me. Sometimes he read passages aloud, and made the book come alive. When I read *Lord of the Flies* again, and I did many times, I could not do so without hearing my uncle's reedy, rasping voice speaking the words in a stately cadence.

■ ■ ■

DEANNY DID GO to school that fall. She was not lucky enough, she said, to be kept home by plague or poison. Her entry into grade six was the first foray she made into the Advocate public school system.

She hated it.

"Dorks and wieners," she told me her first day when she came over to our house after school. My mother made her sit down, got her a snack, and asked her to tell us all about it. The litany of complaint was dizzying in its detail and description. She was in Mrs. Burns' homeroom. Mrs. Burns had too much black hair piled up on her head in a bun, and looked like a tawdry tart — Deanny's words. She made Deanny get up in front of the class and introduce herself, and everyone snickered, because they knew she came from Meadow Pond Lane and was as poor as dirt.

Deanny had new clothes that first day. My mother and Jeanette made sure of it. But they made fun of her at recess and noon hour anyway.

One girl had seen Deanny smoking out behind the school at noon hour and threatened to tell a teacher.

"You do," said Deanny, "and I'll wipe the blackboard with your face and beat your ears together like erasers."

This she did not tell my mother. She saved it for me when we went up to my room.

"You're lucky," she told me. "I tried to tell my Mom I carried plague too because I went over to your house so much, but she isn't buying it. Maybe I should tell the principal."

I admit I enjoyed listening to her. There was little regret in me at not being allowed in school. I hated it almost as much as Deanny, and for the same reasons. The kids. Instead of calling them dorks and wieners, I would have said bullies. The sentiment was the same.

Deanny was a grade behind me, and so was not reading *Lord of the Flies*. She was reading "some piece of crap book I've never heard of by some piece of crap author I've never heard of."

I told Deanny what a wonderful teacher my uncle was. When she came over, always just after school let out at three o'clock, I was released from my studies. We ranged about the town. Deanny was correct that it made no sense to keep me away from the schoolhouse and not her. We hung around so much that whatever I had she was sure to get.

But prejudice, if it is anything, is unreasoning. It consistently kills the Piggys in its midst. I suppose if the principal had to bar students based on association, he would have no one in his school. If what my uncle had was indeed catching everyone would have it by now.

My mother and Jeanette were more concerned with making my uncle comfortable than worrying about the town. The atmosphere, which had been so depressing over the summer, changed. We went into contingency mode. The idea was we would accept this, for the sake of my uncle. We would try to remain cheerful.

Even my grandmother began to rouse herself somewhat. She

still was not wanted at town functions and meetings, but she began to bear this stoically. Fall housecleaning went ahead as it always did in September, but with an unusual vengeance. She wanted the attic and the basement and the garage cleaned, and every wall and floor in between. Deanny and I were engaged in this endeavour. Money changed hands.

The cinema still ran matinees, but Deanny and I no longer went to them. We used the opportunity to walk about the town on Saturday afternoons when practically every kid in Advocate was at Milo's cinema. When they weren't, we stuck to our neighbourhood and the old mill. We stuffed ourselves on penny candy and potato chips. We played basketball in the garage driveway, using an old peach basket with the bottom removed that we'd nailed above the door. My grandmother complained we were beating the shingles to death with the ball.

We rarely went to Deanny's house.

It was a wonder her parents remembered they had a daughter, she was there so seldom. Deanny too was now allowed in my uncle's room. She seemed to amuse him. He would ask her questions just to hear her sarcastic answers, and once or twice she made him laugh so hard he had trouble catching his breath. Deanny claimed to like my uncle.

"He's got guts," she told me. "I don't think I could be so happy if I were in his shoes."

This made me proud. I was beginning, because of my lessons and all we had been through with him, to claim my uncle as my own.


## 2


ONLY A FEW days after we met in Halifax, Pavel calls me up and asks me to dinner at his house. I refuse. Then Deanny calls.

"I'm not going to let you say no," she says. "He really likes you, Jake. I'm not going to let you ruin this one."

"It's his house," I say. "It's my invitation."

"I don't care," says Deanny. "You need someone to look after you. Someone to help you make the right decisions. I'm going to hound you until you agree to dinner with Pavel."

"What will it take for you to *stop* hounding me?"

"Go to dinner. After that, if nothing happens, I won't say a word."

I agree, if only to get Deanny off my back. I borrow my aunt's car and drive into the city the following Saturday. Pavel does not at all seem phased that Deanny had to force me to see him. He doesn't mention it. He lives on the second floor of a Victorian home on Inglis Street. His apartment has very few furnishings and lots of books. No TV. He prefers to read, he tells me when I ask. "TV is a form of mind control. If the Romans had had televisions," he says, "we'd still be ruled by the descendants of Nero."

I realize for the first time Pavel reminds me slightly of my Uncle David. The thought disturbs me. Dinner is awkward, despite a bottle of wine and constant discussion. I am nervous and Pavel seems so as well. He is not his usual garrulous self. He does take an honest interest in my work. And because I don't have to talk much about myself, I respond to him, doing the topic justice.

"It is good work," he says. "But does it not tire you? So much trouble all the time. So much despair?"

"Not really," I say. "The job has its own rewards."

"But it is sad, is it not? When you lose someone?"

"Yes, it's sad. But you get used to it. Find ways of coping."

This is a lie, and I wonder if Pavel is sensitive enough to know it. I never quite get over any client I lose.

Each one leaves a fresh wound on my psyche, so that I am now a mass of scar tissue of longing and regret. I take responsibility for each loss. What could I have done differently? How could I have saved them?

It is this, as well as my penchant for getting too close to clients, that makes me ill-suited for my job. When anyone dies at the agency we have a grief circle. Each of us discusses how the loss affects us, how we plan to cope with it, how it will make us better counsellors. I always lie. I am rational and phlegmatic. I give all the right answers, but inside I am seething. Each death is a replay of that first senseless death. Each death is unacceptable to me, and so I lug it around with me like a load upon my back that gets heavier with each passing day. I often worry over the fact that I am in a job that requires distance, perspective, and emotional discipline, when I lack all three. My boss, Anne, is aware of this. We have had many conversations about it, but she has yet to fire me, and I wouldn't dream, lousy counsellor or not, of quitting.

After dinner, Pavel sits beside me on the sofa in his sparsely furnished living room, and puts some jazz musician I am unfamiliar with on the stereo. He asks me what is wrong.

"Nothing," I tell him. "Dinner was very good."

"Of course," Pavel says. "Excellent company."

"I mean the food. I'd like the recipe for the borscht."

Pavel ignores this. "I don't understand you," he says. "I can't figure out what you want."

"In terms of what?" I ask.

"In terms of anything," Pavel says. "Yourself. Your family. Your work. You seem to be full of contradictions. You give off, how do they say, mixed signals?"

"Ask me what you want to know," I say. "And I'll tell you if I can answer."

Pavel nods. "Okay," he says. "What do you think of me?"

"I think you're very nice," I say automatically. "A wonderful person, really."

Pavel smiles slightly. "That's not what I mean."

"I know," I say. "But there's really no point in starting anything, is there? I live in Toronto. You here. My work. Your work."

"Work is not important," Pavel says.

"It is to me. It's my life."

"To have work as your life is very sad," says Pavel. "It's no life at all."

I do not like where this conversation is going. I feel threatened by it. I've had similar discussions with my mother, and I always shut down. I try to explain to Pavel why my work is more important than most. "Lives depend on it," I say. "Just as minds depend on yours. Would you leave your work if someone asked you to?"

"It depends," Pavel says. "Who is asking, and what they are offering?"

"Are you offering me something?" I say. The question is forward, but I am annoyed at him. For impugning me. For impugning my job, which is the same thing.

"Perhaps," says Pavel.

He is staring directly at me now. Unsmiling. Achingly handsome. I feel no compunction to throw myself into his arms, but something in me stirs. Something much deeper and more fundamental than anything that has stirred before. It occurs to me I am an adolescent, experiencing the complicated equations of longing and desire for the first time in my life. I don't know how to deal with them. I do as I always do. I turn off.

"I should go," I say.

"No," says Pavel, and then he leans over and kisses me. He places a hand on the inside of my thigh of my jeans, near my crotch. It is not grossly sexual, but the invitation is unmistakable. I don't know what to do. I do not move away, nor do I move his hand, but I can tell before Pavel will act I must make some concession of my own. Just a shift of the body slightly towards him will do it. The door will open, and I know, from the little I understand of Pavel, that a shift like that would mean everything. An entire future would open itself up to me.

I cannot do it. I subtly shift away from him. He smiles.

"Do you want to go?" he says.

"Perhaps," I say. My hands are trembling. Pavel notices, but says nothing. He gets up, and takes our empty wine glasses to the kitchen. Just that quickly, it is done. All the potential in our relationship is expunged in that moment. Pavel seems to understand. When he shows me to the door he is wearing a maddening, enigmatic smile. I try to convince myself the relationship is not over, but that smile tells me everything. I truly do not know what he wants from me. I look forward to the drive home. I want to think about what has just happened. The kiss. His opening up to me. I should have shifted towards him. I wanted to, but could not bring myself. What if he wants sex? What if he wants a relationship? One of the reasons I never have luck with men is I simply don't know how to act around them. They either want baseball scores or blowjobs, and I don't know how to give either with any skill or authority.

My mother is waiting when I get home and asks me how it was.

"Fine," I tell her.

"Just fine?" she says.

"What do you want from me?" I ask, now equally annoyed with her. "Do you want me to say we're getting married and you have a new son-in-law?"

"That would be nice," she says.

I shrug, and tell her I am going to my room.

"Your grandmother is awake," my mother says. "That's why I'm sitting here waiting for you."

In the time I have been home, Grandnan has been awake a very few times. She has never been lucid. I ask my mother if she is so now.

"As she is going to get," my mother says. "Jeanette and the nurse are with her now. You should go see her."

"I will," I say, and climb reluctantly up the stairs to my grand-mother's room.

■ ■ ■

I NO MORE like coming into my grandmother's room than I did going into my uncle's all those years ago. Many times, I have stepped into the room of one of my clients who was dying, and I always thought of my uncle. I dread the day when I will be forced to witness something similar with my aunt or my mother. As selfish as it is, I sometimes wish I could go before them. I simply cannot imagine a world without them in it.

My grandmother is sitting up in bed. This is remarkable for a woman who has been near comatose for the last three weeks. Jeanette is sitting beside her, stroking her hand above the coverlet. The nurse is changing the IV. I stand by the door, and listen as my grandmother speaks. She seems confused and sluggish. She keeps looking around, as if searching for someone.

"I don't get half a minute to do what needs to be done around here," she is saying. "The beds. The floors. You girls always up and down the stairs and makeup stains in the sink in the upstairs lava-tory. You think it all gets cleaned up by magic, but it doesn't, I tell you. Someone has to clean up after you."

This is the grandmother I remember. The grandmother of complaint and derision. Except what she is complaining about is all in her head. She hasn't cleaned this house for years. Jeanette and my mother do all of it. She is living in a different time, twenty years before, when she did her "little work" — those daily cleaning jobs in between her large housecleaning projects.

She looks over at me, and barely sees me. When she looks at me again she asks, point blank, "Who are you?"

Jeanette turns and sees me. She motions for me to come closer to the bed. "That's Jacob, mother. Your grandson."

"Jacob?" says my grandmother. "Clean up your room. It's a pigsty! How many times have I told you not to leave your toys lying about. I'll step on one, fall, and break my back!"

"She's not really thinking straight," says my Aunt Jeanette. "But it's better than what she has been."

"I hear you!" crows my grandmother. "Don't you think I don't!"

My mother steps into the room, and my grandmother glares at her. "Shame!" she says. "Shame on the family!"

My mother sighs. "This is about as good as it's going to get, I'm afraid."

My grandmother stays awake for hours. It is almost possible to imagine she was never sick. Dr. Fred arrives after my mother calls him. It is a Saturday. He was not in his office, but we have his home number and instructions to call him whenever needed. He examines my grandmother, and asks her questions. He wears no white jacket or stethoscope, but my grandmother seems to mistake him for her dead husband. She calls him "dear."

"This is remarkable," Dr. Fred tells my mother and Jeanette. "She's surprisingly responsive."

"Does this mean she's getting better?" asks Jeanette.

"No," says Fred. "Her heart is still terribly laboured. She still needs the oxygen. It's a phenomenon, I'm afraid."

The rest of that evening we spend as much time in my grandmother's room as we can. We do not know if she will ever be this lucid again. She still has no idea who any of us are. I am tempted to ask her about the eulogy, but my mother already warned me not to. "She won't remember," she said. "And if she does you'll just upset her." And so I reluctantly stay in the room with my mother and Jeanette while my grandmother cycles between prattling on and falling asleep. Whenever we think she is about to go under for good she wakes up again and starts talking gibberish, or about disconnected events.

I am getting tired of it.

Dr. Fred and the nurse have left. Jeanette decides to go downstairs to make a snack, and tries to ask my Grandmother — who hasn't eaten in days — if she wants anything. But my grandmother's eye falls on me and she waves Jeanette aside. Jeanette stops speaking and my grandmother softens, her eyes going from accusatory to contrite. Almost fearful. She holds out her hand towards me.

"Take it, Jacob," my mother says. "Take it."

I do not. I cannot. I stand there with my grandmother reaching out to me from her position on the bed.

"David," she says suddenly. "David my darling."

And my grandmother starts to cry.

# NINE

∎

OF ALL THE friends my uncle had in Toronto, none came to visit him. No one called. My mother told me years later David had a lover in Toronto, who left him just before he came home. She regretted not asking him more about it. The signs my uncle's life was unravelling were there before he got on the train back to Nova Scotia. But the long-lost lover was just that. Uncle David never mentioned him. I didn't even know his name. It has occurred to me I would have liked to get in touch with him. I could have called him up and asked him how undying love gives way before sickness and stigma. How "until death do you part" is conditional upon the kind of death, and "in sickness and in health" mere empty sophistry.

My uncle, had he been alive, would not have approved. He was not a confrontational man. He did not enjoy protest.

I have heard the terminally ill, confined to their beds while the rest of the planet spins, can become difficult. They get jealous of the living. Hateful. This did not happen to my uncle. I remember him as being serenely complacent. Then again, I may have made him out to be too saintly, given the circumstances of my meeting him. He was often tired, and in some pain as various infections swept through his body. Dr. Fred had him on pain medications which he took in moderation — not enough to impair his perceptions. He told my mother he'd rather not spend his final days a drooling idiot.

My uncle continued to give me lessons. Some days he would be lucid, and some days either confused or just not up to it. My mother took over on those days.

Some days he was so exhausted the walker would not do. He had to be helped to the bathroom by my mother and Jeanette, who wore hospital gowns and gloves and face masks when they did. After each bathroom visit, my grandmother made them scrub down every exposed surface with bleach, which they did, still wearing the hospital gowns. All of us, even my grandmother and I, began using my grandfather's toilet off the study. Upstairs was only to shower. Even then, I worried the germs had somehow crawled to the downstairs toilet seat, so I held myself above it with my hands on the seat proper — a remarkable feat of strength it seems to me now — and relieved myself that way. My grandmother draped tissue all over the seat to use it, and sometimes forgot to remove it.

Deanny often visited with my uncle. Of all of us she was the only one who had the nerve to touch him. Deanny had never known my uncle as a well man. He was always an invalid to her. But she liked him. On his good days he would joke with her and call her Bernadette. No one called Deanny Bernadette. If I had tried I would have been eating five-knuckle sandwiches. But my uncle got away with it. When I asked Deanny why, she looked at me like I was the stupidest person on earth. "Because he's dying, idjit. Dying people can get away with a lot."

Despite this justification, I sensed Deanny actually liked it when my uncle called her by her full name. He asked her questions about school, and home, and her life. She often made him laugh, which could be painful to watch if he was having trouble breathing. Once or twice he laughed so much his face turned purple and he had to be given oxygen out of the canister that sat beside his bed. Jeanette asked my mother if Deanny's presence might not be more harmful than helpful. My mother said no.

"Deanny's good for him," she said. "He's not going to laugh himself to death. And I'd rather he die laughing than any other way."

Outside the bedroom, Aunt Jeanette and my mother discussed the possibility of his death nearly constantly. They knew it would be soon. Dr. Fred had told him so. The antibiotics were no longer fighting the infections.

The incessant pneumonia bothered Dr. Fred the most. "If I can't get it under control, it will take him. He could go tomorrow, or weeks from now. But he will go, unless I can stop the rising tide."

"Has anyone ever stopped the rising tide?" said my aunt.

"No," Dr. Fred said. "It's a matter of when and not if."

■ ■ ■

IN THE SMALL hours of the morning on July 24, 2008, I awake to alternating red and blue light spilling into my room through the bedroom window. I dress and go into the hallway, where I find my mother standing outside my grandmother's room talking with Dr. Fred.

"Jacob," she says, as if I am still a young boy. "I was going to let you sleep."

My mother tells me that Jeanette got up at two o'clock to check on my grandmother, as either she or my mother did at least once through the night. When she turned on the light, she thought at first my grandmother was just sleeping heavily. But there was something too blank about her expression, something too limp about the way her head lay sideways on the pillow. She checked her mother's pulse. Unable to find one, yet still uncertain of her mother's status, she laid her ear against her mouth and nose and tried to feel her breathing.

She could not.

Her forehead felt cold.

Jeanette woke my mother from her sleep. "Caroline," she said. "I think Mom is gone."

"Gone where?" my mother asked, in sleep-induced stupor.

We wait while the paramedics prepare my grandmother. Dr. Fred pronounces her dead and signs the death certificate. I watch in fascination as they carry the body into the upstairs hall-way, sealed in a black body bag. My mother gives a single, muted cry as it goes by, and when Jeanette emerges from the room her eyes are red.

"Will you all be okay?" says Dr. Fred.

My mother nods.

He says he will be back to check on us later today. "I could give you something to sleep, Caroline," he says. "If you think you need it."

"No thank you," says my mother.

After a fifty-year reign, my grandmother is no longer in the house. Nor will she be returning. This is hard for me to accept. There will be no more sleep for us that night. Jeanette makes coffee, and we go downstairs to drink it with her. It is four in the morn-ing. As soon as we sit down at the kitchen table I notice Jeanette lighting a cigarette. My mother gets her an ashtray from under the sink. No longer will grandmother be there to tell her she can't smoke indoors. No longer will my grandmother be there to tell them anything.

They can do anything they like in the house.

Eat in the dining room.

Track mud on the floors.

Princess the cat has long been dead, and my grandmother never got another. But Jeanette can get a dog, which is something she has long wanted to do. My grandmother hated them. "Slavish, dirty beasts," she said. "The Bible dismissed them as curs, and so do I."

Jeanette could now get a whole houseful of dogs if she wants them. I'm sure my mother won't mind. The two of them have waited for dominion over their own lives for decades, but now it is here they don't know what to do.

"I can't believe she's gone," says my mother.

"Truthfully," says my aunt, "I never thought she would be. I kept thinking she'd come out of it somehow, and start bossing us around again."

"Stubborn to the end," my mother says. "She compromised nothing in her whole life. You know, it's hard not to admire that a little."

The three of us sit and talk about my grandmother until dawn. We remain respectful, discussing her attributes and relating anecdotes about the days when my grandmother was young and headstrong. Occasionally my mother or Jeanette cries. I remain dry-eyed, not necessarily out of any hardness of heart, but because it is hard also for me to believe she is gone. Like Jeanette, I too half-believed one day my grandmother would rouse herself from her stupor and start ordering the house again. It is hard to believe that domineering personality is gone from the world.

Death always makes me relentlessly existential. It does everyone I suppose. I probe myself to see if a portion of my resentment has died with her, but my own emotional nature, at this point at least, is unavailable to me. I feel sorry for my mother and Jeanette. I can barely comprehend the reality of my grandmother's death. I drink my coffee and bum cigarettes from Jeanette. I rarely smoke, but this occasion seems to call for it. I can hear my grandmother screaming the house is blue with smoke, and insisting we go outside, and I do feel a slight satisfaction at the thought, which tells me my resentment is not gone completely. None of us able to sleep, we sit for four hours in the living room.

Then, at eight o'clock, and somewhat predictably, the phone begins to ring.

■ ■ ■

NEWS OF MY grandmother's death spreads about the town as quickly as Spanish Influenza. She was a paragon. Phone call after phone call offers sympathies, from the high born to the low. Deanny calls at ten o'clock. She is a mess. My grandmother had been a champion to her. Helped pay for her schooling. Always held her up as an example. Always kept in touch. Deanny's emotional reaction is stronger than my mother's and Jeanette's. She weeps noisily into the phone, and says she will be home as she soon as she possibly can.

"The funeral is Thursday," I say.

"I simply can't believe it," Deanny says. "I thought she'd never die."

"We all did," I say. "Mom and Jeanette are still shaking their heads."

The funeral home calls our house at ten o'clock sharp. They inform us that Grandnan took care of all the arrangements several years ago — what kind of service she wanted, right down to the casket.

Dalton Freeman is my grandmother's lawyer. He called once to express his sympathies, but he did not discuss particulars of the will. I can't help but compare these arrangements to those of my uncle twenty-five years ago. The alacrity versus the reluctance. The constant ringing of the phone compared to the silence. I try not to think about it. This is no time for advocacy. There are times even the spirit of protest should not be given free reign.

Dalton says there should be a reading and discussion of the will before the funeral, and before I go back to Toronto.

"Before the funeral?" I say. "Doesn't that usually come after?"

"Your grandmother requested this specifically," he tells me. "I'd like to do it tomorrow."

I get off the phone and tell my mother what Dalton said. "That's odd," she says.

"What's odd?" says Jeanette, coming into the kitchen. My mother tells her about the reading. "Is that normal?"

"Not at all," I say. "I wonder what she's up to."

"Jacob," my mother says. "She's dead. She's not 'up to' anything."

I can't agree. Even from beyond the grave I do not trust my grandmother entirely. It feels like she has a final card up her sleeve. One last attempt at control. Perhaps a posthumous improvement project. Perhaps she is going to dictate what we should all wear at her funeral.

For the first time since her death, I consider her eulogy — and for the briefest of moments I feel angry at her again for putting me in such a position. My mother would have given her a fine eulogy. Or the mayor. Or even Deanny or Henry Hennsey, as old as he is. What have I to give her? My old resentments still stand. Anything I do say — either accusation or accolade — will feel false, because a part of me feels the opposite.

■ ■ ■

AFTER LUNCH, PEOPLE begin to come. It is a tradition in Advocate when someone dies for visitors to come expressing their sympathies and carrying plates of food — sandwiches and squares and cookies. It is a bad tradition, in my opinion. My mother, Jeanette, and I are exhausted from sitting up all night and answering the phone all day. We would like nothing better than to retire to our rooms for a nap.

But we have to entertain.

Pot after pot of coffee and tea are made.

The squares are eaten, the sandwiches demolished. Some people bring roasts and casseroles, assuming for the next few days we will be too grief-stricken to cook. My mother appreciates it. I notice how she assumes by default the position of head of the household. Jeanette hangs back, taking a secondary role. My mother does not intend for this to happen. The potential lay dormant in her in all these years perhaps, and comes to the forefront out of necessity.

At seven o'clock we push the last visitor out the door.

"Thank God," my mother says. "I'm beat."

Another knock comes at ten after seven.

"You get it," my mother says. "Entertain them if you wish, or tell them we're tired and send them away. I'm going to rest." She disappears up the stairs, as Jeanette already has.

I open the door. To my surprise, Pavel is standing there. He carries no sweets or sandwiches. He hands me a sympathy card and says to give it to my mother. "Deanny told me," he says. "She gave me directions."

I honestly believed after rebuffing his advances the weekend before I would never see him again. I had underestimated his persistence. Or maybe he was just following convention. Maybe in Russia you drove an hour out of your way to give sympathies to a man you barely knew.

"My family is tired," I tell him honestly. "They've gone to bed."

"How are you feeling?" Pavel asks me.

"Fine," I say. "You want to come in?"

"Let's go for a walk instead," says Pavel. "It would do you good to get out of the house."

Once again it is a glorious Advocate evening. July-warm, with the sun setting on the Protestant side. Pavel and I walk towards downtown.

"How do you feel?" he says.

"Fine," I tell him. "It's hard to believe she's gone."

"Old people," says Pavel, "hold sway over our lives for so long, that it's not just they that die. Ideas go with them. Principles. Ways of life. In some ways the death of someone old is more shocking than the death of someone young."

"Yes," I say.

Pavel has touched upon exactly what I've been thinking and feeling. But I don't want to discuss it.

"I suppose," he says, "you'll be going back to Toronto soon." It isn't a question.

"On Friday," I say. "After the funeral, and as soon as I make sure Mom and Jeanette are okay."

"Have you made a decision about the eulogy? Have you prepared any notes?"

This is the first time that day anyone has asked me that question. Faced with the blatant reality of my grandmother's death, it seems harder to think of myself up there at a pulpit accusing her of things. But neither do I feel disposed to shower her memory with kind words. I am wavering. I can feel that. I tell Pavel I simply do not know yet, but I am leaning towards the negative.

"You haven't got much time," says Pavel. "Perhaps this is a time for healing."

"That only happens in novels," I tell him. "Real life is more complicated."

"Novels can sometimes be true," he says, and grows silent.

I appreciate Pavel's romantic streak, but tonight it annoys me. I refuse to discuss it. We walk to the end of Tenerife Street and turn around and come home. When we reach the door he asks me if I have considered his offer.

"Of what?" I say. "A relationship? Now is hardly the time, is it?"

"Don't hide behind convention, Jacob," he said. "It doesn't suit you."

"Fine," I said. "Where would we live? Here or in Toronto?"

"Details," said Pavel. "Unimportant incidentals."

"It's not unimportant to me."

"Give the eulogy," Pavel said. "Let it go."

"I'll think about it," I say.

I leave Pavel on the doorstop and close the door behind me. Then I call Deanny and accuse her of playing matchmaker on the day my grandmother died.

"He wanted to come," she says. "I only gave him directions."

"He asked me about the eulogy. Did you put him up to that?"

"I did not," said Deanny. "Maybe it's just his common sense. Why do you hold on to things so, Jake? All that is ancient history."

"Not for me. I see it every day at my work. The same sickness. The same bigotry and intolerance."

"Give the eulogy," Deanny said. "Don't you understand that it is your grandmother's way of asking forgiveness?"

"I understand that. But you assume I have it in me to forgive her. I don't. I don't *want* to forgive her. I don't want to let it go. Someone has to keep the memory fresh, otherwise we'll forget."

Deanny sighs. It is deep and resigned. Perhaps that is how it sounds after she loses a case. "All right," she says. "I won't bother you anymore about Pavel. Or your grandmother's funeral. Just answer me one question."

"Which is?"

"Do you think your uncle would have wanted you to behave this way?"

"I do," I say.

"You lie," says Deanny. "David forgave everyone at the end. Even your grandmother. You've made a protest out of your life, in the name of a man who didn't believe in protest. Who believed in forgiveness. What would he say if he were here to see this?"

"I don't know," I say. "And neither do you."

"I could guess," says Deanny. "And you can too, if you're honest with yourself. He'd tell you to give the eulogy. He'd tell you to forgive your grandmother. He'd tell you to forgive yourself."

Deanny continues talking, but by then I have hung up.

■ ■ ■

I'VE MADE ARRANGEMENTS for funerals of our agency's clients, men who had no one to handle them. Most have no money or insurance. If they do, they drew on it long ago using the viatical companies, who parasitically advance people dying from AIDS a portion of their life insurance benefit if they name them legally as beneficiaries upon their death for the remainder. Many take this option. Who can blame them? The moral ambiguity of these companies aside, the men need the money, or want to live in comfort as they die. In some cases, family and friends have abandoned them and they have no one to leave their policies to.

The funeral arrangements for my grandmother are different. She took care of everything. She did not want to be buried in a nice dress, but simply a pantsuit she often wore around the house. My mother was baffled why she would want this. She wanted a nice casket, but did not want it lined with plush or velvet. The undertaker had to rip the lining out of the casket, which came preinstalled, and put in the cotton to adhere to my grandmother's wishes. She also wanted my grandfather's medical degrees buried with her. No one, not even her old friends, could fathom the reason for this. Nonetheless, her wishes were carried out

■ ■ ■

TWO DAYS AFTER my grandmother died my mother asks me about the eulogy. I tell her I haven't written it.

"It's not hard," she says. "And it doesn't have to be very long. Just a few nice words about her life."

"I don't think she wanted nice words. I think she wanted the truth."

"Tell the truth then," my mother says.

"I'll be damned," I say, thinking of Deanny, "if I'm going to forgive her. She's trying to force me."

My mother shakes her head. "We should have never let you

stay here back then," she says. "We should have sent you away until it was over. It affected you too much. You have become hard."

"*You* do the eulogy then," I say.

"She didn't ask me," says my mother.

She rarely gets angry at me. Even as a boy I don't remember her punishing me. She is a perfect mother, as far as I am concerned. But she is unhappy with me now. She tells Jeanette I am still vacillating on speaking at my grandmother's funeral. Jeanette is less perturbed; she says I should humour an old lady's final request and stop taking it so seriously.

The atmosphere of grief that overlaid our house is starting to evaporate. Jeanette and my mother still cry a little, turning off and on like faucets, but no one seems completely heartbroken. Grandnan had been sick for months. Perhaps it is a relief not to have her lying comatose in the upstairs bedroom anymore.

I tell Jeanette I didn't know Grandnan well enough to give a fitting eulogy. "You and Mom knew her better," I say. "Why don't you write it?"

"That's not what she wanted," Jeanette says. "She wanted you."

"Maybe she did," I say. "But I can't write it. I've tried, and I've got nothing to say."

"I don't understand," says Jeanette, "why it's so hard to write a few words!"

"It isn't. But don't you understand? It's a betrayal to the men I work with who have mothers and grandmothers like her. And to Uncle David? I'd be a hypocrite."

"You're one now, in my opinion," says my Aunt Jeanette. I don't think she meant to say it. It just slipped out.

"Jeanette!" my mother says.

Jeanette looks at me, and then my mother. She shrugs. "I just meant he counsels people on how to get a life, right? And then he refuses to get one for himself."

This upsets me, and I challenge my aunt to show me how my life is less valid than hers.

She mentions Pavel. "I talked to Deanny," she says. "Why don't you just date him? He sounds like an amazing person."

I go to my room, angry. Two more days and I can leave Advocate behind. It isn't just this drama playing out over my grandmother's death. There's also an old drama playing out underneath. It is as if the two times have merged — my grandmother's death and my uncle's.

Eventually my mother comes into my room. "Jeanette says sorry. She wasn't thinking, and she's distraught. We're all a little thrown by your grandmother's passing."

"It's okay," I say.

"Can I sit down?"

My mother sits on the edge of my bed, as she used to when I was a boy. I notice how old her hands look, how her legs are mapped with blue veins. I tend to think of my mother and Jeanette as still young, but they aren't. My mother will soon be sixty. Jeanette not long after. Neither one of them will have to work again, if they don't want to. Grandnan will have left them enough money to get by. Knowing them, they will choose to work. They are good daughters.

My mother says she is not going to trouble me about my life any longer. "We're just concerned," she says. "Jeanette and I. We know how lonely you are in Toronto. You can try and hide it from us, but all you have there is work, and that is never enough to sustain anyone."

"I know," I say.

"Have you ever thought," my mother says, "of starting something here? A small agency like the one you have there? To help people in this region?"

"No one is dying here," I say. "No one is sick."

"Not now," says my mother. "Or not that we know about. But perhaps you could help prevent those sorts of things from happening.

Counselling children. Going into schools. Educating them, before they go off to big cities on their own."

I had never thought of this. I do not want to live in Advocate, but this would be a noble project. A useful one, though I know I'll never do it. I tell my mother I will think about her proposal.

"Now about Pavel," says my mother.

"That was none of Aunt Jeanette's business."

"I agree," says my mother. "But you know your Aunt Jeanette, and small towns."

"I'm mad at Deanny too," I say. "She should never have told her. I know Pavel likes me. And I like him. But we live in different cities for God's sake. I don't plan on travelling a thousand miles every weekend, and I don't think he does either."

"Fine," says my mother. "Just make sure that's the honest reason, and that you're not fooling yourself."

"I'm not," I say.

"You're not a city boy, Jacob. Do you know that? Some are. But you're not. Your aunt and I have always known that. You went to Toronto to get away from us, not because it was the place you wanted to be."

"Not from you," I say.

"Her then," says my mother. "I meant what I said. We should not have allowed you to stay here when Uncle David was dying. It was too horrible for a child of your age to see. You were old enough to register and yet not old enough to fully understand. Jeanette and I both feel it harmed you. You would likely not have done the work you do if it wasn't for it, do you agree?"

"So?" I say. "I do good work. I make a difference."

"Yes," says my mother. "And I've always been proud of you for it. I think your grandmother was too, if you want to know, though I don't think she could have said it. But a person must have more than work in his life. You must have some happiness."

I do not lie to my mother and say I am happy. It would cheapen the moment. Before either of us can say anything more we hear the doorbell ring below.

"That will be Dalton," my mother says. "Come on. Let's go listen to the old woman's final words."

■ ■ ■

DALTON SMITH HAS been my grandmother's lawyer since he opened his own practice in Advocate years before. She chose him because he is Catholic; her lawyer before had been United. There hadn't been a Catholic lawyer in Advocate since the fifties. My grandmother liked to say this was because Catholics usually didn't go in for such morally ambiguous jobs.

"Except for the pope," Jeanette said on one occasion, though out of my grandmother's earshot.

Dalton is not a stereotypical sharp lawyer. Although his suit is dark and crisp, he is short, and corpulent, with a beet-red complexion which my grandmother suspected was the result of secret drinking. He eases his bulk into one of my grandmother's antique wing chairs — I could almost hear her protests it would collapse under the strain — and lays an expensive leather briefcase across his lap, opens it, and draws out two manila folders.

"Please let me get through the broad strokes of the will," he says, "before you ask questions. Most of them will likely be answered by the document, and what aren't I'll field when we're done."

He begins to read. The language is dry and technical, but it is plain enough to be understood. My uncle used to say professional language was designed to exclude, a kind of linguistic old boys' club, and anyone could learn it if they were willing to spend the time.

There are surprises in the will. She left the house to her daughters, and to each of us, including me, she left three hundred thousand dollars.

We all knew my grandmother was loaded. We expected her to leave us *something*. My mother expresses surprise it is this much.

"You don't understand," says Dalton. "Your grandmother was worth almost five million dollars. The sale of your grandfather's practice, their savings, and his insurance she invested in dividend-bearing bank stocks. She lived frugally, and never touched the principal. After her donations to the church, and the town, and her heirs the remainder of the estate is three million dollars."

Jeanette whistles. "And she was always complaining she was broke."

Dalton doesn't smile. He seems professionally incapable of it.

"So who is the rest going to?" asks my mother.

We expect, I think, the Catholic Church for the conversion of the Protestants. Perhaps a donation to the town to ensure a park or public building is renamed in her honour. None of us are expecting what he says.

"The remaining money is to go into a trust, which is to be administered by Jacob McNeil, her grandson," Dalton says.

There is an expression that a room is so silent you could hear a pin drop. In this case that would be an understatement. You could have heard a single molecule of air bump against a feather. Dalton shakes his head, and for a minute I think I do see a smile there. A ghost of one, at least, though fleeting and soon replaced by his official deadpan. "It would be more accurate, I suppose, to say your grandmother wanted to donate the remainder of the estate to charities, with you as charitable executor."

"Which charities," I ask instantly. A part of my brain is processing this quicker than my conscious mind. I know what is coming.

"Any charities," Dalton says. "Whichever ones you choose. You are the sole trustee. You can do with it as you want. You have carte blanche."

I am stunned. I think we all are. After a few minutes trying to organize my chaotic thoughts I say, "Surely she knew where I will put this money?"

"I think she knew exactly," says Dalton. He truly is a good lawyer. Sixty years of family history do not phase him at all. He continues on with the business at hand. My grandmother was smart getting him to do this instead of my mother and Jeanette, who, I can tell by their bewildered expressions, are as blindsided as I am. "I believe that's why she's doing it. But it is conditional."

"Upon what?" I ask.

"Father Harry told you about the eulogy?"

"You know about that?"

"Yes," Dalton says. "She wanted to give you time to prepare, and so she instructed Harry to tell you before she died. In order to become trustee for the remainder of the estate, you have to do the eulogy."

"I won't do it," I say suddenly. "I won't be subject to posthumous blackmail."

"Understand," says Dalton. "The money she is leaving you personally is not conditional. You will get that, regardless. It is only the charitable money in question."

"And what happens if I don't take it?"

"It goes to the town," Dalton says.

"I can't believe this!" I say. I turn to my mother and Jeanette. "Are you okay with this? She cuts you and Jeanette out entirely, and makes mine conditional?"

"Don't exaggerate," says my mother. "We're not cut out entirely. We're well provided for. What do we, at our age, need with three million dollars? Are you upset about it?"

"Of course I'm not," I say. "I don't care about her money. I've never wanted it. But she's being just as controlling in death as she was in life! What does she want me to say? She was a great person? To forgive her for what she did? I can't!"

"I can't tell you what she was thinking," says Dalton. "She also stipulated that a further ten thousand was to be used to do something here."

"Do what here?" I say.

Dalton shrugs. "That's all she asked me to write down. *Do something here.* I believe she figured you would know what she meant."

I don't. I can't fathom my grandmother, now that she's dead, any more than I did when she was alive. And right now I have trouble seeing the largesse past the manipulation.

"I have to get back to the office," says Dalton. "I'll see you at the funeral. The decision is entirely yours, Jacob. But if you don't mind me making a personal comment. It's a small thing she's asking, weighed against the benefit of all that money channelled into the right causes."

"And what do I have to sacrifice to get it?" I say.

Dalton shrugs. "It's your decision."

He adds, rather insensitively I think, that this is the first funeral he will attend as a work requirement. He means, of course, he has to be there to make sure I give the eulogy in order to become trustee of the money. I wonder if he will bill the estate for the hour.

## 2

AS MY MOTHER had guessed, living in the same house as my dying uncle that year did scar me. The process of suppression I learned then, I have practised ever since. After my uncle died, I found no relief. I was scared. My fear of the virus became pathological as it translated into an equally powerful fear of intimacy. I became overly sensitive to the injustices of the world, tutored as I was by the hostility of our town. This grew into a reasoned fear of the world at large, where evidence of such prejudices was abundant. I chose a job that reinforced my childhood experience that human beings are cruel. I identified with the struggles of my clients in a world opposed to them. I was still locked in combat with my own fear, and my resentment of my grandmother.

Though it has cost her three million dollars, money she will not be needing, my grandmother has in one swift, broad stroke mastered me. She has pitted my personal life against my public one, my general passions against my specific principles, my past against my present. If I get up and speak about her life I will be betraying the men I've worked with. If I don't, I will regret the loss of the money, and all the good it would have done.

The day before the funeral, I try a technique I have often used with my clients. I tell them to write a letter to the object of their resentment, to get out on paper what they can't, or won't say, in person. What often happens in these letters, I am informed, is what starts out as resentment or invective ends up in tenderness, understanding, and forgiveness. I am not such a bad counsellor that I encourage my clients to retain resentment the way I do — another reason I feel I am a hypocrite.

The process of writing things down somehow makes things clearer. Though I am not necessarily ready to give up my resentment towards my grandmother, I do want to see things more clearly before I go to her funeral.

*Dear Grandnan,* I write. *I have resented you for a long time. For what you did to Uncle David. For what you did to me. For how you ruled our lives with an iron fist and never let us be who we wanted to be. You always needed to be in control. You always put the needs of the town above those of your own family, and when uncle died you abandoned us completely and showed a side of yourself I had never seen before. Complete disloyalty. Utter inconsideration.*

I do not soften my letter. In a way, I think, I *am* writing her eulogy. The one I would give had I the guts to say it in front of the church and the townspeople.

I read the letter to my aunt.

"For God's sake Jacob, don't be silly."

"You write it then," I say.

"She didn't want me to write it," says Jeanette. "Dalton was very clear about that."

I realize with some excitement that this isn't entirely true. "I'm to give the eulogy, not necessarily write it." I say. "There's nothing in the will that says the eulogy couldn't be written by someone else. Come on, Aunt Jeanette. I really am blocked."

I am like a child again, begging for help with my homework.

My aunt sighs. "Fine," she says. "I'll write the goddamned thing. Get a pen."

I come downstairs an hour later and my aunt, who is smoking at the kitchen table, hands me her letter. My grandmother's eulogy. She asks me to read it over. I do. It is standard and uninspired. Perfectly suited to the occasion.

"It's fine," I say. And then, just as I am about to hand it back, I see something. I pull it back and scan through it again. My aunt continues just sitting at the table. "You don't mention Uncle David," I say.

"No," says Jeanette. "I don't."

"Jeanette! You can't not mention him!"

"I don't know what to say," says Jeanette.

"Well, say something, for God's sake. This goddamned town has ignored him for twenty-two years. Surely you're not going to leave him out now."

"That's the thing Jacob," she says. "None of us know how to do it."

My mother is standing in the hall, listening. She steps in. "Why do you think she asked you, Jacob? You would be the only one to do it. She knew that. Even at the end she knew it."

I hand the papers back to my aunt. "I know what you're doing,"

I say, "and it's not going to work." I leave them, and go back up to my room. Before I get in the door my phone rings. The call display says it is Anne, my boss.

■ ■ ■

MY UNCLE GAVE me school lessons until mid-September, but he had to give them up. He started forgetting things. His breathing became more laboured. Sometimes he'd look at me after I'd been sitting with him like he didn't know who I was. He was taken to the hospital for three days when his breathing became too difficult. It was no better while he was gone. The sound of laboured breathing had stopped, but its absence was almost as bad. It reminded us of the final absence that was to come.

My grandmother, at this time, went into heavy denial. She forced cheerfulness. She baked, and made meals, and cleaned the house as if nothing at all was wrong upstairs. One day she decided the church needed to ensure that Uncle David receive Extreme Unction. He'd been christened and confirmed. He was Catholic. He needed the last rights, including final confession, then all would be forgiven and he'd be on his way.

Suddenly the idea obsessed her. This too was denial, just a different form of it. Her daughters tried to tell her Uncle David wasn't lucid enough for confession. And if the priest managed to get one out of him, would it count? Who would know if he was really contrite?

"Everyone wants to be saved," said my grandmother. "If you had a choice between heaven and damnation, which would you choose, right mind or no right mind?"

"Attention K-Mart shoppers," said Jeanette pointlessly.

"It's the choice that matters, Mother, not the end. David is in no position to make it."

But my grandmother would not give up. She used the fact that he had not, even in the worst of his illness, removed the St. Jude's medallion from around his neck as proof that my uncle still had vestiges of the religion in which he had been raised. Neither my mother nor Jeanette had the heart to explain to her that it was an irony. My grandmother called Father Orlis and asked him to receive David's confession and provide the last rights.

He refused.

This should have been my grandmother's breaking point. She pleaded with Father Orlis, but he declined. Extreme Unction involved touching and getting very close. It was my aunt and mother's opinion Father Orlis was afraid to touch Uncle David.

"Some priest," said my mother.

"Some religion," said Aunt Jeanette.

Even in the face of such damning evidence, my grandmother refused to believe Father Orlis was afraid. My mother and Jeanette could have asked Deacon Harry. They were sure he would have come. But my grandmother did not want the deacon because, though he could hear the confession, he wasn't qualified to give the unction. One without the other, she told them, was useless. "Bread without butter," she said.

"As I remember it," countered Aunt Jeanette, "Jesus ate bread without butter all the time."

My aunt and my mother did not care about the last rites. They were both certain if there was a heaven David would go to it, with or without the Catholics.

Now that he could no longer give me lessons, my mother once again wanted to keep me out of David's room — this time for his sake. But he insisted I be allowed in. Deanny and I went almost daily.

I know, from my experience now, and my observations then, what he was suffering from. He had *Pneumocystis* pneumonia. He had candidiasis, also known as thrush, a fungal infection of the throat and mouth and bronchial tubes. Another fungal infection of the feet and hands. His toenails and fingernails were practically eaten away. Guillain-Barré syndrome, which paralyzed part of his body. Retinitis, hairy leukoplakia, splenomegaly, stomatitis, toxoplasmosis, and tuberculosis.

He had neuropathy in his hands and feet that caused him pain. The Kaposi sarcoma lesions were now over his body and face. The harmful bacteria in his gut were multiplying; it was hard to keep anything down. A fungus was eating his stomach lining. His eyesight began to fail due to the cytomegalovirus.

I went into his room to watch him struggle for breath, his chest rising weakly up and down, his eyes closed, his gaunt frame on the bed. I counted lesions. I looked at his toenails. I was horror-struck, in part because I was certain I would end up like him. I stood for a half hour or more, marking the progression of the disease. I felt terribly sorry for him, and sometimes wanted to shake him and ask him to get up and walk again as my grandmother told me Jesus had done to a cripple.

When he was awake, David tried to smile at me. Sometimes, he'd ask me for a drink of water. When I gave it to him, he would talk to me. He spoke of his childhood. Picturing Uncle David as a boy who would one day grow into a man of this description was especially sad. I didn't like to hear it, but I let him go on. I became, in a sense, his confessor, and I noticed he stopped talking as much to my mother and Aunt Jeanette. He seemed to reserve his reminiscences for me. Sometimes he would fall asleep, mid-sentence, and then wake up to continue where he left off. I had to move close to his bed, as his voice became softer and softer. He no longer sat up. The life was slowly leaking out of him. It was both fascinating and horrifying to watch.

Once, my mother found Deanny standing quietly beside his bed, holding his hand. Deanny was, despite her experience, just a child; she saw nothing wrong with this, nothing taboo. But the reaction of the adults around her, even my usually phlegmatic mother, was swift and unequivocal.

"Deanny!" my mother cried. "Don't do that!" It wasn't just the health risk that alarmed my mother. There was something more to it, related perhaps to Deanny being a healthy young child so near to my doomed uncle. But Deanny was adamant.

"I won't get anything," she said. "And someone needs to hold his hand."

Deanny would not let go.

My mother gave up. Later, she discussed the possibility of keeping Deanny out of David's room with my Aunt Jeanette. They decided that, for as much risk there was to Deanny if she continued to touch my uncle, it would be worse if she no longer kept him company. And so they let her stay, but suggested if she wanted to touch my uncle that she wear gloves. This seemed unnatural to Deanny. She continued to hold his hand in hers. And as much as this worried my mother, it ensured, paradoxically, that Deanny would forever remain close to her heart. For this, if for no other reason, Deanny is always welcome at the house on Tenerife Street, and they consider her a part of the family.

My grandmother thought it was morbid a little girl should daily be visiting the bedside of a dying man, and told my mother so.

"Hush!" my mother said. "At least she does visit him."

My grandmother didn't enter David's room. She kept up her charade, her forced good nature. She baked and cleaned and listened to the radio and would not engage in any discussion that might "bring her down."

Jeanette and my mother ignored her, but Deanny said my grandmother was like a rat deserting a sinking ship.

"Problem is," said my mother, "it's her ship. She owns it."

Deanny shrugged. She did not much care about the machinations and goings on of the adults in our house. But she was fascinated with my uncle. She never said how her parents were taking all this, and when my mother asked her about this she said they hardly even noticed. "Dad's drunk all the time," she said, "and Mom is busy taking care of him. They never ask me about it."

"But aren't they afraid you might catch something?" Jeanette asked.

Deanny shrugged again. "I guess not. Mom asked me once what Uncle David looks like, and I told her. She said she was sorry for you folks."

"That's refreshing," said Jeanette.

"Having people feel sorry for us is refreshing?" said my grandmother, who had been doing her best to ignore the conversation. "In my day that was a tragedy."

"Clearly," said Jeanette, "we're no longer in your day."

But out of this my grandmother cultivated a respect for Deanny. Though she was a "little urchin," mannerless and coarse, she and Henry Hennsey were the only townsfolk who darkened her doorway. It was as much for this reason as for any other that, after everything was over, my grandmother became her champion and helped put Deanny through law school.

■ ■ ■

MY UNCLE HAD his good days, mentally at least, and my mother and Jeanette took these opportunities to spend as much time with him as possible. He asked Deanny and me to read to him, as his vision was no longer good. He had given up on *War and Peace*, and asked us to read *To Kill a Mockingbird* instead. My uncle's favourite novel would be the last one he would hear, and perhaps he knew this. Deanny read slowly, stumbling over the bigger words. My uncle didn't seem to care. Sometimes he called us Jeb and Scout, and this designation pleased Deanny. She liked Scout. My mother and Jeanette also read to him. When my mother choked up at certain points in the book, David would ask her to stop.

Deanny spent hours telling my uncle what was going on in her school and in the wider world. He talked to me seriously about math. He asked me once what I would like to do with my future. I had no good answer for him. I was not like other boys. I didn't want to be a fireman or astronaut or police officer. I had no idea one could wrangle mathematics into a career other than being an engineer like Cameron's dad, and I couldn't see myself being a teacher. I told him in words I'd never spoken that I'd like to become a physicist like Einstein and discover a new theory, like relativity. My uncle did not laugh.

"A noble goal," he whispered, because it hurt his throat to talk loudly. "You're a purist, Jacob. Whatever it is you choose, be sure you have a passion for it." On the afternoons and evenings he was feeling up to it, he spoke like this to me. I wonder now if my uncle was not trying to pass on some kind of legacy, to expound his philosophy to me before he died, never having had any children of his own.

I listened readily.

I too held his hand, once, when he had drifted off. I was terrified, but felt compelled. I wanted to let him know that I loved him. For love him I did. I had *come* to love him, not as the healthy robust man he had been, and who I had never known, but as this sick, dying person, helpless in his bed. His hand was warm, and though my heart was pounding at the thought of the germs transferring from his hand to mine, I needed to do it. It was a test of mettle, an initiation or rite of passage, only with much more at stake. I held Uncle David's hand for five minutes — it twitched lightly in his sleep, and it was sheathed in hot sweat — but I did not let it go.

I spent half an hour in the bathroom afterwards scrubbing my hands; in the end they were pink and almost raw. But it made me feel good later on to know I had touched him, perhaps when he needed to be touched. I could deport myself with honour later on in my life just knowing I had done this. That, for some reason, meant more to me than almost anything.

■ ■ ■

MY FIRST THOUGHT when Anne calls is that it is Randy. I would like to think I am being alarmist, but I can hear in Anne's voice I am not. She says she is sorry to bother me at this time. I ask her what the problem is. "It's not Randy, is it? Did he tell his lover? Did he get kicked out?"

"Worse," Anne says. "He tried to kill himself yesterday. We just got the call."

"What?"

Randy, Anne tells me, left a note. He had ultimately decided he could not tell John about the HIV and he couldn't live with it. He had been hoarding Ativan for anxiety from his doctor and had taken them all in the morning, after his lover left for work. John found him when he came home at noon, comatose but fortunately still alive.

"He had been planning it for months," Anne says. "John knows now. He's devastated. Randy has been asking after you. He'll be in hospital until Monday, then likely he'll be moved to a facility."

The sense of guilt I suddenly feel, knowing Randy had been planning his suicide the entire time he's been seeing me, is overwhelming. I am enraged, inwardly railing against my own stupidity and lack of insight. How could I have been so blind? Suddenly, I am doubly angry at my grandmother. If it wasn't for the money I would get on a plane immediately. I tell Anne about the eulogy and the money. I tell her all the problems I am having fulfilling my grandmother's request. "I have half a mind to just come," I say, "and forget about the money."

"That's your decision." Anne says, ever the social worker.

"I could try and get the money anyway. I could cite a work emergency. Or I could just take the money she left me personally and donate that. There are no conditions on it at least. It would be enough, wouldn't it?"

"Three hundred thousand does not compare to three million," Anne says flatly, now the administrator.

I don't quite have the guts to make this decision on my own. If Anne were to say the word, I would make the arrangements right then. I need, I tell her, to sit by Randy's bedside and atone for missing his pain. I don't want to be in Advocate anymore. I want to be home, where I belong, in Toronto, doing the work I was meant to do.

"You mean," says Anne, "you'd consider skipping your own grandmother's funeral, and leaving behind all that money, which we can desperately use, for the sake of seeing a client?"

"A client who is in the hospital. A client who almost died because I was negligent."

"He didn't almost die because of *you*. He almost died because he swallowed a lot of pills."

"Same difference," I say.

Anne says nothing. But just when I think she has hung up, her voice comes back. "Jake. I hate to say this to you now, but if you were to do that you should consider yourself dismissed from this agency."

"Pardon?" I can hardly believe what I am hearing.

"I'm serious," says Anne. "Randy is your client. I realize this must be difficult for you. But this is your grandmother, Jake. Even if you do go to the funeral, you still might not keep your job here. You are not the most effective counsellor on staff precisely because you can maintain no personal distance from the clients. Randy is a case in point. You have little social interaction outside of your work. You have no balance. There has been talk of letting you go before."

I am incredulous. "So you're saying that if I don't stay I lose my job? And if I do, I lose my job anyway?"

"No," says Anne. "If you give the eulogy, which is what this is about more than the money, you keep your job. But if you come back to it, after having done what you need to do, you need to work with an outside counsellor about issues in your own life. If you do that, and develop some perspective, your employment here will be fine."

"Thanks loads," I say.

"Those are the facts," says Anne. "We can take care of Randy. Stay and do what needs to be done."

I hang up. I don't want to hear any more. I stay in my room, depressed. The funeral is eighteen hours away. The grandfather clock downstairs, even after all these years, continues to tick inexorably away.

## 3

BY THE TIME October arrived, my mother and Jeanette were still refusing to admit that their brother was as seriously ill as he was. They maintained some hope that David would rally and recover. But he was so weak, Dr. Fred wanted him to have a nurse's care. The problem was, no one from the local Victorian Order of Nurses would come to the house. "I'm going to arrange something from the city," Dr. Fred said. "Give me a day or two."

My grandmother did not want a nurse hovering in her house at all hours. "Especially a foreign one who doesn't live in Advocate. I've got some very nice things here," she said. "I would like to keep them."

Jeanette and my mother pointed out the unlikelihood a VON would moonlight as a burglar. In the end, they didn't have to worry. To find a public nurse willing to work with my uncle, even from Halifax, was rare enough. To find one also willing to travel that distance was impossible. The only alternative was a private nurse.

"Who's got the money for that?" cried my grandmother.

Jeanette and my mother quickly pointed out that she did.

"You kids think I'm made of money," she said. "You always have. But I'm not. I'm just as beholden as anyone else."

My mother worked on Grandnan to fulfill Dr. Fred's request. He, on several occasions, took me aside and asked if I had told my mother that Deanny and I had been to see him.

"No," I told him.

"I think you should. She may be able to answer some questions I can't. And you'll never get those answers until you ask them."

But I had answers enough. I sensed rather than understood Dr. Fred disapproved of what was going on in our house. The conflict between my grandmother and her daughters. The refusal to discuss the problem. He waded in on the argument about the nurse. In his opinion my uncle was beyond the point of being cared for by his sisters alone. He needed a professional.

"What he needs," said Jeanette, "is to be in a hospital."

"I agree," said Fred. "But they will send him home."

"What if you admitted him?" asked my mother.

"The administrators and other doctors overrule me. I could report them to the board or the province, but that takes time. And in this situation time is a precious commodity."

Faced with no choice, my grandmother agreed to pay for a private nurse — on condition she be allowed to interview her, to rule out thieves and wantons. My mother and Jeanette agreed. There were no private nurses in Advocate so Dr. Fred arranged for an interview with one from Halifax. Her name was Cassandra. She took one look at my uncle after she was hired and clucked her tongue. "He's in rough shape," she told my mother. "I've heard of it, but I've never seen it."

"You're not afraid of him?" my mother asked.

"Why should I be afraid?" Cassandra said. "It's just an illness, honey. They come and go. No different from dealing with someone with TB, or syphilis."

Cassandra was older than my mother. More matronly. She had no time for Grandnan, even though she technically employed her. She knew what my grandmother thought of what was happening to my uncle. This did not matter to her; my uncle was sick and she took care of him, calling him "honey" and bathing him, cleaning his feet and hands. She did her best to make him comfortable. My mother and Jeanette appreciated her. My grandmother stayed out of her way; she tended to stay in her room when Cassandra was working. The rest of us looked forward to her visits, for, like Deanny, she brought an outsider's perspective into the house, an uninfected energy.

When Cassandra wasn't there, my mother and Jeanette cared for him. They begged my grandmother to sit with him occasionally, if only to give them a break. She refused. "He's fine," she said. "Someone's always in the next room, so what do I need to be there for?"

This kind of denial was frustrating to my mother, and she told my grandmother she was being a coward.

"I'm busy," my grandmother said. "I'll stay in the house with him, but I'm not going to sit in his room holding his hand." This was a figure of speech. My grandmother would no more hold my uncle's hand than sit in a hot fire.

Eventually my mother and Jeanette employed Deanny and me to sit with him when she and my aunt took breaks. We were ordered to stay by the door and not go near the bed. Deanny didn't mind; she had already been holding David's hand and she was not afraid of him now.

I no longer touched him, after that one time I held his hand. Not so much from fear of contagion. I had examples in Jeanette, my mother, Cassandra, and Deanny that this was no longer to be worried about. But I still could not shake the feeling one day I might end up like him. It horrified me. I was also stricken with pity for my uncle; even this had an effect upon me. To this day I do not know which was more damaging — the fear or the compassion.

■ ■ ■

I HAD LITTLE with which to fill my days. Deanny was in school and I was not. My uncle was in no condition to be giving me lessons anymore. To care for him, my mother and Jeanette had entirely given up on home-schooling me. My grandmother said I would turn into an uneducated savage and fall so hopelessly behind the other students I would never catch up.

"What do you expect us to do about it?" said my mother. "Lay siege to the school? They won't let him in. I can't help it, can I?"

"Well, someone's got to take responsibility for the boy," my grandmother said. "A child left to his own devices is a recipe for trouble and corruption. You don't mind if I take him in hand, do you?"

"What do you mean," asked my mother suspiciously, "by 'take him in hand'?"

"Educate him!" cried my grandmother. "Give him his lessons!"

My mother agreed, if only to get my grandmother out of her hair. But if my mother and Jeanette were too long out of school to be of much use to me, my grandmother was doubly so. It had been forty-five years since she had stepped into a classroom. I was as suspicious as my mother as to what my grandmother's lessons would consist of, and my suspicions were confirmed the first morning we met in the kitchen. She took one look at the stack of books I carried and said I wouldn't need them.

"What are we going to be learning about then?" I asked.

"History!" said my grandmother. "Geography. Music and theology. There are some things, Jacob, that cannot be learned from those books."

When I sat down at the table she told me to take a pad of paper and a pen and take notes.

"This might be useful someday," she said.

It *was* useful, if only as an example of how to twist history. My grandmother gave me a full account of the founding and settlement of Advocate, drawn from a life filled with gossip and the church's teachings. She did not mince words. Into them she poured all her bias and vitriol. She never mentioned the removal of the First Nations people from their lands, and their relegation to the reserve. She exalted the Lemon Day parade, and made particular reference to an edict from the first Nova Scotia assembly in 1792 that banished all Catholic priests on pain of death. Eventually her history dissolved into the naming of personages and families, with the McNeils chief amongst them. She traced the ancestry of my grandfather directly back to the Catholic side's founder, Nathan McNeil. She kept me there almost two hours until my mother came out and asked me how it was going.

"He's a quick study," retorted my grandmother. "He'll go far."

In fact I had said nothing during the lesson, and after the first few minutes barely took a note. My grandmother seemed less interested in teaching than expounding. After the first half hour I doubted whether it would have mattered whether I was there or not.

Looking at an empty notebook, my mother said, "That's enough for today."

"I've barely started," objected my grandmother.

"Until tomorrow," said my mother. "Jacob, run upstairs and see if your Aunt Jeanette will drive me to the post office."

"Same time same place," said my grandmother to me. "Don't you be a minute late."

I hadn't known until that day a formal educator lay so shallowly beneath my grandmother's bosom. She trapped me for a few hours each morning to espouse more history — a detailed description of the inner workings of the Catholic Church, and a brief history of Thomas Aquinas, whom she had never read but knew secondhand from my dead grandfather. I cannot think of any subjects that would torture a twelve-year-old boy more. For my grandmother this was a way to distract herself. By way of teaching me, she could immerse herself in the past, when sons did not die of mysterious diseases upstairs and neighbours and friends did not turn their faces away from what had once been one of the most respected families in town. She wanted to teach me history because history was all she had left.

# 4

THROUGHOUT OCTOBER, MY uncle's health continued to deteriorate, and we — my mother and Jeanette, myself and Deanny — spent more and more time in his room. There were two more hospital visits, and again he was given minimal care and shipped home. In the second week of October, Cassandra told Dr. Fred two days a week were not enough, and that in her opinion David should be moved to a hospital for around-the-clock care. Fred had been dreading this day.

"At this rate," Cassandra said, "he's going to go into cardiac arrest."

Dr. Fred knew Cassandra was right. But he also knew the hospital wouldn't take David. Fear of contagion had not abated there. Rooms were scrubbed, Hazmat suits worn, and sheets and towels burned. Nurse Jones would do for my uncle what she could when she was on duty, but none of the other nurses would. Even the doctors balked. Dr. Fred explained this to Cassandra.

"What of their Hippocratic oath?" Cassandra said.

"It's a small town," sighed Dr. Fred.

"If it was me," said Cassandra, "I'd march in there and make some heads roll."

But Cassandra was from the city. She was enlightened, and a consummate nurse. She understood the fear of contagion, but she couldn't condone it in the medically trained. She suggested my uncle be transferred to Halifax, where he would be cared for by more experienced and seasoned professionals. She told Dr. Fred she was surprised he had not thought of this himself.

"I did," said Dr. Fred. "But it won't make a difference now. His sisters want him close. They don't want him to die by himself."

"Do they want him alive as long as possible?" said Cassandra. "Or do they want him to die tomorrow?"

Dr. Fred discussed the choices with my mother and Jeanette.

They decided to wait for a lucid moment, when they would ask my uncle what he wanted. Dr. Fred insisted he be there as well, to explain the medical considerations, so David could make an informed choice. When that day came, David was groggy from the medications, but lucid enough. Dr. Fred checked him over, changed his iv as my mother and aunt stood looking on. I slipped into the room to hear the conversation. Deanny was in school.

"David," Dr. Fred said. "There's something we want to discuss with you."

And he laid it out on the table. He told David if he didn't go to Halifax his life expectancy could be shortened. He needed care that couldn't be provided at home.

"What kind of care?" croaked Uncle David.

"A morphine drip, for one," said Dr. Fred. "To keep you out of pain. I'm hesitant to give you one in home care environment, and I think we can both agree that the pills and injections we're giving you are no longer sufficient."

As if to prove Dr. Fred right, Uncle David winced. I was unsure of where his pain came from. When it subsided he said, "What else?"

"Antibiotics," he said. "The local hospital doesn't have the necessary compliment on hand. If you're admitted to the hospital in Halifax, they will have everything — and the doctors there can try things I haven't."

"Will they save my life?"

Dr. Fred didn't answer immediately. He looked at my mother.

"They will prolong it."

"By how much?"

"I think you know the answer to that."

"Months?"

"Possibly," said Dr. Fred.

"More likely," said Uncle David, "days."

"Most likely," said Dr. Fred.

"If it's a matter of days, I stay here."

He drifted back to sleep.

Dr. Fred turned to my aunt and mother. "That's it, then. Keep giving him the pills, and I'll keep up with the iv antibiotics. Someone must be with him at all times now."

"Thank you, Fred," said my mother.

"I wish there was more I could do."

"You've done plenty," said Jeanette. "You've done more than anyone else in this damn town."

As if on cue, we heard my grandmother whistling from the kitchen below.

"I better get going," said Fred. "Call if you need me."

■ ■ ■

IT WAS AROUND that time something very strange happened to uncle's mouth. Houseflies began to gather about it. Since my uncle was mostly asleep, or groggy when awake, he did not notice. But my mother did. Sometimes there would be seven or eight of them crawling in and out of his mouth and nose. My mother would shoo them away.

"It could be the thrush," Dr. Fred said, "though I doubt it. They must smell something. It could be because his stomach lining is deteriorating and they smell the carrion."

"It's disgusting," said Jeanette. "Isn't there something we can do?"

Dr. Fred could think of nothing, short of sitting beside his bed and waving them away. Although we were not forbidden from his room, my mother no longer asked Deanny and me to pull watch. She and Jeanette wished to do it, I think because they were afraid he might die and they wanted to be with him. My grandmother kept a fold-up cot in the upstairs hallway closet; they rolled it into his room and made it up, each of them taking turns on it.

My grandmother was incensed when she found out they passed on a chance to move my uncle to Halifax. "You've doomed the man!" she said. "He won't last the week!"

"Spare us the outrage, Mother," my mother said. "This is not about you."

My grandmother said no more. The news that David would stay home to die made it harder for her to keep up her senseless prattle. She stopped baking. She spent most of her time in her bedroom, on the phone. I didn't feel sorry for my grandmother during this time. David was imprisoned by circumstance. My grandmother by choice.

Only once, when I was just coming out of his room, did she corner me in the hallway and ask anxiously how he was. I was surprised, I admit.

"He's sleeping. He always sleeps now."

"Dear God in heaven," said my grandmother. "How did we ever get into this fix?"

"What fix?" I said innocently.

"Never mind," said my grandmother. "Just tell your mother I've made up a tray. It's on the kitchen table."

"He won't eat it," I said. "He hasn't eaten in days."

"He hasn't?"

Although I didn't know it, one of the ways my mother and Jeanette punished my grandmother was by not telling her about

David's condition. "If you want to know," Jeanette had said, "go in to see him yourself."

She wouldn't, of course. But she did want to know how he was.

When I told my mother Grandnan was pestering me for information about Uncle David, she told her to stop. "If you want to know something, come to us. Not Jacob."

"But you won't tell me anything!" Grandnan cried.

"I told you, come see for yourself. Say goodbye to him, before you regret it."

"I don't regret anything," said my grandmother, "except raising two daughters who don't respect me."

But these arguments no longer worked. She lost credibility every day as long as she refused to help her only son. I think she saw, clearly, how the situation had got away from her. I've often wondered if my grandmother's refusal to acknowledge her son's illness came from its origins. Since it was a sexually transmitted disease, and from a "depraved" kind of sex, she couldn't think about him being sick without picturing the acts that gave it to him. I have a theory this is a lot of the reason the disease was so roundly ignored in those first few years. It offended. It wasn't, in the eyes of many, a blameless disease. My uncle had brought this on himself by acting on his perversion. My grandmother never came outright and said that AIDS was God's judgment on the unrighteous, as so many others did in those years, but I know she thought it.

My grandmother had lost so much face that Jeanette started to smoke in the house, and ignored her when she tried to say anything. In the end my grandmother said, "Well use an ashtray at least. Don't get any ashes on the floors."

In retrospect it was a wonder Jeanette didn't butt them out on the floors, just to annoy my grandmother.

# 5

IN THOSE FINAL days it was not uncommon to find all of us in my uncle's room at the same time. He was often asleep, and we rarely spoke to him or each other. Deanny and I sat on chairs near the door. My mother and Jeanette sat on either side of my uncle. We'd stay for hours this way, taking breaks only to go to the bathroom and to get something to eat or drink in the kitchen. My grandmother still did not come in. My aunt and mother stopped asking her. Occasionally David would wake up and ask for water or more morphine. He was often groggy, and there was a terrible silence in that room I shall never forget. My uncle's feeble whispering punctuated rather than relieved it. Deanny and I finished *To Kill a Mockingbird*, and my uncle asked for no other book. That part of his life, the teacher, the reader, was over. I marvelled over the fact that Uncle David had read his last book, had had his last conversation about literature after a life devoted to it.

*War and Peace* still sat on his night table, but it was unfinished. I opened to where he had stopped reading, marked by a strip torn from the *Advocate Gazette*. The strip was from the article "Strange Contagion Strikes Town." When I showed it to my mother she wondered how my uncle had laid hands on it.

"Henry," said Jeanette. "He doesn't believe in keeping the truth from him."

The page my uncle was on was halfway through the book. There was a conversation between two soldiers, and a man praying. My uncle had underlined in pencil a single line. *Lay me down like a stone oh God, and raise me up like a new bread.* This I never showed my mother, or Jeanette, or even Deanny. I felt it was my uncle's last communication, his final words, and I have shared them with no one until now.

■ ■ ■

ON ONE OF those days, when we were all in his room, my uncle woke up and asked to be propped up by a pillow. He was so terribly thin that just watching him move, however slowly, I felt as if he might break. He was barely awake, and he looked at none of us directly when he began to speak. Occasionally his head would droop, and we would think he'd gone to sleep again. But he kept talking.

"This town," he said, "has been good to me. It has nurtured me, made me who I am."

"Good?" said Jeanette. "That's hardly the word I'd use."

My uncle acted as if he didn't hear her, and perhaps he didn't. My mother told her to hush. "When I was a boy," he said, "I fell off my bike. Did I ever tell you that? The wheel came off and I spilled into the road. I was hurt — cuts and scrapes and in pain. And the neighbours came out and helped me. I remember that now, more than anything. Isn't that strange?"

No one said a word. It was as silent as death. "So don't hate the town," he continued. "The town is doing its best. And especially don't hate her."

Deanny sat up straighter in her chair. She knew who my uncle was speaking of.

"You must tell her not to blame herself. You must tell her I don't forgive her because there is nothing to forgive. Do you promise to do this?" He was looking down, not at anyone in particular. I saw my mother and Jeanette nod. "None of you should feel any guilt. And you must make sure she doesn't feel any either. She is old. She will eventually need your help."

And with that my uncle closed his eyes again, and fell asleep. I've often wondered if my mother and Jeanette repeated his final words to my grandmother. I know I did not. I suspect my mother and Jeanette felt the same way at first, but may have passed them along later.

Nonetheless, she did feel guilty. She did regret. Her insistence that I give the eulogy and the money she left says that much.

...

THE NEXT DAY, on October 21 at six a.m., my mother came into my room and woke me as gently as she could. "What's wrong?" I said.

"It's your uncle," she said. "It's time."

When I got into the hallway, I saw my grandmother just emerging out of her room, with her face thickly creamed with her blue facial mask. "For heaven's sake, what is going on?"

Jeanette was coming up the stairs. She looked distraught. "I've called Dr. Fred. I think it's better than calling an ambulance."

"What's wrong?" said my grandmother. "What happened?"

"He's dying, mother," said my mother. "Something happened to him during the night. He looks awful."

Jeanette went into his room, and came back out, face blanched. "He's still breathing."

I tried to go in too, but my mother grabbed me and pulled me aside. "No Jacob," she said. "You don't want to see your uncle like this. You don't want to remember him this way."

Dr. Fred came and examined my uncle while we waited in the hallway. Less than five minutes later he emerged. My grandmother had rubbed off her mask. We were all in our nightclothes.

"He's awake," Dr. Fred said.

"How?" said my mother.

"He says he feels fine. He can't feel any of his extremities, which is why I suspect he's not in any pain. It's sepsis. One, or more, of the infections have moved into the blood. His body has swollen to three times its normal size. The redness in his skin is due to the infection." I know now the condition Dr. Fred spoke of, and my uncle had, is called *Pneumocystis jovecki* pneumonia. He never mentioned that name to us then. Perhaps he knew we were not interested in the purely clinical.

"He looks like a monster!" said Jeanette.

"He's not in pain," said Dr. Fred. "I assure you."

"Is there anything you can do?"

"No. His immune system is gone, and he has nothing to fight this off with. I suggest you say your goodbyes."

My mother started in, but Fred laid a hand on her arm and stopped her. "Don't burden him," he said. "You might be tempted to talk about the past, but don't, unless he brings it up. He may not even be awake for very long. He may go at any minute. In fact, if you don't mind, I'd like to stay."

"To help him?" said my mother.

"If I can," said Dr. Fred. "But more as a friend. I've grown to know David quite well."

No one saw it but me. I'm sure of it. My grandmother winced, as if Dr. Fred's words were anathema, or accusation, to her.

"I'm going to call people," said Jeanette, and she was crying. "There are others that should be here." She looked at my grandmother. "We can do for him what your town wouldn't."

And my grandmother, who at other times would never have allowed such impertinence, went quietly back into her room.

■ ■ ■

THAT DAY WAS the longest of my life.

Jeanette was determined to have a deathwatch for my uncle, and she called the same people she had called for the Lemon Day protest — Henry, Deacon Harry, and Darcy from the reserve.

Deanny came over at nine, but my mother told her it was no place for children. She was upset that she had been called a child, and wanted to know why I was allowed to stay and she wasn't.

"You have a point," my mother said. "In fact I should send Jacob to spend the day at your house." But she didn't — she was too distracted — and eventually she relented. "Just stay out of his room," my mother said. "He's very sick, and we're doing for him what we can."

Darcy arrived soon after. We did not know, at the time, that the band council on the reserve had been watching the actions of the townspeople. They felt they should somehow participate and show compassion. It would be years before anyone from the reserve told Jeanette this. Many reserves during the eighties dealt with the AIDS crisis no better than other communities, with the same fear and prejudice. Some went so far as to kick sufferers off traditional lands when they came home to die. But the reserve outside of Advocate was not one of those. Darcy was delegated to come and act on their behalf.

He brought with him a deerskin drum, an eagle feather, bunches of sweet grass, tobacco, sage, and cedar. He wore traditional Mi'kmaq dress, buckskin leggings, a vest decorated with dyed porcupine quills and beads, and a small rawhide medicine pouch strung at his hip.

When my grandmother saw him she whispered to Jeanette, "What's the godawful getup for?"

"Medicine," Jeanette answered. "Rituals."

"Not in my house. This is a house of the Lord."

"This is a house of death and dying," said Jeanette. "And your Lord has nothing to do with it. I've asked Darcy here to ensure the safe passage of David's soul, which is something your church refused to do."

My grandmother, her position weakened, said nothing, except to fall back on the petty tyrannies of a lifelong housekeeper. "I hope he knows I don't allow smoke in my house. It discolours the drapes."

Darcy looked at my aunt. She shook her head. "Go upstairs," she said. Don't worry about her."

■ ■ ■

MY AUNT'S ESTIMATION that my grandmother's church would not make an appearance at my uncle's deathwatch was not entirely true. Deacon Harry did come, as he had on many previous days, though he had not given my uncle the last rites because my grandmother had not wanted him to. He wasn't, in her understanding, up to the job. My mother and Jeanette discussed with each other whether Deacon Harry should administer what rites he could.

The deacon did not condemn Father Orlis for refusing Uncle David the last rites; he reminded my mother and Jeanette that Father Orlis was old, and that David's case put him "a little out of his depth."

"Will you get in trouble?" my mother asked. "For doing things you're not qualified to do?"

"As far as I'm concerned," Deacon Harry said, "only God makes those kinds of judgments."

If he thought anything untoward about Darcy being there with his Mi'kmaq rituals he didn't say. They were more than polite to each other. Harry, dressed in his black rabbat, and black shirt, but no collar, stood in sharp clerical contrast to Darcy's colourful Mi'kmaq dress.

My mother asked David if he wanted to give confession.

"Why not?" he supposedly said. "Might as well."

I still do not know if my uncle at this stage began believing in the possibility of the afterlife. He had made no noise about extreme unction and confession. Darcy burned sweet grass inside, against the prohibitions of my grandmother. We could smell it all over the house. Deacon Harry asked everyone to leave the room at ten o'clock to hear my uncle's confession. It only took a few minutes. When he came out of the room he was grave.

"It is given," he said. "David is free from his sins."

Aunt Jeanette said, as far as she was concerned, it was those who had sinned against him that needed to worry. She was still angry, and my uncle's impending death had not softened her.

The last person to arrive was Henry Hennsey. Like Darcy and Deacon Harry, Henry brought his own form of absolution: a book.

I couldn't see its title, tucked as it was beneath his arm. To this day I don't know what book it was. Henry asked, if the family didn't mind, if he could read to Uncle David for a few minutes.

"That is," he said, "if David wants it."

They gave him a half hour. Deanny and I hung about outside the door to see if I could hear what Henry was reading. It is one of the few details surrounding my uncle's death I do not know, and it has always niggled at me. I asked Henry once, but he shook his head and said that it didn't matter.

"It was a book we often discussed," Henry said. "I thought it fitting he should hear some of it."

"Did he talk to you?" I asked.

"No," Henry said. "He just listened. I like to think the sound of someone else's words comforted him. He loved good writing, your uncle. We had that in common at least."

■ ■

THE NIGHT BEFORE my grandmother's funeral I stay up to work on her eulogy. The same problems remain. How to tell the truth without vilifying her completely? How to maintain the sense of decency and decorum required? It all seems false. Deanny said once that you can't be both a pragmatist and an idealist, and she is right; but I have never been either. I am an evader. I have long been such, lacking the courage of my own convictions. I march in parades with like-minded people, but I have yet to prove I can march by myself, as Deanny and my aunt did all those years ago.

By three a.m. I give up and go to bed. I will get up in the morning and try again. If nothing comes to me, I will give the eulogy based on my aunt's sanitized version and take the money and run. My uncle David will not be mentioned, except as a footnote.

When I come downstairs in the morning, I am defeated. Jeanette and my mother are already up, having breakfast in the kitchen. My mother fetches me coffee.

"So what have you decided?" my mother says.

"I've got nothing," I tell her. "I'll give Jeanette's version, and I'll insert a few words about Uncle David."

My mother looks at Jeanette and says, "Should we tell him?"

Jeanette nods. "We should."

"Tell me what?"

"We promised your grandmother we never would," says my mother. "Even your uncle never mentioned it. We always thought one of them might say something about it — to you, to each other — before they died, but they didn't. It never seemed our place."

"We held it as long as we could," says my aunt. "It seemed so unnecessary, so much ancient history."

So here was the thing that was hidden, the thing that had always lain beneath the surface. I am determined to stay unmoved. My mother and Jeanette ask me to come into the living room, where, when my grandmother was alive, all important discussions took place.

# TEN

∎

DEANNY AND I lingered outside the door for most of the afternoon but we were not invited back inside. Occasionally one of the participants would come out to get something or use the downstairs bathroom and Deanny would ask how he was.

"No change," she was told.

Darcy continued to beat his drum and chant. Although he was very quiet, he could be heard all over the house. My grandmother — who had gone to her room, and did not come back out even when my mother and aunt told her the end was near — asked, loudly but with no authority, "What is that awful racket?"

No one paid her any attention.

Over the next hours, David's vitals and blood pressure dropped. He became unconscious. My mother sat on one side of the bed holding his hand, my aunt Jeanette the other. They watched as his chest rose and fell, a wheezing coming from his mouth and nose. Someone in that room gave a cry. Deanny and I heard it. We sat up rigid on the rumpus room sofa, listening. Later, my mother told us David had vomited "coffee grounds," blood that had backed up in his system after the kidneys shut down. Years later, I would understand, from my work with my clients, what this meant. The vomiting of coffee grounds spelled the end. Fred cleared his throat and passage-ways with his fingers.

At five o'clock, my mother, ever the watchful parent even in the midst of such a tragedy, came downstairs to make sure Deanny and I had eaten. Under her supervision we were forced to fill up plates from the food in the fridge. On the way back up she went into my grandmother's room to once more see if she could coerce her into saying goodbye to David. Deanny and I heard them from the hallway.

"I can't," said my grandmother. "Don't you understand that?"

"I cannot," my mother said. "And I will never be able to. He's your son. He's dying. I can't think of one single reason why you should not go in and say goodbye. You owe him that much."

But in my grandmother's purview, she owed her son nothing. She had long ago disowned him, and he only came back under her roof under false pretenses, which she had allowed in a weak moment.

At eight o'clock, fourteen hours after we had first discovered him swollen and near death, his vitals and blood pressure dropped dramatically. He vomited once more, again mostly dark blood. The redness of his skin faded suddenly, and the swelling began to go down. He began to suffocate in his sleep. Dr. Fred tried to open his airways again but to no avail. He took one more heaving breath, coughed, and more blood came up. Finally he lay still, his head fallen to one side. His heart stopped. His brain, finally, had shut down.

It was a horrible, painful death.

There was no dignity or nobility in it at all.

■ ■ ■

ONE OF THE most delightful things about my uncle when he was a boy, my mother says, was his capacity for learning. He started speaking when he was a little over a year. It surprised everyone, and even shocked a few, that such a little child could string together sentences with an almost mature eloquence. My grandfather, who in his practice saw many children and was aware of patterns of their development, knew there was something unusual about his son. He put him through a number of tests, with words and symbols printed on cards. When David was older, he administered psychological and intelligence tests. The results of this testing, he pronounced to my grandmother, was that he believed they might be raising a genius.

I saw no evidence of this in my uncle when I knew him. He was intelligent, yes. And articulate. But I detected no stratospheric IQ. My mother says this was for two reasons: David hid it, and actually denied it. He was a precocious child, he said, but he had grown into his abilities, which were barely higher than normal. He pointed out that he had actually achieved little in his life, and as much as he loved being a teacher, it was hardly the place where geniuses ended up.

My grandmother didn't argue with him. Granddad asked him to read books at the age of seven and eight that most people don't tackle until adults, if they ever do. They discussed them, and my uncle made cogent arguments for and against points my grandfather raised. Everyone was delighted. My grandmother insisted he would become a doctor or a lawyer or a politician. But by the time my uncle entered the disappointing profession of teaching, she no longer cared where his star rose and how high. My grandfather was dead and my grandmother no longer spoke to him.

My mother and Jeanette continued to idolize David. It was he who had read to them each night before bed, and he who had chosen the books.

"He spent half of one year," my mother tells me, "when he was sixteen and we were still in elementary, reading us *David Copperfield*." She laughed. "Jeanette and I were usually asleep in minutes."

David had few friends in school. It had bothered my grandmother that he wasn't as interested in people as he was in books. When he was small and she took him to play with other children, he stood off to the side and refused to get involved in their games. He wasn't arrogant. There was a natural timidity in him that bothered my grandmother. She complained to my grandfather that he was antisocial, but my grandfather said she should give David time, that he had to grow into himself.

My mother is telling me all this as she sits on one side of me on the sofa, Jeanette in the wingchair across. I tell her I don't see the point. I had gathered all of this anyway, if not in detail.

"Of course you do," says my mother. "But don't you see?"

"See what?"

"How much she loved him."

"She had an awfully strange way of showing it."

"I'm not finished yet," says my mother.

"*Gay*," my mother says, "was not a common word in those days. And homosexuality was never spoken about. Your uncle David told me once he knew about himself by the time he was thirteen. This was when he began to withdraw into himself. He became absorbed in books and his school work. It bothered your grandmother. She was becoming surer by the minute that David was a misfit. Dad began asking David to spend more time in his study to talk things out, and he did, though I don't think they resolved anything. David knew what he was. He knew how the news would be taken if he decided to tell. It was much more difficult in those days than it is in your generation."

"It's a wonder he came out at all," I say.

"But he did," my mother says. "David got a certain thoughtfulness from Dad, but he could be stubborn like your grandmother. The fights the two of them had over small things when David was a teenager. The angrier your grandmother got the more your uncle dug his heels in. Your grandfather rarely interfered, and if he did attempt to intercede, it was almost always on the part of your uncle. I think he knew David was struggling with something, though

I'm sure he didn't know what. The only book he could find on his condition, David told me later, was a book from the library. He stole it rather than be seen checking it out. It was called *Being Homosexual*. The book described homosexuality as a disease. No wonder David's teenage years were a misery."

Listening to my mother, I have a visual image of my young uncle, an angst-ridden teenager, lying on his bed, the same bed on which he would later die, reading Wilde's *Epidemics of Ireland* or Lucretius's *The Nature of Things* from my grandfather's collection in his study. My own pangs about my sexuality when growing up were less about what people would think of me than contracting the plague my uncle had. I denied my sexuality because I was fearful of it, not of people. My mother would accept me, I knew. As would Aunt Jeanette. My grandmother would hate that I wasn't normal, but she would be kept at bay because of her daughters. The world, however, could not be kept at bay. The sickness that was killing gay men by the thousands, and that we heard about on the news nightly through most of my teens, could not be ignored. It was this that would force me into myself and, unlike my uncle, I would not recover.

I listen as my mother continues her story. I am impatient, and I can't imagine what she has to tell me would change my mind about much. But she is my mother, and I can't deny her.

At eighteen, when he finished high school, my uncle announced he was not going to university. He wanted to travel the world. My grandfather asked him where he wanted to go. David answered that he wanted to see everywhere — the US, Europe, maybe Asia. My uncle was ahead of his time. The mass migrations of young people from west to east in search of spiritual enlightenment would not begin for another five or six years. He anticipated it.

My grandmother scoffed. She asked him if he intended to pay for these voyages with buttons and wishes. He had a college fund, but my grandmother would not let him have the money to pay for travel. On this my grandfather agreed, pointing out that David would need something when he came back. He gave his son money to start out with, on the understanding that David would have to earn the rest.

My uncle took a job for a year as a sawyer at the mill. He saved every penny. His mood, according to my mother, improved. He came from work at night tired but satisfied. He was going away. He had long talks with my grandfather in the den on the weekends. My grandmother complained that he did not go out, that he knew no one his own age. He told my grandfather that the things other teenagers cared about — cars and women and alcohol — didn't interest him. He found them puerile, he said. My mother remembers the word specifically because my grandmother had to look it up.

No one questioned why my uncle said he was not interested in women. Later, my grandmother would say this was their first clear indication, and that something should have been done about it right then. She remained convinced she could have saved him. This made my uncle wonder later if maybe Grandnan hadn't also read *Being Homosexual*.

David's work at the mill didn't diminish his brilliance one whit. He read voraciously. He talked to his sisters, told them that one day he would send them postcards from all over the world. He kept this promise. My mother still has those cards, and has shown them to me. She guards them as jealously as my grandmother did the wartime letters of my grandfather.

My grandmother, a few weeks after he had been working, began demanding he pay room and board. She didn't need the money. She was, she said, teaching him life lessons. David believed she was attempting to sabotage his trip. My grandfather put his foot down, informing my grandmother and everyone else in the house that no son of his would pay to live under his roof. He was the provider and it was up to him to say who paid what.

My grandmother retracted, and David got to keep all his money. He barely spent a penny of what he made, and after a year and a half, he had saved up almost four thousand dollars. In the early nineteen sixties that was a lot of money. In July of that year David bought a ticket to New York City. He'd always wanted to see it. From there, he was going to work his way across the US.

The night before he left, David and my grandfather spent all night in the den with the door closed. When my grandmother got up the next morning grandfather was not in bed with her. He was still with David. She scolded them both, informing them that they were sure to get sick, staying up all night without sleep, behaving like children.

David smiled, according to my mother. That day, he was free.

He would end up in Paris, teaching for a few months at a language school. He lived in Montparnasse, rubbing shoulders with ex-pat Americans and Spanish novelists. On one of many postcards he sent, he wrote: *I feel as if I'm living in a literary dream. The home of Hemingway and Fitzgerald and Parker and Joyce and Stein. You should see the Pont Alexander at night! A golden-lighted vision!*

The romantic in my uncle came out. Advocate could not contain him, and not just because of his sexuality. For years he had been reading about the world, but unlike my grandmother and grandfather, he wanted to see it. My aunt Jeanette had also dreamed of seeing the world, but for all her bravado at home, she was, in the end, too timid. Some people grow out into the world, and some grow down into it. Jeanette is one of the latter.

But David's true liberation did not result from his having left Advocate. He began mentioning in his letters from Europe a young French man he was travelling with. Gaëtan figured more and more in his stories and my mother realized later he was in a relationship. He never said as much, but some of the postcards he sent home from Europe only talked about his companion. My grandmother was suspicious, believing he would be robbed because the French couldn't be trusted.

My grandmother had never met a French person in her life.

My grandfather responded to these letters and postcards, saying he was glad David had a travelling companion. My mother tells me she thought Granddad might have been troubled by it as well, though not to the extent Grandnan was. It was around this time that he started to need more rest and quiet. He had always had a weak heart, and he was feeling ill or tired more frequently.

My grandmother claimed he began sneaking away for these breaks after postcards from David more than any other time. The postcards, according to my grandmother, were too enthusiastic. They did not remind her of a nineteen-year-old boy and his travel buddy. There was too much yearning. Too much romance. From the beginning she smelled a rat.

In the end, my mother tells me, David stayed away nearly five years. My grandfather, according to my mother, started to feel hurt. My grandmother, as usual, was only angry. "There's finding yourself and there's losing yourself." She thought David had done the latter.

Not once, after those few thousand dollars he took from my grandfather to add to his own meagre pile, did David write home and ask for more. He worked his way through Europe, as a farm hand, or teaching English, and once at a turnip pickling factory. That could be done more easily in those days, when work visas were not required or if they were no one worried about them. After Europe, he went to Turkey, then to India, and then to Japan. He wrote a post-card from the Hiroshima Peace Memorial Park. The picture was of the A-bomb Dome. He scrawled, *The evil that men do* on the back. My grandmother got tired of the postcards and refused to look at them any longer, but my grandfather, mother, and aunt enjoyed them.

Eventually, grandfather stopped saying what a good thing David's trip was. Perhaps it was because he missed his son, or perhaps because he'd begun to wonder what world David was actually exploring.

The last postcard David sent was from Hong Kong, and it informed them that he was coming home. *I'm flying into Toronto,* he wrote, *where I'll set up an apartment and then come back for a visit.* My mother and Jeanette had practically forgotten what their brother looked like, and were excited. They jumped up and down like the schoolgirls they were when they were given the news.

But not everyone was pleased. My grandmother harrumphed when shown the card. She had developed a fierce resentment against her oldest child in the time he was gone. Partially, my mother figured, because of what she believed David's absence had been doing to her husband. His heart seemed to bother him more and more. He missed David, and may have wondered what he had done wrong to keep his son away so long.

They had to wait two months for David's arrival, while he set himself up in Toronto. This, too, bothered my grandfather. He wanted David to go to medical school, so that he could take over his practice. David, for his part, had made no mention of wanting to be a doctor. He told my mother later that teaching English as a second language in Japan had convinced him that he would be a good teacher. And since he loved books, it seemed natural to him to be an English teacher. I sometimes wonder if his homecoming that summer was anything like his final homecoming in 1984. My mother tells me that the entire family was there to meet the train. Then too they had been shocked by David's appearance — not because he was thin, but because he had filled out and become a man. He was heavier, though still fit, and he had a beard and long hair.

My grandmother told him that he looked just like the wild man of Borneo. My uncle responded that he had been to Borneo and that it was a nice place. My mother and aunt laughed. Grandnan did not. She still thought David "looked a fright."

Far from being put out by my uncle's looks, my grandfather swelled with pride. His son was his own man, and actually looked it. All my grandfather's worries about school and medicine went out the window, my mother said. He was plain happy to have his son back.

David seemed to have changed completely. The unhappy, insecure, withdrawn boy that they had known was gone, replaced by this confident, self-assured young man. Unlike most people who travel looking for answers only to discover that their problems follow them, my uncle really had found himself.

My grandfather hugged him, then David hugged his mother and sisters. Once home, he gave gifts from his travels: a carved wooden Buddha for Jeanette, a pair of amber earrings made in Germany for my mother, some books for my grandfather — one of them Lucretius in the original Latin bought in Rome — and a Turkish carpet for my grandmother.

One of the first things my grandfather did was to pull David into his den. My uncle laughed and said "Christ, Dad. More Lucretius?" My grandmother heard and informed her son that he may have spent time in godless places, but hers was still a house of the Lord. David apologized to her, but before entering his father's den he leaned over to my mother on the rumpus room sofa and whispered, "She hasn't changed."

Perhaps she hadn't, but my mother says Grandnan was still happy to have him home. She hung the Turkish carpet in a place of honour on the wall in the living room, and prepared a meal. David and my grandfather spent two hours in the den, until my grandmother called them out for supper. It was a joyous occasion. Uncle David recounted his adventures, and my grandmother ran down every place he had been as dirty, uncivilized, and godless. David baited her. He talked about Hindus and Moslems. He described using pit toilets in India. He told about a murder he had witnessed in New York.

My grandmother pointed out to her daughters that they should be grateful to live in a civilized country.

Apparently New York, to my grandmother, was "uncivilized."

David stayed one week. He told his parents he'd been accepted at University of Toronto in Education. He wanted to be a teacher. This was no doctor's position, and Grandnan, my mother says, wanted to dissuade him of the choice, but could not. It's hard to argue with a man who wants to be a teacher. My grandfather was delighted. If he was disappointed, he never said.

It was partially to get his college fund that David came back to Advocate. His father and mother had been proved right; the day he would need that money had arrived. They agreed to give David his college fund.

My mother says that was the best day of her youth. Even my grandmother was caught up in the atmosphere of celebration. A young life had been nurtured and brought to fruition and the boy was now a man, about to embark on his own life. It was apparent, my mother says, how proud my grandfather was of the man my uncle had become.

My uncle, of course, asked after my grandfather's health. Was he still taking his nitro? Did he still get his heart checked regularly? All was well there, my uncle was told. My mother still wonders, she says now, if my uncle was testing the waters, seeing how much his father could take. Because it was true he had found himself. He knew who he was, and he knew that he could never fully be that person if he kept it from his parents, whom he loved. He planned on telling them.

The morning his train was scheduled to leave, he asked if he could have some time alone with both of them in the den. My grandmother was instantly wary. She was never invited to den discussions.

"I made a promise to your grandmother," my mother says at this point, "that we would never talk about what I'm about to tell you. Jeanette and I were never allowed to bring it up. Even between ourselves. I guess we got so used to it that we never did. We should have told you sooner."

We have been in the living room for an hour, and the time of my grandmother's funeral is bearing down upon us. My mother and Jeanette seem no closer to the point of this story.

I got to know my uncle backwards instead of forward, like most relationships. Our association before he became sick was brief, and I saw him as someone who had interrupted my life. I did not have enough time to develop a lasting relationship. David was, more than anything, a symbol to me — of injustice, of disease, of small-town narrow-mindedness and fear. He made me an advocate for the cause, much as the Protestants had been urged to be advocates for their faith. Our brief association had determined the entire course of my life. His insistence on being his own man despite the opposition impressed me, though I have never been quite able to manage this myself. And of course he was the first gay man I knew. Hearing about his youth, and my grandmother's relationship to him, is interesting, but not a game changer. I tell my mother this.

"A few more minutes," she says. "And we'll be done."

"Good," I say.

■■■

THE WORD GAY, my mother says, was not common then. David might have planned on telling his parents he was homosexual or queer. The truth, my mother admits, is she and Jeanette have no idea what words David used.

They were hanging around at the door, the voices were too low to hear, when it was suddenly flung open and David came stomping out. Grandnan and my grandfather followed. My grandmother commanded David to come back, he wasn't to run off as if he'd just given a weather report.

"What's the point?" shouted my uncle. "You won't listen!"

"The Bible is very clear, David Owen McNeil. This is an abomination."

My grandfather, according to my mother, looked waxy and white. He stood behind my grandmother as she and David faced off in the living room. David was flushed. My mother says she had never seen him angry before that day, but he was then.

"I told you," he said, "because I thought you had a right to know. Not because I wanted you to change my mind."

"You don't have a mind," cried my grandmother, "if this is what it's telling you!"

My grandfather put a hand on his wife's shoulder. Whether it was to steady himself or calm her was unclear, my mother says. She and Jeanette still had no idea what the argument was about. More calmly, perhaps because he seemed to be struggling for breath, he explained to his son that something such as this was not unheard of to him. He had had patients.

"But David," he said. "These men live lives of secrecy, even blackmail. Diseases. Never knowing the warmth of a loving family, or having children. Do you want to live your life in that manner? "

"I won't hide it," David shook his head. "I won't." He said this was not something that he could just change, like an old pair of socks. There were no treatments. It wasn't an aberration. Or an abomination. It just was. "And there's nothing wrong with it either. Even if your Bible says there is."

"Blasphemy," cried my grandmother. "The poor boy is lost already!"

My grandfather looked pained. He removed his hand from his wife's shoulder to steady himself on the back of the sofa. My grandmother took a step towards my uncle. She said if this was the way he was then he wouldn't be that way in her house. He could leave and never come back again, as far as she was concerned.

"Is that really what you want?" said my uncle.

"Yes!" cried my grandmother.

"Millicent," my grandfather said. "Don't. He's our only son."

"No son of mine will be this way. Not in my house."

"It's my house too!" my grandfather said, now holding on to the back of sofa with both hands, and his face, my mother says, blanched white. He was wheezing.

Uncle David looked at both of them unhappily. "I hate this," he said. "But I can't be something and then lie about it. I'm not built that way."

"You should have lied," said my grandmother. "You should have gone off and had children and a wife and never spoke a word of it."

"You would have me put a family through that?" David said.

"Yes," my grandmother said. "I would have."

"Well, I won't," he said. "I am what I am, and all the arguing in the world is not going to change that. I wish you would just accept it."

"Accept it?" cried my grandmother. "I will not!" My grandmother again informed my uncle that if he did not recant and live a normal life he would no longer be welcome in their home. "This is not a home of blasphemy and perversion," my mother tells me she said. "It is a house of God, and Christian values."

It was useless for my uncle to argue, but neither could he allow himself to be kicked out of his home as so many gay men had been before him. He loved his father. He loved his sisters. He loved his mother. He could not imagine living his life without them. He had to make his parents see reason. He asked his father to say something.

My grandfather did not. He held on to the back of the sofa, his head down, and when David asked him what he thought he only shook it briefly. "I don't know ..." he said, and stopped.

David pressed him. Did he want him to leave or did he not? Could they not sort this out?

Many years later, David told my mother it was foolish of him to come into the house and expect his parents to accept what it had taken years for him to accept himself. He was young, he told her. Idealistic. It was the sixties. Europe had taught him that there was so much more going on in the world than Advocate had let on. He had developed his own set of principles and expected his parents to live by them. He realized only later that this was wrong.

As he and my grandmother waited for my grandfather to answer, Jeanette saw him sag, and stumble. She cried to my grandmother, who turned around and caught him just as he was about to collapse to the floor.

"For God's sake, Hal," my grandmother said. "What's wrong?"

"Got to lie down," my grandfather croaked.

My uncle and my grandmother assisted him to the sofa, where he lay on his back breathing shallowly with his eyes closed and his hands folded upon his chest. My mother suggested calling an ambulance, but my grandmother refused. She blamed my grandfather's spell on shock, brought on by the disgusting news her son had brought home. David tried to argue, pointing out his father's pallor and blue lips.

My grandfather groaned, and tried to speak. The only word that anyone could make out was "David."

As my mother relays the story, I again see how my grandmother could think there was a devil at work in our lives — never more apparent than when my grandfather was stricken at the same moment his only son came out to his parents. I do not think it was anything more than an unfortunate coincidence. My uncle's news was certainly a shock, but not one big enough to stop my grandfather's heart — especially as he seemed, even in those brief moments, more willing to accept it than my grandmother.

My mother admits now that my grandmother may have felt some guilt herself for what happened. If she had recognized right away he was having a heart attack instead of simply reacting violently to David's news, she might have called the ambulance sooner. Over my grandmother's protests David checked his father's pulse. It was weak. He was having difficulty breathing. When he didn't rebound after ten minutes, she began to get concerned. She shook him gently, and when he didn't respond, she asked my mother to call the ambulance.

When the ambulance came, he was loaded onto a stretcher and taken to the hospital. Before getting into the vehicle with her husband, my grandmother told David that when she and his father got back, he would either recant his nonsense or he would no longer be welcome in her house.

My uncle said nothing. He and my mother and aunt stayed around the house. An hour later they received a call from Dr. Bodsworth, my grandfather's physician. He'd had a heart attack but he was still alive. Two hours later they received another call from Dr. Bodsworth with the news that he'd had a second one in hospital and was dead.

When my grandmother returned home, she blamed my uncle.

"And what did he say?" I ask my mother.

"Very little," she says. "He was as stunned as the rest of us. He told me later that even he thought it was his fault, at first. She said your grandfather could not live with what David had told them, and died as a result of it. She truly believed this. She never changed her mind about it. She kicked David out of the house and told him never to come back."

"And he listened?"

"Not at first," says my mother. "He begged her not to do it. He said he was sorry, and that if he had known he would never have told them. Even Dr. Bodsworth said it was unlikely David's news had killed her husband, but she wouldn't listen. While David stood there she tore the Turkish carpet from the wall and burned it in the backyard along with all the things he'd given us. He never made a move to stop her. He was crying, and Jeanette and I had never seen David cry before. Even as a kid he didn't cry. The whole situation was awful."

"So what did he do?" I ask.

"He left. When he saw that she wasn't going to settle down. She threatened to call the police and have him removed. She said, 'Take your soul sickness and leave here. I never want to see your treacherous face again.'"

My mother pauses.

"He was confused. Grief-stricken. Guilty and horrified. He left for Toronto and did as my grandmother asked. He never cashed his college fund cheque. Perhaps he thought she would soften one day, but she never did. Even when he got sick she didn't forgive him. Now do you understand? Why she hated him so much? Why she couldn't be there for him, even when he got sick and came home?"

"It was foolish," I say, "to think that Granddad died because of Uncle David. And even more foolish to be resentful after he got sick."

"Yes," says my mother. "It was. Your grandmother was. She blamed most of her problems on other people, and she categorized human beings into acceptable and unacceptable lots. But your Uncle David forgave her, because he knew she thought he had killed her husband. He hadn't, of course. But it explains a lot."

"It doesn't justify it," I say.

"Jacob," my mother says. "The world is not a balance sheet. I've given you this information so that you can find it in your heart to forgive her. Your aunt and I have. We think it's high time you did."

"I can't," I say. "Even if I wanted to, I can't bring myself to do it."

"Can't or won't?" My mother sighs, and shakes her head. "You're so much like her, do you know that?"

"I know," I say. "Believe me, I know."

## 2

AFTER UNCLE DAVID's body was removed from the house by ambulance, Dr. Fred drove Deanny home, though she hadn't wanted to go.

"Go home, Deanny," my mother said. "You can come back when things settle down."

My mother and I and Jeanette sat in the kitchen and drank tea. There were no phone calls, no offers of condolence, though certainly the news must have spread. My grandmother had not left her room. No one checked the extension to see if she was making calls. Once, my aunt checked on her to see if she was okay. "She won't open her door," she came down and told us.

"She'll have to open it sometime," my mother said. "She can't stay in there forever."

"She should have said her goodbyes to him," Jeanette said. "I can't believe she didn't."

"She'll regret it," said my mother. "To the end of her days and beyond she'll regret it."

The phone rang at ten o'clock. It was Dr. Fred. He had signed the death certificate and since there was no need for an autopsy the body was to go directly to the funeral home. It had been refused.

"What?" said my mother.

"They're worried about contagion. The staff is afraid to work on it."

"Well, where is he?"

"Still in the ambulance. The paramedics are none too happy about it. They're afraid the virus will jump hosts once the body is dead."

"What are we supposed to do?" said my mother. "Bring him back here?"

"I'll ask the hospital to hold him for a while. But we have to find a mortuary that will take him."

"It's ten o'clock at night!"

"Have you thought of cremation?"

"David didn't want that," my mother said. "We discussed it."

"Try Trenton, then. Or Halifax if need be." Dr. Fred then suggested putting all David's sheets in garbage bags and burning them. "Just in case," he said.

My mother related all this to Jeanette when she got off the phone. Her eyes were irritated from crying. "What about his funeral?" she said to her sister. "How's that going to go?"

"Get Mom to call Father Orlis at the rectory," Jeanette said.

My mother went upstairs and, after what seemed like a very long time, came down. "She's calling now."

A few minutes later my grandmother's feeble voice drifted down. Jeanette went up to see her. When she came back she was more upset. Those brief hours of grief had been replaced already by frustration. "Father Orlis says that they will have a memorial for Uncle David. But they can't have his coffin and body in the church. And they can't bury him in consecrated ground."

"My God!" my mother cried. "Why has thou deserted us?"

■ ■ ■

THE REST OF the morning of my grandmother's funeral, I pace the house in a welter of nervousness, dreading the noontime. I tell myself all I have to do is get through this day and then I can leave Advocate behind. I am uncomfortable with the half-truths and evasions in the eulogy; I am certain they will ring as false and untrue in the church as they do in my head. I can't wait to get back to the familiarity of my office in Toronto. Into the comfortable confines of my life in the city.

I vow that after this I will force my aunt and mother to visit me, rather than having me come home. I try not to think about the story my mother and Jeanette just told me.

"For God's sake, Jacob," Jeanette says. "Sit down. You're making me nervous."

I do. I have already dressed, in the black suit I brought with me for this day. At eleven-thirty Deanny arrives. She is dressed in simple black dress, and she does not mention Pavel, the eulogy, or our argument the last time we talked. She hugs me in the kitchen. I don't think Deanny has ever hugged me before. I notice that the top of her head only comes up to my chin. She sits with my mother and Jeanette, consoling them until the car arranged by the funeral home comes to pick us up.

My mother asks Deanny to sit with us. "You are as much a member of this family as Jacob," she says. "Mom would have wanted you to be with us."

Just before we are scheduled to leave, I ask my mother if she has Uncle David's St. Jude's medallion. I know she removed it from his neck shortly after he died, but she never said what she did with it. "I think so," she said. "Why?"

"I just want to have it with me," I say, "if I am going to do this. Could you get it?"

"I'll look," she said. "Though God knows if I can find it."

Ten minutes later my mother comes down the stairs with the medallion in her hand, and gives it to me. She expected, I think, that I would put it around my neck, but I do not. I drop it into the side pocket of my suit. We do not speak in the car on the way to the church.

My grandmother had dictated what she wanted for a funeral, but I found myself subverting her by allowing an arrangement of lilies to find its way to the altar. She hated them. She said lilies were God's way of reminding us that nature isn't perfect. Jeanette and my mother had also arranged for a bouquet of yellow roses. She had always loved yellow roses, and refused to give away a cutting of the bush that grew in her yard no matter how many times she was asked.

The only thing for me to do as we enter the church is to act bereaved. Even this I find difficult.

As we step inside, the congregation rises and stares at us as we walk in procession down the aisle. Father Harry stands at the altar, waiting for us to take our seats in the front pew. He wears vestments of grey and white and black that look, I think, like a Halloween costume of a newspaper column. My grandmother lies within the coffin, her body concealed by our angle, and I have no wish to look upon her.

Once we sit down, Father Harry does not immediately start the proceedings. Perhaps he wants to give us time to survey the casket. The entire town has turned out. There are people standing outside because there is no room. My mother takes my hand and squeezes it. Jeanette and Deanny cry softly on the other side of her. There are others sniffling in the church. My eyes are dry. It is still hard for me to believe, in one sense, she is dead, though the evidence lies right before me.

Father Harry begins the ceremony. "Eternal rest give to them, Oh Lord, and let perpetual light shine upon them." An altar boy steps forward and lights candles around the coffin. Father Harry offers a series of prayers known as The Office of the Dead. We sing "On Eagle's Wings," a hymn based on Psalm 91. My grandmother chose it. I am not much of a singer, and I don't know the words or tune. I fumble through it. Father Harry says the Mass for the Dead, then sprinkles holy water over my grandmother's casket. Finally, he motions for altar boys to blow the candles. All in all, the rites take only a half hour, but prayers, the lighted candles, the music have bewildered and exhausted me. When he is finished, Father Harry nods at me.

■■■

THE DAY AFTER my uncle died, my grandmother did not leave her room except to eat and go to the bathroom. I believe she had some inkling of the difficulty my mother and Jeanette would have in arranging the funeral, and she did not want to be a part of it. Whenever my mother or Jeanette called on her for some bit of information she gave it, but she would not come out.

My aunt and mother ceased mourning, for they could not be angry and bereaved at the same time — those are incompatible emotions. Both of them thought, naively, that when my uncle died the persecution would stop. But the town was still fearful of him, and since they had shamed themselves by refusing to support him while he was dying they could not very well step out of themselves and offer help now.

Henry came over. My mother asked him point-blank in the kitchen what they should do.

"It seems to me," Henry said, in his laconic way, "that you should call a funeral home in Halifax. Maybe they could prepare him."

My mother had tried the funeral home in Trenton, and they too had given her a feeble excuse. She took Henry's advice, and had Jeanette call Halifax. It took her a while, but eventually they found one that would do it. "They'll pick up the body from the hospital, take it back to the city, prepare him, and bring him back for the funeral. It's going to cost a pretty penny," my aunt said.

"Mom can pay for it," my mother said. "It's the least she can do."

"As for the funeral," Henry said, "I can call Lutheran and United on the other side. I know the ministers there."

"Would you?" said my mother.

Henry spent a half hour on the phone with each of them. "The Lutherans," he told us, "won't do it at all. Said he's not a member of the faith. The United said they would, but not with the body, like the Catholics. The pastor was real sympathetic, and said he very much wanted to, but his congregation wouldn't let him. Seems they've already discussed it. Too many of them think having the body in there will contaminate the place. The pastor called them 'foolish,' but said his hands are tied."

"Idiots," my mother said.

"Not so fast," said Henry. "The pastor said he'd officiate if you need him. He suggested you try the church on the reserve if others don't do it."

"Forget the church," Jeanette said. "We'll just do it outside."

"You can't do it outside with the body, Jeanette," said my mother. "Think, would you!"

My mother didn't mean this. She was tired, and so busy fighting the town even now that she wasn't allowed to grieve properly. Henry asked if it wouldn't be better if he dealt with all these details. "I know I'm not family, and I don't know if your brother would have wanted it, but …"

"He loved you, Henry," said Jeanette. "I'm sure he'd be honoured."

"Okay then," said Henry. "I'll get back to you."

After he was gone there was nothing to say, and the house was quiet again. Jeanette said she was going for a nap. My mother asked what I wanted for supper.

"Nothing," I told her. "I'm not hungry."

"You'll have to keep your strength up, Jacob. The next few days will be trying."

They were. The next few *years* would be, as far as I was concerned. I went back to my uncle's room. The bed was still unmade — sheeted and forlorn. I pressed play on the ghetto blaster — my ghetto blaster — Jeanette had placed in the room for my uncle in his final days, and listened to the sweet sounds of Haydn. He was my uncle's favourite composer. I was not a wistful boy. I did not think in terms of kind recollections and soft memories. I saw only death in that room. The strongest memory of my uncle I would carry in the album of my mind was of the flies around his mouth. I shut the tape player off and retreated into my own room, which is where I would stay pretty much for the next six years.

# 3

"MILLICENT MCNEIL ASKED in her final days," Father Harry says to us, "that her grandson Jacob say a few words at her Mass. So I'll ask him to come up here and do that."

Every eye in the church is upon me as I stand before the casket. There must be two hundred people, and they all must be thinking the same thing. What is he going to say? They all know the relationship. They all know what I do for a living. Perhaps they expect vitriol and anger, the way I expected it myself when Father Harry first told me about this.

I do not give them what they want.

I should be nervous. I am not good in front of people at the best of times, and to be up here should be terrifying. But it is not.

I am not a religious man, or even a spiritual one. I believe we make our own destinies, and I do not believe we should put ourselves or our power in the hands of others to absolve us, to let ourselves off the hook. But I feel calm, almost guided.

I'm not sure when the idea came to me, or when I decided to leave Jeanette's eulogy folded up in my blazer pocket and go it alone. I certainly had no idea of it when I entered the church, and through the Mass I was thinking only of the past, as I always did when it came to my grandmother. But when I got the cue from Father Harry it came to me.

I knew, and perhaps I'd always known, exactly what to do.

■ ■ ■

MY GRANDMOTHER STAYED in her room for the three days before my uncle's funeral. The reserve had indeed offered its church and cemetery. My mother and Jeanette picked out his spot. The band council didn't charge them for the space.

"You can visit whenever you like," Darcy told them. "Your family is always welcome here."

It was then my mother and Jeanette asked if they could, one day, be buried beside him. They were told they could. I have been to visit my uncle's grave, to lay flowers. My mother and Jeanette and Deanny and Henry also go.

As far as I know, my grandmother has not once been to see it.

She could not give him this much.

My uncle's funeral was at two on a Wednesday. There was no eulogy planned. There was no point, because very few people who knew him would be there. And no eulogy could be given that didn't mention the awful events surrounding his death, so my aunt and mother decided against it. It was to be a simple funeral. The casket was closed. No one wanted to see his ravaged body. The word AIDS was never mentioned.

After the reserve offered their church, the United pastor made good on his promise to officiate. My mother had called Father Orlis herself and asked if he was going to attend, but gave up on him when he did not give her a straight answer. Deacon Harry wanted to go, but Father Orlis forbade him. It wasn't proper, he was told, as Uncle David had been a sinner and had not been given the last rites. Apparently the deacon had not told him about hearing Uncle David's last confession.

The most noticeable absence was not Father Orlis, or the deacon, or anyone from town. On the morning of the funeral my mother called out the time to my grandmother several times to make sure she was getting ready. When it was time and she was still not downstairs, my mother and Jeanette went to get her. They found her in her housecoat, not prepared.

I was not there for the conversation. I heard shouting from where I sat in the kitchen. When they came down I asked where Grandnan was.

"She's sick," Aunt Jeanette said. "She's not going."

My mother was crying, and I got the distinct feeling it was not over my uncle. I was only twelve but I understood how wrong this was. I ran past my mother and Jeanette and up the stairs into my grandmother's room. She was sitting on the side of her bed in her housecoat. It looked as if she had been crying also.

"Grandnan!" I said. "You have to go." It was my first act of protest, after a lifetime of quiescence.

"I can't, Jacob," she said. "I'm too sick."

"But it's his funeral!"

My mother came back up and pulled me from the room. "I can't believe you're doing this. Your own son, for heaven's sake. Even Jacob knows how wrong it is."

"What am I to do, Caroline? Do you want me vomiting all over the floor?"

"If you're sick," said my mother, "you've made yourself sick."

"Go," said my grandmother. "You'll be late."

"All the world you care," said my mother.

My grandmother's motivation for not going to that funeral is still obscure to me. Perhaps it was her sickness. Or her guilt. Or her fear. Perhaps she didn't want to face her behaviour those last few months. Her refusal to acknowledge or help her son. I've no idea. But it was the final blow.

We went in Jeanette's Pinto. No one, not even the pastor, asked where my grandmother was. The service was short, as unadorned as the little church itself. The pastor read the more obvious passages from the King James Bible. *Whoever believeth in me* and *In my father's house there are many mansions* and the Twenty-Third Psalm. It wasn't true.

Not a word of it.

David did not believe in God, so he couldn't have been comforted by the last rights. I realized then, for the first time, and in exactly the same manner as I knew I was gay, that I did not believe in God either.

The only people we knew in the church were Henry, Darcy, Deanny — who wore a purple dress, because she didn't own a black one — Fred, Nurse Jones, and Nurse Cassandra, who had driven down from Halifax. Everyone else was from the reserve. No one from the town had come.

When it was over, my uncle's casket was carried out of the church and across the road into the cemetery by six men from the reserve. This part of the ceremony was most memorable by who was *not* there. It was defined by absence rather than attendance. When the pastor said the ashes-to-ashes I was stricken by anger. It was then I began to build my most serious resentments against my grandmother and the town, as I watched my mother and Jeanette go through what they did. I hated the town. I swore that when I got older I would make noise. I would never let them forget this.

I kept that promise, after a fashion. I think my grandmother knew, in later years, I could never forgive her for not going to Uncle David's funeral. She was contrite around me. She let me argue theology and evolution all I wanted, because she knew that I had been watching, that I was, in a sense, the only one who kept the memory fresh and alive long after her own daughters had forgiven her. I did not respond to her authority after that day, and she did not try to enforce it on me.

■ ■ ■

WITH THOSE EVENTS from the distant past in mind, I begin my grandmother's eulogy. Not to shame her, but to place her at the funeral she should have been to.

"On a warm summer afternoon in late July of 1952, a day not dissimilar to today, my uncle David was pedalling up Tenerife Street as fast as he could go. He was eight years old."

The congregation suddenly sits up straighter, galvanized by my words.

With no doubt about what to say, I continue. "I know this story, for I heard my uncle telling my mother and my aunt about it before *he* died. He talked a lot about his childhood, and my friend Bernadette and I listened. I think he was trying to relive it, to make some sense out of what his life had become, to explain what he knew was a senseless death."

I look at Deanny in the front row, sitting beside my mother. She is smiling. Perhaps she knew what was coming. She may have done the same if given the chance.

"The front wheel of my uncle's bicycle fell off," I say. "My grandfather had assembled it earlier that afternoon, and he had not tightened all its lug nuts sufficiently. When the wheel flew off, the bike collapsed onto its front forks and David sailed headfirst out over the handlebars and landed in a crumple on the street. His arms and legs and face were scraped. Two of the neighbours heard him scream. They — you — came running out of your houses. And more neighbours came. Soon there was a knot of people gathered around young David. You soothed him. You brushed him off. You brought out warm water and face cloths and cleaned him up and bandaged his hurt. There were no serious injuries. A few minor scrapes.

"My uncle was very sick when he reminded his mother of this story. 'How good it felt,' he said. 'Having all those people worried about me. Taking care of me. I've never forgotten that.'

"I wish you had been there. Maybe you would have understood why what was done to my uncle was so wrong. It was a betrayal of the child you helped to raise. I wish sometimes I knew who those neighbours were exactly. I would ask you if you remembered my uncle as a boy and taking care of him that time, if you remember your refusal to do the same when he really needed it."

And so I give my uncle's eulogy instead. The one he never had. I tell them more stories about his childhood. The fishing derbies. The brass and the cinema. How when he was fourteen he had a poem published in a national teachers' magazine. The town was so proud of him then. His picture had been published beside his poem in the *Gazette*. It had hung framed in my grandfather's den. I tell them about his travels. To France, Germany, Japan. I wonder, as I'm speaking, if David knew that one day I would bear witness to his life. I talk about his job, his passion for teaching, his love of literature, his failed effort at reading *War and Peace*, which somehow now seemed symbolic of something but lay just beyond my comprehension. I talk about his homosexuality, and my own. And then finally the AIDS virus. I hold nothing back. I educate them. I quote statistics. I examine the town's reaction to him, and to the virus, in 1984. The cancelling of the parade, the manner in which they reacted to his death, their absence at his funeral. I tell the story and speak the words that my grandmother never allowed to be spoken. I expect some of them to leave, but none do. Many lower their heads and refuse to look at me, but all stay in the church.

"In Toronto a few days ago a man I know tried to commit suicide because of the same disease that killed my uncle David. Schooled by people like you into thinking what he had was shameful, that it was somehow his fault. We should be forced to make up to these people for how we have treated them, and for what we have done. My grandmother left me a substantial amount of money, which I plan on using to help those living with AIDS in the city in which I now dwell."

Suddenly it strikes me. What my grandmother had meant when she said in her will *do something here*. It was a private communication, from her to me, no one else would understand it. It was her final act of contrition, her final admission; her last confession, and a way to buy salvation. Suddenly I am certain this is what she wanted.

"Of the money my grandmother left me, she wished me to take some of it and build a monument in Founder's Park dedicated to those who have been affected in Advocate by AIDS. On it will be inscribed the names of our victims of the AIDS crisis.

"I think my grandmother knew when she asked me to deliver this eulogy what I would say and do. I speak now on her behalf, what I think she wanted to say at the end of her life but could not. Advocate is a small town, and what happened here certainly happened elsewhere. But I am giving you a chance to redeem yourself. She was seeking forgiveness not just for herself but for all of you. Do as she asked. Build the monument. Honour my uncle David. Do for him now what none of you could do for him then. Thus far, and to my knowledge, the only name that would be inscribed on such a monument will be David Owen Angus William McNeil, born August 17, 1944, died October 21 1984. Let us hope there is never another."

I run out of words. When I sit down beside my mother the church is silent. They wait for Father Harry to continue. He seems moved by my eulogy. He does not immediately rouse himself to the task of finishing the Mass. When he does, he stands, clears his throat, and says the final prayers. The casket is lifted and carried out by the pallbearers.

The rain falls on us as we make our way out of the church. It is a cold benediction.

■■■

AS WE PASS from the church commons into the cemetery, as lovely and peaceful now as I found it all those years ago, even in the rain, Jeanette catches up with me. She is unable to contain herself. "When did you think of a monument?" she whispers.

I shrug. "Right then, as I was speaking. It was what Grandnan wanted, I think. A public way to atone."

"It's brilliant," Jeanette says. Of course my aunt would think so. Ever the radical. Ever believing words emblazoned on signs and etched in stone could make a difference.

I have decided what words will be inscribed on my uncle's monument. The quote I had come across in *War and Peace*.

"Lay me down like a stone oh God, and raise me up like a new bread."

At the last, my uncle would be a better advocate than we were. His words would never be drowned out, or burned in the fire pit behind my grandmother's house. They would stand long after the rest of us were dead.

Father Harry intones the words for the committal of the dead, as the mourners stand in the rain and watch my grandmother's casket being lowered into the ground. She will be the last person buried here, and with her goes a certain way of looking at and dealing with the world. When the prayer is finished the mourners, led by Jeanette and my mother, reach for handfuls of dirt to throw on the casket while Harry recites the Lord's Prayer. Long ago my grandmother had explained the significance of the dirt to me. "It's a reminder of our own mortality," she said. "A goodbye to the person we have lost. An act of burying the dead, and a realistic view of our life on earth." I reach into my pocket and take out the St. Jude's medallion my mother had given me that morning. I throw it into my grandmother's grave. The Lemon Day and Orange Day parades are over. The marches have begun.

# ACKNOWLEDGEMENTS

■

I would like to acknowledge the Canada Council for the Arts and Arts Nova Scotia for their generous financial support during the writing of this novel. I would also like to thank for their ongoing support Alison Smith, Barb Lush, Jo-Anne Lenethen, and my parents Charles and Yvonne Greer.